5 star reviews

A high octane, adrenaline-powered debut novel. Lewis puts the reader into the most important issues we face today. He tells the story in a way that puts us there naturally with well developed and intriguing characters at war with a smothering and corrupt government. It's a powerful argument for individual liberty that kept me reading until I finished. And still, two weeks later I can't stop thinking about it. Lewis has created an exceptional novel that leaves no doubt he is a writer with a bright future. **David Thomas Reida**, Denver, CO

Mr. Lewis did a great job of not siding with either of our two political parties. He stayed on track as it pertained to the topic of term limits. His book was exciting to read and has motivated me to rethink my political loyalties. My intrigue was enhanced by the author's ability to effectively present both sides of the issue. I found myself switching from one side to another which kept me engaged, entertained, and provoked. **Ormand T Galvin**, Corvallis, OR

Erne has created a memorable and remarkably exiting story that will grip the reader regardless of their political persuasion. I could not put this book down, even after the last page, and will look forward to his next, "Drug War." **Fran Wickeham**, Port Ludlow, WA

Apparently this is the first novel of Erne Lewis, but *An Act of Self-Defense* is the work of an excellent writer. It is hard to believe it is his first. It is far more than a political thriller and will be hard for any reader to forget. The issues are enormous. The themes are as basic and important as are our lives: liberty vs. power, the individual vs. government organized society. These are juxtaposed in characters that we love one minute and fear the next. I cannot imagine anyone reading this novel without their heart hammering as mine was. I had a hard time putting it down and even when I did my mind was still in the story. The author's opinions are plain to see. He fears individual liberty is being lost as government gains power, but the characters on the other side have credible arguments too—they are not straw men. We readers are sympathetic to both sides as this novel builds suspense all the way to the last page. I hated that it ended. And I cannot believe any reader will be disappointed. **Dave Harris**, Palm Desert CA

More 5 star reviews at Amazon.com and B&N.com

". . . experience has shown that even under the best forms (of government), those entrusted with power have, in time, and by slow operations, perverted it into tyranny." **Thomas Jefferson 1779**

An Act of Self-Defense

An Act of Self-Defense

Erne Lewis

Plicata Press

An Act of Self-Defense is a work of fiction. Names, characters, places, and incidents are the product of the author's imagination or are used fictitiously. Any resemblance to actual events, locales, or persons, living or dead, is coincidental.

Published by Plicata Press, LLC, Gig Harbor, WA
Cover design by Mythic Design Studio

Library of Congress Cataloging-in-Publication Data

Lewis, Erne
An Act of Self-Defense : a novel / by Erne Lewis
ISBN: 978-0-9828205-0-6
1. United States—Future—Fiction. 2. Tyranny—SWAT—Fiction.
3. Patriots—Fiction. 4. Revolution—Fiction. 5. Term Limits—Fiction.
6. Congress—Political Aristocracy—Fiction.
7. Libertarian—Fiction.
I. Title.

813'.54
Library of Congress Control Number: 2010911349

Printed in the United States of America

for Marti

Prologue

Professor Stewart stared at the computer monitor, re-reading the paragraph he had just written. *Thomas Jefferson, the author of the Declaration of Independence and the third president of the United States, was a strong advocate of citizen-legislators. He feared the failure to include term limits for members of Congress was a fatal flaw in the Constitution. He argued that even the best men are naturally corrupted by the power of high office held too long. They become arrogant, he said, and self-serving in proportion to the time they hold office. They come to love power and to believe they are better than the citizens who elect them. He warned that over time a self-serving political aristocracy would evolve, persistently increasing their power and the power of the federal government and thereby destroying individual liberty. He believed another bloody revolution would be necessary to regain the individual liberty lost to those power-loving politicians.*

As he reviewed the paragraph, he became convinced Jefferson would not propose revolution today. He would certainly be appalled at the recent loss of individual rights. And he would be angry. But he would also see the impossibility of challenging the federal military power on a field of battle. Revolution, in the sense Jefferson meant it, was now impossible. The federal government would smash the uprising without difficulty and without a second thought. However, he thought he knew what the founders might do if they were presented with this problem.

Well, maybe such men could make it work, but he could not. He was not the person to organize it because he didn't know what would be required. He knew no one who could or would help. And without a high probability of success it would be a stupid, viciously immoral disaster. It would only advance tyranny.

He pushed the idea to the back of his mind and returned to his writing.

Monday, June 2nd
Deliver the Message

10:20 a.m.

She followed the old Ford sedan as it turned east on Leesburg Pike, stopping when it stopped, moving forward when it did, barely aware of its presence. She gripped the wheel to keep her hands from shaking and cursed herself. *Two years in planning, four lives and two million dollars invested, families wrecked, and careers ruined to make this work. And now when it's up to me, I'm shaking too damn much to drive this car, never mind the rest of it.*

Shut down strip malls, run down residences, government office buildings and pedestrians went barely noticed. She was supposed to be a little fearful, but still brave and proud of herself. Where was the pride she felt when they planned this?

She struggled to recapture it, reminding herself of the importance of their goal. It sounded pretty hollow now. *I'm so damned naïve.*

Anna didn't notice when the car in front of her went through the amber light. She drove through the intersection too late. A beefy guy in a red truck was stopped for the light in the oncoming lane. As Anna drove past he leaned on his horn, stuck his head out the window, gave her the finger and screamed, "Wake up, Blondie!"

That started her shaking again. She gripped the wheel harder but then thought, *the wig works.* With a nervous laugh she glanced at herself in the mirror. *Jesus.* Long blond wig, lipstick so red it screamed sex, a mouthpiece that pushed her lips out and made her cheeks fatter, her jaw a little wider . . . *and my skin. Unbelievable.*

Her skin, normally an Italian olive, was Swedish white. Chris assured her it would go back to normal in two or three days. He got the dye from the BND, the German spy agency. She wore a 'hair pull' band that ran behind her head, and under the wig, grabbing hair from above her temples to pull her eyes up at the corners—and it hurt like hell. Her dark eyebrows and eyelashes were lightened and with the blue eyes she was a Barbie doll. She hardly recognized herself.

She remembered getting ready, her hands shaking so much she spilled her coffee. Putting the damn contacts in was a nightmare. Chris offered lots of advice and that made it worse. And what the hell did he know about eye shadow?

He was stone-faced as if this day were no big deal. Jacob was wide-eyed and barely talking. She hated dressing this way. And she didn't think it was realistic. "Department of Justice agents aren't Barbies, Chris."

But he had the last word. "Oh hell, yes. Some DOJ agents look like hustlers. And they get away with it because sex discrimination charges scare the hell out of federal managers. And anyway, we're using the sexy blond disguise to make damn sure you don't look anything like Anna Carpenter. Okay?"

Concentrate, dammit. If she were stopped by a cop now, the disguise would be blown and the whole damned operation screwed up, maybe for weeks. She gripped the steering wheel harder.

The Safeway came into view on her left. She passed it and made the next left turn onto Henry, then a block later a right into the warehouse lot. She opened the garage door with a remote and closed it as she drove in. She found an empty space and parked. There were twenty-two in all. She had helped to drive them here from the car lot five months earlier. They used a dummy corporation to purchase the used car business and its inventory. The metal warehouse was owned by another dummy corporation. Today she would use and abandon the first car.

She removed the mailbag from the back seat, closed both doors, started to walk away and remembered the purse and gloves in the front seat. And the garage door opener. *Dammit, think.* She retrieved them and walked to the first car in line, a white Ford Thunderbird. There was a note from Chris on the front door handle. *GLOVES*

Actually she had already remembered, but it was good he left the note.

The key was in the ignition, the engine started easily and after making sure the door closed behind her, she was soon back on Leesburg Pike headed east toward I-395. At first she felt relief at getting the switch made, but almost immediately the looming task started another round of the shakes.

She pulled onto a shoulder and put the car in park, while cursing and fumbling through her bag. Finally, close to tears, the bottle of valium emerged. Her mouth and throat were dry, which made the pill go down hard. It would need time to kick in. A minute later, still trembling, she put the car in gear. It took forty minutes to cross the

Potomac and find the underground parking garage near the J. Edgar Hoover Building, pretty typical for a Monday morning at 10:30. The valium seemed to help.

She removed the credit-card size Department of Justice ID from her purse and put it in the Radio Frequency ID initializer. The ID had a tiny electronic signal chip embedded. It now transmitted its position to the NSA satellite parked permanently above the Northeast US. A federal computer at the NSA facility in Fort Meade was downloading a new ID and its precise location in Washington, DC.

She hung the laminated ID from her neck. It identified her as Sue Thomas, Postal Crimes Division Specialist in the Department of Justice New York City office. All federal employees throughout the world were now required to carry these special RFID chips on them or have them nearby. In two years every citizen would be required to carry them. From this point every movement she made while carrying the ID would be tracked at all times and a history kept. She put some gum in her mouth—a prop for the role she played this morning—got out of the car, removed the bag from the backseat and placed the strap over her shoulder. She locked the car, put her gloves in the purse and put on her sunglasses. *Okay, Sue Thomas, here you go.*

At 11:10 she stepped from the air conditioned lobby of the parking garage into D Street, now a furnace with heat radiating up from the sun baked concrete. The stone buildings and lack of breeze trapped and intensified the heat. Halfway there, she felt the perspiration under her blouse and began to worry the cosmetic cream might fail. She saw the Starbucks a few yards ahead. The room was crowded and noisy, but the air-conditioning was an immediate relief. She would wait a minute or two.

As her eyes scanned the room they locked with those of a computer programmer she sometimes used. Her knees went weak, but in the same instant he looked away while talking to someone whose back was to her. She moved out of his vision. After her heart slowed and she was cool enough for the two block walk, she continued toward the DOJ building. *I can do this. I damn sure don't look like me.*

She passed the FBI building on Ninth and crossed Pennsylvania Avenue, looking at the gray and oppressive Department of Justice Building. Two guards stood in front of the North entrance. A tiny panic gripped her, but she remembered Chris saying, "The outside security guards are there to send the tourists away. They'll see your ID and say Hi. Just smile big and walk right past them." She began chewing the gum, put on her smile, and her confidence increased. *Showtime.* She flashed her ID, said, "Hi, fellas," and walked past them through the inner doors to face the real security check. Chris had given her a role to play, a voice and accent to use and made her practice until it was easy. He wanted the voice recordings to sound unlike Anna. She dropped the bag on the security check table and pulled off her sunglasses.

"Howsit goin', guys?" The big smile helped.

Their eyes followed her appreciatively as she stepped through the metal detector, just as Chris promised. "Guys can only think of one thing at a time, Sis. If you wear the short skirt and tight blouse, they'll look you over carefully. They won't be minding the store."

She stepped over to the eye-scan and face-scan cameras as if she had done it a thousand times. She knew what was coming; Chris had shown her a video of the technology. The eye-scan and face-scan technology were unbeatable, passing only those whose face and eyes were in the DOJ database. She put her head against the bar and looked into the camera. It only took five seconds. It seemed to take longer but she passed. The face and eyes of Anna were in the database, but as Sue Thomas, DOJ Postal Crimes Inspector. *Garbage in, garbage out.*

She stepped away and watched as another computer aided device sniffed her bag for anthrax, drugs, bombs and chemical weapons; another X-rayed the bag, but since it contained nothing but one page letters from the Department of Justice to 378 members of Congress, and because her ID indicated she had high clearance, the security guards waved her past with "Have a nice day, Ms. Thomas."

She had only gone a few steps, her high heels clicking along the marble corridor when a guard asked, "Ms. Thomas?"

She stopped breathing, turned, but couldn't speak. He walked toward her. "You forgot your sunglasses."

Anna breathed and said, "Thanks a bunch," but it didn't sound right. Oklahoma was back in her voice.

She started down the hall, hearing the clack of her own shoes, but she did not hear him. She desperately hoped he was looking at her butt. She stopped to put the sunglasses in her purse as an excuse to look back. He grinned. She barely smiled and he turned and walked back to his station. She felt better until she remembered she almost left them her DNA. *Deliver the damn mail and get out of here.*

It seemed like a mile down that long hallway to the stairs. She looked up to see the surveillance cameras. Chris said they were excellent digital cameras; they picked up and recorded every detail. "But every detail will be wrong, Anna. The cameras will only confirm what the guards will say—a good-looking blond, slender, maybe five eight, brought the letters in at such and such a time." A picture of Sue Thomas would be in the papers and on television—not Anna Carpenter.

Chris provided a floor plan of the area and photos of every hall and doorway. She knew the route. Down one floor, left near the bottom of the stairs. Finding the mail room was no trouble. Once inside, the mail tubs were where they were supposed to be. No one seemed to notice as she emptied the bag of envelopes into one of the tubs. A minute later she was back up the stairs and headed for the courtyard exit. It would look a little suspicious going back out the same door three minutes after going through security.

There were a few cars parked in the courtyard—late models and limos. The heat had increased a notch, but she was almost feeling relief. Almost. She made herself walk at a normal pace across the courtyard to the special personnel auto entrance, every step bringing her closer to freedom. She said, "Bye, fellas" to the guards as she stepped through the gate.

She worried she was being watched for the first few yards then became almost composed and even a little proud as she crossed Pennsylvania headed back to the car. As she turned the corner toward the parking garage she removed the ID, wiped her fingerprints from it, put the ID in the mailbag, rolled it up and before entering the building, dropped it in a trash container. She imagined the satellite now staring hard and stupidly at the trash container—no longer following her.

By the time she found the Thunderbird in the cool, dark garage and pulled the gloves on, she was shaking again. It made no damn sense. She fumbled with the keys and dropped them before getting the door open. Why now? She should feel great, but the inexplicable trembling bothered her.

She let her head fall against the back of the seat, reminding herself why they couldn't have just mailed the letters from a postal box. *Unofficial letters to members of Congress are delayed weeks to check for anthrax and other viruses or for chemical weapons. The letters she mailed would be delivered tomorrow. And tomorrow every member of Congress will know he is, or isn't, on our list. Using the DOJ mail system sends another message. We're inside your system. No matter how well you're protected, we can get to you.*

When the trembling eased, she drove to the top of the ramp, paid for parking, ignored the camera recording her departure, and headed east toward the freeway entrance. She drove carefully, stopping at yellow lights.

She forced herself to drive under the speed limit, and was careful changing lanes. Chris had said, "The Thunderbird will be immediately known to the FBI as the vehicle driven by Sue Thomas. They'll have it on the traffic cameras and in the parking garage. Sue Thomas will be recorded on cameras going into this garage and coming out."

She couldn't come out of her disguise because of the cameras that were on bridges and street corners all over the area.

Two blocks from the freeway entrance two police cars pulled in behind her. In the rearview mirror she could see the officer in the car directly behind her talking on his car radio. And looking at her license plate? She barely saw the Third Street traffic light in time to stop. She squeezed the wheel. The cop put the radio down and looked at her just as the light changed. She started forward, watching him follow, forgetting the freeway ramp on her right until almost too late. She turned, but she hadn't signaled. She looked in her rearview mirror. *Don't turn, please don't turn.*

They didn't. Both police cars continued east on D Street. She felt like weeping with the relief.

As she crossed the Potomac a few minutes later her hands hurt from gripping the wheel. She pulled a cell phone from her purse and speed dialed Chris. She needed to talk.

He answered immediately. "Are you okay?"

"No, damn it I'm scared." There was a short silence while he waited for her to continue and while she waited for a little encouragement. Finally she said, "But I made the delivery."

"That's terrific, Sis. We knew you could do it."

She heard the relief in his voice and knew he had been worried.

"Jacob is opening a vintage Cabernet. He'll let it breathe until you get here. He says 'great job'. He's been a little nervous. I don't know why."

"Very funny. This project better get easier." When he didn't respond she added, "That's what I'm thinking, too."

Chris said, "We better get off these phones. Okay?"

The call helped move her thoughts elsewhere. As she crossed the Potomac she considered the curious relationship she had with her brother. They had fought from the earliest she could remember, but they also defended each other on the playground at school and at home when dad or mom was angry with either of them. She could not remember a time when either expressed affection for the other, but it had never been in doubt.

When they were apart they called or wrote often. She didn't see him for nearly a year when he served in Panama. That was several years ago. Ten or twelve maybe. He showed up in Arlington unannounced and with a huge grin immediately after leaving the Army Rangers. He hadn't intended to stay more than a week, but he met

Karen and stayed. The father of an army buddy got him hired at FedEx, he married Karen after a short but intense courtship and never considered leaving the area.

He didn't go back to Oklahoma until he had an apartment, a job and an emotional tie to Karen. She smiled as she remembered calling him a coward, afraid to go home until he had roots here, afraid he'd get stuck on the farm. Of course he had sheepishly agreed. The family had begged him to come back for a visit and he did want to see them, but it had been spring, there was a mountain of work to do on the Carpenter and Ribisi farms and he feared he would never escape. God, he hated farming.

Henry Street appeared on her right and as she began to look for her turn she thought, *Maybe that would have been for the best. Maybe it would have all turned out different.* She drove two blocks past Henry and turned right on Harrell. *Or maybe Chris would have ended up in jail, instead of Nicolo.* She stopped the what-if torture and drove to the apartment building they'd selected earlier.

When she was certain no one was near enough to notice, she parked and opened the paper bag. As she backed out of the car she shook the sweepings from beauty shops and fabric stores with the DNA of hundreds of people and with thousands of micro fibers, over the back and front seats.

She had probably left trace amounts of her DNA in the Thunderbird and microscopic fibers from her clothes. After she verified she had her bag and garage door remote and left nothing in the car, she walked away, leaving the key in the ignition to entice a thief.

As she got farther from the Thunderbird and closer to the warehouse her confidence grew. A slight breeze made the noon sun bearable, but she was desperate to get out of the wig. She heard the burbling trills of wrens as she walked under the shade of a huge oak tree. The shade and the wrens perked her up. Then she smiled as the pride kicked in.

She was two blocks from the warehouse when she heard the tires of a car behind her in the left hand lane and approaching slowly. Too slowly. She stepped off the road, walking through sparse grass and weeds.

A silver fender eased into her view, a new BMW Z4 convertible with the top down. The tanned driver wore a silver sport shirt open at the neck. He looked to be ten years younger than her. He wore driving gloves, silver sunglasses, a large head of styled blond hair and a smug arrogant face that instantly pissed her off. One arm was on the wheel and the elbow of the other draped over the door. He was going to try to pick her up and it was just too goddamn much. Before he could begin, she gave him the look of disgust that usually wilted jerks and said, "No!" emphatically.

His face didn't sag as much as she'd hoped. He pulled his sunglasses off and gave her a smile he probably practiced in front of a mirror. She had her cell phone up and pointed at him by the time he said, "Now is that any way to talk to a . . ."

"Tell it to the officer, slick." She began punching the keys on her cell phone. "Your photo is on the way."

"Dumb bitch," he said and sped off.

Anna almost laughed, but remembered her picture would be in the newspapers and on TV. That jerk would recall that she was in this area walking in this direction, only two blocks from the warehouse. She walked faster, as fast as she could without attracting attention, but looking over her shoulder to see if anyone was watching.

Tuesday, June 3rd
The Only Way You've Left Us

10:11 a.m.

Bobby sorted through the pile of letters, opening and separating them according to source and importance. Letters from constituents were usually weeks getting through the security checks. No hurry on those, but a letter from the Attorney with the *open immediately* stamp got his attention. His first "Oh, shit" occurred half way through the letter.

He was standing and still reading when he said it again. He grabbed the envelope and rushed past the open-mouthed staff to the office of Bill Morrison, Senator Parler's Chief of Staff. Morrison was on the telephone, but Bobby interrupted. "Sir, you have to see this."

Morrison ignored him, then glared, but the staffer kept saying, "Please, sir." and with such a damn whine that Morrison finally made his excuses and got off the line. He had been Chief of Staff for twenty years and a political professional for forty-three. At first he didn't take it seriously. All senators received threats—the bigger they were the more threats they received. But when the staffer showed him the envelope with the Department of Justice postmark, Morrison returned to his reading with more concentration.

"Get copies to the leadership offices, Republicans, too. I'll call the senator."

While Morrison read the letter to Senator Parler, the Senate leadership also received copies. The Capitol Hill message system alerted the other offices and within twenty minutes 83 threatened senators and 295 representatives had read or heard the letter.

Long term members of Congress:

The president has been limited to two terms by Amendment XXII to the Constitution. Voters have limited the terms of their state legislators and their governors in every state where legislation did not block them. In every poll taken in recent history, the voters have indicated their fervent wish for a term limited Congress. In 1994, twenty-two states voted to limit the terms of their members of Congress and more were preparing to vote when the Supreme Court ruled, wrongly, that the state actions were unconstitutional. You have refused to offer the people a Constitutional amendment limiting your terms.

You are about to rectify that.

In the next few days you will approve the following term limits amendment to the Constitution and immediately offer it to the states for a decision as provided in the Constitution.

Amendment XXVIII
To insure that future members of Congress shall be citizen legislators and not professional politicians:

Section 1. No person shall be a member of Congress who shall have served for a total of more than eight years in elected state and/or federal political office.

Section 2. With respect to existing senators and representatives this amendment shall be effective in the first election following approval of this amendment by 3/4 of the states.

You are receiving this message on Tuesday, June 3. If this amendment is not approved before midnight on Thursday, June 5, we will begin the process of removing long-term incumbents from office in the only way you have left us. If you have not resigned by that time, you may be one of those removed.

On Friday, June 6, if the amendment has not been approved, we will take the lives of two of the long-term incumbent members of Congress who have not resigned. We will continue to remove two members each day until the proposed term limits amendment has passed both houses of Congress.

When the amendment has passed the Senate or the House of Representatives, we will lay down our arms with respect to the members of that body. When it has passed both houses we will withdraw, leaving the final decision to the people. If the proposed amendment is rejected by the voters and if you have not previously resigned, you may retain office.

Thomas Jefferson believed the failure to include term limits in the Constitution was a fatal error. He predicted another bloody revolution would be necessary to regain the individual rights lost to the power-loving politicians who would, over time, increase their power at the cost of our liberty. Jefferson could not have foreseen that the federal government would today be capable of tracking our every move and communication. Neither could he imagine the unimaginable instruments of destruction that this government, and the interest groups that control it, would willingly use to maintain power.

For the people to regain control of Congress and then their liberty, this is the only form of revolution now possible. It has an added advantage. Instead of the millions of innocents that might otherwise die in another American Revolution, our method has the advantage that if blood must be spilled it will be the blood of the political aristocracy that stole our liberty, our lives and our property. Or perhaps it will be our lives that are taken. If so, we die for the noblest cause we can imagine.

Members of Congress, you have the ability to make this revolution bloodless and we beg you to do so. However, to preserve your lives—and perhaps your office if the amendment is eventually rejected by the voters—you must move quickly to approve the amendment and send it to the voters for their decision.

We believe the American people will join us—with their vote—to regain control of their Congress. If so, this will be the nation's second revolution against a ruling aristocracy.

While we await passage of the amendment we will explain in better detail directly to the American people who we are and why our actions are necessary. For now consider us,

the *T*erm *L*imits *R*evolution.

10:23 a.m.

Morgan Harlowe, with thirty-eight years in the Senate, did not have to see his copy of the letter to know that he was on the list of long-term incumbents. The news raced through the Capitol building and the Senate and House office buildings within a few minutes. The Department of Justice and the White House could not handle all the telephone calls received from frightened, angry members of Congress. The pervasive anxiety was understandable. If the lives and careers of 378 Congressional leaders were threatened, so were the futures of those who served them. Citizen legislators would not require the 14,000 congressional staff whose only purpose was to get their bosses re-elected. The press was aware of the letter moments after the congressional staff began alerting their bosses and each other. The alarm and the apparent fear put the press in a feeding frenzy.

Reporters raced down the halls with notepads, cameras, tripods and microphones to get comments from the most prominent senators and representatives, but until they made up their minds what they would say, most avoided the press. Morgan Harlowe would not hide. He directed his staff to tell the press that he would hold a press conference on the Capitol steps in fifteen minutes. The reporters turned and ran again. In a press conference, position is critical, especially for the TV cameras.

He selected the Capitol steps for this press conference so that majestic structure would be background—he would be speaking of the nation's need for statesmen—but as he stepped into the sun, Harlowe knew the Capitol steps were an unfortunate idea. Hank should have warned him about the sun—he was squinting. Bad angle for the cameras, too. Hank had been his Chief of Staff for thirty years and a long time employee of the Harlowe family before that. *Goddamn it, he should know better.*

His exertion together with the heat made him sweat. *Damn it, let's get it over with.* He stepped to the microphone, conscious of his appearance. Five nine and sixty pounds overweight did not look very statesmanlike, but he also had a head full of white hair that reporters described as leonine, made for the camera. And they were friendly, as they should be. He gave them access in exchange for interviews that made them both look good. They rarely put him in an unflattering light.

He looked directly into the TV cameras. "Today I and 377 other members of Congress received letters containing the threat of assassination unless we immediately pass a constitutional amendment that these pretentious terrorists have written. They demonstrate their contempt for the Constitution when they presume to force its alteration with a gun to our heads. They show their disregard for this nation by attacking Congress at a time when we are working feverishly to straighten out the financial disaster that greedy unregulated free markets have forced upon us. They expose their scorn for the voters of this nation when they propose to blackmail its Congress, a Congress freely elected by those voters in the fairest elections in the world today and in the finest democracy the world has ever seen."

He looked angrily into the CNN camera. "How dare these evil right wing fascists presume to dictate to this great nation? Their threat is cowardly. They hide in the darkness of anonymity hoping to terrorize us from office. Let there be no doubt about their purposes. They intend nothing less than the overthrow of the greatest democracy that has ever existed. They attack this nation's elected leaders because they hate democracy, they despise majority rule and they feel threatened by a free society. Their real purpose is to remove the statesmen from government so *they* can achieve its overthrow."

He turned to the ABC camera. "They will not succeed. They accuse us of being an aristocratic political class. I for one plead guilty, guilty of being a member of a family that has served this country with honor, distinction and with enormous self-sacrifice for 60 years. My father and my brothers have served the nation. I have been returned to office with large majorities because I serve the voters and they know it. The terrorists call it aristocracy; I call it the Harlowe tradition of political public service. So let these vicious terrorists hear me now. Yes, I fear the assassin's bullet. Nonetheless, I will continue to take my seat in the Senate and serve this nation for as long as I have life and strength to do so. I will never resign." He turned to the FOX News camera, and said, "Never," the NBC camera and said it again and then again to the CNN camera.

He paused to wipe the gathering perspiration from his face. "Now I will tell you what I *will* do. I will introduce legislation, but it will not be a term limits amendment. I will offer a bill to insure that guns are no longer available to would-be assassins. Far too many of this nation's leaders have died from assassins' bullets. It is time to end the killing that easy access to guns makes possible."

As the sound from a distant fighter jet threatened to cover his voice, he paused, wiped his brow, and envied the reporters wearing short sleeve shirts. "I'll take your questions now." Pointing at an AP reporter, he said, "Clyde."

"Senator, do you believe Congress will consider the term limits amendment"?

"Of course not. That would be cowardice. No one would dare to offer it in the Senate. We must never yield to terrorist threats."

"Do you feel that you are personally targeted?"

"I assume I would be high on the wish-list of any anarchist madmen. But I also doubt they have the capacity to carry this out. They may be able to get a letter into the Department of Justice, but that doesn't mean they can carry out assassinations—especially when we are expecting the attempt."

The Washington Times reporter asked, "Senator, would you comment, on the TLR accusation that Congress has increased their power while taking the rights of the American people?"

"That's insane. The people of this nation enjoy more rights now than they did when the Constitution was written. Now they have a right to decent housing, and to healthcare, and food. Society has made great progress in recent years. A few years ago only the elderly could expect

Social Security and Medicare. Now it is enjoyed by all as a right. Congress has not limited freedom. It has increased it. Can you imagine how our people would manage in these terrible economic times without those programs?"

He shook his head in answer to his question. "We are here to do the peoples' work, to provide the services they require and to preserve liberty as the voters think best. My constituents do not ask for protection of theoretical rights, but I am flooded with mail demanding more and better health care. They also want to be free from the fear of being murdered. That should be the next item on our calendar. Not *term* limits, *gun* limits."

He added, "Thank you," before turning to start up the steps. His staff fell in behind him to prevent the television cameras from showing that unflattering view and to prevent reporters from getting to him with more questions.

The air conditioning was a huge relief. As he walked through the outer office several aides turned from the television to congratulate him on a powerful message. He thanked them and handed Murphy his jacket as he entered his office. While the senator changed shirts, Murphy closed the door, crossed the room to the bar, put three cubes of ice in a highball glass, filled it with Glenfiddich and brought it to the senator.

Murphy sat in the chair at the side of the senator's desk. "Where the hell do these TLR idiots come from? Do they really expect us to take the Constitution literally in the 21st century?"

After a sip of his whiskey the senator said, "Yes. They do." He shook his glass to make the whiskey colder as he considered the issue. "I love the Constitution, but it placed ridiculously small limits on the power of the federal government. Taken literally, our total powers include coining money, raising money, budgeting for the various federal departments and agencies, declaring war, controlling federal elections, controlling and taxing imports and exports, and a few other minor things I can't recall at the moment. We can also regulate commerce. But even that probably just meant making commerce *regular* between the states—prohibiting tariffs between states, which had been a problem before the Constitution, and establishing standards to be common for all states."

"That's it?"

Harlowe smiled, knowing how this would sound. "Taken literally, almost everything we do here is unconstitutional—education, healthcare, social security, housing, labor laws, minimum wages."

"But those are covered under the general welfare clause?"

"That's the argument we make, but think about it, Hank. Why did they bother to write a Constitution specifying the precise limits of the Congress, guaranteeing all other powers and rights to the states or to the people and then insert a small phrase in a very general paragraph, which means, 'create any laws you think appropriate for the general health and welfare?' What was the point of writing the Constitution if that phrase was meant to give us an excuse to ignore the rest of it?"

"So why did they include the welfare clause?"

"It's one word in a long sentence that probably meant, 'Do everything you can for the general welfare *within the limits of your designated powers.*'"

Hank smiled. "But?"

"We work around it. They weren't perfect and there's no need to pretend they were. We can take inspiration from the Constitution's words, but Americans today need and want a strong government with strong leaders to control the complicated problems of modern society. They want us to organize society, define its goals, and give direction to the nation. And it's natural, Hank. Government has always been the place for true power. It always will be. The Constitution was an attempt to protect the common man's right to control his life. It didn't work because it's unnatural. Government is power. The strongest will always find a place in it. Hopefully that power will be held by statesmen who will use it for the common people."

"Can you imagine the chaos if these nuts get what they want?"

"They won't. Individual liberty scares the hell out of most people, and we work for the majority. Whatever else the Constitution says, it provides for majority rule. Most people want to elect their leaders and then they want those leaders to help them organize and direct their lives. And they want security even if it means the loss of a few liberties."

Hank nodded, "And if we had term limits, your replacement would have to give the people whatever they wanted or he would be replaced by someone who would."

Harlowe was about to tell Hank he had missed the whole point. A citizen legislator couldn't run for re-election, he could vote as he damn well pleased. But his line was buzzing; that would be the first of the many companies and interest groups that depended on him. He shook the empty glass of ice cubes and held it up for a refill. "Get me an update from the Department of Justice and then help me with some of these calls."

10:54 a.m.

The CNN newscast paused for a commercial and Anna ran a nervous hand through her hair as she leaned back to stare at the ceiling. So far it was going as expected. The mail was received creating political panic and pompous speeches. Now they had three days to worry how they would handle the really hard part. Jacob seemed no more intense than usual. He wrote in his notebook, stopping occasionally to watch TV or think. He brought his left hand to his face—a fist with the index finger softly touching his mouth—while he seemed to stare at nothing. His appearance was altered enough that she probably wouldn't have recognized him on the street, but his mannerisms were still the same as the day she met him.

He was Professor T J Stewart then and working on lecture notes when she entered the room. By the time she got to the lectern, he was staring into the distance, his hand to his mouth. It was a few minutes before his economics history class was to begin. Out of the hundred or so students that would later arrive, only a few were seated. His head was turned, his blue eyes seemed to look through her, his pen still poised to write. She asked if she could monitor the class. She meant to first tell him she loved his book on the relationship of economic and personal liberty, but he had hardly glanced at her. "Yes, of course, but sit at the back and please do not ask questions—it wouldn't be fair to the students who are paying." He returned to his notes without giving her a chance to speak. She was not offended; she had liked him immediately. His nose was slightly bent, as if it had once been broken. And he had a couple of scars on his face. She wondered what that was all about, but somehow it just added to his appeal. He was tanned and his skin was weathered—he didn't spend all his time at a desk.

She found a seat in the back and, in that trimester, never missed a class. She loved the course and Professor Stewart's presentation. It was a year later and after auditing two more courses that she was introduced to him. Burton Alan, a graduate student and teacher's assistant, invited her to Professor Stewart's home for what she discovered was a regular Thursday evening gathering. She had met Burton for coffee and been out with him a couple of times. He recognized her interest and asked permission to bring her. The wine was good and plentiful, and the antipasti that Angela served reminded her of meals at her grandparents' home. The discussion drifted, but always came back to political and economic issues—power versus liberty. She felt unable to contribute anything meaningful to that evening's conversation—just questions—but she loved it. And Angela—Mrs. Stewart—invited her to return next week.

She was smart and attractive, just as Anna expected, but also fun to be with. They hit it off immediately. Over the next four years they became close friends, or as close as they could be with the difference in age. And both were busy. Angela was a prolific and published writer of children's books. Mary, their oldest daughter, was a junior in George Mason and unmarried; Carol had dropped out after a year, married and was that year the mother of a two-year-old—named Angelina—who her grandmother adored and frequently cared for.

Anna, and a few months later, Chris, became frequent guests of the Stewarts. They were treated and felt like members of an extended family. By then he was TJ to them both. The Stewarts lived in a large older house in Alexandria, a short walk from his office at Higgs University. The comfortable living area and nearby kitchen made for great discussions. Sometimes there were only a few at the Thursday night gatherings; at other times as many as twenty. Former students were invited, as were other professors, friends and some graduate students. The common denominator was politics and economics philosophy, not that the opinions were held in common, but even heated arguments were serious and respectful. Usually. That period had been wonderful. For all of them.

Jacob set his notepad aside and asked, "Coffee?"

"No thanks. Maybe later." As he headed for the kitchen she thought he looked younger now, but he wasn't. And he seemed older. The plastic surgeon hid the suffering in his face but it was still in the eyes. Angela's death was a tragedy for all them, but it was far worse for TJ—worse even than for Mary and Carol. If it had not been for his granddaughter, he might have taken his life. Carol finally saw that her daughter could help and began leaving Angelina with her grandfather. Making excuses for why it was necessary and never accepting his pleas that he wasn't up to it. And it worked. His love for his granddaughter pulled him back from his deepening depression. It was no match for her relentless joy.

He still missed Angela but no longer with the dark desolation he once did. Unfortunately, as a result of the project, his granddaughter and two grandsons were cut from his life, probably forever, and for the rest of his life he would long for them, too.

She grabbed the volume control. *Dammit, we'll all miss our families before this is over, and they'll miss us.* She cranked the volume up to take her mind off that thought.

1:24 p.m.
Attorney General John Hammar looked across his black granite desktop at his visitors. "Our telephone system can't handle the calls I'm getting from Congress and K Street. The president has called twice in the last hour." His eyes bored in on Assistant Director of Counter Terrorism, Lance Bullard—he ran the FBI's Joint Terrorism Task Forces—and then back to FBI Director Raymond Proctor.

Proctor said, "Members of Congress receive threats all the time, but almost always from simple-minded nuts without the capacity to do any real damage. They are usually easy to find and put away; although in the last few years we are getting a great many more. I believe . . ."

"But this threat came from someone inside this building, someone who was a few yards down the damn hall. And she walked in and out free as a damn bird."

"I meant to say, sir, this is not a typical threat. We know we will need our best people and we will need all the resources we can muster from outside the department."

Hammar had personally never been bothered with the apprehension of would-be assassins. He would be involved this time. He pointed at the file just placed in front of him. "This is your best?"

"Yes, sir." Bullard said. "Special Agent Michael O'Brian is our top choice for this assignment."

The attorney general opened his file, checked the color photo and nodded. He liked the look of O'Brian, green eyes under thin, straight, black eyebrows, short coal black and almost curly hair, small nose and mouth and a small scar above the left eye. Hammar noted he was six feet and 180 pounds. He was also attractive. Hammar didn't like dealing with unattractive people. "Tell me about him."

Assistant Director Bullard looked at his prepared synopsis. "Seven years on the Joint Terrorism Task Force, 230 arrests—all clean, respected by other JTTF agents, good investigative skills, excellent team manager and a natural leader. Most important, he seems to know which rocks to turn over."

"What's his personal background?"

"Only son of a Pittsburgh street cop, tough working class neighborhood. His school chums included some future hoods—a couple now in prison. O'Brian stayed straight, good student, no problems. Graduated high school at the top of his class, joined the army for the GI benefits, graduated University of Pittsburgh in three years with a BA in History, and two years later from Pitt Law School. Passed the bar first time. Assistant Prosecutor for the City of Pittsburgh three years. Joined the Bureau eleven years ago and JTTF six years ago. Lots of arrests from his investigations or from informers he developed."

Bullard closed his folder and looked up.

"Any family problems that will affect this assignment?"

"Parents are dead. He's divorced and lives alone. Supports a daughter who lives with her mother in Arlington."

Hammar picked up his phone and told his secretary to show Agent O'Brian in.

O'Brian knew when he got the call that Bullard must have suggested he head the task force. He hardly knew the Director and he had never met the AG but he knew that they wouldn't have anything else on their plate. He intended to accept the position, but there was no way he could promise to find these nuts in three days.

Attorney General Hammar rose and walked around the desk to shake his hand. He said, "John Hammar." He wasn't smiling.

O'Brian introduced himself and turned toward the director who acknowledged O'Brian with a nod and "Agent O'Brian." Bullard smiled.

Hammar motioned O'Brian to the chair directly across. O'Brian thought he had seen farms with less acreage than the AG's granite desktop.

"You'll be Special Agent in Charge of the TLR investigation."

O'Brian heard himself say, "Thank you, sir."

"We'll give you all the resources you can use, but these nuts must be caught quickly. The president and the congressional leadership want us to use any methods necessary to catch them before they panic Congress and the nation. Whatever it takes." He paused, staring with piercing black eyes beneath thick white eyebrows. "Do you understand what we're asking of you?"

O'Brian nodded. "Yes, sir."

"They won't play by the rules and neither can we. I don't like to ask that of you." His eyes did not reveal any embarrassment or sympathy. "It goes against my Christian grain . . . it really does. I know it does yours too. But these people mean to bring our government down." He put his hands flat on the desk and leaned forward. "They claim to be defending freedom, but term limits would destroy the leadership that keeps it safe. We must do whatever it takes to protect our American way of life."

"Yes, sir."

"As I'm sure you know, I served in the Senate for twenty-two years before accepting this post. Many of the threatened senators and representatives are long-time friends. Good men and women. Their job can't be done by a new crop of freshmen every few years. You'll need to smash this radical group before they kill or scare off some of our most important leaders."

"Yes, sir. I would like to pick the members of my task force."

Bullard said, "Give me your list."

At least they weren't telling him how to organize his team.

"You'll also have the help of the OITC. General Faedester is the director. The president ordered him to drop his other assignments and devote his full attention to discovering any information that may be helpful to our task force. He'll be in touch."

O'Brian knew OITC was the Office for Interception of Terrorist Communication, one of the organizations that made up the National Security Agency. In fact that was about all he knew. "I've never worked with them," he said.

"More than 1100 terrorists were apprehended last year as a result of the National Security Agency."

"Yes, sir," he said, but he was pretty sure that none had stood trial.

"They're authorized to use investigative methods we can't," Proctor said. "Because they're involved with espionage their budgets are unsupervised. Not even Congress knows what they are spending. Or doing. We do know they use super-computers to examine data and cross check it against data from other sources. And apparently they get it all, Agent O'Brian, all the data on every computer of interest everywhere. Unless it's encrypted."

"That will be illegal in another year. It's too easy for terrorists to use," the AG said. "Get your task force organized and moving. I want to hear tomorrow how it's going." He stood to indicate the meeting was ended, but as he walked O'Brian to the door he said, "One more thing. These term limits terrorists will almost certainly be involved in Term Limits Now or libertarian organizations like the Jeffersonian Freedoms Institute. If they aren't active in those, they will be known to people in those organizations. Lean hard on everyone pushing the term limits issue. Start with the Jeffersonian Freedoms Institute and Term Limits Now. Get a list of their members. And get a list of the cranks and rabble-rousers that send them money. General Faedester will know what to do with those names."

2 p.m.

Jacob watched Anna at her laptop. Her skills and natural aptitude for everything mathematical or related to the computer were astonishing. He knew she had taken a job several years ago without any interest in the field. It was happenstance. Entirely. But computer science became her passion.

Before that she worked as intern to Senator Penny but quickly became disgusted with the sycophants, lobbyists and politicians attracted to Washington. Senator Penny offered her the internship when she graduated from high school—her father was a lifelong friend of Senator Penny. She had no college, so when she left it was to apply for a job she found in the classifieds—an entry level office job at Tandem Computer Company. One thing led to another. They nurtured the talent they found in her. She did, also. She took computer science courses in the Arlington area and studied constantly. She stayed with Tandem for several years, until a change in management prompted her departure four years ago. She opened her own consulting company and was immediately profitable.

Until last Friday, she was consulting to several federal agencies and to a number of private companies that contracted to the federal government. The rest of the private sector was in an economic crisis but her customers were not. There were few problems in the information technology field—hardware or software—she could not identify quickly and resolve. Her customer's technical support staff relied on her to make them look good.

They and her friends believed she was on a chartered sailboat cruise in the Aegean Sea. She packed a bag as if she were leaving for three weeks. She made appointments for the period after that, but when she walked out of her apartment it was for the last time. Jacob suspected she nursed a slender hope Congress would capitulate quickly and she could go back to her consulting. If so, she had better get over that notion. Too much was at stake.

They both worked on a long desk-high worktop supported by file cabinets and built against the wall in the room that had been his office for the last two years. Now it was her office too, and at night, her bedroom.

She was turned slightly away, her head in profile. He tried not to make a habit of it, but often found his eyes pulled to her. A twisted smile almost found his face. *I'm still a man even if she is young enough to be my daughter*. The phrase brought back a memory, a conversation he and Angela overheard. They were in the kitchen. Anna had arrived early for a Thursday evening get-together.

She was in the living room on her cell phone. He had not noticed the conversation until she said, "Oh my god, no! That's so stupid. She could almost be his daughter."

He exchanged glances with Angela—her soft smile and gentle shake of her head suggested she agreed with Anna. He went back to uncorking the wine.

Anna said, "Doesn't she get it? He's nearly 20 years older. He's 50, right?" There were brief pauses as the caller spoke. "Doesn't he get it? He must be a father figure to her? I know he's a nice guy but what can they have in common? They both need to get a life."

The conversation went on in that vein another minute or so, her repugnance for the young-girl/old-guy romance apparent. And he agreed of course. She came into the kitchen afterward without mentioning the call but he caught her looking at him with a quizzical almost startled expression.

2 p.m.
Jerry Young, the White House Press Secretary, looked over the sixty-eight news and TV reporters crammed into the briefing room. Three years ago he was one of them. Now he had the daily problem of assuring the public that the administration and the Congress were working together to invigorate the economy, get the 20% unemployment figure down, reduce the surging inflation, eliminate waste, fraud and abuse, and bring unnecessary spending under control. He was pleased to have something else to talk about. So was the president, who didn't really believe that the TLR was capable of carrying out their threat.

"Good morning." He glanced at the clear Lucite prompter hanging from the ceiling above the reporters. "The president has spoken with the congressional leadership about the assassination threat. He assured them, and he wishes to reassure the nation, that each of the threatened senators and representatives will be fully protected. No one," he emphasized, "will be assassinated. The president, as authorized by the Patriot Act, has designated the TLR as terrorists. He has directed the Department of Justice to use all the powers granted under that act to find and apprehend, or destroy them."

His eyes swept briefly over the prompter before looking into the cameras again. "The president asks for the public's help. Those who may know a member of this organization should understand that the law requires that you immediately come forward with any information they may have. Under the Patriot Act those who knowingly fail to report information that may help with the apprehension of terrorists, are by that Act's definition, accomplices to that terrorism. This includes family members. All federal police agencies have been placed on the highest alert. The Secret Service will be responsible for protection of threatened members of Congress. They will supervise and coordinate the actions of the Capitol Police, Washington DC Police Department and other federal agencies providing manpower and equipment. The president is personally following the situation to insure that every possible resource is used to protect threatened members of Congress and to bring the terrorists to justice. He will be speaking to the nation soon."

He pointed at a reporter from the New York Times. "Howard?"

"Is it possible that someone in the Department of Justice is part of this group? And if so, how will it be possible to protect Congress?"

"The Department of Justice cameras recorded the TLR courier from the time she arrived at the North entrance until she left at the East entrance. The cameras followed her into the building and observed her as she put the letters into the mail bin. They are certain she is not a Department of Justice employee, but she was wearing what appeared to be a Department of Justice badge. As we speak, the Department of Justice is preparing to post photos of the courier on its website. They will also be transmitted to other police agencies, news organizations and television stations. A substantial reward will be offered for information leading to her arrest or the arrest of any of the terrorists." He instantly selected another reporter before the frantic waving and shouting could pick up steam. "Bill?"

"How did she get through the staff entrance if the badge was not real and if she was not an employee with security clearance? The DOJ uses face-scan and eye-scan technology to verify identity. How could she get past that? And if the badge wasn't authentic, where did it come from?"

Jerry Young nodded. "She is not with the Department of Justice, but obviously her access must and will be explained. The badge appeared to be legitimate, but wasn't. We need to determine how that was done and how she could deceive the face and eye-scan technology. We expect to have those answers within a few hours."

Bill could not resist asking, "Does the president feel the accusation of incumbent political aristocracy is deserving of comment?"

"The president believes voters are able to select whomever they want."

2:30 p.m.
Jacob thought nothing important had happened at the White House press conference or at Harlowe's press conference. Anna seemed transfixed by Young's comments and by the TV journalists afterwards. She was probably a little frightened to see the reaction the letter had provoked. "Worried?"

She looked at him as if she couldn't imagine what he meant and turned back to the television. She sat slumped at one end of the brown leather couch in a loose gray sweater, faded jeans and sandals, her long legs crossed and extended onto the worn Persian carpet. No makeup; not that she needed it. They watched CNN. Two other televisions, volumes muted, were tuned to NBC and Fox News. The same snippets from Senator Harlowe's press conference were repeated every thirty minutes together with news from the battles in the Middle East and the latest announcements of layoffs and closings. Jacob had never met Jerry Young but he knew Harlowe personally. He knew many of the people who had received the letter. Some were easy to like, personable, intelligent and without apparent conceit. Some were as overbearing as they appeared. But almost every damn one of them, on the left and right, were arrogant enough to believe they personally could create a better society by commanding it. The others just wanted the power that came with their office. He thought the omnipotent social engineers probably did more damage than the corrupt group.

He turned the television down and tried again. "Will the photos bother you?"

She shrugged.

"It was a good disguise. You won't be recognized." When she didn't respond, he leaned forward. "Will you be able to handle this?"

She continued to look at the television. "What's the alternative?"

"If you can't, we rethink the plan."

She threw her head back in exasperation. "We're way past rethinking anything."

"I mean if you can't handle the task . . ."

"What are you doing?" Her face stiffened and grew a little red. "A change now would be a disaster." She hesitated a moment. "I'll do my part. I promised I would and I will."

He shrugged. "Good."

For a long minute the only sound was the television. She got up with a cup of cold coffee and started to the kitchen. "Forget it. I'm just feeling sorry for myself."

He went to the bedroom-office, just a little pissed but he wasn't sure why. He sat at his laptop but looked at the photo of Angela standing at the helm of their ketch; it was taken three months before the accident. They had been married for thirty-two years; she had been gone for nearly four. Her eyes looking back at him from that photo stopped his heart. The photo of Mary and Carol and his three grandkids had the same power. It was taken a little more than two years ago, shortly before his "death at sea," almost the last time he saw them.

Their photos reminded him why he was sitting at the desk. He began editing the second message; the basic text had been ready for weeks. Anna would download it from his laptop to an internet-capable cell phone and, at midnight, send it to a hundred news organizations. Over the last two years she learned everything she could about privacy software, encryption, and hacking. Because she consulted at the programming level she had access to the federal computer systems and, as a result, to the personal computers of members of Congress. She had dropped contact handshakes in their firewall software that made her access appear to be from a sister agency.

Their cell phone system was also her design. Each of them used a different phone with a different number and service provider every day—she had purchased a hundred phones from various vendors in multiple cities. Conversations were short; terms or phrases that might catch the attention of the NSA were avoided. Instead of TLR they referred to the *project,* and *task* was the word used instead of assassination.

She could also send internet messages without leaving a return path. She established a hundred internet accounts and twenty websites. They and the phones and laptops were purchased under bogus names. They could not be traced, Anna assured them, if they used the cell phones and laptops as she designed them. She was as important to the project as Chris, maybe more so.

Jacob heard the increase in the television volume as Anna called to him. "I think this is it."

Over the Department of Justice logo the screen displayed the message. *In accord with recent changes in the Patriot Act and to keep the public aware of planned, potential or ongoing terrorism, the Department of Justice presents the following information. Each radio and TV station in the nation is required to make this information available immediately and without alteration. Failure of any station to do so may result in the loss of their broadcast license.*

The message disappeared as Attorney General John Hammar appeared at the Department of Justice pressroom podium. "Yesterday morning a woman, using false identification, entered the Department of Justice building and used the Department of Justice postal facilities to mail assassination threats and demands to 378 members of the House and Senate. The letters were from a group that identifies itself as the Term Limits Revolution. Our cameras captured multiple photos and videos of the woman. They will be shared with the public. Because of their ability to gain access to our facilities with false documentation we must take the threats seriously. A reward of fifty million dollars is offered for information leading to her capture and or the capture of any member of this organization."

Jacob held both hands aloft. "Thank you, Jesus!" and was grinning until he noticed Anna's shock and fright.

As various long and close-up views began appearing on all three of their television screens, the attorney general continued, "She is approximately five feet eight, slender and probably in her mid-thirties. The blond hair may be a wig or she may wear a wig at other times. The blue eyes may be contacts. Please look carefully at the face. If you believe you know this person, do not approach her. She should be considered dangerous. Call your local FBI office or your local police department immediately."

The screen went momentarily black and the Fox News reporter was back. Jacob turned the volume down and said, "They will be overwhelmed with false reports."

"The guy who tried to pick me up will recognize me."

"But the DOJ will get a thousand such calls. More! And in any case, what could he say that would hurt us?"

"What if they blanket the area with cameras and people?"

"Chris will know and we will find a way around it."

"What if someone saw me go in or out of the warehouse?"

"Do you think they did?"

She shook her head. "I'm frightened, that's all."

"We all are. We knew we would be. We have to get past it."

3 p.m.
O'Brian stopped before crossing Pennsylvania Avenue and looked up at the J Edgar Hoover FBI building—three million square feet of office space and seven thousand employees in that building alone. Imposing.

He made his way through the security system up to the Joint Terrorism Task Force on the sixth floor. He shut the door of his office, hung his jacket on a hook on the back side and, with his hands clasped behind his neck, sat at his desk and thought. The Secret Service and a bunch of agents untrained in body-guarding couldn't possibly protect 378 political prima donnas. If TLR has done their homework and if they're only half as capable as they claim to be, then some Congress members will get term-limited. Unless we get a break.

O'Brian reread the TLR letter. They could have someone inside the DOJ, maybe someone in the bureau, but lots of federal officers had DOJ access.

He would have to build a task force fast and needed help designing it. He made his first decision. Katherine Bradley. She was smart, maybe smarter than he was. And she wouldn't get in his way. He'd have to wear his blinders though. He was reaching for the phone when it rang.

"This is General Faedester. I believe Attorney General Hammar told you I'd be calling?"

"Yes, sir. He said you could help with the TLR investigation."

"I think you may be surprised at how much information we presently have for you. For example, we can give you the financial sponsors and activists within the term limits movement, those fervent and wealthy enough to finance this operation. At this moment we are running cross-checks on those and other names in our database."

"I look forward to getting my hands on it. But I just got the assignment a few minutes ago; before I can do anything with your information I need to select my staff and organize it. That will take most of the night. I'll want to meet with you as soon as that is done, perhaps tomorrow morning."

"This is Tuesday afternoon and, if we can believe the threats, the assassinations start Friday. My team can deliver more leads in a few minutes than a hundred agents can find in a year. We have ways of getting them you simply don't have."

"I'm sure that's true, General. Can we meet tomorrow morning?"

General Faedester said, "Yes," and disconnected.

O'Brian shrugged and called Bradley. She arrived seconds later; her desk was down the hall.

Special Agent Katherine Bradley was tall, but three inches shorter than O'Brian; a distance runner with short platinum blond hair and dark gray-green eyes that partly explained the "Kat" that friends used. She was liked but kept her professional life separated from her private life. Most days, like today, she wore a dark pants suit with a blouse or sweater, no makeup and no jewelry.

His phone rang again as soon as she was seated. His face tightened when he recognized the caller ID. He lifted the handset, but before he could identify himself, Attorney General Hammar said, "General Faedester has the ear of the president. I want you to meet with him today."

The line went dead as soon as he said, "Yes, sir." He was losing control before making his first decision.

Bradley waited. He said. "I've been asked . . . told, to put together a task force to find the TLR. I want your help."

Bradley raised her eyebrows and nodded.

"You'll be surprised to know, the AG wants them caught before anyone gets hurt."

"Which means we have three days . . . if we can believe their message."

"No problem. General Faedester, the AG, Congress and the president will be working closely with us."

She laughed, but O'Brian wasn't smiling.

"You'll be second in command, the Assistant Special Agent in Charge."

She looked suspicious. "ASAC? Why me?"

"You're competent." He smiled before adding, "Anyway, I didn't get a choice, and neither do you."

She nodded. "Thank you. I think."

"Make me look good. Help with decisions. Anytime I'm out of pocket, you're in charge. If I get a chance to sleep for a few minutes in the next few days, you make any decision you think appropriate, or that you think I would make."

"Where do we start?"

"Help choose our team." He turned his monitor so she could see it and brought up the personnel files of every JTTF agent in the District. She came around to sit on the corner of his desk to see it better.

The JTTF is composed of agents that come from the FBI and from 23 other federal agencies as well as the military and the Coast Guard. Port authorities, city and state agencies also provide agents. The purpose is to make coordination with those organizations as fast as possible and to have the special expertise of those agents.

They selected agents from the CIA, Secret Service, ATF, DEA, Coast Guard, US Border Patrol, and the Bureau. They chose one agent each from the Virginia, West Virginia, and Maryland State Police, and several detectives from nearby cities including the Capitol police. Over the next hour they selected thirty-eight agents for the nucleus, another ninety-six were chosen to bring on board tomorrow. They could add to that team after they developed some ideas of where and how to look for the TLR.

O'Brian attached the agents files in an email to Assistant Director Bullard. *My initial selection. I need the first 38 in an organization meeting this evening at 7 p.m. Tomorrow I need the other ninety-six. I may need more.*

He leaned back from the keyboard. "We'll move faster with two teams, each team under a separate leader and following different hunches, but both teams sharing information."

"This will be a super high visibility case. Everyone will want to be the agent who caught the TLR. They'll need a reason to share."

He thought about that. "Anyone caught holding potentially valuable information will be terminated. After obtaining information, they have thirty minutes to get it to Central Communications."

"And CenCom will report it back to both teams, with credit to the agent. I like that. Who do you want for your leaders?"

"What about Getz and Barnes?"

"I like Barnes."

"But not Getz."

She shook her head. "He's the agent I had in mind when I asked about sharing. What about Ward?"

"He's good. And Ward and Barnes will have different approaches."

She got up and moved to her chair. "Now where do we start looking? Who are these guys? How many are they?"

"It could be one crazy lady with DOJ access or a thousand para-military."

"I wonder if they have federal law enforcement agents on their team. Or someone from the military."

"And what is their real motive? Hammar says he thinks they're trying to bring the government down."

She frowned. "No, its term limits. Their argument was too damn good."

O'Brian wondered where that came from. She must have read his concern. She laughed. "Don't worry, O'Brian. I'm not TLR. But I do read."

"Hammar wants us to question Term Limits Now."

Her smile vanished. "That figures. They've been attacking Hammar for years."

He was impressed with her knowledge of politics. He didn't know that.

She shrugged. "I don't think we'll find TLR members in Term Limits Now, or in Jeffersonian Freedoms Institute and they've harassed the attorney general, too."

O'Brian rolled his eyes. "That's the other one."

"The other one?"

"JFI is the other organization that Hammar wants us to investigate."

They were both disgusted. O'Brian ran his hands through his hair. "Okay, he has personal reasons, but they're still worth checking out. Both organizations want Congress term-limited and someone in one of those outfits may have heard something, or may know someone."

"Right."

O'Brian saw the flashing email alert, a reply from Assistant Director Bullard. *"Your personnel request is approved and each is being notified to report to your 7 p.m. meeting. Please let me know what other resources you require."*

They spent the next hour organizing. Bradley took charge of moving agents that were on the new team into O'Brian's area. Some agents were moved to make room for the new task force. It was standard operating procedure, accomplished quickly. Files, chairs, desks and electronics rolled to new locations. Bradley moved to the cubicle nearest O'Brian's office and across from his secretary, Rita.

While Bradley was organizing staff, O'Brian read her file. She was thirty-five, nine years with the FBI, married two years but divorced eight years ago, the same year he was. No children. Before joining the FBI, she was a CPA with the IRS investigating tax evasion. She enjoyed detective work and applied to the FBI. Good marks at the academy; worked bribery and public corruption investigations out of the NYC office. Commendations and posted to Washington JTTF three years ago.

O'Brian glanced at the yellow telephone slips from his former wife. He sent her half his pay every month. Most went for his daughter Meg's private school and he was glad to give it, but damn he hated dealing with Nancy. He'd have to call her later. It was 5:25, time to call Faedester's office. He smiled when he got his answering machine. "General, this is Agent O'Brian. I'm very sorry to have missed you. I've made up the task force and we are having our first meeting this evening at 7 p.m. Excuse me, sir. That would be 1900 hours. I wish you could be here for that meeting but I can certainly meet with you at your pleasure when you get this call. We should get together ASAP." He was still smiling as he opened his notepad to make notes for the meeting.

A few minutes later Bradley came in carrying sandwiches, cokes and a notepad with ideas for the meeting.

O'Brian realized he was hungry. He bit into the sandwich as he looked over her list. Some items did not duplicate his. *Artist to work up photos of blond with dark hair, no makeup, etc. Check for photos taken by street cameras, parking garages or banks in the area that could identify the car she drove.*

He asked what she knew about the Office for Interception of Terrorist Communication.

"A little. OITC is a division of the National Security Agency. The Department of Defense NSA to look at every signal in the ether, all the time and everywhere. OITC looks at all the data that is digitized. They're hi-tech, digital super snoops with a file on everyone. NSA records phone conversations, emails and blog sites. They search it for the key words and phrases that terrorists might use, keeping those and discarding the rest. Anything worth keeping goes to OITC. OITC puts it into the extensive and detailed personal files they have. On everyone."

"Hammar wants us to work with them."

She shrugged. "Whatever it takes."

O'Brian picked up the television remote. "Rita said we should watch this." He found CBS in time to hear reporter Maggie Lister say, "Today the nation learned of a plot and threat to assassinate long-term incumbent members of Congress by a group calling itself the Term Limits Revolution. According to polls, most Americans are displeased with Congress and support term limits. At least one man seems to favor the TLR." As she spoke, a video appeared of a tall skinny man dressed as an American Revolution soldier with a tricorn hat. He stood in front of the Capitol next to a large sign. Maggie said, "He wouldn't identify himself, but the sign appears to speak for itself." The sign read, "54 HOURS REMAINING." In the video, he looked at his watch, smiled and changed the 54 to 53. Maggie said "Following these messages we will talk to Cal Jackson, the president of Term Limits Now."

O'Brian hit the mute button. "Maybe Mr. Jackson will give us the names and addresses of the TLR leaders." They ate their sandwiches until the advertisements finished. O'Brian started the sound again as Maggie introduced Cal Jackson. He sat on her right, a thin face with short blond hair, blue eyes, frameless glasses and a determined expression. He appeared to be in his late thirties. "My guest this evening is Calvin Jackson, president of Term Limits Now. Welcome to the CBS Evening News, Mr. Jackson."

He leaned forward, his smile seemed eager. "Thank you for this opportunity."

"Before we discuss the TLR and their demands, may I ask why *you* believe the term limits issue is important? I mean, there is probably a great deal about our government that should be changed. Why the focus on term limits?"

The smile faded. "Because our government and our economy is a mess and getting worse. Our professional politicians caused the problems and the longer they stay in office the worse the problems get. They blame economic liberty—free markets—for the mess they made. Their laws and regulations have destroyed good productive businesses and forced the layoffs of millions of workers. As the economy spirals down the professional politicians claim the only solution is more of the regulations, laws, and controls that are killing us. At every session of Congress, they gain power and we lose liberty. We can only expect graft, corruption, political payoffs, earmarks and constant re-election from long term incumbents."

"But Mr. Jackson, we have the ability to elect good people now. Don't we? And we have seen major shifts in political power in the last few years."

"We have seen a change from one corrupt power-grabbing political party to the other. And back again. That is not real change. We see a few seats in Congress move from one party to the other. It's almost always exceptionally wealthy professional politicians replacing politicians caught in scandals. The fact is the laws for re-election so favor the incumbent that in most elections they run unopposed. The longer they stay in office the more powerful they become within Congress. Most voters tend to see removing their member of Congress as a mixed blessing, like removing a fat leech to replace it with a skinny one. It's not really much of an advantage."

She seemed taken aback at the mention of leeches. He added, "We need thoughtful individuals serving in Congress, people willing to dig deep into issues and make hard decisions without regard to how it will look and without concern for getting re-elected."

"And you think term limits will give us those thoughtful individuals? Why? How?"

"People attracted to politics have multiple motives. Power, money, ego; some begin with a sincere vision of a better society. But a political career requires compromises long before an election is won. On the day they enter office they tell themselves they will recover their principles later, that the political deals they must do today are temporary. But they never are. Politicians are as adept at deceiving themselves as they are at deceiving us. Term limits removes the need for deceiving us or themselves. Citizen-legislators, after serving, will have to return to private life to live under the laws they passed or removed."

"Why would anyone seek office if it was a dead-end job?"

"Liberty is at the core of every human's self interest. I personally know a hundred intelligent, liberty-loving, Americans willing to take a break from their private lives to serve four or six years in Washington. They are far better qualified to serve in Congress than the professionals who make a career out of it. Professional politicians are not interested in our liberty. Their power is derived through government growth. Increasing or even protecting our liberty is a conflict of interest for them. Their interest is in the power to tax and regulate us, in writing laws favoring those who keep them in power. And frankly, they enjoy directing our lives. Only term limited citizen-legislators would be interested in protecting the individual rights that will protect them when they return to their communities."

Maggie seemed astonished. "You assured me before the program that you do not support the TLR."

"That's true. In fact, I had never heard of them before today. I don't know anyone in that organization—at least not that I'm aware of—and I most definitely do not support their cause. I still believe this can be done within the law. The American people can force Congress to change if they become angry enough. I fear . . . If these people are serious I fear it will get out of hand. Once assassination starts there's no telling where it will lead. We can find a better way. We would have term limits now if the Supreme Court had not stopped the individual states from term limiting their Congressmen. Term limits has passed everywhere the people have been permitted to vote on the issue."

"What do you think of the term limits amendment proposed by the TLR?"

Jackson seemed to consider his answer. "It's extreme, more extreme than anything I have seen proposed. I think if it were enacted it would stop professional politics dead and would produce true citizen legislators. Most term limits proposals are a compromise. They barely restrain professional politics but . . ." His jaw tightened. "But I do not support their methods."

"Do you think the American people would support the amendment if it was passed by Congress and it came to a vote?"

"That's where the TLR may be miscalculating. The power and money supporting the status quo is enormous. Corporations, the teachers union, labor unions, other government unions, federal agencies with huge budgets and a million contractors are dependent on growing federal budgets. There is no limit to what they will invest to kill the amendment." He paused before adding, "The TLR may also be miscalculating in another area. If there is too much bloodshed, the voters may turn against the amendment before there can be a vote."

"The Department of Justice appears to be taking the possibility of assassination seriously."

"I'm sure there are some in government who would not be sorry to see blood shed. Many people despise Congress. And within government there are many who will see an assassination as an opportunity to increase federal power."

She looked skeptical and offended. "That seems a little strong."

"When the nation is threatened, government grows, politicians gain power, liberties are lost, and taxes raised. Always, always, always. Afterward some of the liberty is returned and some of the power reduced and some taxes decreased, but never to the pre-threat level. Sometimes politicians find a threat to justify increases in power or taxes. The War on Poverty and the Drug War and the Global Warming Crisis and the Financial Crisis are continuing examples. I think the TLR threat will be enthusiastically used to expand power."

Maggie said, "I'm afraid we'll have to leave it there. You've . . ."

O'Brian turned the television off. "I want to ask Mr. Jackson who he knows in government, especially in the DOJ." He took a last bite of his sandwich as he stood. It was time for the meeting.

Bradley smiled and pointed to the right side of her mouth.

O'Brian wiped the mustard from his face. "Thanks, Mom."

6:50 p.m.
They both enjoyed Cal Jackson's interview, grinning at every point he made. Jacob loved Anna's enthusiasm as much as Cal's answers. Cal's concern, that their actions might be used to excuse more grabs for power, had long been one of their concerns. He wished Cal could have heard Anna's response. "It's happening anyway. If this doesn't stop it, nothing will."

Jackson was a good friend, or had been two years ago. They had frequently traveled together pushing term limits everywhere they were invited. Presenting those ideas on prime-time television had long been a goal. He wished he could congratulate him on a job well done, but Cal was one of the many friends he must lose forever. He turned to the message instead. And found it hard to concentrate.

Anxiety is the result of conflicting values. He had a surplus of conflicting values. Their actions were justified and necessary and if successful would be the source of the greatest personal pride imaginable. And so long as it might possibly succeed, it must go forward—no matter what their personal cost. But he had walked away from a very satisfying life and from people he loved passionately. So the anxiety was matched by guilt. He had guilt enough to shrivel the soul of any man. His daughters and grandchildren paid a price for his decision.

They thought he died at sea two years ago. Because of his previous work for term limits he would have been one of the first to be questioned when the threat was received. His death had to be convincing, which meant his family and friends had to believe it.

On a summer afternoon in a 15-knot southerly breeze on his 35-foot sloop *Liberty,* Professor T. J. Stewart sailed out of their lives forever. Out of Hampton Harbor, Virginia, he steered out into the Chesapeake and then south and east into the Atlantic. She was a sleek, fast sloop he sailed at every opportunity—twice in solo voyages across the Atlantic. Except in severe conditions, she was a forgiving boat that would let him leave the wheel for a cup of coffee and return to find her steady on course. And that day she steered herself without need of his touch to the appointed spot. As darkness came on he went through the chart table and storage areas. He found grandkid's things, and went over charts of voyages and anchorages where the family had spent wonderful days and nights. He discovered an old lipstick of Angela's that had rolled back into a folded chart and Angelina's doll's shoe in the pocket of a slicker. The wind held steady and he continued sailing after it grew dark, using his GPS to make course corrections and trim his sails. The bow rose and fell in a rhythm that had always produced a hypnotic comfort—until this trip. This trip the waves parted too easily, as if drawing him to the place where Chris would meet him, as if inviting him to the end of everything he loved.

Several hours after he left Hampton Roads, Chris left Little Creek in a fast powerboat, rented under another name. They maintained radio silence but easily found each other at the agreed coordinates 16 miles west of Cape Henry. At midnight in four knot southerly winds with two foot swells, Professor T. J. Stewart put *Liberty* on a beam reach headed east, letting his jib and mainsail run almost free. As Chris pulled his bow alongside her stern, Professor Stewart stepped off onto the powerboat, abandoning *Liberty* and his former life.

He would never again see his daughters or his grandchildren. He would never again laugh and argue politics with his many friends and professional associates. And he would never again teach. As he sailed toward the meeting with Chris he had wept for the life he was giving up and for the terrible pain he would be causing his family and friends. But he never considered abandoning the plan, not even for a moment.

Liberty was found the next day by the Coast Guard after a fishing boat reported her drifting, unmanned and with sails flapping. The vessel was towed to the Coast Guard dock in Norfolk. Before it arrived, the Coast Guard knew the owner was Professor Thomas Jacob Stewart and that he had left the marina, as he sometimes did, about 3 p.m. for an evening sail. He was reported missing and presumed drowned. An attempt to locate the body was unsuccessful and his daughters—both living in the Arlington area—were notified, as was his employer, Higgs University.

Chris took him back to shore where a rental car, a false passport and an airline ticket from Miami to Brazil waited. When he returned two months later, his passport indicated that he was Jacob Morgan; his trimmed beard was replaced with a stronger jaw and chin; his battered left ear and bent nose—mementos from protecting his brother in high school—had been repaired; contacts made his blue eyes brown; his short white hair was much longer and light reddish blond; his face was wrinkle free and he had lost a few pounds with exercise.

He looked younger than his fifty-six years.

The name Jacob felt natural. It was his middle name and the name used as a child. The change in his appearance was dramatic enough that it wasn't likely he would be recognized, but he tended to stay inside and away from public places. When he did go out he watched for his daughters and grandchildren and his friends—both fearing and hoping he would see them. His children had moved to California after his death. Mary to San Francisco and Carol to LA, but they had friends here and he knew they visited. He did see former friends and associates but they never recognized him. T. J. Stewart was a nationally known advocate for term limits, a frequent speaker at civic clubs, who made many guest appearances on talk radio and TV. He had been frequently recognized on the streets in that previous life, but no longer. His circle of friends had shrunk to three. Now he had the guilt of their sacrifice to add to that of his family. Not that it changed anything. They might all lose their lives or spend them in prison, but there could be no turning back. Liberty has always come with a high price, guilt has always been part of it.

Anna broke into his thoughts. "I found a few blog sites that seemed receptive, but most think we're just evil. Even libertarian websites are attacking us."

"They don't know us yet. But they will."

7 p.m.

Bradley followed O'Brian out of his office but nearly ran into his
back when he stopped abruptly. Two men, obviously waiting for
O'Brian, stood outside his door at Rita's desk. O'Brian wondered how
they got in and why the hell he hadn't been told. He looked at Rita who
looked wide-eyed back at him.

The younger man stepped forward to introduce himself. "I'm
Assistant Attorney General David Koberg. Attorney General Hammar
asked that I help you with the TLR matter. He nodded toward the man
standing next to him. I believe you've spoken with General Faedester."

The micro-managing had just kicked into high gear, but O'Brian
shook hands and introduced Bradley.

Koberg looked to be ten years younger than O'Brian but was equal
in rank to the Director of the FBI. He was blond with steel-gray eyes,
five eleven and 180 pounds.

Faedester was stocky, with short military cut gray hair, bushy gray
eyebrows, small intense black eyes and no visible emotion. "Thank you
for inviting me to your meeting."

O'Brian said, "Glad you could make it, General. Let's get it
started."

The meeting room, large enough for 200, seemed overlarge for the
38 JTTF agents sitting at chair-desks with built-in writing areas and
outlets for their laptops. Three large flat screen monitors on the wall
behind the raised podium connected to a computer-media controller.
Their laptops would record everything said at the podium and displayed
on the monitors.

O'Brian stepped to the podium but Assistant Attorney General
Koberg was beside him. "Agent O'Brian, let me just say a word or two
about the purpose of this task force."

He looked the agents over for a moment, *assessing my choices,*
O'Brian thought.

"I am Assistant Attorney General David Koberg. Attorney General
Hammar asked that I introduce myself and make sure you understand
the special gravity of your mission. You're aware of the threats made to
Congress. We must assume they have the ability to carry them out.
That places the nation in danger. If members are actually assassinated,
Congress and the nation may panic, with great damage to the economy.
You must not let that happen. You must find them quickly and take
them down.

"The terrorists involved in the Term Limits Revolution almost
certainly have links to the Jeffersonian Freedoms Institute and Term
Limits Now, the organizations that have been pushing that concept for

many years. Look for connections between the officers of those and similar organizations and the TLR; and look for contributors to those organizations. They may be financing the TLR. Those people may consider themselves patriots, but if they are financing terrorists or know who the terrorists are and keep it from us they are also traitors and terrorists." He glanced briefly at O'Brian. "I'm sure we all wish we could do this by the book, but we must do . . ." he paused for emphasis, "whatever is required to protect our nation.

"The attorney general and the president have prayed over this issue. They have not made their decision lightly. If we fail to break the TLR within the next three days we may all be witness to far more devastation than the loss of one or more members of Congress or the temporarily damaged rights of a few weak minded libertarians. The president, the attorney general and Congress know there may be collateral damage in your hunt for these terrorists. They have asked that I assure you, your efforts will not be reviewed by Monday morning quarterbacks. They know they can count on you and they wish you to know, you may count on them."

Koberg added, "Thank you," as he stepped to the side. Two agents started to applaud but quickly stopped.

O'Brian stepped to the podium with his jaw set and his face red. *How the hell can I control this task force after that?* But he had no choice. "Most of you know me. For those who don't, I'm Michael O'Brian, Special Agent in Charge. When I'm unavailable," he nodded at Bradley who stood off to one side, "Special Agent Katherine Bradley is agent in charge. You have read the message. You've seen the TV footage of the messenger. Beyond that we have no idea how large the TLR organization is. It may be a single angry woman, without the means to do anything, or a hundred trained and capable assassins. We have to assume they mean to carry out their threats. And we must assume they have the means, the knowledge and the will to do it. We will need leads and quickly."

He glanced at the general. "General Faedester, the Director of the Office for Interception of Terrorist Communication is here to tell us how the NSA and OITC can help with our investigations." He turned to look at Faedester. "General."

General Faedester, ramrod straight, stepped to the podium. "Thank you, Special Agent O'Brian. I will make this brief. OITC is authorized to discover, examine, compare and analyze all digital information that might lead to the discovery of potential terrorists. We work with the National Security Administration to monitor all electronic communications. That includes the internet, wire and wireless telephone lines, telegraph and radio broadcasts. And it includes all stored data that has been digitized, or that can be, all the data gathered by local, state and federal government agencies, including the military, IRS and Social Security Agency. We also have the electronic data recorded by substantially every private company and corporation. We have a digitized file on every person in the United States and a great many outside the US. We have their medical records, welfare use, parking tickets, car licenses, airline travel, train travel, insurance and internet usage—literally everything ever recorded that might be of use."

"Holy shit," someone muttered. Other agents chuckled nervously.

The General managed a fleeting smile. "Indeed. But I want to emphasize that our efforts help to secure the safety of the nation's citizens. We aren't interested in digging up dirt, although in the course of our work we certainly discover some."

Another agent asked, "But some companies must hold out?"

"When we mention the investigations and audits we can bring down on the company and its officers, from the IRS and other agencies, they usually discover their patriotism. Of course technically we can't capture every bit of data generated, but we capture nearly all of it. Our resources include nearly five-hundred of the largest and fastest super-computers that have ever been built and the finest talent and skills the nation has to offer. Algorithms that imitate human reasoning are used to find relationships between the names in our database and suspicious transactions. "When the computers raise a flag, that data is immediately routed to one of our technical analysts, to determine if the suspect needs further examination. If so, we dig deeper. Perhaps credit card records indicate the purchase of materials that might be used in making a bomb. Telephone records may indicate calls to someone who has dealt with someone belonging to a revolutionary organization. An email, or internet activity, may connect the suspect, or an acquaintance of the suspect, to a weapons dealer."

The General turned to O'Brian. "The OITC is presently compiling a summary of organizations and individuals that are worthy of your closer examination for this particular case."

Bradley asked, "How did you select these organizations . . . and individuals?"

"Oh there are many characteristics that are red flags for this group. Persons with militant or rabid views on the Constitution or term limits for starters."

"So," Bradley asked, "this is a list of organizations or people who have strong opinions on the Constitution and the federal government?

Do you separate those who call for the overthrow of the federal government from those who call for radical change?"

"There is an obvious difference, I suppose, but someone who calls for radical change may well support the violent overthrow of government."

O'Brian asked, "So when do we get your list?"

"Tomorrow. It will contain everyone that deserves your attention, and it will be prioritized by the number and ranking of hits."

"Hits?" Bradley asked

"The number of times and the strength with which they have complained about government. The phrases or words they have used to describe our government—tyranny, totalitarian, socialistic, fascistic—that sort of thing."

O'Brian asked, "Will we be able to see what those hits were . . . what caused you to rank them as you did?"

"Only a computer equal to those we use could digest the information." Faedester smiled for the second time, but his eyes remained cold and intense.

Over the next half hour O'Brian divided the TLR task force into two teams with each group split into two twelve hour shifts. He named Sam Ward to lead one and Bill Barnes the other. He told the assembled agents to "report to your team leaders as soon as you discover anything of note. Information will not be withheld for even a minute. If you withhold information that I think might possibly be useful to this investigation, you will lose your job and your pension. I want several eyes seeing the same material. One person may recognize a pattern or a clue that others miss."

He checked his notes. "Let's look at what we know. We have photos of the female who delivered the messages." A monitor showed a sequence of color photos of the TLR courier from the moment she began walking toward the security guards until she left the building.

"Almost certainly she is in some disguise. She may be heavily made up, the blond hair may be a wig, and it's possible she's padded." There were snickers from agents who thought her tight fitting clothes made that unlikely.

Bradley asked, "Could she be faking the great legs?"

Agents laughed, Koberg frowned at Bradley, the General continued rigidly at-ease and O'Brian smiled, but pointed at Sarah Murphy, a forty-five year old agent with ten years on the JTTF and with special training and experience in fugitive disguises. "Agent Murphy, I would like you to work on these photos with a staff artist. We need some educated guesses of what she might look like with different makeup, haircuts and color. If we can get her identified we can take this group apart."

"If she isn't wearing a disguise in these photos," Murphy said, "we should have her ID'd tomorrow. If she's wearing a disguise, we have photo manipulation tools that will produce some close approximations of what she might look like before the wig and makeup and, or, with other wigs and makeup. But in that case, we'll have at least twenty-five or thirty approximate looks. At least."

O'Brian's pained expression caused Murphy to add, "It's just the nature of make-up and disguises, sir."

Koberg said, "The Department of Justice will insure her photos appear on all television channels and often. Perhaps someone will recognize her as a term limits hothead, or maybe a co-worker will identify her."

O'Brian asked Murphy, "How soon can we have them?"

"Tomorrow morning. I'll get our staff artists on it tonight."

He looked around the room. "Good. Anything else?" O'Brian checked his watch. "Yeah, well, tonight we start with the two groups that deserve our immediate attention. Ward's team will visit Term Limits Now. I'll go with that team for the initial investigation and interviews—if anyone's at home. Barnes' team will look into the Jeffersonian Freedoms Institute. Bradley will go with them."

O'Brian gathered his notes and said, "Be ready in twenty minutes. Ward's team in meeting room A, Barnes' team will gather here."

Agent Johnson stopped O'Brian as he started away. "Sir, I don't think you want me on this task force."

"Why not?"

"My brother is a member of both organizations you'll be raiding tonight and I'm on their mailing list."

"These aren't raids. We're just searching for leads. But I see your point."

"Yes, sir. I also think the people in the organizations you're going to interview are really good people."

O'Brian nodded. "You can return to your former assignment. Just don't discuss this with anyone. That includes your brother."

"No, sir."

After Johnson walked away, Koberg asked, "An agent with qualms?"

"Possible conflict of interest."

"Perhaps we should watch him."

"He's one of our best. If we have to start watching agents like Johnson, we are truly screwed."

"Some of us believe the TLR may well have a mole within the Bureau, perhaps even within the JTTF."

"It's not Carl Johnson. And if he were TLR he would sure as hell want to stay on the TLR Task Force."

"Unless he's concerned that he's already on General Faedester's list."

O'Brian thought *Bullshit* but said, "Yes, sir. I'll watch him."

A minute later, as he donned his bullet-proof vest, he had a mental image so vivid it stopped him—standing on a beach on an island in the Bahamas where he fished five years ago, the warm water up to his crotch, his toes curling in the white coral sand.

8 p.m.

Soon after Senator Orville Hackman began talking, Jacob lost interest. Orville seldom had anything interesting to say. But Anna appeared to be interested. Now he was talking about the TLR. "They're anarchists, Bill. Term limits is just a quick way to get there."

Jacob didn't know the interviewer, Bill somebody. He said, "According to polls, many Americans want term limits."

"That's the problem with polls. How was the question asked and in what context? I don't believe it. My email is running 100% opposed to term limits. If we yield to these terrorists and tie up Congress and the nation with this ridiculous demand, the people would vote it down overwhelmingly. It would be a terrible precedent. Imagine the future if we yield on this one. Every nutcase who wants government to change will threaten Congress. We send our brave troops in harm's way to protect our nation. Congress must summon the courage to face these terrorists. Public service has always required courage."

"Would you like to respond to the charge that Congress has passed laws making it all but impossible to challenge the incumbent?"

Hackman smiled. "They don't have their facts right either. I defeated an incumbent."

Jacob knew he had been a governor with a strong political machine and several million dollars to invest in the campaign. Bill said, "I believe you defeated Senator Narley and that he had recently been indicted."

Hackman did not seem to take offense. "He was a powerful opponent, but I had the support of my constituents. And since election to the Senate, I have worked hard to produce good legislation for the

American people. I'm very proud that my constituents have continued to re-elect me to the Senate for 28 years."

"And you served in the . . ."

The senator interrupted him. "The voter wants seasoned statesmen in these very important positions. I, and most of my colleagues, strive to be statesmen. With term limits the nation would lose the knowledge and abilities we have developed in its service over the years."

"How is your family reacting to the threats, Senator? They must be worried?"

"They are. Myrna and the children want me to retire. Myrna believes I've given enough to the nation." He looked into the camera, brave and proud. "But there is so much left to do."

Jacob didn't bother to take notes until Hackman said, "Term limits were intentionally rejected by the Constitutional Convention, and for very good reason. You don't throw your best players off your team if you want to win." The interview lasted two or three more minutes. Jacob was disgusted by Hackman's posturing. Anna seemed transfixed, but understandably. If the amendment were not passed Hackman would be first.

8:17 p.m.

The offices of Term Limits Now were dark. O'Brian would have preferred to question Cal Jackson, but he wasn't disappointed either— he might discover information that Jackson would have withheld. He authorized a surreptitious-entry, the door was opened and the room carefully photographed so everything could be put back the way it was. The JTTF team followed with computers to make copies of everything digital. Guards were posted to apprehend anyone attempting to enter the offices.

While O'Brian wouldn't be able to question Cal Jackson that night, evidence gained during a surreptitious search could be especially useful. Giving false testimony to an agent investigating a crime was itself a federal crime punishable with a long prison sentence. And catching Jackson in a lie, even a very small lie, based on information discovered in his files, could be a great lever for gaining cooperation.

The Constitution required that a search warrant be obtained from a federal judge after showing probable cause and naming the papers or effects being sought. Until the Patriot Act, judges assumed the owner of the property being searched was to be presented with the warrant. The Patriot Act authorized surreptitious entry wherever there might be evidence involving terrorism. Better yet, the Patriot Act found a way around the inconvenient rights protected by the Constitution. It simply required that federal judges sign search warrants upon presentation. Their opinions and approval were not required.

O'Brian told the team if they were interrupted by a janitor or night-watchman or even an employee of Term Limits Now, that person would be told they were not to mention the break-in or the search to anyone, not even to an attorney, under penalty of a very long prison term. Not that he liked any of that, but O'Brian assured himself no one would be hurt by it either, not while he was in charge.

He discovered Cal Jackson had a meeting scheduled with Don Hayes at 10 a.m. tomorrow. Good time to come back for a talk.

They left at 11:03 p.m. with a copy of every hard drive and CD in the office, including Cal Jackson's computer address book. They also had a list of members, donors, prospects and contacts. Everything was replaced exactly as it had been when they arrived. No one would know they had been there.

As he drove away, he called Bradley to see how she was doing.

"It's a big organization, O'Brian, and it's full of personal computers, laptops and servers. We'll be busy for another two or three hours getting copies of everything. How's it going at your end?"

"They were gone. We made copies of everything. They won't know we were there."

"This place is busy. There was a seminar on free trade underway. Lots of important people, maybe 200 altogether, including a senator and three representatives. We didn't interrupt the seminar but I pulled Don Hayes aside and let him know what we needed and why he would give it to us."

"How did that go?"

"He was disgusted and angry. JFI constantly attacks the Patriot Act and the Department of Justice. Hayes knows what powers we have. He read them off to me. He also knows what rights he's lost, and he read those off, too."

"You're just doing your job."

"Yeah, that's what I said. Anyway, we're interviewing the staff that's still here and copying data."

"What's your instinct . . . about the organization?"

"I asked for a membership application."

"Funny."

"I doubt they're connected to the TLR. But maybe someone here knows someone with the TLR."

"So what's happening now?"

"We'll be copying hard drives and paper records for another 3 or 4 hours."

"Let the team handle that. Get some sleep. That's where I'm headed."

11:16 p.m.

Months earlier, Anna had hacked into the personal computers of their targets. She knew almost as much about their lives as the OITC. Tonight she used a cell phone she had registered to Senator Mahoney at his home address two months ago. She liked the irony. Mahoney authored the Patriot Act requirement that every owner of a cell phone or computer register it using their Social Security number.

She downloaded the message from Jacob's laptop to the cell phone and attached it to an email message from a free Hotmail address, also acquired in the name of Senator Mahoney. The message, sent at midnight, went to 100 major news organizations, and to the office of each member of Congress.

The following is the second message from the Term Limits Revolution. If your news organization makes this message available to your readers and viewers in its entirety, we will continue to make future messages available to you. You may comment as you wish, but if any part is deleted or amended, we will not provide you with our future messages.

Wednesday, June 4
Yesterday we explained what we require of Congress. Now we will begin to explain why.

The American people despise the political aristocracy in control of Congress. They want to retake control of their government. They wish to restore to themselves the rights and liberty they have lost. They want Congress term limited. None of these changes can occur so long as election to Congress is controlled by the long-term incumbents, the professional politicians who can only be voted out of office under extraordinary circumstances.

The election laws are their diabolical creation, making an effective challenge all but impossible. In recent years 98% of Congressional races were won by incumbents. The contest is so lopsided that 25% of incumbent members of congress run unopposed. Even in those years when the majority party is swept out of office by an irate public, the change amounts to only 30 or 40 seats, less than 10% out of the 535 seats in both houses.

Incumbents use the federal treasury to give themselves enormous financial advantages, such as paid staff to compose, print and mail their letters; free printing of brochures and surveys mailed to every voter in their state or district; use of government film studios and professional public relations staff; paid travel with staff; constant television and radio coverage; and other advantages worth millions of dollars to each incumbent.

They have written campaign finance laws preventing challengers from raising enough money to overcome their financial advantages. These include restricting the contributions individuals or companies can make to amounts so low as to predictably prevent a challenger from mounting a successful campaign.

They have created campaign laws that prevent ads that attack them over radio, television or in newspapers within 90 days prior to an election—the clearest violation of freedom of speech, while incumbents may continue using the media to reach their constituents.

They have created an election bureaucracy and made the campaign reporting requirements so complex and expensive only an incumbent with government paid staff, or a person of exceptional wealth, can afford the attorneys, accountants and office staff needed to run for congressional office.

They have required that all contributions to a challenger be immediately and publicly declared, thereby insuring that the contributor will be immediately known to the incumbent and can be properly punished with regulations or legislation. Many business owners have learned the hard way. Never contribute to a challenger and, if asked, never fail to contribute to the incumbent.

These are some of the tools incumbents use to retain office. But they have also used their offices to buy votes and secure financing to buy more votes.

To gain votes from trade unions, they have written laws granting special rights and powers to them in contract negotiations with employers. In the process every individual's right to freedom of association and freedom of contract has been damaged.

To finance their elections, they have written laws and authorized subsidies and tariffs favoring businesses that financially support their re-election and damaging businesses that failed to support them. That extortion has distorted the marketplace, driving prices higher for all consumers and damaging the nation's economy.

They have, with exorbitant and crippling taxes, stolen wealth created by some taxpayers and 'redistributed' it to constituent groups that support their re-election.

They have passed laws enabling harassing lawsuits without financial risk to the plaintiff, in exchange for re-election contributions from trial lawyers who use those laws to blackmail potential defendants with continuous lawsuits. Businesses have been destroyed and industries damaged as a result, with a consequent loss of jobs for individuals and damage to the nation's economy.

They have increased the size of government and in that process created their largest and fastest growing constituency—government employees, government contractors and those that depend upon them. Maintaining that constituency and maintaining themselves in office has increased the national debt to the point it cannot be paid without destroying our currency.

Congressional incumbents have all but destroyed our nation's economy and our personal liberty. Most of their abuses are clearly unconstitutional. However, presidents have named and the Senate has confirmed to the Supreme Court those compliant justices willing to interpret out of the Constitution our individual rights while ignoring every limit on the growth of government and every constraint on the power of Congress that document was meant to provide.

At every opportunity the American people have made clear, they do not want professional lifetime politicians in Congress, but citizens from among the American people who will serve a short time in Congress and then return to live as ordinary citizens under the laws they created.

Pass the amendment, Congress. Only two days remain.
the Term Limits Revolution.

Wednesday, June 4
Force Them

1:32 a.m.
O'Brian had slept for a couple of hours when the jangling phone forced him awake. "Sorry, O'Brian." It was Bradley. "Another TLR message."

O'Brian said, "Hold on" as he sat on the side of the bed, looked at the clock, and rubbed his face to wake himself. "Okay, read it."

She read it but after the fourth '*They have*' he broke in. "Hey, you don't have to read it like it's the Declaration of Independence."

She laughed, "Yeah, I do. Whoever wrote this did that intentionally—it's the same phrasing. Does that make us the redcoats?"

She finished reading the message and he asked, "So how did we get it?"

"They sent it by email to lots of newspapers and news services."

"That may be our break."

"Maybe, I'll get our computer geeks on it."

Now he couldn't sleep. He thought about phrases used in the TLR message. Maybe the phrasing could be used to identify the writer, if they published anything before. Searching for phrases should be easy for Faedester's team; everything written is digital and on the internet. He spoke with Ward and with Barnes while driving from his apartment in Alexandria. They told him of the leads their teams were following up on—none hopeful—and would join him at the meeting.

O'Brian drove past the Capitol Mall on his way to the office. The Minuteman's reader-board indicated *40 HOURS REMAINING*. O'Brian didn't need the reminder.

Bradley followed O'Brian into his office. "The message was sent using a cell phone. It's off now. We have three helicopters on the roof ready to go if they're dumb enough to turn it on, but I wouldn't bet on it. They've been working on this for some time. The cell phone and e-mail address were purchased seven months ago, in Senator Mahoney's name."

"Cute."

"The senator didn't think so. He thinks it's a warning."

"Maybe it is. We need more techs . . . Bureau and OITC."

At nine a.m. they walked over to the central meeting area. O'Brian was talking to the now 200 agent task force before he reached the podium. "Last night we recovered more information than we can digest. I'm bringing in data specialists from the Bureau to go over that material. Both teams will appoint agents to work with them and with OITC. If there's anything in that data, we need to find it fast." As O'Brian spoke, he noticed he had lost the attention of the task force. He turned in the direction they were looking to see Hammar, Koberg and Faedester step onto the stage.

O'Brian stepped away as the AG took the podium. "Sorry to intrude, Agent O'Brian. This needs to be said." He turned to the agents. "You know that last night the terrorists made another attempt to turn the public against their government. Their message intentionally twists the truth to shake the nation's faith in its leaders. They may succeed if they are allowed to continue to send these messages. They must be captured very soon. Our government and the freedom of all Americans are in great danger."

He looked in the direction of General Faedester. "General Faedester will provide you with a list of people that must be thoroughly and quickly investigated. Many of the people on his list are politically, or financially powerful, but the General has also shown me his reasons for placing them on the list and I can assure you, some of these people are TLR and others almost certainly know members of the TLR. Some are well-known people. Do not be intimidated by them." He paused to let his own gaze fix each of the task force agents. "Your nation needs the information they certainly have. And be assured the president and Congress stand firmly behind you. We will protect you. I know you won't let your nation down." He seemed to be almost shaking with emotion.

O'Brian glanced at Bradley who stared back at him with disgust.

Hammar looked at Faedester. "General, please tell our task force what you told me earlier."

"We have developed a list of persons whose complaints and goals are in close alignment with those of the TLR. There is a high probability many of these people are TLR supporters and some will be members of that group. Our list contains the 500 most likely names. Most live within driving distance of the Capitol. The names are prioritized in proportion to the anger of their statements and the number of their pleas for radical change in government, or for other treason-inciting statements."

He handed a CD to O'Brian. "I believe you will find the people you seek on this list. Not surprisingly, numbers one and two are Donald Hayes and Calvin Jackson."

O'Brian would have felt better if Faedester had not been smiling. "Thank you, General. We'll get started immediately. May I ask your help with analysis of the data we recovered last night? The OITC could sort through it faster than the Bureau."

The general smiled. "I can make our supercomputers available—with your people present—to analyze the data and compare it to the information we have. But I suspect we will discover that their names are on this list. In any case our computers will take no more than an hour or so to digest it. If additional names appear or even if they are simply confirmed, then . . . all the better."

The attorney general interrupted to thank Faedester and O'Brian said, "I'll send two agents from each team and someone from our computer group to help with the data transfer. Will you loan us six members of your staff to work here within our two teams?"

Hammar smiled, "I see I can leave this matter in your good hands." He looked over the agents in the room. "Good hunting." He left, but Koberg and Faedester remained.

O'Brian took the podium again. "Does anyone have anything to add to our knowledge at this point? Bad leads, goods leads, dead-ends, whatever?" He pointed to Agent Murphy.

She said, "The eye-scan and face-scan technology at DOJ has a few bugs. The TLR female was passed because, somehow, she is in the approved database. We don't know how or who put her in. Could be a DOJ employee or an outside contractor. Maybe someone just hacked in, or maybe they had help. Lots of questions still."

She looked at her notepad. "The guards certainly remembered her. She came through the employee entrance with an ID that was top security and with lots of Department of Justice envelopes in her bag. A guy in the mail room also remembered her. He didn't speak to her, but noticed that she was unusually attractive. Actually that's not an exact quote. They all described her as a natural blond, approximately five eight, about 35 years old with blue eyes, white skin and long legs. She chewed gum and had maybe a New York accent, although one security guard thought the accent wasn't quite right. He also said, and I am now quoting," Sarah opened her notebook and read in the huskiest voice she could manage, "We woulda caught the bitch if the fuckin' data server'd worked."

Everyone laughed. Except Koberg. O'Brian asked, "What about the photos and artist sketches?"

"They'll be ready later this morning. We're working on several possible "looks" with different hair styles and colors. Also we found some traffic photos that may be her. If so, we may have the car's license and ownership. I should have all that in a few minutes." She started to sit down and remembered. "One more thing. She ditched her badge and RFID tag in a trash container on Ninth Street. We found it at the landfill, still transmitting. We're checking it for prints."

8:33 a.m.
Anna overslept. The sun, shining directly on her face, woke her. She knew it was late without looking and she felt good, until she remembered where she was and why. The sound of the television coming through the closed door was barely audible—Jacob was up. She opened her eyes, stretched and covered herself with the sheet. She slept in the nude and sometime during the hot and humid night had pushed the sheet away. She lay on her side, her eyes on the desk when the thought occurred, his laptop was gone. Startled, she sat up in bed, her eyes wide. Horrified and embarrassed, her first reaction became anger a second later. But that too, died quickly. She was sleeping in his office. In a few more seconds she found herself smiling as she imagined him turning from the desk to see her and what? Blushing? Or offended? Or outraged maybe? The idea of shocking him brought a grin. Then she wondered if she was sunny side up or what? She laughed at the thought of asking him as she slipped on a robe and selected fresh clothes from the closet.

As she headed for the shower, she said a cheerful, "Good morning" in the direction of the kitchen and living room.

Jacob had fresh espresso waiting when she joined him. He didn't have his contacts on yet, so his eyes were blue. She loved his blue eyes; he reminded her of Paul Newman in his early fifties. She said, "Jacob?" so he would look up and when he did, she looked directly into his eyes. He blushed and she knew he had seen her. She asked, "Did you sleep okay?"

"Yes." He felt the blush and turned away to sip his espresso. The door had been ajar. Jacob didn't knock because he didn't want to wake her. Of course he expected her to be covered and didn't know she slept in the nude. Because the opened door blocked the view of the bed he didn't see her as he went in. Not until he picked up the laptop and turned back to the door.

She lay on her side, face on her arm, her long hair a dark pool on the bed. He didn't know he had stopped breathing until he heard himself gasp for air. He was hard, strongly aware of it and moving toward her before he realized what he was doing. He regained control, stopped and walked from the room, cursing himself for a voyeur. He quietly shut the door but heard himself say her name and was shocked at the plea in his voice. He shut his eyes to better see the image he thought might be burned forever in his brain.

Still smiling, she said, "Good. I slept well, too."

He sipped his coffee, his face still hot. *She knows. She is laughing at me.*

He was obviously angry. It hadn't been her fault. After a long silence she said, "I stayed up to see the reaction to your message . . . our message. All the websites posted it immediately—even the warning about printing the entire message. CNN and Fox News published the entire message in split rolling screens with the talking head reading it. Most other radio and TV began airing the message soon after that. Some blog-sites were posting opinions in the first thirty minutes."

Jacob was glad for the change of subject. "Morning television barely covers anything else."

"Are they beginning the countdown? Some of the blog sites can hardly wait for us to . . . to get started."

Jacob leaned forward to look at her, "Our countdown began two years ago."

She crossed her arms. "Maybe it would be best if I drew the short straw . . . so I wouldn't have to worry an extra day, or two, or three."

"Yes, that's what we agreed, but Chris, Burton or I would take your place if you let us. If Congress passes the Amendment quickly, you might not be required."

"No. We draw straws as we planned. Damn it, Jacob, we can't change the plan now."

He looked at her with real sympathy and she liked that. "I'll do my part," she said.

His cell phone rang. Chris, parked two blocks away, was on his way over. Jacob started another pot of espresso.

Anna gave Chris a hug as he came in the door. Jacob was always surprised to notice how alike they looked, dark brown hair and eyes, olive complexion, straight noses and full lips. Their Italian ancestry was obvious. Chris was as handsome as she was beautiful. But Chris was six two, muscular, a big neck and wide shoulders. His face was more oval than Anna's, his mouth smaller. His hair was very short. Jacob shook his hand, glad to see him, but with a question. "So what's going on? You should be at McLean, right?"

Chris looked at Anna, his face troubled. "It's just a heads up. Friends at the Bureau tell me artists are working on photo touchups of Sue Thomas. What she might look like if she'd been wearing makeup and a wig Monday morning. I don't think we have a lot to worry about. They'll have to produce many different looks. And even if they come close, it'll be one of many. That doesn't mean someone will identify you. The mouth-piece changed your jaw and cheeks; they won't get the shape right and they sure as hell won't get the combination of all your features on the same photo."

Anna seemed resigned. "When?"

"Later this morning. The good news is the Bureau is swamped with positive identifications. Several women have been captured by mobs who think they've won the lottery when they spot anyone resembling Sue Thomas. A few have been roughed up."

"If I'm identified, it won't take five minutes before they come for you."

He nodded grimly. "I don't think you'll be identified, but I'm glad Karen and the kids will be in Oklahoma."

Jacob asked, "They're still leaving tomorrow?"

"At noon. I don't want them here on Friday." Chris changed the subject. "Any resignations yet?"

Jacob said, "Not yet. They'll wait until the last minute."

There was a moment of silence. The espresso pot began to gurgle and steam. Jacob went into the kitchen. Anna and Chris sat on the couch. He seemed down. She said, "It is going pretty much as we expected."

He nodded. "We need to keep it that way. No holding back. If we hang around long enough we'll screw up and get caught. We may get away with twenty or thirty days, but if we want a chance at a future, we have to finish this thing quickly."

Jacob walked in with a cup for Chris. "Anna noticed some favorable reaction from blog sites and letters to the editor."

Chris looked at her and she said, "Some are using Jacob's terms, really blasting the Congressional aristocrats. A couple said they've got it coming." She didn't mention the attacks from libertarian groups.

"I wish Karen thought that. She hates the TLR terrorists." His face sagged. "Anyway, there isn't much chance Karen and the kids will be coming back here."

The conversation stopped. Chris was sweating. He moved nervously, running his hands through his hair, then sitting on them.

Anna let her hand run over his shoulder on her way to the air-conditioning control. "Let's hope Congress takes up the amendment soon."

Jacob shook his head. "Someone might try to introduce it, but leadership won't allow it to be considered. At least not yet. It partly depends upon public opinion."

Chris stood. "Sorry about the photos." He walked into the kitchen with his empty cup. "I gotta go."

Jacob reminded him, "We're still on for tomorrow night?"

"I'll bring the hardware in the back of my pickup." He turned to Anna. "How are you holding up?"

"I'm doing okay." She looked him in the eye and added emphatically, "I have no intention of backing out."

Chris looked at Jacob, who shrugged.

After he was gone, Anna asked, "If something happens to us, is there money to help Karen and the kids?"

"That's arranged, and he knows it." From its beginnings the TLR finances had been a non-issue. As an author of text-books on economics and history, he had done well, his wife even better. She authored a popular series of children's books. The money had been wisely invested, much of it offshore to avoid taxes. When he 'died' two years earlier, his will provided a substantial amount for Mary and Carol. The remainder of the estate went into a trust for the grandchildren. However, another two million dollars was in an interest bearing offshore account unknown to the family and probate attorneys. That had been done through 'losses' to companies owned by his offshore account. Anna, Chris and Burton had the offshore account number and password. If something happened to Jacob, the others could carry on, or start new lives. In the event they died, or more precisely, in the event they did not withdraw the money within a year, the account in Zurich would be closed and the money distributed to Chris's family, and Burton's son.

The houses, cars and other physical assets in the US would be abandoned. They were owned by dummy corporations, but eventually they might be traced to the operation, and then somehow to them, especially if they tried to use or sell it. There was $200,000 in a briefcase in the Arlington house and a like amount in the waterfront home. Money wasn't the problem.

9:47 a.m.

After the JTTF meeting broke up, O'Brian called Bradley, Ward and Barnes into his office and brought up Faedester's list on his computer, a long list ranked by the hits assigned to each name, but with nothing to indicate what caused the hit.

Bradley asked, "So what does it take to get a black mark, accusing a senator of voting for an unconstitutional bill?"

O'Brian said, "Let's assume they know what they're doing. Okay?"

She shrugged. Some of the names did have notes attached. Hayes and Jackson were among these. They spent a half hour discussing various people on the list. They went through the files on Don Hayes and Cal Jackson. O'Brian asked, "How are we coming with the information we got last night?"

"We got names and information, but nothing suspicious," Barnes said. "They've written articles, but . . . Jesus, nothing tying anyone to anything like this." Barnes, a bald, burly fifty year-old former Secret Service agent, had been with JTTF since it formed in 1990. "The JFI destroy letters they receive after they respond to them. The response letters are in the data. No one talks about overthrow or shooting anyone. They bitch about the DOJ and Attorney General Hammar. Not flattering, but it's not treason, either."

Ward agreed. He had twenty-two years as an FBI agent. He was tall, lean and quiet with a reputation for thoughtful analysis. "Obviously all of the contributors to Term Limits Now are contributing to the term limits movement. But we have no letters or emails indicating they want to overthrow the government. And the replies from TLN to the donors are pretty bland. I haven't seen anything that would cause me to suspect anyone."

Bradley asked, "What about the other names?"

O'Brian said, "Let's put an agent on each of the top 100 names. See what they can dig up."

"We need more people," Ward said. "At least a hundred more."

"Pick anyone you want." He looked at Barnes. "You, too. Anyone on the east coast. Send me your lists and I'll get a fast approval from Bullard. Our main effort now has to be Don Hayes and Cal Jackson."

"Guess we have to start somewhere," Barnes said. "But I don't get the motive. All this for a term limits amendment?"

Ward said, "Its not just power, money and sex, brother Barnes. You've met lots of terrorists willing to die for a bad idea. Why not a good one?" He turned to O'Brian and asked, "Where do we go to coordinate with the OITC? Not the NSA building in Fort Meade I hope."

"Sorry." They all knew the NSA building was several times the size of the Pentagon and had probably more than 100,000 people at work there at any given moment. At least half were computer tech contractors with exceptional salaries that compensated them enough to attract them from more exciting positions in hi-tech. They finished laying out the assignments. O'Brian was still hung up on the search for terms and phrases used in published books and papers. "Maybe we'll identify the author." He looked at his watch, ejected the CD and handed it to Barnes. "Ask Rita to send copies to each of you. Bradley and I are going to visit with Mr. Jackson and perhaps Mr. Hayes."

It was 10:15 a.m. before they were in the car and pulling out of the Hoover Building. O'Brian worried they might be late for the meeting. He was headed east on E Street NW, when Agent Murphy called. O'Brian used the car's speakerphone.

"It's a good news / bad news story," she said. We have great pictures of the blond in a 2000 model white Ford Thunderbird coming and going. Also we got pictures of the New York license plates. But the car is registered in the name of R. Charles Fargin, meaning of course Representative Fargin."

"Another dead end, but confirm it wasn't stolen. What about the badge?"

"No prints on the badge. She wiped it clean."

"Give the car info to CenCom. Let's get state and locals looking."

Bradley asked, "What about the photos?"

"They're finished. In ten minutes the AG's office will have the reworked photos. I think the AG wants to personally present them to the public."

He turned left onto North Capitol Street and glanced at Bradley. "How is it you know so much about these TLR types?"

"Former boyfriend. He belonged to JFI and we argued a lot."

"Maybe he'll recognize her. With her face on every television in the nation, somebody will identify her."

The receptionist at Term Limits Now barely looked up from her PC as they entered. Two people were at work, one at a copy machine, the other sorting mail. To the left of the entrance was Cal Jackson's office. Beyond that and opposite the work area was the large glass-walled conference room where two men sat talking, the door open.

Both looked up to see O'Brian and Bradley. The receptionist asked, "May I help you?"

They flashed their badges. "No, thanks," O'Brian said. "We can find our way." They started back and the receptionist rose, her eyes wide.

He recognized Jackson from the television program. As they walked back, he asked, "Don Hayes, right?"

"That's him."

Hayes wore a light blue-gray business suit, white shirt and blue tie. He appeared to be fifty years old, five nine and twenty or thirty pounds overweight. His thick blondish white hair was brushed back. He didn't look happy.

They displayed their badges and introduced themselves. Hayes said, "I've met Agent Bradley."

O'Brian asked Jackson, "I'm sure you're aware we are searching for the TLR."

Jackson nodded and gestured at the chairs. "I'm sure you have some questions."

Hayes asked, "Did you want me in this conversation?"

"Definitely."

The battered oak conference table was big enough for ten people, but half was taken up with printed material. Hayes and Jackson were on opposite sides of the table when O'Brian and Bradley came in. She moved around to sit by Jackson. O'Brian sat next to Hayes. "We are not accusing either of you of belonging to the TLR, but we think you may know members of that organization."

"The hell we do." Jackson's thin face was grim.

"We think you might know them without knowing they're members of the TLR."

Hayes turned to the side to catch O'Brian's attention, "Precisely the subject we were discussing before you arrived. If either of us knows any member of the TLR we are unaware of that fact. Neither can we guess who among our friends, contributors and associates may be a member. What leads you to believe we do know such people?"

"Your organizations are focal points for the term limits movement. And you are both active in inciting public action for term limits. There is an extremely high probability that one or both of you know, or have met, or have heard of some members of the TLR."

Don Hayes was shaking his head before O'Brian finished. "You accuse us of inciting public action, demonstrating that you have no idea who we are, or our purposes. There is a profound difference between those who encourage forceful overthrow of government and assassination and in those who believe liberty and the Constitution need and deserve a reasoned defense, using political dialogue and education.

Both our organizations are working to change the direction of democratically elected government. I suggest you look more carefully at our literature. That philosophy is apparent in every piece published by both our organizations."

O'Brian shook his head. "You don't seem to be listening, Mr. Hayes. I don't care whether you incite or educate. You and Mr. Jackson know everyone who is passionate about term limits—or know of them. You can tell us where to look, if you want to stop the assassins. Unless you are protecting them—and that would make you an accomplice."

Jackson leaped up, sending his chair flying back. "You don't believe that. You know damn well we aren't accomplices."

"You are right, Cal," Hayes said softly, "he doesn't believe we are associated with the TLR . . . but he intends to make us suggest people for him to investigate, so that he appears to be doing his job."

O'Brian slammed the table with his right hand. "My job is catching terrorists. That's what I do. And I use whatever resources it takes. These bastards will be killing congressmen in two days and you nit-picking idealists are helping them do it by stonewalling us. Well it won't work. I'll find them and you will help me. Do you understand that?"

Bradley looked at Hayes. "Don't you consider it your obligation as an American citizen to help stop the TLR from killing Congress members?"

"Yes, I do. But that is irrelevant, isn't it? Agent O'Brian is unconcerned with our intentions, or our guilt or innocence. He will make our lives miserable until we give him the names of people from whom he can force confessions or more names."

O'Brian's face burned from the anger, but he knew better than to speak now.

Hayes continued. "I have been saying for years now that incumbent members of Congress have all but captured that institution. But I believe the TLR will not succeed and in fact they may do a great deal of damage. Their probability of success is so small, it may even be morally wrong to attempt it."

O'Brian stood. "We don't have time for you to wrestle with the morality of it. I want a list of your ten most likely before 3 p.m. or I will begin an investigation of you and your organizations that will shut you down and keep you down."

He stood. "I'm officially warning you both that you will be prosecuted if either of you hides or destroys any information that we believe may be helpful in our investigations of the terrorists. That also applies to employees of both your organizations. You'd better warn them."

A secretary leaped aside as O'Brian stormed through the office with Bradley in his wake. They had driven a couple of blocks before she said, "Hayes really got to you."

"Get the warrants. I'll bring the world down around their ears If I don't have names by 3 p.m."

She thought about it, decided not to say it, and then couldn't stop herself. "Which won't do any good, but Hammar will be pleased."

"What the hell do you mean by that?"

"He wanted you to get tough. This is just what he wanted."

O'Brian was so pissed he ran a light, which embarrassed him more. Neither spoke until they stepped off the elevators. O'Brian said, "Let's talk in my office."

After he closed the door he said, "I'm not doing this because Hammar told me to, or to make him happy. I'm doing it because it's our best option now and time is running out."

She nodded, considering his statement. "If Hammar demands that you name the ten most likely agents on your team that might be TLR moles, I don't think your reaction will be to sit down and make a list. Hayes and Jackson won't either." She won the staring contest.

He turned to his monitor. "You have work to do."

CenCom called as the door closed behind her. "The Arlington police found the white Ford Thunderbird five minutes ago in front of an apartment building off Leesburg Pike. Windows down, unlocked, the key still in it. An Arlington police car is watching it."

"Get the forensic lab on it before anyone touches the car." He hoped she had panicked, leaving evidence behind, but he knew better. He punched in the AG's private line and got his voice mail. "Sir, this is Agent O'Brian. The car used by the TLR courier has been found. I've asked forensics to go over it and I'll let you know what we find. With regard to the ongoing investigations of Term Limits Now and JFI, an hour ago Agent Bradley and I met with Don Hayes of JFI and Cal Jackson of Term Limits Now. The meeting produced nothing that will help the investigation, but we need their cooperation. I've given them until 3 p.m. to furnish me with a list of the ten people most likely to be working with the TLR. If they fail to offer us that help, at 4 p.m. I will bring sufficient pressure to induce their cooperation."

O'Brian added. "Please get back to me ASAP. I will not move ahead until I am sure you approve."

He was pleased he had thought to add the last statement, in case the raid backfired. He noted the time was 11:51 a.m. The call would be automatically logged at Hammar's end.

Bradley came in. "Legal will have the National Security Letter and warrants ready in thirty minutes."

O'Brian barely nodded.

"And you won't have to explain the National Security Letter to Hayes or Jackson. They've testified to House and Senate committees about its unconstitutionality. The attorneys in the legal department got a big laugh. Hayes and Jackson know that if we say 'terrorism investigation,' and write an NSL, their rights disappear."

"Goddamn it, if we have to pussyfoot around with legal niceties while the TLR kills Congress members, we aren't doing the job we were hired to do. Maybe we should rethink your position, Bradley."

Her eyes narrowed and her mouth tightened, but her voice was soft. "You're better than this, O'Brian."

11:13 a.m.

Anna worried someone would recognize her from the artist-edited photos, if not this week then eventually. It must be eating Chris, too. He would be identified if she was.

Jacob was on the treadmill again, his feet slapping the rubber surface with a steady rhythm. He would run another ten minutes and then use the stretch bands—his Wednesday schedule. Two years mostly stuck in this house. How did he not go crazy?

She clicked the icon that let her see the front of her apartment. It would be some hours after the photos were released before she could be identified, but she looked anyway. The cameras she and Chris installed one night allowed her to look at the front of her apartment from across the street, from a block down the street and from inside. Chris acquired the tiny cameras from the CIA. Two covered his home, two Jacob's and two showed their Maryland house. Each was battery-operated with a satellite controlled sending unit she could turn on and off from her laptop. After a few seconds she shut it off. No point in draining the camera batteries.

She joined Jacob, who was watching Fox News. A grim-faced Senator Jack Mahoney was announcing his decision to retire. She and Jacob exchanged smiles as he said, "I regret that my announcement must come at this time. The decision was made some months ago. But after discussing it with my wife and family, I decided to announce that decision today. If my 34 years of service are about to come to an end anyway, then this will at least remove the concern my family has for my safety."

Anna was revolted. "You pious, pretentious bastard." She knew he didn't give a damn about his family. He was screwing three women she knew of.

"But I also want to say to the TLR. You stand directly in the way of more than 200 years of democracy. You seek to reverse the development of magnificent institutions developed over that period by its great statesmen. And you will fail." The senator's voice quavered and his eyes were bright with tears as he added, almost inaudibly, "You will be destroyed." He turned from the microphones and cameras. The Fox News reporter commented, "Senator Mahoney is obviously overcome. He served twelve years in the House of Representatives and twenty-two years in the Senate."

Jacob turned the volume down. "Our first."

"I hope we get a lot more today, and tomorrow."

"They may not see it yet. They should approve the amendment. Their best hope is convincing the public that term limits is a bad idea. They could raise enormous contributions from all the groups that use the political power of Congress."

She shook her head. "No. It's their best hope, but it will still fail. I suppose they know that, too. The more money that's thrown at it, the more apparent the problem will be. Big government is also big labor and big corporations. They pretend to fight but its really just about using federal power to steal from consumers and taxpayers."

As he spoke, the stern face of Attorney General Hammar at the DOJ press room lectern appeared on the television screen. "Thank you for allowing me to come into your homes and offices for this announcement. I am appearing to urge the American public to help the Department of Justice with the capture of the TLR. As you may know, we are offering a reward for information leading to their capture. It is my pleasure to make the first award. It will go to Charlene Teague who called the Arlington police to report the location of the white Ford Thunderbird driven by the TLR courier. The car is being investigated by our forensic lab. We are confident that their efforts will soon produce additional leads. A check for $100,000 will be awarded to Mrs. Teague for her help with this investigation."

Hammar pointed to a map behind him. "Mrs. Teague discovered the car in front of an apartment building at 3713 Olen Street. The people living in the area of the apartment building are being interviewed and hopefully will remember something about the car and its driver. Anyone who comes forward with information that helps our investigation will be rewarded."

As Hammar spoke, the television screen was filled with a series of photos—each shown for five seconds—Anna in the blond wig, with short blond hair, long dark hair, short dark hair, red hair long and short, and each with and without makeup. Far more combinations than either Jacob or Anna had expected. "As you know we have extensive photographs of the courier who delivered the TLR assassination threat. We believe she may have been wearing a wig and makeup to disguise her identity. She may also be in a different disguise now. FBI artists have altered the photos taken earlier to present some of the many ways she may now be disguised. Or the way she may have looked at an earlier time."

Anna's stomach knotted, as she leaned in to see the photos.

"These photos are examples of the way she may appear now, or as she may have appeared in the recent past. If you believe you know her, or if you see her on the street, please contact your local FBI office, the state patrol, or your local sheriff. Please do not attempt to restrain her; she may be armed and should be considered dangerous. The Department of Justice will pay $50,000,000 for information that leads to the capture of this woman or any of the other members of the TLR."

Anna squirmed as the various photos appeared. Some seemed too close. By the time the attorney general finished she was close to tears. Jacob tried to console her.

"Anna, they're not as close as you think. They look something like you, but they look something like lots of women. The FBI will be flooded with calls, more than they can possibly handle."

"Maybe so, Jacob. But many of my friends and business associates will see me in those photos. For $50,000,000 they will call, too. It's a matter of time before the FBI notices several calls identifying one person." Her eyes filled with tears. "Don't you get it? I can never go back. They will recognize me. If not now, then tomorrow, or the next day, or next week, but eventually."

He said, "Yes, eventually they will identify us. It may take months and hundreds of agents for the FBI to follow up on those calls, but in time they will identify us. You knew that going in."

She slumped on the couch, her eyes moist and her arms crossed. "Maybe I didn't really believe it till now." Her life, at least her former life, was gone. And their grand plan was collapsing.

In the bathroom she tried to wash away the red eyes and nose. Still despondent, she went to her laptop. Jacob looked as if he were going to preach to her. She turned away. "I'm okay. I want to work."

She stared at one website after another, but retained nothing. Eventually though her self-absorbed misery turned to anger. *I thought about it for two years. It was my damn decision. I knew what could happen.*

3:20 p.m.
Cal Jackson called. O'Brian didn't realize he was anxious until he heard Jackson's voice on the other end.

"I'm sorry, I have no names for you. I cannot think of a single person that I believe could possibly be associated with the TLR."

"You don't know what sorry means. But you're about to learn."

"Please. You're asking me to name innocent people to protect myself."

O'Brian exploded, "That's not what I'm doing! I'm asking you to select ten people from your list that are more likely to have some relationship with TLR than the others on that list. You'd better have ten names by the time I see you . . . in your office, in one hour. And your employees will be there too, Cal."

"And if I pick ten names you'll terrorize them as you're about to terrorize me. Dammit, it has to stop somewhere. It stops with me."

O'Brian was angry after speaking with Jackson, and dejected at the same time. Angry at himself for starting a pissing match and dejected because he couldn't stop it. When the phone rang a few minutes later, he knew it would be Hayes and the conversation would be a replay. It was.

Hayes said, "I wish I had some names to hide from you. Perhaps I just don't know them well enough."

"You wish you knew someone willing to assassinate members of Congress?"

"I wish I knew people willing to take up arms to defend liberty. I don't think I know anyone who feels that strongly. Certainly no one who would help the TLR."

"Oh, you're helping them. Thirty-three more hours and they start shooting."

"Listen to me. I don't know anyone. Do you hear me? I don't know anyone."

"Are you at the JFI office now?"

"Yes."

"Stay there."

Hayes sighed, "Very well."

"And Hayes . . . when we get there you will have remembered a name or two worth our talking to, because if you don't have some suggestions of who may be in the TLR, or who may know someone who knows someone, I'll find a way of helping you remember." O'Brian slammed the phone down.

A few minutes before the scheduled 4 p.m. meeting, O'Brian looked up to see Assistant Attorney General Koberg walking into his office with General Faedester close behind. *Shit!*

Koberg smiled and Faedester did his imitation of a smile, but both remained silent. O'Brian was even less enthusiastic, but asked them to sit. He turned back to Koberg after calling Bradley. "It's important she hear this."

Koberg sat in the chair opposite O'Brian. "Have we heard from them?"

Bradley stepped inside the door and leaned against the jamb as O'Brian said, "They can't think of a single person who might be involved."

Faedester said, "You asked that we use our computers to search for matches to the unique phrases and terms in the TLR messages. The strongest matches were with Don Hayes. Only one other person, who died two years ago, used language that is closer to the language of the two messages. The messages could easily have been written by Hayes or Jackson. They both sound very like the TLR author."

"Who was the dead guy?"

"A professor who taught at Higgs U."

"And other than him, Don Hayes and Cal Jackson are the only persons who use phrasing like that in the messages?"

"I didn't say that. But only a few living authors use such phrases and they are often quoting Hayes or Professor Stewart. Their names are also in the report."

He handed O'Brian a single page that listed 34 people, each with the number of times they had used phrases identical to those used in the messages. Stewart had a score of 239, Hayes was 198, and Jackson was at 91. Others, only a few of whom lived in the Washington area, were at lower levels. A footnote indicated that the total number of people who had used at least one of the phrases was more than ninety-eight thousand.

"It's time to turn up the heat," Koberg said. "Hayes and Jackson are your strongest suspects and we are out of time. Attorney General Hammar asked me to personally convey his approval of your plan. He directs you to bring all necessary force to uncover any evidence Don

Hayes, Cal Jackson and the people in their organizations may be hiding. We believe that evidence may lead us to the rapid capture of the TLR. He wants this done as quickly as possible."

O'Brian glanced briefly at Bradley before he said, "I don't believe either of these guys are members of the TLR." She arched an eye.

"A hunch," Koberg said. Perhaps you should rely on your superiors in this matter. We *know* there is some level of involvement. Trust us, O'Brian."

O'Brian did not trust Hammar or Koberg. John Hammar had risen from City Prosecutor to senator by manipulating a willing press in three high profile prosecutions of easy-to-hate criminals. As with all senators, his rise in power within the Senate was directly related to seniority—winning re-elections. His post of attorney general was for promising to back the president's expanded executive powers. But they weren't really asking. He stood up. "Let's do it."

As they walked out of the office, O'Brian asked Rita to distribute a copy of Faedester's list to each agent ASAP. It would be done electronically and on their laptops before the meeting ended.

O'Brian stepped to the podium wondering if Koberg would push him aside again. "All right, before we discuss today's mission, do we know anything new? Anything else we should be following up on?"

Barnes stood. "The fifty million dollar reward was way too much. People are reporting thousands of sightings. Women are being grabbed in shopping malls and off buses. It's nuts. CenCom is swamped with calls. So are the state and locals."

Several laughed when a black agent said, "I thought seriously of turning in my sister."

O'Brian glanced at Bradley, who nodded. Yes, she knew about the problem. He was disappointed. He hoped the photos would help break the case. Koberg's face seemed a little red. O'Brian guessed it was his idea. "We can't fix that. But the Bureau will bring in as many agents as it takes to follow up on the call-ins."

Barnes said, "That will take days and . . ."

O'Brian interrupted. "Let's move on. Anything else?"

"Forensics struck out on the car," Ward said. "Apparently the TLR expected the car to be found. They left a pile of hair and fabric that forensics couldn't wade through. Dr. Galvin said there was DNA from hundreds of people, maybe more. No way of knowing which one was the driver. However, the registry of the car indicates that it was traded in to a car lot about eight months ago. The Bureau is tracking the owners of the car lot."

It was all bad news. Barnes and Ward said their agents were interviewing everyone with any connection to term limits but there were so many and the connections so thin that nothing seemed worth following. O'Brian told them of the list they had been sent and directed the agents to pay special attention to those names when questioning anyone. He reminded them that most cases rested on someone digging up a name or relationship. "It never works until it does. Keep at it. Something will break."

He wasn't sure what he was going to say until he said it. "We are about to revisit JFI and TLN. We will use intensive interrogation techniques." A few faces turned sullen. Most agents didn't like using it. Intensive interrogation was a term described by the attorney general to describe the questioning used for witnesses who were reluctant to testify and possibly innocent, but were thought to possess vital information. Standard questioning required observance of the witness's rights. Intensive interrogation used a swearing-in oath, intimidation with threats of prosecution, tape recorders to catch them in apparent contradictions, long periods of questioning by multiple agents and the direct accusation of lying, always followed by reading the line, *Martha Stewart served time for lying to the FBI. I will caution you one last time, you must tell the truth, the whole truth and nothing but the truth or you will face prosecution.* He hated intensive interrogation.

"TLN has a staff of five and JFI has about ninety-five so I want ten members of Ward's team at TLN again. The others join Barnes' team at JFI. We don't leave either place until we get some names."

He hadn't mentioned the National Security Letter. Bradley must have noticed. She almost smiled. Koberg sneered. O'Brian tried not to be bothered by either. "Look for anything we can use to get into TLR. Get their ideas. Ask where they would look. And get names."

He motioned to the large screen behind him. "These are people you should mention to the people you question tonight. Watch for their reactions. One name on the list is Professor T. J. Stewart from Higgs University. He's dead, but he pushed term limits hard. Maybe he started something. Who did he know?"

As the meeting broke up, Koberg approached O'Brian. "Attorney General Hammar expected this operation would be more aggressively advanced. Hayes and Cal Jackson are unlikely to give you the information they have as a result of this effort."

"If they have anything to give, we'll get it. And if I see anything justifying it, I'll use the National Security Letter."

4:05 p.m.
"I have decided to resign effective the end of this session."
Representative Marcus Ray was being interviewed by the FOX news
reporter somewhere in the Capitol. "Of greater importance, and if the
Speaker will recognize me, I intend to offer the Term Limits
Amendment to the Constitution exactly as proposed by the TLR."

Anna grinned and looked to Jacob, who did not appear to be
pleased.

Congressman Ray continued, "Now to my reasons. Last night
Attorney General Hammar sent his Joint Terrorism Task Force to raid
the Jeffersonian Freedoms Institute. Their officers and employees were
questioned through the night until this morning. Computer and paper
files were copied. Today the Special Agent in Charge of the task force
visited Term Limits Now and threatened Don Hayes and Cal Jackson—
two great Americans who deserve this nation's applause for their
constant work for liberty. The JTTF treated them as if they were
terrorists. They've been insulted and threatened with prison sentences.
Both are as patriotically American as they can be. The actions of the
Department of Justice are as un-American as they can be."

The reporter asked, "You think the Department of Justice doesn't
have information that would justify their . . . visit?"

"Don Hayes and Cal Jackson have long been demanding the
Attorney General's resignation and that the administration stay within
the powers granted by the Constitution. I have encouraged Jackson and
Hayes in those efforts. I suspect the Attorney General hopes he can find
a link between the TLR and JFI or TLN. It's a witch hunt that must be
stopped before it gets completely out of hand. I also fear that if the TLR
takes the lives of any members of Congress the administration will use
that as an opportunity to expand its powers still more, crushing more of
our individual rights. In any case, the public must be allowed to make
this decision."

"Do you believe that the House will approve your amendment,
Congressman?"

"I hope to find additional sponsors tonight and tomorrow. I hope
the speaker will allow the amendment to be offered . . . to prevent
bloodshed."

Anna was thrilled with Marcus Ray's announcement and a little
angry with Jacob. He had been groaning, looking at the ceiling and
nervously running his hands through his hair. "At least our amendment
is being proposed," she said. "I'm glad Marcus Ray had the courage."

"I'm sorry it's Marcus. And I was sorry to hear of the raids on JFI
and TLN. I don't want to see Marcus or them hurt."

"We knew the Department of Justice would lash out and people would be hurt. This can't be done without good people getting hurt."

"The other members will heap scorn on him and they may resist the amendment more than if it had been proposed by another member. He has principles. . . and nothing goads the other members more than their own self-comparisons." He seemed to notice his remarks were depressing her. "But you're right, at least a member will introduce it. Or try to."

4:35 p.m.
O'Brian, Bradley and 51 JTTF agents entered the once impressive wood paneled lobby of the Jeffersonian Freedoms Institute. O'Brian ordered the phone system shut down and all doors guarded to prevent anyone from leaving without his permission. Agents rushed to make that happen as he and Bradley approached Hayes and a group that were probably staff and attorneys. They seemed appropriately wide-eyed. Among the group was Senator Tobler.

O'Brian looked at Hayes, ignoring the senator. "Do you have any names for me?"

"I know no one that I believe might in any way be related to the TLR. But if you wish to know the names of those who believe strongest in the need for term limits I can offer this list." He handed O'Brian a list of ten names. "They are here and prepared to answer your questions."

"What the hell do you think you're pulling?"

Hayes' was also angry. "I told my staff that you were coming to interrogate us and why. I got a lot more than ten volunteers. I selected the strongest proponents of term limits that I know. And yes they work here. Were you expecting I would give you their names secretly, so you could raid their homes in the middle of the night?"

"Agent O'Brian." Senator Tobler stepped forward to shake O'Brian's hand and turn the heat down.

O'Brian kept his eyes locked on Hayes, but said, "Senator."

"The Jeffersonian Freedoms Institute has done wonderful work in the protection of America's values and principles. I can personally assure you, the TLR has no friends here. Let me assure you, Agent O'Brian, we have only patriots here."

O'Brian was unmoved. "Thank you, Senator, but we believe they have information we need. And the Attorney General has ordered me to investigate."

"Are you aware of the enmity the attorney general bears Don Hayes? Do you know that JFI has challenged Attorney General Hammar on a number of issues?"

O'Brian said, "Thank you for your advice, Senator," as he walked to his waiting team.

"Thank you for listening," Senator Tobler said to his back.

Over the next few minutes O'Brian and Bradley organized the interviews of the JFI staff. He wanted the interviews conducted with maximum psychological pressure. During the questioning, there was to be at least one agent for every staff member with alternate agents interrupting the interviews to ask questions and whisper to the agent in charge. Those waiting to be interviewed were not allowed to talk.

Most of the staff were in for a very long night. Some, office assistants and others who knew nothing, were released. O'Brian directed that Hayes and the ten people on his list be given especially intensive treatment.

He left Bradley in charge and drove alone to Term Limits Now. The questioning was underway. There were only five staff members, which meant two agents for every person. Jackson was made to wait in the hallway.

O'Brian stepped out of the elevator and walked over to Jackson, who was seated beside the closed office door.

Jackson put his angry face in O'Brian's. "You swore to defend the Constitution. Instead, you're helping destroy it. But so long as they pay you, you don't really give a damn, do you?"

"Do you have any names?"

"They aren't names, O'Brian, they're people. I won't identify those people who feel strongly about term limits, liberty and a government that's out of control—because you will do to them what you are doing to my staff and me."

O'Brian wished he were as angry as Jackson. It's a lot easier being an asshole with someone you dislike. He managed a sneer and walked past him into the office.

Sam Ward met O'Brian at the door. "There's been some tears but we got some names."

"Any names keep coming up?"

"Depends on how we ask it. If we ask, 'Who do you know, or know of, that has spoken of term limits as the only way to regain liberty?' And if we then ask 'Has that person ever said or written anything to make you think that person believes extreme actions are justified to gain liberty?' We get two or three names but the only name that seems consistent is that Professor Stewart." Ward shook his head. "They're just desperate to get out of here."

"Yeah, that's what I'm thinking."

"Why are we pushing these two outfits so hard? The AG's idea, right?"

"We'll quit looking at these people when we have something better to look at." He didn't mean it to sound angry. He tried to back off a little. "These people may not know anything, but they might. We may get lucky. Someone may suggest a name that develops into a lead. You can shut down when you think you've got everything."

"Give us another hour."

He stopped before turning right on Constitution. Two sign-carrying protestors crossed in front of him. He liked the sign, *"Invest in America, Buy a Congressman."* He almost smiled but then saw the other. *"Thank you TLR"*

He found a CD on his desk and a note to call Agent Linda Morrow, who ran the Cyber Action Team. They did computer and internet forensic investigations. He had asked her for an independent Bureau report. While he waited for her to answer he read the news clip at the bottom of his monitor, *Representative Fargin resigns.*

Agent Morrow said, "Yes, sir, we found 28,131 internet users who have said something in support of congressional term limits during the last 4 years. The guys from OITC gave us the names. Of those, 3,912 seem really angry, cursing and threats. Their names and addresses are listed separately. Of those, 1,291 have also used phrases that were contained in the two TLR messages. Of those, 237 live within 200 miles."

"And Hayes and Jackson are at the top of the list?"

"They aren't on the list."

"How could that be?"

"They've never even inferred threats. Others on the list have. *Somebody oughta shoot the bastards,* is typical. There are several local names."

"Did my name show up?"

She laughed and said no.

9:00 p.m.

The president appeared live from the Oval Office on all major networks. He wore his concerned face but Anna thought he seemed to be almost smiling. He was probably glad for the opportunity to discuss something besides the worsening economy.

In a ten minute speech he praised the members of Congress for their bravery and encouraged them to refuse the amendment. He promised the nation that their statesmen servants would receive the strongest possible protections and the TLR would be quickly caught, tried and punished.

A long dull speech, Anna thought.

Jacob followed her into the kitchen. "I'll have the message finished in a few minutes. How will you send it?"

She was pouring a glass of wine and wondered if that was why he asked the question. *Like I can't even have a single damn glass of wine?* She poured it full and took a sip. Then asked, "Can I pour you a glass?"

"Yes, thanks." He reached for a glass and handed it to her.

Maybe she did have a chip on her shoulder. "They'll be watching for a cell phone email tonight. I'll download the message text to a new cell phone with high-speed internet capability. I'll drive to a good signal area, park and leave the cell phone while its sending. Last night I gave them an encryption key to prove future messages are ours. It shouldn't take more than 90 seconds. I'll be gone when they find it anyway."

She liked that he said, "You're amazing, Anna." And she liked the way he said it. She wished he hadn't added, "Don't forget to wipe it down."

Jacob was finishing message three when Anna heard her computer beeping. Someone was calling her apartment phone. She stepped into the office in time to hear the answering machine, "Hi, this is Anna's machine. Leave me a message."

"This is Preston."

Her stomach was in her throat because she knew why he was calling. They hadn't spoken for years.

"Is it you, Anna? Are you the one they're searching for? It damn sure looks like you." He mumbled something she couldn't understand, cursed and said, "Call my cell phone. We need to talk."

She screamed, "God damn it," and raged around the room, her arms waving and hands balled into fists. "He knows, Jacob. That sleazy bastard Preston Pruitt knows."

Jacob was almost as shaken as Anna, but after a moment he said, "He wants you to call. Does that make sense, Anna? I mean calling him . . . does that make any sense?"

"Why? He would sell me for a hundred dollars, never mind a million." She sat heavily on her desk chair with her arms folded tight, her anger bitter, as she was forced to think of Preston.

"If he would sell you for a hundred dollars why did he bother calling?"

She hated Preston. She didn't want to examine his reasoning. She waved her hands in exasperation. "I don't know. Just to make sure, to twist the fucking knife."

He shook his head. "I heard fear in his voice. Does he still love you?"

"He never loved me. He never loved anyone but himself. He's in politics, Jacob." She hesitated, remembering. "How could I ever . . . ? He's everything we hate, Jacob. He wants a House seat. He'll do anything for Senator Cranshaw's blessing."

"He wants to run for office, but his former lover is maybe a terrorist?"

She could see what Jacob was seeing now. She nodded to him and began thinking of how they could divert Preston. It wasn't that difficult. She came up with the plan over the next hour and ran over it with Jacob. She would call Preston, making it look as if she were calling from Turkey. He might believe it. "In the long run it doesn't matter. We'll be identified soon anyway. But . . . it may give us a few more days."

"He'll want to believe you, Anna. He doesn't want it to be you. And if you can buy us those few days, we may get our amendment. We may even see Americans take back their government."

A few minutes after 11 p.m., she downloaded the completed message into a cell phone. Three minutes before midnight she parked in the shopping center at Seven Corners. At 11:58 p.m., she connected to the internet, pushed the send button, wiped it down and dropped it in a trash container as the messages went out. In the eight minutes it took to drive back to the house and bring up the internet, the message had been received everywhere and published immediately.

Thursday, June 5,

Today begins the last day of the three day warning period. We dread the task in front of us tomorrow. We beg Congress to begin immediate consideration of the Term Limits Amendment to reduce the bloodshed their delay has made inevitable.

Many Congress members, reporters, editorialists and others have asked where we get the right to demand the Term Limits Amendment. And why we believe we have the right to take the lives of Congress members to accomplish that goal. When Senator Harlowe said Tuesday, "the threat of terrorist actions demonstrates once again the need for serious gun control," he demonstrated why this amendment is necessary.

The founders feared government, including the government they were creating. They understood that over time, politicians would assume unconstitutional powers over us, damaging or destroying our individual rights and liberties in that process. They recognized that every human has a natural right of self-defense against the use of force, but that government cannot achieve complete power until it has stripped its citizens of weapons for self-defense.

The Second Amendment recognized our natural right to defend ourselves and gave us the means to defend our lives, liberty and property from criminals and from our government, if it became criminal. Senator Harlowe would prefer us to be defenseless. If we will not rise up now to defend our right to self-defense we deserve to be the serfs of the political aristocracy.

Tomorrow we will take the first of our acts of self-defense.

We assert that our natural rights have been stolen, the protections for those rights written into the Constitution, have been ignored by a political class of aristocratic incumbents who have turned our government into an extortion racket. If you want to operate a business, you must get permission. If you financially support incumbent members of congress with significant sums they will produce legislation that will enable you to charge more to your customers or damage your competitors. Is it any wonder why Washington is full of lobbyists? They facilitate those arrangements. Incumbents control Congress. They and the lobbyists write laws requiring businesses to enter into contracts with unions and requiring workers to belong to and pay dues to that union. Workers and businesses have lost their choice. They must take part in this extortion racket. It is the same for every individual, industry, and occupation. We are either a victim of this protection racket, an unwilling partner or a willing partner. Congress created this monster and feeds it constantly.

Our lives, our rights and our property have been stolen by the institution charged with their protection— Congress. Our actions tomorrow are in self-defense.

To restore our rights will require major changes to existing federal law. We are not demanding those changes now. Such changes must be thoughtfully considered by members of Congress who are truly representative of the American people. We seek no more than that.

Now we will answer the question many ask. Who will be removed first and how are they to be selected?

Each targeted member of Congress was selected at random, by a computer, more than a year ago. The order in which they were chosen by the computer will be the order in which they will be removed from office. The probability of a member being chosen was roughly proportionate to the time they held office, but with an added element of chance. For example, it was less likely, but very possible, that an incumbent who has served twelve years was chosen before an incumbent who has served thirty years.

We have taken this course reluctantly. If we survive, for the rest of our lives we will be haunted by the acts now before us. Unfortunately there is no longer any other way to restore individual liberty. The election process has been captured by the incumbent aristocracy and the two political parties. This is liberty's last chance.

Others are beginning to agree. Those who would like to join our effort can best help us by demanding that Congress pass the term limits amendment.

We hope no one will attempt to help us by taking the life of a member of Congress. After two years of careful preparation we have the necessary resources. We will remove no more than we must to get the term limits amendment in front of the voters. At that point, with your vote for the Term Limits Amendment, you will make this a successful revolution that will unseat the political class that has stolen your government. In the final analysis, you will play the most important role in this revolution—you will actually change your government.

Tomorrow we will begin removing the long-term incumbent members of Congress who have not resigned and we will continue removing them until the amendment is offered. We beg those long-term incumbents who have not resigned by midnight tonight, please do not endanger your family or friends by going near them. If you have been selected to be removed, you will be. Nothing will stop us.

*The **T**erm **L**imits **R**evolution*

Thursday, June 5
Punish the Innocent

12:06 a.m.

Jacob was watching CNN coverage of the message when Anna returned. They both moved into the office to see the reaction on the internet. The message was being covered by news organizations everywhere and thousands of blog-sites were commenting. Everyone noted the first assassination would be tomorrow. Most believed the TLR would not be up to the task, the incumbents would prove to be too well protected—unless it would be a mortar attack on their home, or a drive-by shooting.

After twenty minutes, Jacob said he was too tired to stay up. He was disappointed in the overall intellectual level of response from most reporters. He told Anna she should get some sleep, too. But she couldn't, not until she knew precisely how she would make the call to Preston appear to be from Turkey. It had to be convincing.

She felt encouraged when she found the Turkish telephone system had a VOIP website—with internet-to-phone and phone-to-internet software programs. And with an excellent translation to help English speaking tourists use their systems.

She tested it using her laptop to sign onto the Turkish network. She used her personal credit card to pay for 100 minutes in advance which covered all incoming and outgoing calls. She called the cell phone sitting on her desk and while she was waiting she turned on the radio near the computer. The cell phone rang after a few seconds and she carried it into the living room as she answered. The connection was good—the computer mike picked up the radio clearly. She could go online to any computer, phone or cell phone anywhere in the world. But when she disconnected there was no record of the Turkish calling number on her cell. *Why will he think I'm in Turkey?*

She was still signed into the VOIP network. After a short search she discovered the phone number to call to get onto the Turkish VOIP for long distance calls. She called the number from her cell phone and was asked in Turkic and then English for her account number. She took it from the screen and punched it into her cell phone and was immediately connected back to her computer. Nothing was said about VOIP or the internet. She walked back into her living room, set the phone near the television and turned the volume up. She hurried back into the office and heard the television as clear as a bell.

She found a video travelogue made in Iran—close enough—and recorded the sound of a market scene onto her IPOD. She plugged that into a small external speaker and played it back. Perfect, all conversation was in Farsi—the Iranian language. Preston wouldn't know Farsi from Chinese. There was even a brief shouting match between a man and a young girl, with street vendors in a public market, and with automobiles and trucks farther in the background. That should do the trick.

She would call him at 5:30 a.m.. The internet clock indicated it would then be 3:30 p.m. in Turkey. She checked Google-Earth to find a small seacoast village on the north side—Ordu. She noticed the temperature there was 88 F. She hoped his cell phone would be off, or in another room, but if not, she would play the Iranian street scene and try to sell him with the first call. She worked on some notes and worried about what she would need to say to stop him and what her attitude should be.

There were many ways it could go wrong, but no alternatives to calling.

She slept, but kept waking. The night took forever. Over and over she hashed out the imagined conversations that always ended in disaster, her dreams continuations of those conversations.

At 5:10 a.m. she dressed and made some coffee, trying to be quiet. But espresso cannot be made in complete silence and when she heard Jacob she knew she had wakened him.

He came out as the pot began shrieking and said, "Good morning" on his way to the bathroom. She said, "Sorry," poured herself a cup and settled in to the laptop. She brought up the Turkish website, signed into her account, was given internet-to-phone access and called Preston's cell phone. While the cell phone was ringing she turned the IPOD on.

"Preston Pruitt." He sounded sleepy and gruff.

"Hi Preston, it's Anna. Sorry to wake you. It's the only time I could call. What's up?"

"I need a straight answer. Are you the woman who delivered the TLR message? You look a lot like her."

"What woman? I don't deliver messages, Preston. What's a TLR message anyway? Until this delightful moment I was enjoying myself. You left a message on my answering machine. Instead of yelling at me,

I think you owe *me* an explanation. Or we can just hang up and I'll go back to enjoying my vacation."

"Vacation?" He still sounded angry. "The Department of Justice is publishing pictures of you, or someone who looks like you, on television and in the newspapers. And there's a fifty million dollar reward for turning her in."

She laughed, "Damn, Preston, lets split it. I'll plead guilty for that much money. And I just delivered a message?"

"The woman who looks like you, or a lot like you, is a member of a group that plans to kill members of Congress."

"What's the crime, though?"

"That's not funny, Anna. These people are serious. I'm sure others have noticed the resemblance. If they haven't called yet, they will."

"Preston, wake up . . . If I look something like this person then so do a lot of other women. The FBI are smart, they'll find the right one."

"Where are you?" He was beginning to notice the sound in the background.

"Today we're in a small city on the north coast of Turkey . . . Ordu. But tomorrow we sail east, maybe Gorele."

"Turkey? Really? Wow. What's Turkey like? Have you been there before?"

He bought it. "It's my first time. But I'll be back. I love it. Listen, I have a cell phone that's licensed here. But it's on a local network. If you need to call me, take down these numbers." She gave him the Turkish phone-to-VOIP number and the account number. If he called, it would come in on the computer.

"I just wanted to make sure it wasn't you. I would hate to see you get into any trouble."

"Thanks Preston." *You bastard.* "That's so sweet. I hear your career is going well."

"You could say that." She heard him turn on the pretentious voice. "Charlie and his friends have promised me the New York Ninth District. Congressman Dan Smith will be retiring at the end of this term, but he won't announce until the last moment. He owes Charlie the favor. Charlie wants my help in the House with the programs he'll be promoting in the Senate."

She knew by Charlie he meant the powerful Senator Charles Cranshaw. "So how can he give you the position?"

"He and a couple of friends control the party in New York City. Smith will wait until the last minute to declare his retirement. By naming me as his favorite my election will be a shoo-in. No one will have time to mount a campaign against me."

"Preston, that's wonderful. But what about this group that's killing Congressmen? Will they affect your plans?"

"They haven't killed anyone yet, but a few have retired. If more resign, or are killed—not that I would want that—the sooner I move onto one of the important committees."

"I guess that would mean some fresh ideas wouldn't it, Preston. Hey, I've got to go. They're yelling for me down on the boat."

"Best of luck, Anna. Look me up when you're back in Washington. Please."

"Of course. Bye, Preston." She signed off, threw her earphones down and leaped back nearly knocking the chair over as she yelled at the computer. "You power seeking asshole. You repulsive low life . . ." But she remembered Jacob and turned to see him standing in the doorway. She wanted to weep and scream, primarily because she had once shared his bed.

She shook, her fists clenched for a moment before she had control of herself. She told Jacob of the plan to put Preston in Congress.

"It's pretty standard," he said. "Long-term incumbents announce retirement at the last moment, to give the chosen heir a head start. Potential challengers have insufficient time and budget to mount a campaign, while the heir apparent hits the ground running, his staff in place, his posters printed, his website up and enough party money to assure a win. Of course he also enters office with a large debt to the exiting incumbent and to all those who fronted his get-into-office cash."

That only made her angrier. "I don't suppose we could go after Congressman Smith first?" Without waiting for his answer, she threw her hands up and said, "I suppose not,"

"What difference would it make? A challenger who beat Pruitt would also be a professional politician looking for power. Our present system attracts the disgusting bastards to both parties and into the bureaucracy."

"Jacob, how could I have ever . . ." She struggled unable to say it. "How could I have let him? Who was I? He's slime, Jacob."

"You were young. He was handsome. You saw in him what you wanted to see. Young people do that, Anna. When you discovered he was less than the man you imagined, you left him. That is what defines you, not your earlier mistake. Many young people would have continued their self-deception."

"I don't want to think I could make such a stupid choice again."

"No." *What more could he say? You've got a great future. You'll do better.* His phone rang anyway.

It was Chris. "You fucked up, Jacob."

Anna heard Chris clearly. He was angry.

Jacob said, "What? How?"

"In the message. You said two years, Jacob. The message said we've been putting this together for two years. God damn it, Jacob. They'll almost certainly put that together with . . . God damn it . . ."

Jacob stammered. "Oh. You're right. God damn it! It was incredibly stupid. Oh Chris, I'm so sorry."

She could hear Chris back off a little. "Yeah, well, I better get off this phone." He was gone.

Jacob was obviously crushed, "I screwed up the message last night. I mentioned two years of planning."

"I heard. I should have caught it too. It won't make any difference in the long run. We'll be identified, but that doesn't . . ." Her cell phone was ringing.

Chris again. "Tell him I'm sorry I yelled at him. I'm headed to Quantico . . . to pick up some toys and find out about the raids on JFI and TLN. I'll call you later."

8:05 a.m.

O'Brian sat across from Attorney General Hammar. The AG called him in an hour ago, after Senator Harlowe had called Hammar at home. Congressional leadership wanted to hear what was being done to catch the TLR. Hammar was nervous and angry. "They'll be here in a few minutes. I want some answers first. What can we tell them? Why the hell aren't Don Hayes and Cal Jackson under arrest?"

O'Brian hadn't slept for twenty-six hours and felt as if it had been a week. "I've looked both of these guys in the eye and interrogated them with every trick I know. I don't believe they're related to the TLR except that they want to see Congress term limited. I also don't believe either one of them is capable of ordering the death of anyone or being a part of it—no matter what they believe. Liberty is a great philosophical idea for these guys. They might sacrifice their own lives for it, but they don't have what it takes to kill—for liberty or anything else. It's just not in them."

Hammar stood and walked to the window, his face and neck bright red. O'Brian hoped he was trying to get control of himself. Hammar changed the subject, but was still angry. "What about the DNA information left in the car? And what about the car?"

"The hair apparently came from barber shops or hair salons, the material from fabric shops. It was left to cover any DNA and fabric clues left by the courier. There were no fingerprints—the car was wiped clean. The badge left by the courier was also wiped clean. That's in your morning report, sir."

"I want to hear it, anyway. Did you trace the car?"

"Yes, sir. It was traded in months ago. The car lot was sold to a Maryland corporation that was owned by a Bahamas corporation that was owned by people who apparently do not exist. An attorney handled the transactions for the corporation. The attorney was paid in advance by someone else who doesn't exist."

Hammar turned back from the window, still angry. "What about the courier? The edited photos were excellent. She must have been identified by now. The reward is certainly large enough to get the attention of someone who can identify her?"

O'Brian glanced at Koberg before answering. "Thousands of women have been identified. More than 3000 have been identified by multiple witnesses. Maybe the courier is one of those, but we have a major logistics problem. We're following up on those names as well as those developed by OITC. We're also following up on the names we got from JFI and TLN. To chase them all down we would need three or four thousand agents and a few weeks. We don't have all the agents we need. The Bureau's available agents are being used to back up the Secret Service."

"You've been given all the damn resources you've requested! If you don't have . . ." Hammar's secretary announced that the congressional delegation was waiting in his conference room. "We'll continue this later," he said.

Senate Majority Leader Harlowe sat at one end, the chair at the opposite end had been left vacant for the attorney general. He pointed O'Brian to a chair in the middle, opposite most of the delegation. The introductions were quick. They seemed anxious to get on with it. O'Brian thought they also looked worried.

Harlowe set the tone. "We have our hands full just running this country, without having to worry about getting shot. How close are you, John?"

Hammar nodded at O'Brian, who told the committee all that he had said to Hammar. He added, "We have a good start, hundreds of agents following up on thousands of leads, but nothing yet pointing to any particular suspect."

"Do your agents understand that we want results." Harlowe paused, his eyes wide, to make sure his next words were heard, "whatever it takes?"

O'Brian thought Harlowe looked like a fat bully, nothing like the talking head on television. "Attorney General Hammar has made that clear to them."

Congressman Gruber, the Minority Leader asked, "Well, why don't we have some arrests?"

Before O'Brian could answer, Senator Hackman interrupted. "We need action, O'Brian. There's less than seventeen hours remaining."

Representative MacDulmie asked, "What did you get out of Don Hayes and Cal Jackson? We all know they're involved."

O'Brian waited until they had stopped interrupting each other. "We questioned Hayes, Jackson, their officers and employees at length. Each interrogation was taped and the information gathered was cross checked. We gathered more information from their computers, data that is being analyzed by the Bureau as well as the OITC and NSA. So far, everything checks out. But we . . ."

Several members exploded at the same time. Harlowe was loudest, "That's unacceptable. We want arrests. We can't wait while you analyze data."

"Senator, I'm getting conflicting advice. When I visited JFI to question Hayes, Senator Tobler assured me Don Hayes was innocent. He said I should look elsewhere."

Senator Reigns grunted his disgust. "A goddamn freshman, a super-rich businessman that put a personal fortune into his campaign so he could play senator. And he still wouldn't have won if Fultros hadn't got caught with his hands in some kid's pants. Tobler doesn't know a damn thing."

"Ignore Tobler," Hackman said. "He has nothing to do with running this country. Break Hayes and Jackson. Maybe they aren't TLR, but they can guess who is. And anyway, they make it impossible for us to run this country."

Representative MacDulmie interrupted. "I disagree, Senator. If you read the TLR messages and the speeches and emails from Hayes and Jackson, you know the TLR messages are coming from them. It's the same crap."

O'Brian wanted to point out that if Hayes and Jackson were not related to the TLR he shouldn't waste his time on them. He was glad he brought the pocket recorder. *If things turn to shit I'll need it.*

Congressman Gruber said, "You need to stop this thing dead, especially those fucking messages. They're fomenting revolution with those messages and the crazies are using the internet to get organized." He looked around the table. "Can we shut down the internet? It would just be temporary, for the nation's security."

Senator Reigns shook his head. "We can't shut down the internet, Congressman. But maybe the DOJ could threaten to shut down the service providers that give internet access to the TLR."

"That won't work either," Senator Harlowe said. "They could use a different service provider every night for the next hundred years." He turned to the Attorney General. "Two incumbents may be killed tomorrow if you don't get this investigation going. We want action, dammit, and this guy," he pointed at O'Brian, "isn't getting it done."

The Speaker of the House, Sam Keith, stood as he said, "Make it happen, John."

Hammar glared until the congressional delegation was gone. He leaned forward, his face florid. "I don't want excuses, O'Brian. You want your pension. You want your badge. I want action. I want results." He slammed both outstretched hands down. "Make them help! They know! They damn sure know!"

8:38 a.m.
Chris regretted yelling at Jacob, but the *two years* had been so damned obvious. The FBI would pick that up in a minute. and it won't be long before they notice the other things that happened two years ago. Then Karen had started in on "those evil TLR terrorists." Why didn't she see the real problem? His brain was a tangled jumble of plans, thoughts and emotions. He felt incapable of logical thought. And at noon, he had to take Karen and the kids to the airport. He tried to think about the drive, and Quantico, and his job. But the thought that he might never see them again slithered around in his sub-conscious.

Quantico, the Marine Corps training camp, was a forty-five minute drive from Langley. The base was also used as the FBI training facility and some CIA agents trained there. He had. His job as Weapons Specialist Liaison was to gather weapons technology developed at the CIA and share it with the Pentagon, DEA, FBI and other agencies—and vice versa. Quantico was where he demonstrated the weapons. He suspected he shouldn't, but he enjoyed the job.

For Chris and the TLR it was the perfect post. It took a little finesse and some luck to get it. He applied to the CIA, in the spring, two years ago—as soon as the four of them decided to go forward with the plan. The CIA accepted him that July; they needed every former Ranger, Seal, and Green Beret they could get.

Chris had all the qualities they sought. His service record, leadership reports and physical condition made his recruitment a slam dunk. He went through the year-long agent training with 'exceptional' reports from all his instructors. The problem came afterward.

He declined overseas duty and insisted on a Washington DC posting and they were so desperate they agreed.

Today's trip was allegedly for the purpose of setting up a weapon demonstration. He could have done that by telephone. He also wanted to pick up a couple of special weapons he had stored there, and he wanted to know what was going on in the Bureau and in the JTTF. Mark Adams would know.

Mark ran the FBI shooting ranges and weapons testing facilities. He was easy to talk to and seemed to always have the latest information.

As Chris pulled off at the Quantico exit he hit a pothole and the photo of Karen and the kids dropped down. It was taped to the headliner and fastened with velcro so that he could pull it down to see them. All three had bright red hair with copper tones. He shoved the photo back up but too late to stop the pain.

The guard at the gate recognized his truck and waved him through with a smile, a smile Chris saw through tears.

Two miles later he turned into the FBI compound. He would normally chat with Bill Miller, the guard at the FBI gate. Bill's son was on the same baseball team as his son Larry. He couldn't take the time. "I'm runnin late, Bill. Catch you later." His stomach knotted when he realized Larry would never play baseball with Bill's son again.

He parked at the main building and went in. More than two thousand people in six acres of floor space was impressive. FBI Special Agents, as well as local, state, federal, and international law enforcement personnel were trained here, in addition to cops from half the countries in the world.

He found Mark in his office and after the required small talk Mark asked, "So what can I do for you, double o seven?"

Mark was ramrod straight and wiry, with short brown hair, intelligent brown-gray eyes and a sun-wrinkled face nearly always in a good humor. Chris guessed Mark was a year or two past fifty. "Just want to confirm everything is set up for tomorrow . . . to demonstrate the laser rifle to the ATF and Secret Service."

"It is." Mark opened a spread sheet on his computer to make sure.

"Can we demonstrate how it works, or doesn't, in rain?"

Mark leaned back in his chair. "I wondered about that. We simulate rain with a sprinkler system, or maybe you got some ideas?"

Chris nodded. "That'll work. How about fog?"

"I can do that at Range A, with a sprinkler system capable of fine mist."

Chris pushed his chair back, as if to leave but said, "Thanks, Mark, I appreciate your help. So what do you hear from the District of Corruption?"

"TLR all day, every day. The only thing anybody talks about. Congress is shaken up and screaming at the Attorney General, and the AG is serving more of the same to his Joint Terrorism Task Force and the Bureauocracy."

"Did you hear about the raids on those think tanks?"

"Yeah, the task force grilled them pretty hard and took copies of their computer files and contributor names, but they didn't find any smoking guns. I have a friend on the task force. She thinks the people at JFI and TLN don't know anything. But the AG thinks they do. He wants the JTTF to go after them."

Chris looked serious and nodded to encourage Mark.

Mark looked a little sheepish. "The task force will uncover some interesting stuff in the data they took."

"How's that?"

"They'll find several agents on the JFI contributors and members list, including mine."

"No shit?"

Mark grinned. "Shocked?"

"Yeah, but I may be on that list, too, although it's been a couple of years." His stomach knotted. He had yelled at Jacob for saying two years.

"They may be asking me questions. I'm a recent contributor. If it's been a couple of years they may not ask you. They're definitely casting the net wider, though. Today they'll be asking around Higgs University."

"Yeah?" He hoped he didn't look as sick as he felt.

"Yeah, I was speaking to my friend just a few minutes ago. The only lead that looks even remotely feasible is a professor who died two years ago. He was big in the Term Limits movement. They think maybe he was in contact with people who are now in the TLR."

"Oh yeah?" His voice sounded weak.

Mark looked at him oddly for a second before continuing. "Mostly they're just shaking the trees hoping something will fall out. Professor Stewart wrote a lot and his phrasing seems to be close to the messages coming out of the TLR. But Don Hayes, Cal Jackson and others used similar phrases. Apparently Stewart made sense too."

Made sense? Chris was racing toward a fork in the road. He made the decision. "Actually I met Professor Stewart. I audited some courses he taught. Good guy, really smart, but I thought he died in a sailboat accident."

Mark nodded. "You went to Higgs U?"

Now he felt like he was digging a hole for himself but he tried to get past it. "Not really. I just audited some courses for the fun of it." But he couldn't leave until he disposed of Mark's concerns. "It's weird. I was a terrible student in high school. I couldn't wait to get out. My grades were about as bad as I could get and still graduate. So I signed up for the army, ended up in the Rangers, got out years later and while I was working for FedEx, decided I would just attend some big-time university courses."

"Late bloomer."

"I guess. Hey I'm holding you up and anyway I have to get back. I'll see you tomorrow."

He stood up. Mark stayed seated "I forgot you were in the Rangers."

"Yeah, I was."

"Why did you leave?"

"We were sent to Colombia to teach a lesson to an out-of-control drug boss who was supposed to be doing undercover work for the DEA. Some of us were assigned to work with pro-government fighters who would help our patrol take out key drug-lord forces. Turned out the pro-government fighters were actually working for another drug lord. We were being used to take out his competitor. More than a hundred innocent people were caught in the crossfire. People in our State Department were in on the deal."

Mark nodded but stayed silent.

"I may never get the killing out of my head. I wake up many nights reliving it again."

"We shouldn't be fighting a drug war." Mark said.

Chris didn't want to get started on that subject. He just nodded

There was a moment of silence before Mark asked, "So what do you think of the TLR?"

How should he handle that. "They seem nice. But last I heard it's against the law to shoot congressmen . . . although I think that law is seriously flawed."

Mark laughed and slapped the table. Chris headed out the door. "Talk to you later."

"See you tomorrow. Be careful, Chris."

Be careful? He drove to the weapons storage facility a half mile away and took two boxes. Bill Miller was still at the gate. He stopped just long enough to say hi. Bill looked put-off, but Chris was desperate to get away. *Time to start writing off my friends, too.*

He headed home, unable to shake the feeling he had screwed up. He shouldn't have admitted that he studied with T. J. Stewart, but he didn't have time to think it out. He feared it would come out later, but what difference would that make? He would immediately be caught anyway. Damn it, I shouldn't have come here.

Looking at the photo didn't help—he needed to hold her—but he let himself think of her for another moment before calling Jacob.

"I'm sorry I blew up. Maybe I just did something worse. I'll tell you tonight. I do have bad news. Someone thinks you're worth investigating. I can tell you more this evening."

He heard Jacob groan. Their elaborate scheme to hide his identity was blowing up. He had every right to groan.

"I'm on my way home. Time to take the family to the airport."

The drive gave him time to think. Mark was a friend. He hated big government. Chris wished he had asked more questions. He should have asked Mark the same question Mark asked. What do you think of the TLR? He sure as hell wasn't angry with the TLR, but he sure as hell couldn't be trusted either—$50 million made that impossible.

He checked his watch. Karen would be almost packed.

They lived in a small three bedroom house three miles from Dulles airport; but the air traffic never passed overhead and could barely be heard. It was a nice neighborhood, with safe streets and lots of good kids for Larry and Maria to play with.

They went to a private school, which was expensive. Yesterday was the last day of school and Karen's last day at the day care. The extra money helped and she enjoyed working with the small kids. Anna was a frequent guest in their home and a favorite of Maria's. Maria slept over at Anna's at least once a month and they sometimes went shopping together.

Chris was a few blocks from home when he called, "Hi, Sweetheart. Sorry I was mean this morning."

"Where are you?"

"Just a block away."

"I've been thinking naughty thoughts."

"Oh, boy." Making up wasn't going to be a problem.

"The kids are upstairs packing. Come in quiet and meet me in your office."

"I just parked and I'm approaching the door, but I can't open it."

"Why?"

"I bump into it before I get there." He heard her sweet giggle before the phone went silent. He was just coming up the walk when she opened the door. He ran his eyes up and down her body. "Oh, good, I get to take them off."

She was still laughing as he stepped inside, put one hand behind her head and drew her to him. The other hand went around her waist and then down over the sweetest little . . .

"Hi, Dad." Larry stood in the inside doorway. "Stop kissing, huh?"

Karen's arms were around his neck. She wanted him, he could feel it; but parenting requires sacrifices. This was a fairly standard sacrifice. He continued to hold her but said over her shoulder, "Hey Larry, what's going on?"

"I can't get everything in my bag."

"Okay, I tell you what. You go upstairs and try to figure out what you can leave here for just a few days and I'll be right up there to help."

"You're going to kiss Mom some more." He didn't look happy with the idea.

Maria had heard the discussion. She raced down the stairs as she squealed, "Daddy."

Karen pulled away smiling wistfully. "We really do need to finish packing."

"Yeah, I guess so."

He went upstairs, helped the kids finish packing and then came down to help Karen. He hadn't said a damn thing, but after she looked at him she asked "Okay, what's up?"

He needed to set the stage for a long separation. "I can't tell you about it, but I'm being given a task that will take me out of the country for a bit."

"No. You can't do it that way. Damn it, you can't just tell me you're leaving for an unknown place and some unknown period of time. You can't do that."

"I don't know what I can tell you yet. I am CIA." He tried to smile.

"Don't you do this. Don't you do this, Chris."

"Sweetheart, I won't do anything that's not the best thing for you and the kids. You know that don't you?" He watched the anger go, then pulled her to him, aware he might never be able to hold her again. He wanted to tell her how much he loved her, but didn't trust his voice.

He picked her up, her arms around his neck and buried his face in her neck. That did it; big mistake. Tears were forming and he couldn't allow that to happen. He kept his face away from her view as he kissed her forehead, turned quickly and left the room.

Of course she would sense his misery. Whatever that special sense, Karen had it in spades.

He shut the door to his office, and through the open window heard Maria taunting Larry and the squeak of rope tree swing. *What the fuck did I get them into?* He had to get out of this mood. He couldn't take them to the airport with tears running down his face. Leaning back in his chair and slumped down, his eyes were fixed straight ahead, seeing his life and theirs in ruins. Eventually he realized his blind stare was fixed on the bookshelf and "Lost Rights," James Bovard's catalog of the rights Americans have lost to their government. He let his eyes run over the other titles and his back began to straighten. Their future was screwed if he didn't succeed. He went out to be with them until it was time to go.

4:13 p.m.
O'Brian lay on his office couch, exhausted but unable to sleep. Last night had been awful. He and Bradley had worked until 2 a.m. ending up in the awkward and embarrassing situation he had been trying to avoid. When he finally made it to bed, he couldn't sleep. This morning, since returning from the meeting with Hammar and the congressional delegation, he had worked with Ward and Barnes getting them all the manpower that made sense and getting the bureau to assign agents to follow up on all the courier look-alikes.

His thoughts wandered between Bradley, Hammar and Koberg, the TLR and his daughter, Meg. He loved his daughter. She was a source of pride, but also guilt—he didn't see her as much as she or he wanted. She wanted him to see her play soccer tonight. He worried about Hammar and Koberg. They were political animals, but there seemed to be something especially threatening about them. Even their religious faith seemed menacing. But he had also seen the pressure Hammar got from the Congressional delegation. They were frightened, but unwilling to give up their power. They also wanted someone else to do the dirty work.

He was glad he had taken the pocket recorder. Those bastards would feed him to the lions without a second thought. Six years to go. The same year Meg enters college he would retire with a pension large enough to help her.

He gave up, got off the couch, strapped on his shoulder holster, opened the door so Rita would know he was available again. Back at his desk, the muted television was showing the Minuteman's signboard—8 HOURS REMAINING. Bradley came in and took a seat.

He hadn't seen her all day. He didn't blame her for avoiding him. Last night had been embarrassing for both of them.

They had worked late. He wanted to quit for the night and said, "Let's go home." Only he said it like a question—meaning he wondered if she thought they should keep working. But she took it wrong.

She raised an eyebrow in a sexy way, smiled and nodded.

O'Brian was speechless. He had blushed.

Her face turned red. She walked out. He sat there a moment, still in shock but knowing she was embarrassed and probably pissed at herself and him.

He grabbed his jacket and ran for the elevator, but too late to get the one she took down. By the time he got down to the parking garage, she was starting her car. As he ran up, she threw the car in reverse without looking back. She just barreled back. He jumped aside pushing off from the car, but his hands hit the car loud enough that she heard it. She looked frightened and angry as she rolled down the window.

He leaned down and said, "I'm pretty screwed up now, for several reasons. I wasn't inviting you home. But anytime you want the complication of me in your life . . ."

She interrupted, her face and voice ice cold. "Let's keep it professional. I'll see you tomorrow." She had driven off before he could speak.

She sat looking at him now without expression, daring him to bring up last night. He wasn't about to.

She gave him a summary of the information developed by Ward's team on everyone connected in the past to Hayes and Jackson. None seemed likely to do anything reckless, for any reason. None were really passionate about term limits, except Professor T. J. Stewart. He had strong opinions about term limits earlier in his career but apparently less so in the period before he drowned. Until the sailboat accident and for twenty-one years he was a very well liked and nationally known professor of economics at Higgs U. "If he faked it, he hurt a lot of people that were really close. His daughters and grandchildren were torn up for a year. They're still getting over it. He had lots of close friends and students who admired and even loved him. They were hurt, too."

O'Brian asked, "What do you think?"

"Maybe he faked it, but I don't think so. I spoke with the Coast Guard investigator. He said it was fairly typical. Most likely, if his body had been found, his pants would have been unzipped. Lots of lone sailors step to the rail to pee and a wave catches them and they go over the side. And Professor Stewart sailed alone often."

O'Brian was about to ask about the professor's friends and associates when the phone rang. Caller ID indicated it was the attorney general. *Shit.*

"My office in 5 minutes," Hammar said.

"Yes, sir." Hammar was going to turn up the heat. O'Brian knew how, but he didn't know how he would handle it. He guessed Hammar had been getting a constant stream of phone calls from worried members of Congress. The Minuteman was on all the channels, clicking off the hours. As he walked out he gave his pocket recorder to Bradley. "You might want to listen to that."

4:14 p.m.

Jacob and Anna circled around the Wal-Mart parking lot until they found Chris. They stopped next to his truck and moved the laptop and groceries.

Anna was depressed and frightened—tonight they were drawing straws. Jacob was obviously struggling with it, too. And Chris looked awful. She took the middle seat and put her hand on his arm to make him look at her.

He glanced at her as he began backing out. "Said my goodbyes." Then he added, "We better make this work."

It was a long drive on a sweltering day with enormous black clouds building. The trip normally took 90 minutes to travel the 80 miles from Arlington to the waterfront house. The gloomy silence was unbroken. Anna tried to find some Country and Western music for Chris, but heard Marcus Ray's voice and stopped at that station.

The newscaster reported, "apparently, in a parliamentary maneuver worked out beforehand, a freshman member yielded his allotted time to introduce a bill on environmental protection, to Representative Marcus Ray. Ray used that opportunity to introduce the TLR amendment to the Constitution." The reporter went on to describe a Congress in turmoil, with Ray and freshman Congressman Terry Greenke being vilified and threatened by several members.

Anna used her wireless laptop to access the internet, discovering several items referring to the "Marcus Ray bill to amend the Constitution." She also discovered he would be on the Tom Paulson News Hour tonight at 7 p.m. "But dammit, Jason MacDulmie will also be interviewed. He's such a jerk."

Jacob snorted with disgust. "That's not a problem. Marcus Ray will handle MacDulmie easily. I worry about the anger he will feel from the House and on K Street. It may get brutal."

5:30 p.m.

O'Brian was ushered in to the AG's office. Koberg again occupied his right-hand-man seat. Hammar, red-faced, pointed to the chair across from his desk. "Congress is in a panic. Some members have left the Capitol, hiding from the TLR. A few are resigning. Some are privately calling for the term limits amendment. We're out of time. We need some names and Hayes and Jackson must give them to us." Hammar started to say something but looked at Koberg and changed his mind. "If they don't help, they are traitors, giving aid and comfort to the terrorist enemies of this nation. For years they have frightened peace-loving citizens with phantoms of lost liberty. They erode our national unity, diminish our resolve, and give ammunition to the TLR terrorists. And they know, O'Brian, they know who the terrorists are, or they can damn well guess."

Hammar seemed to be waiting. O'Brian said, "Yes, Sir."

"I don't like doing it this way, but we're out of time. Do you have what it takes to do the job?"

O'Brian felt himself slipping. He heard himself say, "Yes, sir, I can do the job." As soon as he said it, he knew he feared Hammar. Hammar could control him like a puppet.

"Break them. Seize and forfeit their property. All of it, their homes, bank accounts, boats, cars, whatever they own, all of it. If they help and if we determine they were innocent we can return their property."

O'Brian slowly nodded his head as he said, "Yes, sir." Hammar remained red-faced, but Koberg seemed to be enjoying himself.

For just a moment the AG hesitated, as if he knew he was observing O'Brian's moral collapse. "These aren't evil people. I know that. They're idealists. On a personal basis, I like Don Hayes; I really do. But I must put my personal wishes and weaknesses aside, for my nation's sake. I think of it this way. If a nation can demand that young men take up arms and even sacrifice their lives for their nation, there cannot be a moral dilemma in demanding the active help from every citizen in this war against terrorists. Am I right?"

There was something wrong with that argument, but O'Brian couldn't work it out. He just felt sick. Hammar didn't wait for an answer anyway.

"Hayes and Jackson are not only failing to help their nation, they're giving aid and comfort to the enemy. By Constitutional definition that makes them traitors. When they discover that this nation will not put up with their disloyal behavior, they will yield. They will quit their traitorous incitements and they will help us find the TLR assassins. We can be merciful at that time, if they are innocent." He leaned forward. "But not before."

Hammar stared hard at O'Brian to make sure he understood what was being said. "Until then we must use the powers Congress has provided and the strength of character God has given us. Arrest them, arrest their wives as accomplices and take their property—everything they own. Put their children in a well-chosen foster home."

Koberg said. "I have one in mind, sir. In the long run it's the least hurtful to the children and the parents, because it insures the earliest collapse of resistance."

"Right." Hammar said, "Break them. Then we can be merciful."

Hammar remained silent, but he leaned forward, waiting for O'Brian. O'Brian said, "Yes, sir. You can count on me." This was that moment he had always feared, when he discovered he was the moral coward he feared he might be. He grabbed for the excuse—*If it's not me, it'll be Koberg, better me than him.* He forced himself to look Hammar in the eye, "Yes, sir, we will make them help us and we will get their confessions. This method always works."

"You know that, don't you, Agent O'Brian?"

They didn't just look at my file. They've been digging. "Yes, sir, it never fails . . . not if they love their families. They'll yield. They always do." He spoke without emotion. "By the time we are through with them they'll admit guilt to any crime we name. They'll sign any statement we put in front of them, if we'll let their wives and children go free. They'll agree to a long prison sentence. They will even implicate their closest friends and professional associates . . . if we tell them to."

As he spoke, Hammar's eyes opened wider, as if he were unsure just how blatant O'Brian would be.

"Well . . . now . . . don't misunderstand me. We don't force confessions from innocent people."

"No, sir, but we know they're guilty, don't we? We don't have to prove their guilt. The president has designated them terrorists. We are required to use these and other methods to obtain their confessions, for the good of the nation. The press and public will accept the confessions. They believe we're protecting them."

Hammar's brow furrowed, an eye cocked. "We have a profound and sacred obligation."

"Yes, sir. We do."

"Congress and the administration have given us these tools to protect this nation and its government. We teeter on a precipice above anarchy and chaos. Can I count on you to carry out the task I have assigned you?"

"I'm your man, sir." And he knew he was.

Hammar sat back in his chair. The condescending smile said he liked that phrase. "I am pleased to see we can count on you. Assistant Attorney General Koberg will help you."

Koberg affected his voice of quiet authority. "Normally we would schedule for 4 a.m. but we are running out of time. Let's schedule the raids for tonight at ten."

O'Brian realized his stomach had been knotted for some time. "I'll call a pre-raid meeting for 9:30."

The attorney general stood to look out the window. Koberg motioned it was time for O'Brian to leave. Koberg said, "I will arrange for the National Security Letters and the seizure orders for the local authorities, banks and brokerage houses."

As O'Brian walked toward the door, Hammar, still facing the window, said, "Agent O'Brian, your support of this nation will be remembered; you should be proud of yourself."

5:41 p.m.
The house sat among trees at the end of Toms Road on Earle Tilghman Cove, three miles northwest of Centreville. The only homes within sight belonged to neighbors across the cove, nearly half a mile away. Anna stepped out of the air-conditioned pickup into a hot, thick humidity and heard the ominous sound of thunder in the distance.

The summer storm would be on them before dinner-time. In Oklahoma she would be worried about tornados. Jacob walked down to watch a small sloop beating to windward tack a few yards off the end of the dock. He waved to the skipper, who waved back. She knew Jacob ached to be on that boat; she did too. After watching it pull away, he turned and followed her inside.

The house was hot and musty from being closed up for too long. Jacob opened windows and doors as she and Chris unpacked groceries and put them away. A few minutes later they heard Burton drive into the gravel parking area. He burst through the door shaking hands with

Jacob and Chris and hugging Anna. His good mood seemed to infect the others and it helped her, too.

Burton was an inch taller than her, red headed and a bit overweight. His face was damaged from acne as a teen. Still, he was kind of sexy—the deep green eyes, baritone voice and sense of humor didn't hurt.

A little after 6:30, they sat down to spaghetti with meat sauce and red wine, a meal they'd enjoyed many times together. Everyone except Burton seemed tense. Chris took a bite and pushed his plate back. The pain in his face meant his stomach hurt. Emotional stress had given Chris stomachaches as long as she could remember. She was also pretty sure he wanted to get something off his chest.

When she pushed her plate back, Chris began describing the morning's conversation with Mark Adams. He told them the Joint Terrorism Task Force was "maybe closer than we thought. They are digging into Jacob's past." He glanced at Jacob. He had stopped eating, too. "Looking at your former friends, your attorney."

Jacob closed his eyes and sighed. Chris said, "I'm sorry, Jacob. I thought the boat accident would throw them off for weeks, maybe a month. They started looking at Higgs University for connections today."

Anna guessed Jacob worried about agents questioning his family, saying he might be alive and a TLR leader. It would tear them apart. She said, "I removed every mention of our names from the Higgs U. computers. They won't find us that way."

Chris said, "But if they try hard enough they'll find someone who'll remember we were close to Professor Stewart . . . and we supported term limits." He walked to the window and looked out for a moment. "They need to find just one little clue that we failed to hide, one thread and things will start to unravel."

He looked out at the dock being battered by waves. "I may have provided that clue." He came back to face them. "When Mark brought up the name T. J. Stewart, I felt I had to admit having known him."

Anna said, "Shit" and was immediately sorry.

"I thought . . . it was bad thinking, but I thought if I said nothing, and they discovered I knew him, but failed to mention it . . . Maybe I panicked."

There was a long silence while everyone considered where this might lead. Anna said, "You did what you thought best. I'll monitor the cameras. If they start watching any of us, we disappear."

Jacob said, "But we don't stop. We finish this! If we have to move here, then let's do it."

Chris said, "The camera at my house won't be much use. If they figure it's me, they'll pick me up at Langley and interrogate me there. Using the tools of the trade it won't take long."

The flash and delayed crack of a lightning strike not far away startled everyone. Anna suggested they go into hiding now, but Chris refused. They needed the inside information, how the targets were being protected and what was happening within the TLR investigation. Burton suggested Chris call in on a regular basis "so we know you haven't been picked up."

Jacob asked. "Why hasn't Mark already turned you in? He knows you joined the CIA two years ago. He knows you know me. The reward is a lot of money."

Anna said, "Maybe he has."

Lightning struck very near with an instantaneous crack and sizzle. The crash of a falling tree came a second later and then the wind and rain struck with a savage violence.

6:42 p.m.

O'Brian stopped at a restroom on the floor below Hammar's office in time to grab the toilet bowl and throw up. He washed his face without looking into the mirror and waited in a stall until the self-abuse hurt less. He no longer doubted himself; he was as weak as he had feared. Hiding on a toilet seemed appropriate.

He made it back to the office without having to speak to anyone and shut the office door to keep Bradley out. The reports on his monitor were mostly cover-your-ass paperwork from agents afraid of having missed something. He couldn't hide in them. He was overwhelmed with shame, the thought of facing Bradley, and later tonight his agents. He had to get it over with. He asked Bradley to come in.

Seconds later she walked in and turned on the News Hour with Tom Paulson. "We have to watch this."

He had worked himself up to say it, but nonetheless it felt like a reprieve. The Marcus Ray and Jason MacDulmie interview had started. She was completely absorbed and obviously assumed he was also. When she turned the television off, he said, "We raid the homes of Hayes and Jackson tonight."

She closed her eyes.

"The ton-of-bricks scenario," he said. "National Security Letter; SWAT teams; seize everything; Hayes, Jackson and wives arrested and take the kids. Koberg is coming." He heard the wimp in his voice and was disgusted. "I could resign . . . but it would still happen."

Bradley was furious. "Those slimy bastards. MacDulmie is one of those assholes on your pocket recorder, isn't he? I recognized his voice. On television he and the others pretend to love civil rights. They strike this noble pose, and talk about freedom and democracy, but they ordered this shit."

They both struggled to find sense in it. O'Brian said, "Let Ward and Barnes pick their men. Twenty each team. Call both teams in for a meeting at 9:30. The raid will be at ten." He paused and added, "Hammar said he'll turn the wives loose and give them back their children, after he gets the confessions."

"What if they won't sign?"

"They will. The only people who don't sign are those who don't give a damn about their wives and children. And there won't be a trial. Trials and evidence for accused terrorists haven't been required since the Patriot Act unless the AG wants the trial."

She looked bitter and her voice was sarcastic. "Everyone's a terrorist if the Attorney General says so."

7 p.m.

The old house sat near enough to the water that, from the large kitchen Anna could hear wind whipped waves crashing on the stone bulkhead. But the old house was comfortable and well built with five bedrooms, a dining room with a massive oak table and a large living room with two couches and several comfortable chairs that faced the television. They had all been here many times over the past two years.

When the News Hour began, Anna took a seat on the couch beside Burton. Paulson described the recent suicide bombs, attacks and counter attacks in the Middle East while a video tape displayed scenes of mutilated bodies and destroyed buildings and vehicles. "And last night the search for the TLR continued here in Washington. The Department of Justice Joint Terrorism Task Force raided the Jeffersonian Freedoms Institute and Term Limits Now."

Jacob leaped to his feet and turned the sound up.

"Many in the Washington political community are shocked by these raids. JFI, a well respected libertarian think tank, has, from time to time, provided political and economic analysis for the News Hour. TLN also enjoys a good reputation, but both organizations have accused the administration and Congress of unconstitutional actions. Today, FBI agents also visited the Higgs University School of Economics in Arlington, Virginia, to question a number of teachers and staff there. The Department of Justice has not commented on the JTTF action other than to say, they have reason to believe that members of the TLR may be associated with people within those organizations."

"In related developments, the Department of Justice announced the car used by the TLR courier to deliver the first TLR message has been found. The white 2003 model Ford Thunderbird was reportedly registered to Representative Charles Fargin."

"Congressman Fargin denied that he owns the car or knows the woman driving it. He believes he is being targeted for assassination by the TLR and announced today that he has no alternative but to announce his resignation effective at the end of this term. Four other members also announced their resignations—Senator Kevin Roble, Representative Daniel Smith, Representative Mary Marlan, and Representative Marcus Ray."

Everyone was pleased with the resignations. Anna was thrilled that Smith's would throw a monkey-wrench into Preston's plans.

"Congressman Ray proposed a constitutional amendment today identical to that required by the TLR. His actions have caused a furor among many Congress members, although a few appear to be reluctantly supporting the amendment. Later in the program we will be speaking with Congressman Ray and with Congressman Jason MacDulmie, one of the members opposed to the amendment."

After the news summary discussed the increases in unemployment and the closings of several corporations, Paulson returned to say "That's it for the news summary and now on to the assassination threats and the Term Limits Amendment." The camera backed away to reveal Paulson seated at a table opposite Marcus Ray and Jason MacDulmie. "Let me begin with you, Congressman Ray. Your proposed amendment to the Constitution has upset many of your colleagues. Why did you propose it?"

Marcus Ray was in his mid-sixties. His hair was white, his mouth wide and thin-lipped. The high cheekbones, sharp nose and leathery face suited his serious manner. "Two reasons, to stop the assassinations and to give the nation the opportunity to make the choice. It is their Congress and they have wanted it term-limited for a great long time."

"But do you think term limits are needed?"

"Of course. Members of Congress have too much power. They love it and will never give it up willingly. The TLR has that much right."

"But they can't have done that bad a job. Isn't life pretty good in the United States? The economy is in a downward trend at the moment, but most people are comfortable at least."

"Thanks to millions of creative hard working individuals, wealth is still being created. But too much is extorted by government. If we don't fix it soon we won't be able to stop the downward slide. To win or retain office, the congressional incumbents promise programs and entitlements like a pusher selling drugs. They continue to make promises that every one of them knows can't be kept. Something must give. If Congress attempts to meet these obligations by increasing taxes, that will destroy the economy. If Congress borrows and prints more money we will suffer hyper-inflation and that will destroy the economy. Either way will produce severe depression with starvation and riots. All of this is obvious to anyone who has taken the trouble to look at the numbers. The entitlements promised by Congress require wealth beyond the nation's capacity to produce.

"We can't even pay the interest on the money we've borrowed. But entitlements like Social Security, Medicare, Medicaid, Veteran's benefits, and the enormous healthcare entitlement added in 2010 aren't even recognized as debt, because Congress must approve the cost each year. They are kept off the books so members of Congress can pretend they are almost balancing the budget every year. But the entitlements stretched out in front of us are a debt. We have promised the people that they are entitled to the future payments. But the nation cannot produce those sums.

"The depressed economy is the result of too many taxes and too many regulations. This is the beginning of the end. Buyers for our bonds are demanding higher and higher rates because our money is worth less and less. I predict that we will not make our interest payments next year. We will be forced to default on our bonds as England did last year and France the year before and Spain and Japan the year before that. We must face the truth. But Congress is incapable of such an act."

Paulson asked, "Do you think our nation is actually failing?"

MacDulmie's eyes grew wider, as if fearful of Ray's answer.

"Yes, of course it is. Our democracy is no longer controlled by the Constitution or the people. So of course it is failing. Ben Franklin said it best. 'Democracy is two wolves and a lamb voting on what to have for dinner.' The Constitution protected us from such votes when the government was bound by it. This government has abandoned that restraint. Americans are encouraged by their leaders to believe it's legitimate and even moral in a democracy to vote on anything and everything. The rights of the individual no longer exist, we are only members of groups now. The choices placed before the public in every election concern which groups will be consumed by which groups, who will be forced to live under whose rules, morals and values. As Americans . . . ."

"Marcus, that's obscene!" MacDulmie couldn't take it any longer. He had been squirming, his face registering horror and his mouth forming unspoken words. Paulson was also visibly upset with Ray's statements, but he stopped MacDulmie. "Please, Congressman, let him finish."

Marcus Ray looked at Paulson, not bothering to consider MacDulmie. "As Americans it's beneath us. In the history of mankind, this was the only nation to be founded on the supremacy of the individual over government—his right to own himself and make of his life what he wanted. Not what the tribe, the chief, the king or even the United States government wanted of him. And not what society wanted of him, but what he wanted of himself. That has been turned on its head. Now as individuals we live in fear of society, because it's controlled by Congress."

Ray looked away from Paulson, straight into the camera. "You don't own yourselves, society owns you, which means government owns you, which means Congress owns you. Congress makes you think you have liberty because you get to re-elect them. You get a choice of two parties. They will let you change from one to the other. It may be democracy, but it is not freedom. That is the great trick played on you by the professional politicians. In the political fight to gain and keep the enormous power of congress, the contenders of both parties have divided you into constituent groups. They promise to take the money or property of one group and give it to the other; or force the values of one onto the other. In such a system you own nothing they cannot take in the name of society for the greater good.

"Our democracy sets everyone against everyone else. Is it any wonder that our elections have become so bitter? While we fight among ourselves over which of us is to be consumed and who will do the consuming, the incumbents in Congress, and those who keep them there, hold our coats and go through our pockets."

Paulson seemed genuinely shocked, unable to move forward. Chris and Burton leaped up and hi-fived each other. Jacob smiled and nodded and smiled and nodded.

MacDulmie found his voice and his anger. "This is obscene! Americans are comfortable with their members of Congress. They like to gripe about Congress but they keep returning their members because they like the way we vote. They like the laws Congress has passed, and by the way, they appreciate the free healthcare we have given them. I have hundreds of letters praising our actions. Thirty million people that had no insurance a few years ago, have healthcare security today."

As if MacDulmie had made a point, Marcus Ray nodded. "Healthcare is your perfect example, as it is mine. To give the public free healthcare, Congress nationalized doctors, other healthcare professionals, hospitals and insurance companies. Then drove the insurance companies out of business with payout requirements that exceeded the fees they could charge. And Doctors that borrowed half a million dollars each to pay for their education and worked eighteen hour days for eight years minimum to get their education, and then worked sixty hour weeks as barely paid interns for two years more to get their licenses, are now government workers earning little more than postal employees.

"Have you noticed how many have fled the country? How few medical students there are? They cannot be called slaves because they can leave, but they were robbed of their professions by their government. Is it any wonder that those with real skills are leaving for countries that reward their skills? Politicians and bureaucrats now decide who is to receive treatment, and when, and how, and who will be taxed to pay for it. Patients wait in line for months or years to be given medical attention by clock-watching civil service doctors who have learned to resent their patients as much as the patients resent them.

"The quality of medical care is not decreasing, it's collapsing— except for the politically connected. National healthcare has helped to destroy the national economy. We are bankrupt. And those who voted for the medical entitlements knew it was a threat."

Paulson seemed genuinely upset. "But you don't mean that, Congressman Ray, you cannot believe members of Congress intentionally voted to bankrupt the nation."

"Not with certainty. And most don't bother to think about such issues. They have advice from people they trust—their political handlers. But the members who voted for it knew it would cost far more than was being admitted. If the vote were whether or not to bankrupt the nation, every member would have bravely voted against it. However, each member knows his or her vote will make no difference to the final vote; its only one vote of 435 in the House, or one in 100 in the Senate. But each member also believes his or her constituents are simpleminded ninnies who believe Congress has lots of money. And when one politician promises anything for free, the others rush to beat his offer. Free healthcare, and subsidized retirement, and subsidized food, and subsidized gas for their car, and subsidized housing and subsidized income for every corporation. Of course they don't vote to bankrupt the nation. But since each member's vote can lose them their office, but will not make a difference in the final decision, they vote in a way that will keep themselves in office . . . and then hope the other members will outvote them, to save the nation from bankruptcy."

Paulson looked at MacDulmie, who didn't wait for the question. "We give the public what they want. That's democracy. That's how it works. The public expects us to give them what they want. It's completely fair for the wealthy to help with the healthcare of the poor and the middle-class. I know many doctors who fought for free healthcare. They don't hate it at all. Most Americans want Congress to lead on these issues. They expect professional leadership. The American people select us in honest democratic elections. They can throw us out any time they wish. Any time they wish. And they frequently do." He made the mistake of looking at Ray. "My gosh, just look at the last election. The power of Congress changed 180 degrees. And it's changed hands many times."

Ray said, "Oh, a great power shift. In the House 34 seats changed hands; 7 of those who lost were under indictment. The 401 other incumbents retained office. Four incumbent senators were defeated and they lost to exceptionally wealthy challengers who outspent them."

MacDulmie glared at Ray. "You accuse members of Congress of placing themselves above the people. At least they are elected. No one elected the TLR. Not only have they placed themselves above Congress, the institution designed by the Founders to represent the American people, they threaten to murder members of Congress if they don't immediately get their way. Those aren't patriots, Congressman Ray. Those are terrorists."

Paulson asked Congressman MacDulmie, "Would you comment on the Congressional resignations and the threat many members will face tomorrow?"

"I know the members that resigned. The nation has lost seven excellent leaders, senators and representatives who understood this complex modern nation. I hope we will not see more resignations before the terrorists are caught. And I hope they will be caught and made to pay for their crimes. The nation cannot afford to lose its leaders."

Tom Paulson turned back to Representative Ray. "Do you believe that Congress will pass the Term Limits Amendment?"

"Yes, and I hope it will be quickly, before many lives are taken."

"Do you think the TLR will actually assassinate someone tomorrow?"

Congressman Ray looked very sad. "I have no idea."

He had represented their views better than they had hoped. All four were grinning, even Chris. This was what they wanted America to hear. Anna's face was wet with tears.

Jacob grinned and nodded. "Let's drink a toast to Marcus Ray. I think he just sold our cause to a hell of a lot of Americans."

Burton poured the wine and they toasted Marcus Ray. Their high spirits lasted until another lightning crash took out their power and reminded them where and why they were gathered. They had decisions to make and it was growing dark. Jacob and Anna found flashlights and lighted the propane lamps. As the rain smashed against the windows, Burton said, "I'll get some straws."

8:33 p.m.

O'Brian was through with phony pretense. He was not a defender of the innocent, or of justice, or whatever he once pretended. He was one of more than a million badge-carrying enforcers of a government that believed anything is justified to protect itself. He would lead a Joint Terrorism Task Force that would terrorize and damage two families. He couldn't stop it if he quit and he couldn't quit, he had a child to support.

The reports on his desk of dead-end investigations didn't help. It had been a bad idea to require all agents to turn in all information. He turned on the television and heard that Congress was almost uniformly opposed to the TLR amendment. According to CNN almost no one in either house admitted they would vote for it, but fear was strong, too. The reporter said there was a rumor circulating that the TLR was a large quasi-military organization, perhaps a thousand strong and perhaps many of its members in federal law enforcement or the armed forces. Some said it was headed by officers in the Pentagon. Another reporter described a public poll where seventy-six percent of Americans were strongly opposed to the TLR while thirteen percent were sympathetic, but seventy-nine percent were in favor of term limits for Congress.

Bradley brought O'Brian a ham and Swiss on rye and told him the meeting was set. They both ate while watching television. CNN cut to a scene on the Capitol Mall. The reporter said a growing number of protestors were gathering. Most opposed the TLR, but she said an increasing number supported the amendment and quite a few supported the TLR. The Minuteman was staying late tonight. His sign indicated *4 HOURS REMAINING*. O'Brian wondered why that seemed to please him.

Shortly after 9:00 p.m. Assistant Attorney General David Koberg walked in smiling. He ignored Bradley. "Good evening, Agent O'Brian. I have the warrants. Are we ready?"

"I called the meeting for 9:30."

"Good, stop by when you're ready. I'll be in my temporary office down the hall, just beyond the elevators."

O'Brian said, "Right." *Office down the hall? Shit.*

At 9:30 the team was assembled. Most were dressed for action with dark JTTF bulletproof jackets, dark slacks, and JTTF baseball-type caps. They knew what was coming. None of the agents wore suits except O'Brian. David Koberg was dressed in an expensive light blue suit, a starched white shirt with gold cuff links and a brilliant red silk tie.

O'Brian divided the raid into two groups. Ward's team would raid Jackson's home, Barnes' team would take the Hayes home. O'Brian told the agents the homes were staked out; the subjects were all at home and appeared to be settled in for the evening. Arrests should be straightforward.

The seizure documents were broad and generic. Anything of value was to be taken. An agent would be sent to each of the banks that held their personal checking and savings accounts. That money would be taken, their safe deposit boxes would be opened and the contents brought to the Department of Justice for examination and eventual sale. Money, jewelry, watches and other items on their persons would be taken.

An agent would visit the brokerages to seize their stocks, bonds and other financial assets. Banks and brokerages are required to provide twenty-four hour access to federal law enforcement. Their homes would be seized and eventually sold, as would their cars, and other personal assets.

O'Brian was well acquainted with the seizure laws. He had used them many times as a prosecutor against accused drug dealers, and more recently against accused terrorists. The law was based on the assumption that anything of value—any money, property, stocks, bonds, cars, or boats that may have been, or in future, might be used for terrorism—may also be presumed guilty of terrorism. The owner need not be tried in a court for the property to be found guilty, and sold.

Money or property that may have been legitimate may be assumed to be mixed with money used or intended to be used for terrorist purposes, making it guilty by association. The assets would be tried before a judge whose salary was paid by the Department Of Justice. His cooperation could be safely assumed. Although citizens have the presumption of innocence—except in cases of terrorism, drugs, tax evasion, prostitution and an increasing number of other crimes—assets do not. If the assets could not prove their innocence, and since the laws had first been tested in the 1970s none ever did, they were forfeited to the government and sold. Hayes may ask an attorney to defend his property, but attorneys almost never take the case—the client can't pay and innocence can never be proven. And in Hayes' case, and Jackson's, they wouldn't be permitted to speak to an attorney anyway.

One agent asked, "So how much are these guys worth?"

He was wondering how much he might benefit from the raid. Federal enforcement agencies don't benefit directly from the sale of forfeited goods, but raises, special hazard pay bonuses and perks seemed always to follow the raids. And it was always proportionate to the value of property seized. Agents had a hard time not being influenced by the size of the seizure.

Another agent said, "For shit sake, Charley."

Ward and Barnes assigned agents with financial backgrounds to inventory and legal work, finding titles to the seized items and transferring them to the Treasury.

Murphy would go with the Jackson raid and stay in touch with Bradley. O'Brian and Bradley would go on the Hayes raid. He was the bigger fish. Koberg would be on the Hayes raid, too, but he had his own car and driver. An assistant to Koberg, also with the AG's office, would accompany Ward's team on the Jackson raid.

When it was apparent that the agents knew their assignments and were ready to go, Koberg stepped beside O'Brian, "Let's remember, tomorrow members of Congress may be assassinated by the TLR. It is essential that we bring the full weight of the Department of Justice down upon Don Hayes and Cal Jackson tonight to gain their help in finding the terrorists. The attorney general personally ordered this raid. It has been approved by the president and congressional leadership. Hayes and Jackson, and their wives, are aiding, abetting and giving comfort to the TLR terrorists. You must help them understand the need to aid, abet and give comfort to the Department of Justice."

Several officers laughed, some smiled, a few looked at O'Brian. He couldn't help.

"And to help in that regard two SWAT teams will accompany us. They will go in first and we follow."

Someone said, "Hooo-haaaah!"

10:04 p.m.
O'Brian watched the SWAT team pour out of their black unmarked vans. He led other teams against desperate and violent criminals. To ready themselves psychologically, they talked each other into an aggressive kick-ass attitude, much like a football team preparing for a game. Get the testosterone flowing for quick reaction time and to get peak strength. They didn't remind each other their target has not been convicted of anything and may well be innocent.

Don Hayes' two-story home was set back and surrounded by trees in a quiet upscale residential area in the Spring Valley area only four miles from the Capitol. The SWAT team wore unmarked ninja-like black clothes and masks to encourage terror and quick submission. Shouting and screaming were also important, as was the battering ram that splintered the front door.

O'Brian knew what to expect, but watched horrified as they went in. Bradley was furious.

Don Hayes was upstairs, preparing for bed and worrying about the donors who were withdrawing their contribution pledges to JFI, not that he could blame them; no one wanted to be hounded by the IRS and the FBI. In the living room, Barbara was reading, while Bill and Eddy, ten and twelve years old, played a video game. Don had just taken a shoe off when he heard a loud crash downstairs, and the immediate screams of his family.

He thought a hot break-in was underway. Thieves no longer waited until people were away. Hot break-ins had become common and the damage was always done long before 911 responded. Hayes kept an automatic pistol in a small safe in a bureau drawer but the hysterical screams and shouts destroyed his coordination. His hands shook as he tore the drawer open, but too far and it fell on the floor. He found the small safe among the clothes, punched in the code, pulled the Berretta 9 MM automatic out and exploded out of the room striking the door jamb with his shoulder on his way out, which threw him off balance. His body and brain were nearly incapacitated by the screams of his family, the sounds of crashing furniture and the enraged cursing shouting male voices. He managed to chamber a round with trembling hands as he approached the corner to the stairs. As he made the turn holding the pistol in front of him with both hands, prepared to fire, he collided with an agent and fell face forward into space, hands flailing. His right hand still held the pistol as he slammed to a spread-eagled stop halfway down the stairs, unconscious.

O'Brian watched as SWAT team members shouted commands at the top of their lungs, "On the floor, on the fucking floor, get down, God damn it." Barbara was jerked down onto the floor with "Get down and shut up". Another team member held an automatic rifle to her head and his foot on her neck as he screamed "Lie still, lie still, God damn it". She was still, but he continued yelling anyway. He noticed Koberg was also watching.

Eddy and Bill were both screaming, unable to move. They too were pushed onto the floor with an automatic rifle held to their heads. The other team members ran through the house accidentally knocking vases and lamps off tables as the regular JTTF agents came running in past O'Brian and Koberg.

Hayes lay face down, unmoving, at the feet of a SWAT team member who was pumped and ready to shoot anyone holding a gun. He did not shoot but took the precaution of smashing Hayes' hand—it still held the pistol—with the heel of his boot.

As O'Brian started toward the stairs, he passed Bradley, who was ordering the SWAT officer to let Barbara sit up. He did but he cuffed her first with her hands behind her back. When he raised her to the sitting position he grabbed her cuffed hands to raise her to her knees, wrenching her shoulders. She screamed with the pain and the officer yelled, "Shut up."

Bradley pushed the officer away and said, "Leave her to me."

Barbara wept but tried to calm her shaking and screaming children. Bill had thrown up and both children had lost control of their bladders.

O'Brian dismissed the SWAT officer who smashed Don Hayes' hand. He called one of his team over and they rolled Don Hayes to his back. Holding him by his shoulders, they dragged him down the stairs to the floor. O'Brian checked his pulse and said, "Get an ambulance."

Barbara saw them dragging her husband down the stairs. She screamed "Don" and tried to rise, but a SWAT officer put his hand on her head and shoved her back down.

O'Brian went to Barbara and the children and said, "He took a bad fall. I think he'll be okay, but we'll put him in a hospital for the night."

Koberg stepped between O'Brian and Barbara. "Barbara Hayes, you are under arrest for terrorism. So is Mr. Hayes. You will be taken to the Federal Detention Facility. Your property will be seized. The children will be taken to the Juvenile Detention Facility and then to foster homes."

Her face twisted in horror. The long, begging scream, "Nooooo," felt like a knife in O'Brian's chest. He wanted to kick Koberg in the nuts, but didn't.

Koberg seemed unaffected. He turned to a nearby SWAT agent. "Take these to Juvenile Detention, until we find foster homes."

Barbara screamed at him, "You bastard. You vicious bastard!"

When she tried to get up, the masked agent who had earlier pushed her down, did so again, while looking at Bradley. The hysterical children were picked up and carried away by two of the SWAT team officers while Barbara wept and begged.

Koberg looked at another agent, pointed at Barbara, and said, "Now this one." Barbara appeared to have reached hopelessness; she wept without other protest as she was led away. Koberg turned toward O'Brian but stopped when he saw the rage in O'Brian's face. O'Brian spun around and walked out the door.

Bradley followed him, and as she stepped outside, Murphy reported in. The radio was clear enough that O'Brian heard it, too.

"Bradley, I'm worried. The SWAT team is about to break the Jackson door in with a battering ram. This looks like it's going to be nasty."

10:14 p.m.

After they drew straws, and while the storm raged outside, Chris explained how each target would be removed. They went over the checklists and examined in detail the photos associated with each plan. He would direct the operation and if the target was out of place, or too well hidden, or the plan seemed in any way compromised, he would select an alternate time or target. Anna was proud of Chris, but sorry he knew so much about killing.

Burton hugged everyone, especially Anna, before he left for NYC. He would teach class again tomorrow, probably for the last time. Chris was on the phone to Oklahoma, while Jacob finished the night's message. She downloaded it to a cell phone at 11:30 and they headed back to Arlington.

The storm was moving on, the flash of lightning still evident on the horizon as they drove toward the Bay Bridge. She had drawn the shortest straw. Her target, Senator Hackman, was scheduled hours from now—before dawn. All of the targets were identified sixteen months ago. The drawing of straws was only about the order of their removal and who would be assigned to which target. Burton volunteered for his target before the drawing of straws.

"I'm glad I drew the short straw. I hate the waiting." She looked at her watch. "In six hours it will be over . . . or anyway the first round. I won't have to dread this anymore."

Jacob said, "My hand trembled when I reached for the straw. I was shocked. I didn't think I was that worried. But I was shaking inside . . . even more than my hand revealed." He smiled ruefully, "I guess we never really know how we'll react."

Anna said, "I try to think of other things, but it's like trying to hear songbirds when a tiger is circling. I hate Senator Hackman. He's such a pious son-of-a-bitch. But I don't want to kill him. He seems to love his family, and apparently they love him."

Jacob asked, "Shall I tell you why he's your perfect target?"

"Maybe . . . yes, please."

"When he first ran for the Senate, Orville Hackman believed in individual rights under limited government. And early in his first term, he spoke passionately for lower taxes and worked hard to reduce the size of government. He tried to cut regulations. But over time he changed. He believes he should make choices for people; they don't have the courage or intelligence to make the right choices. After 27 years as a senator he still talks about limited government, but he has helped to grow the federal government far beyond the limits he once thought extreme. And he has backed nearly every confiscation of liberty proposed."

"They're all like that," Chris said.

"He's also a drug warrior. He supported the laws allowing police to seize and sell property that might be related to drugs, without charging anyone—even if the only witness against the property is a convicted criminal who will share in its sale. He helped write the laws giving the federal authorities the right to determine if doctors were over-prescribing drugs and if so, arrest them as drug dealers and take their property."

Chris asked, "How the hell can he stand himself?"

"Power corrupts. If they stay in office long enough, even those who arrive with strong principles come to believe they are empowered by God or nature to make our decisions. Orville Hackman began discovering excuses for growing government because it increased his power." Jacob looked at Anna as he said, "He is more responsible than most members for the laws that put your brother in prison."

She nodded slowly as she thought of Nicolo. He was six years younger than her and built like Chris with broad shoulders and strong arms. But unlike Chris and Anna, Nicolo had always loved the farm. Although quiet and a little shy, Nicolo had also been the favorite of their grandparents. Francesco and Maria Ribisi, their mother's parents, had lived across the road for fifty years. Until three years ago Nicolo did most of the work on the Ribisi farm. It would be his someday. Life had been so good.

She looked at Chris and knew from his clenched teeth and angry mouth he was thinking the same thing. How had it all gone so bad so fast? And it was so unnecessary. Grandmother Ribisi had back pain from a farm injury that occurred twenty years ago. The pain had been increasing, but Oxycontin took away enough of the pain she could still do all of the cooking and enjoy working in her flower gardens. It was the only drug that worked and it was relatively cheap. But then the Drug Enforcement Agency began looking for doctors who over-prescribed Oxycontin—they were so much easier to find than real drug dealers.

They arrested her doctor in a drug raid, accusing him of being a drug dealer because he prescribed Oxycontin for long term use in too many patients. They didn't seem to care that he made no money on the sale of the drug. The pharmacist made very little but it was the pharmacist's records that led DEA to make the arrest. The DEA definition of drug dealer did not require that the dealer make money. He had only to have made the sale possible—written the prescription. It was upheld by the lower courts and Dr. Thompson went to prison. Grandmother Ribisi could no longer get a prescription for Oxycontin. Doctors would prescribe it only for short periods and never for chronic long term pain.

Grandmother Ribisi was in agony for several weeks. She wanted to die. Nick attempted to get Oxycontin from a drug dealer. It was a sting; he was caught with the drugs in his hand. He had to plead guilty; extenuating circumstances are irrelevant in drug cases. Because it was a first offense he received the minimum sentence allowed, five years, no parole. He couldn't deal with prison life. He was now in a mental ward.

Anna leaned against Jacob and said, "Thank you. I will remember what that self-righteous bastard has done to Nicci and our family.

"How is your grandmother doing now?"

"She and grandfather miss the farm and our family, but they have friends there, too. And in Italy the Oxycontin is available with a pharmacist's prescription. She doesn't have to live with the pain now."

11:01 p.m.

Bradley was livid. She watched as the hysterical boys were placed in two separate cars. "Why can't they at least go in the same car?"

"Its part of the plan," O'Brian said. "To break Hayes we terrorize his family. He won't be able to take it. He'll sign anything we put in front of him. And he'll start naming people who might be involved with the TLR."

"They can't even ride in the same damn car?"

"Koberg doesn't want them comforting each other."

The boys screamed and begged for their mother. Barbara was pleading they be given to her parents, but she too, was pushed into the back of a car—Koberg's car. He would take this opportunity to interrogate her.

As the cars vanished up the street, the night grew quiet, except for the sounds of two laughing agents from the SWAT team. One was imitating the screaming children. She heard a voice in the darkness and realized the neighbors were watching. The night was moonless and clouded, but the lights from the cars and vans, aimed toward the house, seemed obscenely bright. The neighbors inched closer to the edge of the lighted area. Some stepped into the lights. They appeared dumfounded, unable to believe what they were seeing, speaking softly or not at all. Most of the task force agents were as appalled as she was, but a few seemed unaffected. A few number-crunchers and legal guys were inside taking inventory. Their work was just starting. Barnes was supervising.

O'Brian looked almost as bad as she felt. He started for her car. "Let's go, there's nothing we can do here."

She followed him into the darkness, using her remote to turn on the headlights. The lights revealed several neighbors who moved away from their path.

O'Brian said, "Nice evening, isn't it?" But he said it with a sarcastic anger.

A neighbor in her bathrobe and slippers was incensed, "What the hell is going on?"

Bradley said, "Just remember, we're from the government and we're here to help you."

A man, probably her husband, asked, "Why? Those kids couldn't have done anything."

O'Brian pulled a note pad and pen out of his pocket. "You care to make a statement?"

The neighbors retreated or looked away, one woman sobbing. O'Brian got into the car and Bradley pulled away slowly as the neighbors parted to make way for her car.

Bradley drove slowly, her mind on the children. O'Brian, slumped in his seat, said, "I'm sorry I got you into this. I'll get you reassigned. It won't go on your record. You can go back to looking for real terrorists." He sounded sad, but also bitter.

"Who'll replace me? Marshall?" Marshall was the agent imitating the boy's screams. That reminded her that Sarah was probably going through a similar nightmare at Jackson's home. She called.

"How bad is it?"

"Oh, my God, it couldn't be worse. Jackson was killed. Someone on the SWAT team thought he was pulling a pistol out. She yelled "Gun!" Everyone started shooting. It was just a cell phone. He was probably calling 911—he didn't know we were police. They were shooting and they just kept shooting. Ward went nuts. He was slugging and kicking the SWAT team guys . . ." Her voice broke with sobs as she tried to report. "He tried to stop the shooting. Oh, God, Bradley. The children . . . they went nuts . . . and Jackson's wife. My God, it was . . . I can't . . ."

The line went dead. They would wait for her to call back. Bradley had pulled off the road as Murphy described the raid. They sat there in silence for a moment before she put the car in gear and started forward, slowly at first but gradually increasing speed as her anger grew. "What the fuck are we doing?" She asked it quietly. "Who the hell are we?"

Friday, June 6
As Promised

12:01 a.m.

After they crossed the Chesapeake Bay Bridge, Anna sent the fourth message, wiped the cell phone down and handed it to Chris in a kleenex. He pulled onto the left shoulder and threw it across the oncoming lane, still on—in case NSA picked up the call and was tracking it.

The news organizations that received the message immediately posted it to their websites. Editorial comment would follow. TV and radio newscasters read it to their viewers and listeners and the next morning it was headline news for every newspaper in the country. The headline for the New York Times was typical. TLR SAYS TWO WILL DIE TODAY.

Friday, June 6

The three day warning period has expired. It is now too late to save the lives of two members who will die today.

We regret the task before us, but it seems obvious Congress will move only when they discover that we are completely capable of taking their lives and that we will.

Over the last three days we have heard several members of Congress explain that the Constitutional Convention considered and rejected term limits. True enough. Even among that noble group there were many who saw political futures for themselves as members of the Congress they were creating. Many others thought term limits silly— who would want a job that paid little and had almost no power, for the powers of Congress were very limited, at that time. They failed to see what Jefferson saw clearly—without term limits, and over time, we would lose liberty as the office attracted power seekers who would find ways to ignore the limits placed on them by the Constitution.

We now live in the future that Thomas Jefferson feared.

He was not present at the Constitutional Convention—he was then our Ambassador to France. In a letter from France, he begged Madison to include term limits in the Constitution. He thought it a grave mistake that the Constitutional Convention failed to include it. He said it was in the nature of politicians to grow government and accrue power at the expense of the individual's liberty. And he predicted a bloody revolution would be required to recapture the liberty individuals would lose to a Congressional political aristocracy.

Senator Harlowe describes us as "a pretentious rebellion at best, and one that will be squashed." Perhaps, but if we succeed in securing for the public the right to require their Congress to be term limited, then this will have been a true revolution. If the public approves the amendment and if citizen-legislators then succeed in restoring individual liberty, this will be a successful and magnificent revolution. And if it comes at the cost of our lives and the lives of a few members of Congress, that will not be very costly as revolutions go.

Yesterday Representative Marcus Ray offered the Term Limits Amendment to the House of Representatives. That brave action provides some hope of an early end to the loss of life that begins today. If the House of Representatives quickly passes the amendment he offered, we will stop the actions now planned for the long-term incumbents from that body.

We beg Congress again. Please give this issue to the American public for a final decision.

The Term Limits Revolution

12:32 a.m.

O'Brian handled two calls from local authorities and another from the agent at Hayes' bank on their way back to the Hoover building. As he and Bradley walked into his office, Ward called from the Jackson house. O'Brian used the speaker phone.

"It was a fucking disaster, O'Brian. The kids saw the whole thing. The shooters were using automatic weapons. The little girl is only five. She'll never get over it. Shit, her sister and mother won't either. I won't. It was fucking awful. They just kept shooting."

"What happened to the kids?"

"The asshole from the AG's office sent the kids to the Juvenile Detention Facility. Their mom went to the Federal Detention Center. Damn it, they need help, not this shit. What the fuck are we doing?"

O'Brian exploded. "What we're told. What the hell else can we do?"

Bradley asked, "How's Murphy?"

"Not good. She asked me to call." He hesitated as if he wanted to say something else but thought better of it. "I better get back to work."

The line went dead. The door was open and Bradley was gone. He noticed the flashing urgent communication light with *TLR message released* and turned his monitor off.

1 a.m.

Sleep was unlikely, but Anna tried anyway. Because she was so desperately tired, she slept a little, but mostly she spent the night alternating between doubting she could do it and fear of what killing the senator would do to her. When she heard Jacob in the kitchen at three thirty, she was glad for the excuse to get up. Jacob looked surprised when she came out of the bedroom. "I'm sorry, did I wake you?"

"Not really. I couldn't sleep."

He stood awkwardly with a pan in his hand, unmoving and looking at her as if he thought she might fly apart. "Some coffee?"

She pulled a chair up to the kitchen table as he poured. "Chris explained what I have to do." She tried to be positive. "It sounds easy. Whatever happens, in another week, I won't be dreading this. I'm sick of dreading it."

"If we could justify the act easily," he said, "we wouldn't have waited so long. It won't be easy. For the rest of our lives, we'll regret the pain we caused. But it's the only way we can make them let go. It's necessary."

"And our goals are noble."

His face turned red and angry. She hadn't meant it to sound as sarcastic as it came out and she regretted it. But she didn't like him getting into such a damn huff either. She left her coffee on the table. She needed to shower and get ready.

When she came out, Jacob was sitting on the floor in front of the television, weeping. She was shocked, briefly wondering if she had caused it, until the newscaster's words penetrated.

She stood beside Jacob as the CNN reporter described the raid on Cal Jackson's home. A video of his home was shown with crime scene tape and police everywhere, as the description continued. The neighbors were interviewed, adding to the emerging picture of a brutal act of retribution. One elderly neighbor wept as he described the children being taken away—to a detention facility. A Department of Justice spokesman described the accident. "The Jacksons were about to be arrested for their part in the TLR terrorism. Mr. Jackson appeared to reach for a weapon as the officers entered the living room. The Officers fired in self-defense as they are trained to do. It was only discovered later that he was reaching for a cell phone, an unfortunate, but in the circumstances, understandable mistake."

Jackson's past was discussed briefly over still photos from the CNN files. Jacob continued to weep. Cal and Jacob had been close friends. Anna had met him once. She remembered seeing a photo of Cal Jackson's children in Jacob's arms.

A few minutes later CNN provided live coverage from in front of the Don Hayes home. The reporters interviewed neighbors who had witnessed the aftermath of the brutal raids. Jacob raged about the room as neighbors described the arrests. A reporter said he received a call from someone claiming to be one of the task force agents on the raid. "The agent told me the SWAT team came in with orders to teach the targets a lesson. He also offered to give me his name, but I stopped him. I told him I would be subpoenaed by the DOJ and forced to give up my source."

Her anger grew as she listened, but Jacob's white-hot fury shook her. She had never seen this side of him, this potential for violence. It frightened her. He was normally careful with language, but now as tears flowed from red angry eyes, he cursed John Hammar and his brutal enforcers. He cursed the power grabbing goons in Congress who would send Hammar to destroy these good people. But as he continued to rave, his language changed, betraying the guilt he felt. "How could I have been so stupid? I should have seen that Hammar would smash Hayes and Jackson . . . and terrorize their families. Hammar . . . and those bastards in Congress, only wanted an excuse, and I gave it to them. They. . . " He began weeping again.

She almost felt betrayed. Jacob was wavering. They had all invested too damn much for him to give up now. In a few minutes, she was supposed to assassinate a senator. *Do we call it all off, or what?*

His hands were over his face. She only understood the last few words, " . . . the suffering we've caused those good people."

"God damn it," she yelled. "We didn't cause it. Stop blaming us. Congress passed the laws that made this possible. And they sent Hammar out to do their dirty work. You knew they would lash out and hit innocents. I'm sorry they were your friends, but God damn it, blame Congress, not us!"

She slammed into the bathroom to get ready, and quickly realized it had been his pain talking. She put on a long black wig, pink lipstick and green contacts. A few minutes later she was ready. And it was time to go. She found Jacob standing in the kitchen, eyes wide, staring at a scene that was only in his mind. She stopped in front of him.

It took a moment for him to see her. Whatever he had been thinking, he shook it off. "I'm sorry. I let my emotions . . ." He ran his hands over his face as if trying to come back to the present. He looked at her, then into her eyes. "You were right. Everything you said was right. We can't stop now and we must succeed." He hesitated before he added, "Please come back safe, Anna."

Whatever effect the morning's news had on Jacob, it galvanized Anna. There was no turning back. She was sorry for the damage done and the damage that would be done, but that made their mission all the more important.

She found the address, a side street strip-mall near Baileys Crossroad's, saw the black 2000 model Nissan Maxima Chris had left for her, drove past it to the intersection and turned right. She parked at the end of the block and walked back in the dark. She had gloves on before she reached the car. The keys were under the mat. A few minutes later as she crossed the Potomac, she checked her watch for the fourth time in ten minutes. It was 5:01 a.m. as she exited the freeway and headed south on Indian Head Highway.

She was definitely stressed, but less than she expected.

The sky was lighter in the east when she recognized the turn coming up. Sunrise would be at 5:40 a.m. She was running a little late. Chris had shown her photos of all the intersections and landmarks in the order she would approach them, including a photo of the senator's house. But in the semi-dark nothing seemed quite right. She took the right-hand turn onto Fort Washington Road and followed it as it curved right for a little more than a mile. She turned right again on Drake Creek Road. Her heart pounded. She drove another quarter mile and recognized the signpost Chris had said was a hundred yards from the senator's house.

Then she saw the house, dark and quiet, set back from the street. As it should be. If the house were lighted she was to do nothing, just come back to the house. She held her breath as she passed a car that looked to be government-issue, parked across the street. She was careful to not touch her brakes or do anything that would indicate she had any interest in the place. She continued driving at twenty miles an hour past the senator's house. Then as she approached the corner where she would turn she opened the glove compartment and removed the device.

She turned the transmitter on as she made the turn, and without hesitation, as Chris instructed, she pressed the red button. Chris said she would hear no noise and she didn't, except for the sound of her own muffled cry.

Had she killed Hackman? Shaking, but still in control she continued driving in a right hand loop until she came back to Fort Washington Road, turned left and left again on Indian Head Road. She realized she wasn't sorry. *Good.* She felt bad for the family, but no remorse for killing Hackman—at least not yet. As the freeway became visible ahead she also saw the oncoming flashing lights. Police, or . . . no, they were ambulance lights. She felt relief that they were not police, and certain she had killed the senator. *Or someone else? His wife? Was someone maime*d*?* Now she felt bad.

For the last two days, except when he was on the floor of the Senate or in his home, Senator Hackman had been surrounded by the damn Secret Service bodyguards. They stood guard at every access point and never gave him a minute's peace. Outside his home, he couldn't visit the john without the bodyguards. He hated that, and anyway he felt he was unlikely to be a target for the TLR. *Those guys may complain about incumbents but they probably like my conservative views. I always fought for limited government and constitutional rights, except where they didn't make sense.*

He chaired the Rules and Administration Committee and that evening had taken calls from important backers that believed as he did. He assured them he would filibuster, if necessary, to stop any vote for the term limits amendment. Later he noticed Mildred looked frightened and worn down. He wished she wouldn't worry so much. *Maybe I'll sleep in her bed tonight. She may need comforting, and tomorrow if someone really is assassinated, I'll send her to visit the grandkids. Help get her mind off this business.*

Chris had gained access to the senator's home three months earlier, using the training and specialized tools provided by the CIA and the Secret Service records. The senator and his wife had been away on a Congressional fact-finding junket to Paris. The magnificent Potomac waterfront home stood on a three acre lot that ran between the wide canal on the back side and Drake Creek Road. The senator had not been wealthy when he took office, but he was damn sure wealthy now.

The Secret Service maintains an extensive file on all members of Congress. With the passage of the Patriot Act, the CIA was no longer prohibited from sharing those files. It was in the interest of both agencies to make file-sharing seamless. Their computers were now linked with all computers in Homeland Security as well. The data held by one agency was available to all.

Chris knew the senator's home was protected with the latest technology. He also knew the type, model and manufacturer. With this particular system the slightest intrusion past the alarm would alert a central system and silently trigger a very fast armed response, unless the system was defeated by the better technology the CIA carried on its shelves, courtesy of that same manufacturer.

The alarm relied on a coded radio transmission at timed intervals. If the transmission failed, the alarm was triggered at the central station. The CIA device would detect the radio code and then reproduce it when the intrusion broke the transmission.

The entire break-in, including the defeat of the senator's intrusion protection system, took less than a minute. The CIA had also trained Chris to pick the lock and provided him with the best possible tools.

He found the senator's bedroom. He knew from their medical records they were light sleepers and tended to keep each other awake. Orville Hackman and his wife no longer slept in the same bedroom. Chris placed a small plastic tube-bomb, with a radio receiver, in the half inch brass stem of the lamp beside the senator's bed. The package was designed by the CIA to escape detection. It even had safeguards to prevent it being set off by unintended transmissions. Four separate signals were necessary. One to turn it on and then three others sent simultaneously—which Anna did when she pressed the single red button.

Anna called Jacob as she drove over the Potomac. She wanted to tell him it was done. But when he answered, she burst into tears.

After she stopped sobbing, his voice broke as he asked, "Are you okay?"

"Yes, Yes, I am. I don't know why I did that. I think I was successful."

"Oh Anna, hurry back and please be careful."

As she dropped the cell phone in her purse she realized she had accomplished the hardest thing she had ever attempted. And she knew she would have the courage for whatever was necessary. She wanted nothing now, but to get back to the house as soon as possible.

She parked the black Nissan two blocks from where she had picked it up, leaving hair and fabric in it as she had the Thunderbird on Monday. She was only a little shaky when she found her car in the breaking dawn light and headed to Jacob's.

Jacob opened the door as she approached. He had been watching for her. She looked up into his face as he stood back to let her in. As he leaned forward to shut the door they were close. Their eyes met. She saw the hunger in his eyes and he must have seen it in hers. The eager embrace almost immediately became a desperate, frantic, hungry kiss. She was shocked that he wanted her, that he wanted her so desperately, but amazed that she wanted him—and she did want him. She wanted him as he did her—a violent, savage, frenzied, and delicious wanting and having.

A kiss that tasted of blood—his or hers she didn't know, but she loved it. His unshaved face tore at her skin and she loved it. His arms crushed her and his hands hurt her breasts and she loved that, too. She loved his desperate need for her as she loved her own need of him.

At some point the need became a demand so intense it did not permit thought, only action and observation. Hands shaking, he struggled at the buttons of her blouse, fumbling gently at first until both lost patience with the buttons and tore off the blouse, shedding their clothes as they went to the floor. He grabbed her shoulders pushing her back. His mouth fixed in a savage grin, his eyes wild, crazed, moved slowly over her body, looking, looking. It was torture as he made them both wait while his eyes fed. Then he lowered his face to hers for a long wet kiss and she pulled him in.

From electric violence to sweet and beautiful and back again. They loved again and again until, fully exhausted and both damp with sweat, they collapsed laughing on the entryway floor, their hearts beating wildly. She pulled his face to her breasts, felt a spasm and heard a soft chuckle that was almost a sob. She rolled on top, her face beaming with pleasure and sitting up so that he could look.

She loved that his eyes seemed hungry to see her and his hands desperate to know all of her and she loved that he had surrendered his always thoughtful, rational mind to a rapture she gave him. And she loved when he looked into her eyes and grinned as if guessing her thoughts.

5:50 a.m.

Jack Daniels provided a soft and comforting fog while he was awake, but as he approached sleep he returned to the scenes and images from the raid. When the Cencom dispatcher woke him with the news of the senator's assassination it was almost a relief. Twenty minutes later he was in his car punching in the senator's address on his mapping system. Traffic was light, the sun just up. O'Brian, with his lights flashing, paid no attention to the speed limits. Cencom would alert the Bureau's Forensic lab. Agent Ward would send ten agents from his team to help with questioning the neighbors. He left a message for Rita to re-schedule the task force meeting to eleven. The GPS gave him the turns as he removed the stubble with his electric shaver.

He parked on the street among twelve cars from various agencies. A Fort Washington officer confronted O'Brian as he walked toward the house. He didn't bother to look at the officer as he showed his badge and continued toward the house.

He introduced himself to two Secret Service agents at the front door and asked, "So what happened?"

Agent Odum answered. "The senator was asleep in a spare bedroom, Mrs. Hackman in the master bedroom. We didn't know he slept there, but the TLR did. That's where the bomb was."

O'Brian heard the muffled sound of Mrs. Hackman sobbing and someone trying to comfort her as Smith said, "She's in pretty bad shape; thinks her snoring drove the senator out of her bed last night. A daughter is with her."

"The bomb was in a table lamp next to the senator's bed," Odum said. "Went off at 5:15 a.m. Death was instantaneous. There wasn't much left of his head. It's good that Toby got to him first. He managed to stop the senator's wife from seeing the body. It's real bad. We both puked. I don't think we touched anything."

They still looked ill to O'Brian. "If the bomb was in a table-lamp it was either timed or radio controlled or both. Did you see anyone who might have set it off?"

"A car came by a couple of minutes before that time." Smith held up a notebook. "The agent got the license and description of the car. A woman was driving, but it was dark, no one got a look at her. We put out an all points, but nothing so far."

O'Brian called dispatch. He wanted the 'all points' to go to local cops within a hundred miles. He handed the phone to Odum to give the description to dispatch. The team from the Bureau's forensic lab had arrived and was preparing to go into the bedroom. Dr. Galvin, the lab's director, was with them. He shook his head. "They were serious. I didn't think they could pull it off."

They put on plastic booties and gloves. The bedroom door was partly off its hinges, the scene gruesome with blood and brains splattered on the walls, the mostly headless body still on the bed; but the blast was entirely contained within the room, except for the missing window. Whoever did it was skilled, probably professional.

It was easy to imagine how it happened, but the gore was getting to O'Brian. He wanted out. Galvin was planning how his team would gather clues and evidence without compromising them.

Ward stopped at the door, saw the gore splattered walls and said "Holy shit" before he greeted Galvin and O'Brian. Galvin was quick to conclude that the bomb was hi-tech. "We need help. Maybe someone from the CIA. This didn't come from a hardware store. There's no shrapnel, no residue from the explosive. I haven't seen one like this before."

"Ward, you have a couple of guys on your team from the CIA," O'Brian said. "Ask them to bring in Langley."

Ward said, "Bernie Schaefer can help."

O'Brian heard Bradley down the hall. The lab team was setting up cameras and lights as he left. Material samples would be next. O'Brian stepped in front of Bradley and said, "Come outside with me, I need some air."

She followed him out, but she didn't look happy. Several of Ward's team had arrived. Some were trying to get in to see the scene but O'Brian sent them out to interview the neighbors—maybe there was a witness to when the bomb was planted. He gave them the details on the car and asked Bradley to come with him.

6:38 a.m.
Senator Reigns pushed the newspaper back, sipped his breakfast coffee and reminded himself of his goodness. He believed he was a man Thomas Jefferson would have understood—they had so much in common. Both tall, angular, fair-haired fellows—men from the soil of southern states—each with a strong belief in the common man.

He wished Jefferson had been able to witness the majestic democratic institution that the United States government was now. Modern democracy, with elected, professional statesmen, smoothed out the unworkable features self-governing citizen legislators would have provided. If he were alive today, Jefferson would certainly recognize that by allowing the people to call upon their natural leaders, the nation had become unimaginably stronger, perhaps not completely within the intent of the founders, but something they would have admired in retrospect.

The senator noted the country had changed greatly since its founding, but so had the times. Crime had not changed, but to combat crime in the U.S. it had become necessary for the federal government to be involved. The Constitution's framers may have believed criminal law was a matter for the states, but with the advent of the computer and modern drugs and business methods and air travel and so on, it was just obviously a federal matter. His people knew that. They relied on him to understand all these complicated things and see to the writing of laws that protected them. And modern democratic self-government required strong statesman like himself to help it along. That's why he was passionate about stopping the use of steroids in baseball.

Baseball was an important American institution; he had played the game himself as a young man. And he had his plate full of such important projects. Because of his seniority, as well as his natural abilities, he was able to bring home a constant stream of excellent projects for the people of his great state. That was an unarguable fact. He knew without a doubt that his people benefited greatly from his service. Let people rant on about pork, but by golly he knew he was appreciated and loved by his constituents.

He would not resign and he would continue to represent his people even at great risk to his life. His people needed him. And that was that. He sipped his morning coffee, returning his attention again to the newspaper.

Chris drove east in a 2000 model Chevrolet Malibu taken last night from the warehouse. The low sun, undimmed by any clouds, shone straight into his eyes, making it difficult to see the traffic lights. He worried more about Anna than about taking the life of the senator. He expected to hear from her, but didn't want to call. Then he heard the radio news that Hackman had been killed by the TLR. There was no mention of an arrest. She must have got away, but why hadn't she called?

She didn't answer until it rang several times. When she did answer she was spaced out, or something. He said, "I was worried."

"I'm okay. It went fine. Really."

There was something odd in her voice. "Good for you. Wish me luck."

She said, "Good luck, Chris. Be careful."

It sounded genuine, but weird. Maybe she was taking something to help her sleep.

He turned right onto Lee Highway and took a left onto Military. The sun was behind him now. At the end of Marcay Drive he parked in the visitor's lot. It was 7:00 a.m., right on time. After removing the gloves and pulling the hood of his forest green sweatshirt up, he jogged the park trail to the turnoff spot. Twenty yards into the brush he stood behind a large rhododendron on a bluff overlooking the area, with a perfect view of the senator's house slightly below and 200 yards away.

He knew from previous visits that at precisely 7:20 a.m. the senator would step from his kitchen into the adjoining greenhouse and begin watering his orchid collection. Each orchid required the senator's individual attention; It was a job the senator would not delegate.

Chris sat on the ground in a place where he could not be seen from the path or from any other home in the area. He checked the time, 7:16 and focused his pocket binoculars on the greenhouse. *Uh-oh.* Sometime within the last two days, the greenhouse glass had been changed from clear to translucent, probably to prevent a rifle shot. That was unfortunate—he would not be able to see the senator. But he was sure the senator would remain a creature of habit. As he waited he heard the traffic below and a half mile away on the George Washington Memorial Freeway. There were a lot of birds in the area; two jays seemed to be angry with him. He realized he was sitting directly under their nest.

He looked down at the house just as the greenhouse light came on. *Good morning, Senator.* Chris removed the device from his pocket, flipped the switch cover off and armed the weapon. He waited long enough to give the senator time to gather the orchids that needed watering and bring them to the drainboard. The bomb, identical to the one that killed Orville Hackman, was located in a large bag of orchid systemic, a feed and disease preventative kept above the drainboard at head level. Chris had placed it there three weeks ago after several days of watching the senator's movements. The male jay's raucous scream and dive did not shake his attention. He pushed the trigger button and the explosion was immediate. He could not be sure the senator had been killed because he couldn't wait for the smoke to clear.

The noise was loud but not as loud as Chris expected. A few shards of glass hit the trees nearby. The greenhouse was completely blown out. As he got up, the jay dived again, barely missing his head. Chris ignored it, quickly retraced his path, listening as he approached the trail. He heard no one and stepped into the trail and began jogging toward the car.

After a hundred yards or so, he saw another jogger running toward him. Chris kept his head down under the hood, not seeing the jogger as they passed and not being seen.

He made his way to Military without hearing any police or ambulance response units. He was clear. He ditched the car two blocks from Seven Corners, after distributing the bag of hair and fibers in the car, walked to the shopping center, retrieved his truck and headed toward Langley.

7:03 a.m.

Bradley told herself she would not say anything, but the car had just begun to move when she asked. "What the hell was that all about? You think I can't handle the nasty crime scene?"

He paused before saying, "Because you wouldn't have learned anything I didn't and we didn't need more people walking around and maybe leaving misleading clues."

"Bullshit. You didn't want me seeing the bloody body."

"I have a whole damn forensic lab team shooting photos, taking samples and gathering clues you and I would never see . . . And, yeah, I nearly puked . . . it was fucking awful."

She felt her anger dissipate. "Don't do it again."

He pulled in to the Indian Head diner. "Now we wait for the other shoe to drop."

After they ordered and the coffee had been served, she said, "The Secret Service guy told me the bodyguard system is stretched way too thin, not nearly enough guards for the job."

"A hundred cops outside Hackman's wouldn't have made a damn bit of difference."

Good point. "What about getting them out of harm's way? The New York Times wants the president to place Congress in protective custody—perhaps on a military base."

He shook his head. "Can you imagine trying to get 378, or 377 senators and representatives herded onto a military base and housed where? In tents? Mobile homes? And the president can't order it— Congress is equal and separate. The president has no authority over Congress."

The New York Times had missed that. O'Brian was an attorney. They sipped their coffee without talking for a couple of minutes. She asked, "What about the Don Hayes interrogations?"

"Koberg will handle it."

"Hayes doesn't stand a chance."

"That's the plan. Break him fast and get a confession signed quickly."

"Koberg might stretch it out for the fun of it."

"I don't think he enjoys it. I think he believes in strong government. So does Hammar. They probably believe Hayes and Jackson were somehow involved with the TLR."

"So you're saying their suspicion justifies what they are doing."

"I said they believe it does."

As the waitress arrived with their breakfast, CenCom called with the news of Senator Reigns' assassination. He asked Bradley to get the bill while he punched the new address into the GPS. She came out with some toast in a napkin.

7:50 a.m.

Chris called Jacob as he drove into the CIA Headquarters grounds. Jacob asked. "How did it go?"

"Should be on the news pretty quick; I left before I could be sure, but I think it went according to plan."

"We'll watch to see."

"How's Anna handling this? She seem a little strange to you?"

"She seems fine to me."

Chris sensed the electricity in the CIA building as soon as he stepped inside. While walking to his office, a number of people commented about the assassinations of Senators Hackman and Reigns. Their reactions varied. Some were incredulous, some angry, and several just seemed to think it was interesting. Chris selected incredulous. "I can't believe it. Who the hell are those guys?" was typical of his reply to comments from others. He wouldn't be there long anyway; today he would demonstrate the laser rifle. He picked up three of the experimental weapons and carried them out to the truck. CIA red tape was almost non-existent compared to the FBI, DEA or ATTF. To get a weapon like this out of those agencies would have taken all kinds of sign-offs. But the CIA budget was not supervised by the congressional budget office or by the General Accounting office. Everything at the CIA is top secret, which reduces oversight to nil.

Chris drove out of the parking area headed west to US 495. He picked up an all news station and listened to the reports of the heinous assassinations and the senators who would be sorely missed. Political killings were always *heinous* and the politician was always certain to be *sorely missed*. Flags at half-staff pissed him off—*they should be at half-staff for our lost rights.*

When he couldn't take any more, he turned the radio off, flipped down the photo and thought of last night's telephone conversation—the kids were having fun. Larry had said, "Bill definitely remembered us, Dad. Granddad said he could tell he did." Bill was the Carpenter's horse and the third horse named Bill, Chris could remember. Karen seemed to be enjoying herself, but she wanted him to commit to coming there soon. He had been evasive. She said his mom was doing better since they arrived, but was still anxious and worried over Nicolo and her parents.

Roast in hell, Frank Reigns.

He arrived at the base a few minutes early, talked to Bill Miller, then found Mark Adams in his office. Mark seemed genuinely pleased to see him. They got through the pleasantries; Mark assured him the range was ready. "We have a sprinkler-misting system for your amazing Star Wars weapon. When the rest of your students are here, you can talk to them in the conference room across the hall before we go out to the range. The DEA guys are in there now."

"Thanks, Mark."

Mark paused a second. He seemed to be considering his subject matter. "Looks like the TLR are making good on their threats."

"Seems hard to believe, huh?"

"The TLR is quite an outfit."

They looked at each other without comment for a bit. Chris heard the Secret Service people arriving. He said, "Better get started, huh?"

They walked into the conference room where Chris introduced himself and Mark Adams before asking the others to introduce themselves. When the introductions were complete he began the video that described the new weapon and showed it in operation. It was impressive. Chris said, "Unlike ballistic weapons, the laser rifle has no trajectory and is unaffected by the wind. If the path is clear air, then it is capable of amazing distance and accuracy."

Chris then showed them one of the weapons. A DEA weapons procurement officer said it looked like a damned boom-box radio with binocular gun-sights mounted on a gunstock.

Everyone was impressed. Chris said, "The weapon can evaporate a cantaloupe or a human head at a range of 500 yards—and do it time after time in the hands of a capable user. There is no sound from the weapon. The cantaloupe explodes but does not make much of a sound." He paused and said, "We don't know about the head yet."

Everyone laughed.

"The accuracy is due to the binocular sight. The computer controlled binocular provides optimum power at the target. At extreme ranges, beyond 500 yards, a rest must be used, but once the laser is locked on the target, the weapon can move some, with the computer retaining the target. Even some pretty bad shots will look good using this weapon."

Someone said, "Hey, Fred, this might be just the weapon for you."

Chris grinned. "Now for the problem. This thing doesn't work as well in fog, mist, snow or rain, because it tends to explode the first object it hits. A cloth, or helmet covered head, would still be exploded, but if the cloth were a yard in front of the head it might or might not work. Rain and mist make a difference depending on how much. There are no firm rules here. You need to get a feel for it. So let's go to the range and try it out."

"Assemble in front of the building," Mark announced. "Use the vehicles you arrived in and if you haven't been here before, just follow Luke Skywalker and me. The range is about a mile away."

As he and Chris walked out, Mark said, "I hear the JTTF is looking hard at the former friends, colleagues and students of T. J. Stewart."

"Thanks for the information."

Mark said, "Let me know if I can help."

7:46 a.m.
The rush hour traffic was bumper to bumper, but the flashing lights, screaming siren and wide shoulder helped. They shared the toast as O'Brian drove and Bradley called for a forensic team and twenty agents to canvass the area. The 17 mile trip to Senator Reigns' home took 23 minutes.

They pulled up in front of the house at 8:09 a.m., only 49 minutes after the explosion, but they were parked behind a TV news truck that had been there for six minutes. As they got out of the car, TV cameras surrounded them and a reporter stepped in front of them, speaking into her mike then shoving the mike in O'Brian's face. O'Brian and Bradley ignored the reporter's aggressive questions, pushed past her and showed their badges to the local police managing the scene.

A Secret Service agent met them at the door. "I'm Ted Moss. This was my show." His clothes were splattered with blood. O'Brian asked for an update.

Moss trembled slightly. "We'd just heard about Senator Hackman. I sent four agents outside to watch the perimeter. As I came back inside and started toward the greenhouse, the bomb exploded. Agent Marler was . . . near the senator. The senator was killed instantly. There was nothing we could do for him. The senator's wife ran screaming to the greenhouse. She saw it before we could stop her—pretty fucking hideous. She passed out on some broken glass. We called for two ambulances. Marler may live, but he'll be badly messed up." Moss hesitated before adding, "He's a friend."

O'Brian noticed that Moss was turning pale. "Let's sit down." He moved them toward the living room. "Anybody touch anything in the greenhouse?"

"No, sir. Except to get Marler out"

"I'll have a look. Agent Bradley will take the rest of your information."

Bradley shot O'Brian an angry look.

Two Secret Service agents outside the greenhouse kept the cameras away; the two inside the house were staying away from the greenhouse. Secret Service agents normally see little in the way of bloodshed and this was a particularly gory scene involving one of their own. They also had blood on their clothes, probably from trying to help Marler.

As O'Brian stepped over the senator's body he observed this bomb had also exploded near the senator's head. O'Brian had an image of Reign's red and angry face yesterday morning. He made his way through the blood and glass strewn area, leaned out over the low wall that had held the greenhouse glass and expelled his toast and coffee.

He waited a moment with his hands on the wall before looking again. The remains of the head were everywhere. Bomb parts would be non-existent here also. And this bomb was probably identical to the one that killed Senator Hackman. But it was set off knowing Reigns was near the bomb. How? He tried to observe without seeing the gore. The glass was not transparent. The killer could not have seen Reigns.

The light switch was in the on position. That would do it. He looked up at the green forested hillside. Someone could have been up there, someone on that bluff could have seen the light come on and set off the bomb. He saw movement and the reflection off something. Someone, two actually, were up there now—with a camera.

His back was to the door, but he heard Bradley's, "Oh," and turned to see her look quickly around and go back inside.

O'Brian couldn't handle any more, either. She was leaning against a wall, her eyes closed. He guessed she wanted to go out the front but didn't want to deal with the TV cameras.

Agents began arriving. He sent the first up into the park to shut down the TV camera. "And take someone with you to help search the area. I think the bomb might have been triggered from the bluff where the TV crew is, if they haven't pounded any clues into the ground. I'll send forensics up." He told the others to "talk to the neighbors, interview anyone who might have seen or heard anything."

Dr. Galvin and two of his lab team arrived. Galvin asked O'Brian, "Same M.O.?"

"Yeah, probably similar to the one that killed Hackman." He told Galvin his theory about the assassin on the bluff.

Galvin agreed and sent a man up to the bluff. "The bombs may be our best clues. I hope the CIA's bomb people can help us."

O'Brian watched Galvin go into the greenhouse and decided he had had enough. He and Bradley spent the next hour organizing the investigation and assigning agents to various tasks. Eventually he and Bradley just weren't needed there.

They headed back to headquarters. He pulled in to a drive up window and ordered milkshakes to get the bad taste out of his mouth. "I'm going to try to see Hayes. You want to come?"

She nodded over her milkshake.

They had just turned onto the Highway 50 bridge when Attorney General Hammar called for an update.

"Yes, sir. Both senators were killed by bombs that were planted earlier, maybe weeks earlier. Both homes were occupied constantly for the last week. We suspect very small radio controlled bombs. Hi-tech. I've asked the CIA to help identify them. So far we haven't found any clues that look helpful. We have agents at both crime scenes canvassing the neighborhoods asking residents what they've seen—this morning or over the last several weeks."

"I'm going into a cabinet meeting in three minutes." His voice rose. "The president is angry, so is Congress, the press is killing us, and O'Brian, we look stupid and powerless."

"Sir, perhaps the CIA can identify the bomb quickly. Meanwhile I think the Secret Service should warn Congress members to avoid established routines. They may not use a bomb next time. But they should be advised to sleep in a different bed, sit in a different chair than they normally use, travel in vehicles they don't normally use, use alternate routes and so on."

Hammar's voice was withering. "That's a great idea, O'Brian. If we want to frighten them and produce more resignations."

O'Brian thought they should be scared.

Hammar asked, "Don't you have anything more?"

"I have some other leads that probably aren't worth mentioning, but we are following up. I'll keep you updated."

"Do."

O'Brian fed onto Constitution Avenue while Bradley called Ward to find out what leads he might have. Ward was meeting with Sarah Murphy. They both got on Ward's speakerphone.

Sarah said, "I met with Roland Fischer, Professor Stewart's attorney. He believes Stewart really died in the sailboat accident. He was pissed when I suggested the accident might have been staged. However, as our conversation went on he seemed to be warming to the idea. He obviously liked the professor; he also likes the TLR's amendment. Here is the interesting part. Stewart made changes to his will four months before the disappearance."

O'Brian asked, "How old was Stewart?"

"Fifty-four, so maybe changing the will was just a coincidence. He was at an age where he might have been thinking of his family. He and his wife had established a family trust several years earlier. It had three million dollars in it at the time he met with Fischer and it provides income for his children and grandchildren for another twenty years. His will provided the remaining estate would also go into the trust in the event of his death. Fischer said they went over Stewart's additional assets which included $2.5 million invested through his private corporation in some foreign ventures. Stewart told him it was a high risk-high reward investment.

"Now here is the interesting part. When the professor went overboard—if that really happened—the estate that was supposed to be added to the $2 million trust had a few pieces of property and some money in a bank account, a value of maybe $700,000. The $2.5 million foreign investment was gone. Fischer—he's also the executor—set out to gather in the funds from the stock investments and discovered $2,457,000 had been invested in a Delaware company for common stock. But that company was acquired by a Bahamian company that has since gone out of business.

"Mr. Fischer says he believes that Professor Stewart may have used the Delaware company as a vehicle for investing in a foreign venture— perhaps for tax reasons—and that his untimely death made recovery of the investment impossible. Fischer says the IRS was very interested in the missing money, but eventually gave up, apparently satisfied with half the $700,000 estate they could get their hands on."

O'Brian asked, "So the kids got $3.5 million and the Professor went missing and so did another $2.5 million?"

Murphy said, "Yes."

"Where did he get that kind of money?"

"His wife died in a car crash four years ago. Her name was Angela, as in Angela Stewart, the author of 33 best-selling children's books."

"I met her," O'Brian said. "At a book signing in Arlington. I think my daughter owns all 33."

"And Stewart wrote a few books that made money. And he invested well, with the exception of that last foreign investment."

"Too much coincidence," Ward said.

O'Brian nodded in agreement. "Did you get the names of anyone we should follow up on? Any former colleagues with a revolutionary streak?"

"None that Fischer thought might be involved. He said Stewart was close to Hayes and Jackson. Fischer was really pissed about the raid. Really pissed. That was the first thing we discussed after I introduced myself. I told him what I thought of the raid and after that we didn't have any trouble talking."

No one followed up with a question or comment. O'Brian picked up on the silence, but he ignored it. "What about Fischer? Is he hiding anything or anyone?"

"I think he was giving it to me straight, because he really believes it doesn't lead anywhere."

Ward asked, "Why does he believe that? He must see the same unlikely coincidences we see?"

"He believes . . . he strongly believes Stewart would not have put his family through the desolation his death caused them." Murphy said. "Fischer was in a depressive funk for a month afterward. He says the professor's family is just now getting over it."

O'Brian said, "Nonetheless, let's assume he's alive, he's a member of the TLR and he's not working alone. Who was he working with when he disappeared?"

Bradley said, "Someone that's good with bombs and computers. Do we have a list of his students?"

Murphy said, "Yes, it's digitized since 2000, and we have a paper record of his previous students since he started teaching at Higgs U."

Bradley said, "Good job, Murphy."

O'Brian said, "Let's run a search on those names, Ward. And crosscheck to see if we have someone with the same name in law enforcement, especially the CIA or the Bureau. Add his colleagues and friends to the list. I want the results tonight. Talk to them. See if they can make any guesses about where Stewart would be hiding, or who he might be working with. If you find someone that seems reluctant put a little pressure on them . . . but just a little—not like last night."

O'Brian heard the silence again. "That was the worst piece of shit I've ever been involved in. I hope you know I would never have ordered that."

Ward said, "I won't take part in something like that again."

O'Brian was sorry he brought it up. "I'll see you both at the meeting at eleven."

He and Bradley were just pulling into the new Federal Detention Facility on D Street. It was nearly as big as the J Edgar Hoover building and provided underground parking on several levels for federal officers and contract interrogators.

10:00 a.m.

Jacob woke with a dull ache in his arm, but smiled as he gently rolled Anna onto her pillow. He watched her from a chair, amazed—at her, at how much he loved her, at how little he understood of himself.

He should have seen it. Why had he not? He could remember the first day she came into his classroom, to ask if she could audit the class. She had affected him that day. Their relationship had been student and teacher for years, but he was always conscious of her when she was in any of his classes. Later Burton brought her to the house and soon Chris began to audit his courses. Their friendship grew quickly from that point. But it had not been friendship alone, not for him. Anna always had attractive men chasing her and Burton was always first in line. And Jacob knew she liked men her own age. Perhaps this, whatever it was, was an emotional aberration, a result of the stress she was under and because she was confined there with him.

He decided he didn't give a damn. *We both deserve whatever joy we can find in the next few days.* He let his eyes caress her and then went into the living room to gather their clothes. He laughed at the way they were spread around the entryway, a few thrown some distance into the living room. As he picked those up, his eyes fell on the muted TV. The caption identified the house as that of Senator Reigns. He dropped the clothes on the couch and brought the sound up as the reporter warned, ". . . by a neighbor. Because this home video has been made public and is being distributed on the internet, we believe many of our viewers may also wish to be informed." He spoke of the graphic nature of the scene and warned parents that it would be inappropriate for children. He described the death of the senator and the maiming of a Secret Service Agent. The home video began with a distant view of the house from a hillside, perhaps a hundred yards away. The video zoomed in to the demolished greenhouse. A man entering the blasted area from inside the house looked around briefly before leaning over a low wall. The reporter identified him as the JTTF Special Agent in Charge, Michael O'Brian. The camera zoomed-in tighter, then panned to a gore strewn scene and a headless body. A woman's voice, probably the person who made the video, began sobbing as the video pointed at the ground. The television cut back to the reporter in front of the house as he continued to describe the few facts that were known and the many questions that were unanswered.

Jacob's immediate thought was *Anna must not see this*. Chris could handle the gore. He would be more upset to hear an agent was maimed. And he worried that the gore could backfire, turning the public against them.

Over the next hour, Jacob made a pot of espresso and watched the reaction to the first assassinations. The White House press secretary was predictable, lauding the senators as statesmen serving the public faithfully with great moral vision for many years." He also attacked the TLR. "The terrorists who murdered these noble men revealed their hatred for the rule of law, our democratic electoral system and the will of the American voter. They claim to be patriots, seeking a return to constitutionally limited government, but they have placed their personal views above the Constitution and the legally elected representatives of the people."

He said the president had ordered flags flown at half-staff and the attorney general has promised quick action in the roundup of the TLR. After a time he mentioned the president was meeting with his cabinet "to consider the various options available for protection of the threatened members of Congress. In the meantime, a doubling of bodyguards has been ordered for every threatened Congressman. To further frustrate the TLR, the Secret Service is ordering a change to their regular schedules."

He asked for questions and the Washington Times reporter asked, "We've known for days that the TLR would attempt to kill members of Congress. How did the bombs get past security?"

"It appears the bombs used were very hi-tech, entirely non-metallic, and contained in a plastic sleeve that prevented their detection. We believe they were placed some time ago but we do not know when. Only a few people have access to such weapons, which may help us narrow our list of suspects. Attorney General Hammar has also assured the president the Joint Terrorism Task Force expects new information today that will help with the apprehension of the killers."

"Has he considered placing the Congress on a military base where the environment can be secured?"

"The congressional leadership believes it would be nearly impossible for Congress to get its work done in that situation. There are several thousand staff and constituent groups that must interact with the members to accomplish the people's work."

Another reporter asked, "Do you have a comment on the shooting of Cal Jackson and the arrest of Don Hayes?"

"The news of the arrest of Don Hayes and the accidental shooting of Cal Jackson was a great shock to the president, but Attorney General Hammar assures us that the evidence against them is compelling. The president has complete confidence in Attorney General Hammar."

"What about the arrest of their wives and the taking of their children?"

"The president does not second guess the manner in which the Department of Justice carries out its legitimate duties. He is comfortable they follow the laws passed by Congress and they have excellent reasons for their actions."

Young ended the questioning. Jacob muted the sound and looked into the future. He hadn't foreseen the attacks on Don Hayes and Cal Jackson. The bloody scene on television could hurt their cause. They should have expected photos from neighbors. What else hadn't they planned for?

10:05 a.m.

O'Brian dreaded the interview with Hayes and was glad Bradley was with him. The Federal Detention Center gave him the creeps. They showed their badges at the security area and then again when they told the desk officer they wanted to see Don Hayes.

"Yes, sir. Assistant District Attorney Koberg is waiting for him now."

O'Brian felt his gut heave. "Where?"

"Down the hall, last door on your left—Interrogation A."

"I better go alone. Wait for me." She offered to go but he shook his head and walked away.

He looked through the small window; Koberg was alone. O'Brian straightened his shoulders before opening the door.

"Good morning, O'Brian. What brings you here?" His face showed no emotion.

O'Brian walked to the opposite side of the table. "I wanted to question Hayes."

"You really don't look well, Agent O'Brian. In any case, I'm not sure you can be of much help."

O'Brian looked at Koberg for a long time before he made up his mind. He sat down. "Oh, I'll be a great help. I know the drill."

Koberg raised an eyebrow.

"When I was Assistant Prosecutor in Pittsburgh I specialized in drug enforcement."

"I know that."

"I was very successful. Everyone confessed."

Hayes walked down the long hall in the short shuffling steps leg chains demanded. The guard stayed behind him and did not speak until he ordered Hayes to "Stop." The guard opened the metal door and followed Hayes in. The interrogation room was gray, dismal, sterile and small, the only furniture a small gray metal table that sat in the middle of the room surrounded by four gray metal chairs.

Koberg stood. He was handsomely dressed in an expensive light blue suit, white silk shirt and dark blue tie. He wore a smug and condescending smile. O'Brian wore his standard dark blue suit. Hayes noticed O'Brian looked shocked as he rose out of his seat a little. In this depressing hellish place their attractive dress felt like an intentional taunt. He wore bright orange overalls with the stenciled white block letters PRISONER spelled out across the front and back. The overalls were humiliating. The sight of Koberg and O'Brian only amplified his depression and hopelessness. He knew what was coming.

The table and chairs were bolted to the floor. The guard chained Hayes' already handcuffed arms to the chair leg—as if he might otherwise leap up and beat someone to death. The bruised and broken nose hurt a lot, but the great agony came from his blue-gray and badly swollen hand. The pain came in waves, hurting all the way up into his underarm and stealing his ability to focus his mind.

The guards had refused him pain medication—for his own good, they said. But they also hinted they might be able to find some if he cooperated.

Koberg began. "So how are you doing, Don? Are they treating you right?"

"What have you done with my family?"

Koberg's condescending smile broadened. He shook his head slowly. Hayes loathed him. "What am I being charged with?"

Koberg asked, "Mind if I smoke?" He lit a cigarette without waiting for an answer. "We won't charge you until we finish questioning you. Eventually, you and your wife will be charged with terrorism. But we are still considering the precise charges. Perhaps you would like to have some input."

"I want . . ." The pulse of pain seemed electric, racing up his arm and stopping him for a second. "I want to see my attorney."

"You know the rules, Don. You're an accused terrorist; you no longer have a right to an attorney. We may eventually appoint an attorney for you. But of course even if we do, you and the attorney will not be allowed to communicate."

Hayes looked at O'Brian for help. Koberg called Don's attention back. "You and your wife have been linked with terrorism. That allows us to remove your citizenship. Do you understand me?"

"I could never understand you."

Koberg turned to O'Brian. "Agent O'Brian, please explain the situation to our friend Don."

O'Brian tried to square his shoulders. "Mr. Hayes, you know all this before I say it. Don't make us go through the steps. The pain will stop when you agree to help us catch the TLR. You must name . . ." O'Brian's voice was weak. He was obviously having a hard time saying it. But then his face grew hard, his tone hard, almost brutal. "Your wife is under arrest. All your assets—your home, property, cars, everything—has been seized and forfeited to the Department of Justice. They will be sold. Your children will go to foster homes, the worst we can find. They will live with abused children, the children of drug dealers. The foster parents that run the place won't give a damn about any of the kids . . ."

"GOD DAMN YOU!"

Koberg half stood his face red with anger. "Do not use that language."

O'Brian interrupted. He seemed to be in pain. "Mr. Hayes, you know the techniques we use. You know what I'm going to say. Don't make me say it. Give up now."

Hayes began weeping. He knew that resistance was hopeless. For nearly thirty years, federal, state and local governments had increasingly used confessions and guilty pleas obtained this way, and he had been fighting it all of that time. JFI had written hundreds of articles and published several books on the subject. The methods were developed while pursuing the Drug War. No one cared to protect the civil rights of drug dealers. The Supreme Court confirmed their legality in a drug case. That became a precedent, allowing its use against those accused of other crimes. But since 2002, the simple accusation of terrorism was sufficient to remove all Constitutional protections and since 2006, torture was redefined to make confessions readily available and trials unnecessary.

He wept for his family and for what he knew he must do to save them. He wept for the horror he was about to cause those who had helped him defend individual rights. He had interviewed others who had been through this. Resistance was pointless. If he attempted to maintain any semblance of self-respect, if he attempted to bargain for some limited benefit for the people he was to condemn, his family would be made to pay the price.

Koberg waited for Hayes to stop weeping before saying, "When you are ready to work with us, we can begin to relieve some of your concerns. Until then you will sit in your cell and consider that your children will be in separate foster homes. They will be moved there from the juvenile detention facility tomorrow or the next day. It is true we selected foster homes in tough neighborhoods. Perhaps that will be good for them—it might toughen them up. I was shocked to hear that Bill was taking it so hard. But we aren't completely heartless. We sent a doctor into his room this morning with a shot to calm him down. I'm sure he is much better now."

Hayes saw the calculated taunt coming. He knew it was intended to break him. But their willingness to inflict malicious brutality on his son to break him was so monstrous he lost control. He lurched at Koberg, enraged and screaming, but his handcuffs stopped him. His forward movement caused his broken hand to jerk hard against the handcuffs and his body shuddered to an instant stop from the pain exploding through his body. He collapsed on the table, his body sliding back toward the chair.

O'Brian helped him into the chair, his own face contorted in sympathy. "Don, don't make this worse than it has to be. You know where this will go. Get it over with, Don. Give up."

Koberg said, "Yes, Don, you do know where this has to go. Don't you?"

Hayes' head and shoulders lay on the table; he sobbed in agony.

After a time, Koberg interrupted his sobs. "Your wife is handling this a lot better than you, Don."

Hayes continued to weep and groan as the pain shot up his arm, overwhelming him.

Koberg rose. "Agent O'Brian, let's leave Don to consider his options for a couple of days."

O'Brian did not rise. Hayes knew he must beg. "I'll sign. I'll sign anything you give me. I'll testify against anyone you want. If you'll release my wife and children, I'll testify against anyone you want."

Koberg returned to his seat and said, "Oh come now, Don. Don't get dramatic on me. We just need you to give us a list of other TLR conspirators."

"Please. Please, I'll confess to anything, but I can't guess who you want next unless you tell me who you want."

"Give us the names, Don. We will help you write out your confession, but we also need the list of co-conspirators. Until then, your wife will be held here and the children will be placed in the foster homes." Koberg nodded at O'Brian and stood. "We will give you some time to think about this."

Tears poured down his face. He was close to collapse—pain and fear had prevented sleep. He thought of his children, now in juvenile detention and headed for foster homes filled with children of drug addicts and criminals. It would kill him if he had to think about it until they returned. "Tell me what you want. I'll give you whatever you want, but let them go. Please don't hurt my children any more."

O'Brian said, "He wants you to . . ." but was interrupted by Koberg before he could complete the statement.

"I call the shots here, O'Brian. We are leaving *now*." Hayes' eyes were glued to Koberg. Koberg was furious.

But O'Brian continued, "You must name Marcus Ray and Cal Jackson as members. The DOJ *knows* they are guilty."

Hayes asked Koberg, "Why? You know they aren't TLR either. How can you do this? And why?"

"Give us the names, Don." He looked at O'Brian again. "Come now, Agent O'Brian, we must go."

Hayes said in a rush of words, "Please, not yet. Don't make my family suffer more. I'll give you names and I'll sign if you'll let them go."

Koberg sneered, "Now there is the problem, Don. We can't bargain like that, as I'm sure you know. It would look bad in court, not that this will ever come to court."

O'Brian said, "If we bargain, if we promise to let them go for your confession, then it can come out in court. If Marcus Ray is tried based on your testimony, his attorney will point out that we gave you something, your wife's freedom, or your children's, in exchange for naming him. We must be able to say, 'There was no deal. He gave us the testimony freely. We released his wife and children, because we believed it was best for the children.'"

"Will you?"

Koberg smiled and said, "No deals."

"How fast will it be drawn up?"

O'Brian said, "Tonight," but Koberg said, "Tomorrow."

"How soon will my wife and children be released?"

"Now that sounds too much like a deal," Koberg said. "I can only promise to plead with Attorney General Hammar. My guess is that he will want the children released as soon as possible. But I give no promises. It is his decision. I believe your wife will remain accused and under house arrest until we have a confession from Marcus Ray."

"And from Jackson, too?"

There was a short silence before O'Brian said, "I'm sorry, Don. Cal Jackson is dead."

Until that moment Hayes thought nothing could increase his devastation.

Koberg said, "An unfortunate accident. The attorney general will be letting Mrs. Jackson off and returning her children, if she admits to simple complicity."

He grabbed at the idea that Sue Jackson was to be released. It could be true for Barbara. "I'll sign and give you the names . . . if . . ." He looked at O'Brian. "if you will promise to have the confession ready for my signature tomorrow morning."

O'Brian immediately said, "Yes."

After they left, Koberg instructed the chief of guards to let Hayes sleep a little tonight, but that he should not be fully rested tomorrow morning. The chief asked about medical care and Koberg said, "Not yet. A few aspirin perhaps."

Bradley walked toward them, but Koberg stopped her. "Agent O'Brian will ride with me."

O'Brian handed her his car key. "I'll see you at the office."

Koberg's chauffer picked them up on D Street. "You have a lot to learn, Agent O'Brian. If you aren't terminated first, you will discover that getting a full confession and full cooperation requires that the accused be kept desperate, wondering if it will actually occur. Hayes would give us the names of ten people now, but none would be TLR. He is not truly broken yet. He knows one or two of the TLR, or he can guess, but he must be even more desperate than he now is."

O'Brian heard himself mumble. "Yeah, I guess so." But it pissed him off that his stomach knotted when he heard the word *terminated*.

"It only prolongs the pain of all involved if we allow them to regain strength and start thinking of the damage they are about to pass on to others. Our task is difficult. It is difficult to play the role I played in there. I hated that. But it is like a surgeon forced to operate without anesthetic. Do it as fast as it can be done. Get it over. I don't want to extend his pain. But if we are sympathetic he will imagine he can negotiate with us and this will go on for weeks."

O'Brian needed air. He rolled his window down. "Do you really believe he's guilty or that his wife is guilty?"

"I am certain of it. But even if they were not members of the TLR team with assigned duties, they can guess who is. They have certainly created the atmosphere that made it possible. They have aided and abetted the TLR with their rabblerousing speeches and papers. And if we shut them up it will be noticed by the other ilk that refuse to be governed."

"Then why not accuse them of inciting crimes and get a jury to convict them?"

"You must be smarter than that. They would be out of jail in thirty minutes and they would not only continue to preach their message, they would have every news organization in the country giving them a forum. We don't have time for that. We hold them as terrorists so we can keep them quiet. Suspension of their citizenship and rights is a warning to others who would attack our nation. Innocent people die in every war, by the hundreds of thousands if not millions, without being given a day in court. People like Hayes and Jackson are not innocent. They undermine society and we must stop them. I hate this as much as you, O'Brian. I suffer as a result of the pain we cause. However, my faith strengthens me. I know that God loves this nation and he has given me the strength to serve his nation. And I know the nation will be saved far greater pain as a result of my willingness to endure this."

O'Brian was exhausted, physically and emotionally. He had not slept ten hours in the last three days. And the future seemed so damned hopeless.

As they passed the Capitol, they saw the Minuteman. His signboard no longer marked hours but the 378 names of the senators and representatives marked for term limiting. Some were crossed off with a gray X. Reigns and Hackman were marked with a red X as term-limited. "That fellow is going too far," Koberg said. "He will be taught a lesson, I'm sure." As they entered the FBI parking garage, he added, "Think hard about what I've said. You won't be kept around if you can't help us."

As they walked toward the elevator, O'Brian asked, "Do you want me to work on the confession?"

"It's already prepared. Get Hayes' signature at 2:30 tomorrow afternoon, but not before."

O'Brian nodded yes but his head hardly moved. Koberg turned to walk down the long tunnel under Pennsylvania Avenue to the Department of Justice elevators as O'Brian said, "We have a task force meeting in five minutes. Maybe you should attend."

10:55 a.m.
The laser rifle demonstration was a big success. Mark provided fifty under-ripe melons for target practice, some outfitted with metal helmets. Various water dispersion devices provided misting, fogs and rainwater effects. The red-meated melons were spectacular. And the computer control could lock-on a target amazingly well if the rain was not present or the mist was light enough. Some participants missed the sound of the exploding bullet and feel of the recoil and it wasn't entirely dependable in anything but clear weather. But everyone agreed it was a deadly son-of-a-bitch in clear air—you just pulled the trigger and splat—no bang, no trajectory, just watermelon and helmet blown to bits. "Damn that was fun," was a typical comment.

There wasn't a good opportunity to talk with Mark during the demonstration, but Chris wasn't sure he wanted to talk. He took off as soon as he could afterward.

He called Jacob's phone, but Anna answered. He told her he would stop by later. She seemed unfocused. Maybe this was all just way too much for her. He would ask Jacob.

He pulled into the CIA complex a few minutes before noon and carried two of the laser rifles back to inventory. The inventory clerk asked about the third weapon and Chris dismissed the request with, "It's still being tried out."

He walked back to his office and found a *see me* note from Sheldon Scribner, his boss. He walked in without concern. "Hi Shel, what's up?"

"Hey Chris, the JTTF wants to talk to you."

His stomach knotted. "Oh, what about?" He tried not to show his concern.

But Sheldon must have seen it. He laughed, "Don't worry, they aren't after you yet. In fact they need your help."

"Can they afford me?"

He laughed. "Yeah, we'll sell you cheap."

It seemed too much of a coincidence. "So what can I do for them?"

"Our bomb technicians are otherwise occupied in the Middle East and you have the most experience with those small tube bombs. Apparently the two bombs that killed the senators may have worked something like those. They need you to examine the scene of the blast and the pieces their lab picked up. See if you see a similarity."

"Sounds like fun, but I was hoping to take a few days off. My family is in Oklahoma now."

"No problem, we can live without you a few days. Just give them an hour or two this afternoon." He handed Chris a name and phone number. "Let me know if it looks like one of ours."

For a few minutes, Chris feared a set up. But if they suspected him, they wouldn't do it this way. He looked at the name on the note. Bernie Schaeffer was CIA, but apparently on assignment to the JTTF. He punched in the number, spoke to Schaeffer and agreed to drop by in an hour or so.

After making a list, he stopped by the weapons storage maybe one last time.

11 a.m.

Koberg exuded power and confidence as he led O'Brian into the meeting. O'Brian was depressed and desperate to escape responsibility. "I assume you'll take charge, sir." He sounded so fucking weak.

"This is your meeting, O'Brian."

"I just thought . . ."

Koberg said, "You're in charge" as they stepped up to the podium area.

Bradley stood waiting. O'Brian asked Ward to report on "what you have going."

Ward checked his notes. "We've interviewed 214 people in the last 24 hours, established a number of leads. None feel really hot, but you never know. Some seem like they're trying to help; others need prodding. Some names keep coming up, Professor T J Stewart is at the top. Murphy and I filled you in on that development."

"Everyone should hear it," O'Brian said.

Ward described the apparent death at sea, no body, the money, his attorney and distribution of the trust. Murphy added to the description and O'Brian asked, "Anything else?"

"We're checking out Stewart's friends. Nothing yet but we're still looking. Agents are meeting with his stock broker and his banker. We'll have more later today."

Koberg decided to get involved. "Shouldn't we be spending our time on the living, Agent O'Brian?"

Bradley jumped in. "One reason for looking at Stewart was to find out who he knew. We shouldn't be giving up on that lead yet. He knew everyone involved in Term Limits. We need to check-out the people he worked on term limits with. Also, he supposedly died two years ago. About the time the TLR says they started." As she spoke she looked at

O'Brian, obviously miffed. O'Brian had sent Ward looking for Stewart's friends and acquaintances.

O'Brian nodded at Ward. "Go ahead, if it's producing leads." He asked Agent Barnes for a report.

"We've interviewed 273 people in the last 24 hours, mostly following up on the list we got from the OITC, but some of our team are chasing leads related to the TLR female operative. A couple of people calling in seem to be really talking about her. One guy said he saw her in Arlington thirty minutes after she left the Department of Justice."

Koberg was pleased. "Excellent. Where was she seen?"

"Two blocks from where we found her car. He said he pulled up beside her and she yelled at him. She acted suspicious, he says, so he drove off, but she was the same person and dressed the same as in the photos."

"Sounds as if he tried to pick her up and she put him down." Bradley said,

"That's my guess too," Barnes said. "He wondered if his picture would be in the paper or if he would get a reward."

Koberg asked, "So where was she going?"

"We don't know. She was walking toward Leesburg Pike, two blocks away. Maybe a bus stop. She left the car parked in front of an apartment building, where we would find it—and we did. The material left inside the car demonstrates they expected it to be found and they didn't want to use it again. So probably she had another car nearby, or was meeting someone, or caught a bus. It seems doubtful she lives in the neighborhood, but we have been talking to people in the area. Nothing so far."

O'Brian asked, "Anything else?"

"Yeah, there's a student organization at Higgs University that's been involved in the term limits movement for many years. Professor Stewart started it. Many of the students still live in the Northeast. We've just started interviewing them."

"Be as persuasive as you need to be," Koberg said. "Two senators died today. The TLR has demonstrated their capability; more may die tomorrow. Exert every possible effort and use every tool at your command. This is a very dangerous period for our nation and not the time to be squeamish."

Murphy said, "The newspapers are complaining that JTTF and FBI agents are roughing people up, arresting them on bogus charges, and threatening them. That's making our job harder. Lots of people don't want to help."

An agent on Ward's team asked, "What the hell were those SWAT team raids about? That seemed way over the top."

Koberg nodded gently to O'Brian, as if to say, *You handle it.*

He tried to look angry. "The decision to use the SWAT teams was made for good reasons. Now do we have more leads, or suggestions?"

Bradley said, "Bernie Schaeffer asked a CIA bomb expert to help the forensics lab with an analysis of the bombs that killed the senators. That will happen in the next hour or so."

"That may be helpful. Anything else?"

Linda Morrow, the FBI agent in charge of the computer and internet investigations said, "We expect the TLR to send another message tonight at midnight. Our group has been working with the OITC and NSA to set up a system to detect the message as soon as it starts and then to triangulate on the site. We have the active help of all the cell and land line phone companies. But can we get there in time to catch them?"

"I think so," Koberg said. "We will have helicopters in the air, waiting to drop on them as soon as you tell us where they are."

O'Brian asked Barnes and Agent Morrow to work out the logistics and make sure everything was in place well before midnight.

11:32 a.m.

They couldn't just let it ring. It had to be Chris and he would worry if the call went unanswered. Anna got up to find the offending phone. While she spoke with him, Jacob enjoyed the view.

"Chris is coming over," she said, "We have to get dressed."

"Did he say why?"

"No. But we have to tell him." Her smile was sweet. "I want to tell him, Jacob." She was looking for her panties in the fold of the bedclothes.

She found them as Jacob said, "He may not approve."

She stopped. "Why not?" She sounded almost challenging.

"Well, it is just possible he will think I'm too old . . ."

"That's none of his damn business."

Her reaction seemed too quick, as if she had already been thinking the same thing. He added, "And he may think our new relationship is potentially complicating for the project."

"He'll like the idea . . . when he has a chance to think about it."

Jacob rolled out of the bed. "We should definitely be wearing clothes."

A few minutes later she worried the age thing might be a problem for Chris. She remembered Chris once said Jacob might be too old to fight. The memory made her angry.

Jacob made toasted cheese sandwiches while she caught up on the internet news. He warned her the Reigns photos were gory and would be on the news and internet. She avoided websites with photos but watched a video clip of the Jerry Young press briefing. He mentioned new clues and leads and that worried her enough to send her to the surveillance cameras.

She watched for a minute, saw nothing suspicious, shut them down and went back to searching the internet using Google to find websites mentioning the TLR and the term limits amendment. She was amazed at the growth of the websites covering those topics. Yesterday at noon, Google found a few thousand mentions for those topics. Now there were 57,463 mentions. She looked at a few and discovered they were getting more support. Editorials were still negative but even some of the negative editorials castigated Congress for failing to pass term limits legislation.

She was delighted. What would be the point if they risked everything, giving the public the opportunity to term limit Congress, only to find that the public didn't really care? That had always been a concern. Do they really care? They do. They want term limits. They want the political aristocrats out of Congress.

11:28 a.m.
After the meeting, Koberg invited O'Brian to his office. Koberg sat behind his desk and motioned O'Brian to shut the door. When it was closed, he said, "Agent Bradley seems unhappy with our methods."

O'Brian remained standing. "I can reassign her back to the Al Qaeda detail." He thought it would be the best thing he could do for her.

Koberg said, "I just wanted you to know my observation."

"She's smart, but I'll let her go if you think she's a problem."

"There is a rumor that you and she are close."

"The rumor is bullshit."

"Rumors can be damaging, even when they are wrong. But I leave the matter in your hands."

O'Brian wondered what the hell he meant by that.

Koberg changed the subject. "Let's hope we catch one of the TLR tonight. If so, we could wrap things up quickly." He leaned back in his chair with his hands behind his head, his expression thoughtful. "But if it takes a few more days to find them, that may also work to our advantage. By then Congress will be desperate to grant us any authority we ask for. Perhaps we should consider what we might need?"

Koberg smiled up at O'Brian. "The expression on your face, Agent O'Brian. My goodness. I wasn't asking for your advice, I was merely thinking out loud."

O'Brian nodded. It was the most he could make himself do. He waited to see if Koberg had more for him. Koberg said, "That's all I had."

"I'll talk to Agent Bradley."

He told Rita to not disturb him, shut the door and lay down on his couch. He couldn't do this shit. Meg needed him, but he couldn't do it any more.

A minute later Bradley walked past the protesting Rita and shut the door with authority. "What the hell's going on, O'Brian?"

"Open the door. People are beginning to talk."

"Bullshit." But then she asked, "What people? Oh, you mean Koberg, don't you? I don't give a damn."

He got up, walked to his desk and sat behind it. She sat down and said, "God damn it, what's he done to you?"

His arms were in his lap, his shoulders slumped, his eyes roamed the room.

"Talk, O'Brian."

"I think Hayes' hand is broken. He's in terrible pain. Koberg won't let him have any relief until he signs a confession. And Hayes is begging to sign a confession if we'll just let his wife and children go."

"God damn Koberg. God damn him! Hayes is innocent and he knows it."

"No. Koberg thinks he's guilty . . . so does Hammar."

"Thinking has nothing to do with it. They believe it because they want to believe it. They're both really good at self-deception. They convince themselves of Hayes' guilt, so that they can excuse the use of extorted confessions. And torture."

"The AG wants Hayes' confession to name Marcus Ray and Cal Jackson."

Her face twisted with anger. "This is sick."

"What can I do about it? Koberg says get on board or I'm toast."

"You think he would fire you?"

"Firing would be the least of it."

A long silence broke when Bradley said, "Shit."

"I've got a daughter that depends on me. Her mother can't support herself and she definitely can't support Meg. I'm not going to fight him. I'll try to do what good I can for Hayes. I may not help much, but I'll do what it takes to look like I'm a team player."

"You'll do his dirty work?"

"And you will, too, or you'll be gone before I am . . . He wanted me to get rid of you today."

She glared at him and he said, "I'm sorry I got you into this. Let me send you back to the Al Qaeda detail. You're needed there."

She left her newspaper on his desk and slammed the door on her way out. The cover photo was of the guy in the three cornered hat with his sign and a flag at half-staff.

1:10 p.m.

Chris was expected at the FBI forensic lab in an hour but he wanted to discuss that development with Jacob and Anna. Jacob's house was in the general direction. He parked his truck two blocks away and carried the laser rifle in its case, not that it looked anything like a rifle. Perhaps he was afraid of being seen or maybe it was the weapon, but he was definitely anxious to get inside. He knocked and opened the door.

Anna half leaped, half fell off Jacob's lap. Her blouse was open, both their mouths wet and red. Chris was shocked. It was just too much to believe. "God . . . damn, well . . . shit . . . I . . ." He stood with the weapon in his hand, his feet planted in mid-stride where they had stopped. Then his shock became embarrassment—for all of them.

She stammered, "Oh, damn it, Chris. I wanted . . . oh . . . damn it."

He recovered enough to smile, and then pretend anger, "Well . . . if you were trying to tell me something, I guess this demonstration pretty much explains everything." He took a step forward and set down the weapon.

She grabbed at Jacob's sleeve, twisting it in her embarrassment. "We made up our minds to tell you as soon as you arrived."

"Yeah, well telling would have been good. I am shocked, though. I mean, damn, how long has this been going on?" He was looking at Jacob now.

Jacob blushed but grinned. "Since about seven this morning."

She took Jacob's arm with both hands, as she looked up at him. "We've been attracted to each other for years." She pulled his arm just a little. She turned to look at Chris. "Each of us was afraid to make the first move. Neither of us guessed about the other."

Jacob looked earnestly at Chris. "We hope you'll accept our relationship, Chris."

Chris shook his head slowly. With a twisted smile he thought, *Not in a million damn years*. But Anna was beaming like . . . whatever. He couldn't stop them, but damn, it felt wrong. Jacob was way too old for her. Shit. What could he do? "I never saw it coming. But damn, it's none of my business . . . I mean, that's fine. I have no problem with this."

Jacob grinned and shook Chris's hand. Anna looked away. Chris saw the pain. She knew he wasn't happy with the situation. He tried again. "Well, too bad we don't have any champagne."

As she walked to the kitchen, Anna said, "Wine will do."

Chris put the laser rifle away and sat in the big leather chair. Anna brought three glasses of wine. She held her glass with one hand and put the other arm around Jacob. Chris stood and raised his glass, "Here's to you both. May you enjoy each other for a very long time." He meant it to be light-hearted, but short futures were too likely a possibility. They must have thought the same thing—their faces turned serious.

She sipped her wine, then looked at Jacob. "I do want a future with you. Let's be careful . . . but get the job done."

Chris remembered why he had come. "I always seem to bring the bad news. Two things." He sat down again.

Anna and Jacob sat on the couch. She put her hand on his thigh and leaned against him. Chris put his wine aside and told them of the JTTF call to Langley requesting a bomb expert. Anna leaned forward. Jacob looked worried but took her hand in his.

Chris said, "My boss told them all the CIA experts are in the mid-east blowing things up, except for me, that I have lots of experience with small tube bombs." He started to get up, but sat back down. "Maybe I can convince them it isn't a CIA bomb." He stood and walked a few feet before turning. "I brought one of our tube bombs with me. I thought I could change the signature of the bomb—the material it leaves behind—so that if they test it, it will look a little different. But I think I've changed my mind."

"Why?" Anna asked.

"If they find material that makes no sense, it will prove I doctored it. I will tell them their bomb has characteristics similar to the CIA version, but there's no way to be sure. They've been duplicated by others."

"Could this be a set-up?" Jacob asked.

"That's not the way they work. If they halfway wondered if I might be TLR, I'd be in an interrogation room now getting my brain chemically emptied."

He picked up his wine. "Second thing. I met with Mark Adams again this morning. The bad news is, I think he really does think I'm TLR. The good news is, he likes the TLR."

Anna asked, "Can we count on his silence?"

Jacob said, "If he suspected Chris and were not strongly sympathetic, he would have turned Chris in. The reward money would be very attractive."

She nodded. "Can he help?"

Chris thought before he answered. "Let's stick to the plan."

Anna pointed to the muted TV and grabbed the remote. The newscaster was interviewing Representative Harry Randall and Marcus Ray in front of the Capitol. Randall was saying, " . . . and a great patriot. The attorney general undercuts our nation and our liberty when he speaks of Congressman Ray as if he were a traitor. I believe his accusation was an intended threat against Congressman Ray."

The reporter faced Marcus Ray. "Congressman, do you feel threatened by the attorney general's accusations today?"

"It is a direct threat. When the attorney general and the administration feel comfortable threatening members of Congress, every American should feel threatened. It is a sad commentary on the state of the nation that it actually took courage for Congressman Randall to come to my defense. And I thank him for doing so."

Randall beamed. "Thank you, Marcus. Now if I could just convince you that running a modern complex society of more than 300 million people and an $18 trillion economy requires statesmen."

"Harry, our job is not to run society or the economy."

"You know I did not mean to say that we run the economy in the sense of a centralized command economy. I only meant to say that we establish a fair marketplace and a level playing field."

"But that's the problem, Harry. We don't. Congress grants favors to some people over others, to some companies over others, to some constituent groups over others. Congress is in the favor-granting business. The favors inevitably go to the politically favored. This," he held his arms out to indicate the Capitol, "is where favors are exchanged for re-election. That problem would be greatly diminished if Congressmen served only one or two terms."

Randall rolled his eyes and lost his good humor. "Term Limits would mean the dumbing-down of democracy. America needs leaders who are giants—and you don't get them out of the phone book."

Ray smiled. "No one suggested the phone book, Harry. We should look to the best people from our communities, people we know and admire. They are the individuals who really built this economy. They are the real giants."

Randall grinned. "Oh you mean people like . . ."

The reporter interrupted their argument to thank them, the studio cut to a commercial and Jacob said, "Marcus needed that help. It was good of Harry to support him."

Chris could see the pain in Jacob's face. Randall would be Jacob's target Sunday and in spite of their disagreements, until two years ago they were friends. "Well, I better get outta here—before you two really embarrass me." He walked into the kitchen to deposit his glass and on his way back into the living room he looked at the television covering CNN news. "Holy Shit." It was muted but the sound was unnecessary.

A close-up showed an agent throwing up over the low wall in the blood splattered greenhouse area. In the foreground the senator's headless body lay on the gore-strewn floor. The blue jay that had pestered Chris was diving at the camera.

Chris turned on the sound in time to hear the home video photographer say over and over 'Oh my god,' before the camera pointed at the ground while the photographer wept. Anna rushed to the bathroom and slammed the door. They heard her retching. "Goddamn it," Chris said, "I'm sorry she saw that. I shouldn't have said anything."

1:23 p.m.

Chris parked in the underground parking and took the elevator to the sixth floor. He had been here many times and personally knew Bernie Schaeffer, who escorted him to the forensics lab area and introduced him to Marla Lamme, the explosives specialist.

"I have the material from the bomb site," Marla said. "What there is of it, and some photos. Hope you aren't squeamish." He and Bernie followed her to her lab. She looked up at Chris as she unlocked the door. "To protect the evidence."

Marla got out two trays with the bits of probable bomb materials used at the two sites. Chris was wondering how he should respond. Both trays were labeled with the time and date of the samples and the name of the senator. She said, "Don't touch, but do you see anything in these materials that you recognize or that would help you identify the bomb? You can use the magnifying glass, microscope or whatever."

Chris breathed out with a sigh of relief. "Hardly. Hey, I can blow things up, but damn, I don't recognize this stuff as even being related to a bomb. These fragments aren't big enough to be identified . . . at least by me." He paused as he wondered how far to go. "But maybe that's part of the identifier. Most bombs leave a lot more."

"We worked that much out," she said.

"We have a couple of bombs that leave no residue—like these. They are a little more difficult to make than most bombs, but we know others have learned to make them. I don't think the information is available on the internet. But still they aren't rocket science, either. Do you have a chemical analysis? "

"We found traces of gold and PVC plastic but nothing remaining of the explosive itself." She pulled out a file with photos. "These photos may be helpful. At Senator Hackman's, the bomb was about three feet from the senator's head. At the Reigns site the bomb was only two feet from his head. His head was removed as was much of Senator Hackman's. The blast carried across the room in both cases but there was far less damage as the distance increased from the bomb."

"The explosion from one of the bombs we make is similar to the blast you've described. Shrapnel is not used. That makes it less detectable."

"So it could have come from the CIA?"

"Yes. Or it could have come from several agencies with access to these bombs. The Pentagon probably has a few; inventories are never accurate; items are missing. But just as likely someone is using their knowledge to reproduce the things. Like I said, it ain't rocket science."

She shoved the trays back as she said, "Shit."

"Sorry." Chris hoped he hadn't overplayed it. If she talked to someone else at the CIA—like Sheldon—she would hear another story.

Bernie said, "You're not off the hook yet, though."

His stomach gave a squeeze. "What's up?"

"Mike O'Brian wants to talk to you. He's Special Agent in Charge. You got another minute?"

"Yeah, sure." He started to walk out but turned back to Marla. "I'm sorry I wasn't more help. I'm not much on the scientific stuff."

Bernie said, "Thanks Marla" and Chris followed him out of the lab. After closing the door, Bernie said, "She's a tiger."

"I noticed."

"She'll play with those dust fragments and talk to people until she has something."

O'Brian was alone. Bernie made the introductions and Chris asked, "How can I help you?"

"Tell us where it came from."

"Sorry. It could be from the CIA. But it could also have come from the Pentagon, a Special Operations Unit, or from outside. It's hi-tech in one sense, but it isn't that difficult to make, if you know how. I saw photos of the bomb sites and some fragments that weren't much more than dust. Only two materials could be identified for sure. When I put all that together, it tells me these were non-fragmenting high intensity bomb blasts. The senators were killed because the bombs were close to their heads—if they had been ten feet away, they would have lost their hearing. That's all I can get from the stuff I've been given."

O'Brian didn't get up. "Thanks for your help."

Bernie followed Chris out. "Sorry about that, Chris. O'Brian's a good guy, but he's really upset today."

"Something's chewing his ass." As they came near the elevator he asked, "You done with me now?"

"You should also meet Agent Bradley, she's second in charge." They stepped around a partition; Bernie made the introductions, then said, "Chris met with Marla and Agent O'Brian. The bomb didn't leave much evidence for him to work with."

"Sorry to hear that. Will you be available if there are more assassinations?"

"Sure. But from the attorney general's statements, it appears you pretty much have them surrounded."

Bradley rolled her eyes, "Yeah, that's what we hear too."

Bernie said, "We might get lucky tonight. If they transmit at midnight again, we hope to pinpoint the location and drop in on them with a few helicopters."

"Well that should work—if you have enough in the air and triangulate the site fast enough."

Bradley stood up and shook his hand. "It was nice to meet you, Agent Carpenter."

Chris gave her his card and said, "Please call if you need me." He turned to Bernie. "What's next?"

Bernie said, "That's it. I'll ride down with you."

As they stepped into the elevator, Chris relaxed a little. When Bernie changed the subject to internal politics in the CIA, the relief grew. When they reached Chris's parking level, he stepped out and Bernie continued down.

Chris backed out as a car stopped behind him. As he pulled forward he checked his rear-view. O'Brian seemed to be looking right back at him and Chris's stomach tied a new knot.

He turned left coming out of the parking. So did O'Brian. And in the stop and go traffic O'Brian stayed behind him. As they entered the freeway Chris changed lanes but the traffic was stop and go. O'Brian dropped back a few cars. But soon he was back behind him. O'Brian changed lanes and was soon beside him. They continued moving forward and back of each other while crossing the Potomac. Finally Chris moved behind O'Brian and then farther right to the exit lane. O'Brian continued ahead and Chris turned off on Washington Boulevard.

The big blue Dodge Ram was too easy to spot. What if O'Brian saw it pulling into the warehouse? He had to get rid of it.

2:30 p.m.
She was embarrassed and it had been her own fault. She knew to look away, but the video had been so grabbing. She still couldn't get the headless body of Senator Reigns out of her head. Her mouth tasted like a sewer, even after brushing her teeth, taking a shower and gargling. She couldn't let Jacob near—her breath must be awful. And she couldn't shake the thought, *I did that to Senator Hackman.*

To prevent Jacob from seeing her and smelling her breath and to avoid hearing the TV descriptions, she went into the office and closed the door. The story would be constantly repeated until they found something more horrific. She stayed in the office until she heard Jacob answer his phone. That would be Chris.

She heard Jacob say, "Better, I think. I don't know, it's hard to tell." And a moment later, "Uh oh," and then, "We better talk again. Yeah, see you in a bit."

Of course she wondered what was going on. By then it had been more than a couple of hours since Chris left. She came into the kitchen and asked, "Was that Chris?" She meant, *what did you and Chris talk about?*

He looked at her for a moment before saying, "He's on his way over." Jacob picked up his car keys. "I'm going to pick up some . . . wine."

Bullshit. They had lots of wine. He was mad at her, or disgusted with her because she was so weak. She couldn't help that. She sat at the kitchen table, the sound muted on all three televisions, the sunny day evident only through the light forcing its way under and around the nearly opaque privacy shades. The house felt dismal and desolate, but it wasn't just the house.

Chris knocked and she rushed to open the door. As he stepped in she threw her arms around his chest and heard herself sob. But just that once. It shocked her as much as it did him; she didn't know she was that wound up. It was good to feel his arms around her. Then she remembered her breath and backed away. "I'm sorry, my breath must smell like Dad's pig yard."

"What's going on? Where's Jacob?"

"Jacob went out for wine . . . maybe. I don't know what's going on." She sat slumped down at the kitchen table. She couldn't tell Chris she and Jacob were already having a problem.

Chris pulled up a chair opposite her. "The gore on television change your mind?"

She was glad he changed the subject. "I hope not. If I don't remember that scene and freeze, up I'll be okay."

"I threw up the first time I saw a bomb mutilated body. Everyone does. If you haven't changed your mind about what we're doing and why, you'll do fine."

"I may never get that image out of my head, Chris."

"You won't. I have several images like that. But we learn to deal with it."

She didn't look as if she bought it, but asked, "What did you think, when you saw that image on the screen? Didn't it shock you . . . and make you sick?"

"No. I planted the bomb so it would blow his head off. Dead is dead, however it happens. I knew the bomb would do just what it did. The image didn't bother me because they brought it on themselves— they stole Nicolo's life, they're stealing our lives and my children's lives. They think they own us. They won't stop until we stop them. If we have to blow their fucking heads off to get their attention, then so be it. How they die doesn't matter. If they refuse to let the nation vote on term limits, if they refuse to yield their power, they will die, one way or another."

She nodded. But she didn't feel any better.

"Now what about Jacob and you? How did that get started? It looks a little crazy, you know." Before she could answer he went on. "Maybe it's an emotional reaction? It's just natural this stuff would get to you."

She pushed the chair back and paced as she said, "Crazy huh? Are you saying he's too old for me? You'd better not be." She was angry and close to tears. "Because you know what? You were right; it's none of your damn business!"

"You're right. If he makes you happy I think it's great. But damn, Sis, he is a lot older." They heard Jacob at the door and Chris finished quickly. "He's almost Dad's age."

That did it. She stormed out and slammed the door to the office.

Jacob saw her disappear into the office and slam the door. The sick feeling in the pit of his stomach was almost more than he could bear. But it pissed him off too. *If she's changed her mind then she could damn well tell me instead of hiding from me.* He knew they had been discussing him from the stupid guilty look on Chris's face. He carried a case of wine into the kitchen and began stowing it. *What a stupid damn mistake. We need to be thinking about the project and stop the personal shit.* He said hi to Chris, without looking at him. The drive had given him time to work the issue out in his head. He would let Anna go. He would make it as easy on her as he could. *But, damn, why couldn't she just admit she had a change of heart?*

Chris turned the Fox TV volume up, maybe not wanting to talk. Maybe she told him how she felt. Jacob felt ill at the thought of losing her, but also angry. We don't need this. We need to talk about Chris's news and how we should handle it.

Why the hell is she still in there? He started to the office door but stopped when Chris said, "Jacob. This is great. The television coverage of Reigns' body has created panic in both houses, lots of resignations. Farley says he'll propose the amendment in the Senate."

Jacob said, "Good," but it sounded like *so what.*

Chris said, "It damn sure is."

Jacob tried harder. "Of course it is." He sat on the couch to watch.

Chris turned back to the TV and a moment later cranked the volume up to hear the names of the five representatives and two senators who resigned today. He cheered with Chris as each name was announced.

Six resignations should be very good news, but it didn't help. Then the television showed the family and the close friends and relatives arriving at Senator Hackman's home. A large crowd watched from behind barricades as the newscaster said, "The senator's sister Bertha is arriving now with her husband, Samual J. Kamp, a Deputy Director with the Department of the Interior. They will join the others inside who have arrived to comfort the Senator's wife." She mentioned a long list of important officials making it sound like a Hollywood premier.

"The oldest daughter of Senator Hackman, Rebecca Sawyer and her husband Brad are just now driving up. Mr. Sawyer, a senior official with the Department of Education, spoke earlier to reporters and strongly denied the TLR claim of a political aristocracy. He also . . ."

Chris switched televisions. Marcus Ray was being interviewed on CNN.

Anna heard Marcus Ray's distinctive voice. She was still angry with Chris but they had decisions to make. As she came out of the office, Ray was saying, "I am especially pleased that Congressman Randall has decided to join the list of co-sponsors."

The camera zoomed out to include Representative Randall standing next to Ray. "I'll be damned," Chris said.

The reporter asked, "Congressman Randall, why the remarkable shift in your position? Just two hours ago you were opposed to term limits."

"My opposition to term limits remains as strong as ever. When the amendment is before the voters, I will advise them to reject it. But Congress must quickly give this issue to the public for their decision, before this administration plunges the nation into a tyranny from which we cannot recover."

"You fear the administration, Congressman?"

"I do. John Hammar is silencing the administration's critics. Freedom of speech is now available only to those with friends in Washington."

Marcus Ray interrupted, "Congress must take much of the blame. With the powers we gave the administration, no one is safe, not even a member of Congress. If they first declare them to be a terrorist, the administration can suspend anyone's Constitutional protections. Don Hayes and Cal Jackson sought term limits because they believed that politicians are naturally corrupted by long-terms in office. Many patriots believed that, including Tom Jefferson. That doesn't make them terrorists."

The reporter moved his microphone to Randall. "I support Representative Ray and I will support this amendment's approval by the House. I suspect we will discover more support as the day wears on."

"Congressman Randall, will you resign? I believe that's required by the TLR to avoid assassination."

"No, I will not. If they assassinate me, then so be it."

The reporter turned to the camera for his close-up. "We have been speaking with Congressman Marcus . . ."

As Chris reduced the volume, Anna said, "We can't take his life now."

"Our rule was, they resign effective the end of this term, or we take their lives. Randall hasn't resigned." He looked at Jacob. "I hate changing the plan. You think we should give him a pass?"

Anna interrupted. "Of course we should. We have lots of people on our list more deserving than Harry Randall. No one besides us knows that his name was next. If he's going to help with the amendment, then we want that, don't we?"

She looked at Jacob, but he seemed to be somewhere else.

Chris answered, "Yeah, I suppose. I just don't want us to be making changes. We have a plan and we need to stick to it."

Anna glared at Chris. "We haven't made a single change until now and the only reason for this change is because it helps the damn plan. Who's next on the list?"

Chris shrugged. "Tom Gruber." He looked at Jacob before saying, "Next item. At midnight, NSA and OITC will be monitoring internet and cell phone traffic, trying to spot your outgoing message and the sending location. They'll have helicopters in the air with SWAT teams waiting to drop when the location is known. They seem to think they can pull it off. I think they have some new technology."

6:30 p.m.

Bradley got a sandwich from the Bureau cafeteria and found a chair in the TV lounge. It was dry and tasteless but she didn't have time to go out and she wanted to catch up on the news. Fox News was covering the demonstrators and protestors on the Capitol Mall.

"Their numbers have increased enormously since yesterday at this time, apparently coming from all over the country. The amendment supporters are obviously disorganized and their numbers are fewer, while those protesting the term limits amendment appear to better organized. Their signs are obviously professional. There has been no violence yet, but there is a lot of anger between the two sides. I spoke with an officer from the Park Department who thought the situation could get dangerous if the TLR is not caught soon. The Capitol police are having a difficult time keeping the two groups separate."

Moments later the news cut to the studio where the newscaster said, "We have learned that in addition to the announced resignations, additional resignations are to be announced if the amendment is not voted on soon. Senator Farley offered the amendment to the Senate a few minutes ago, but apparently leadership is refusing to schedule a vote on the bill. The president has offered the use of government housing at local military bases to the threatened members of Congress. He also directed that the Secret Service increase the number of bodyguards assigned to each member."

Ward took a seat opposite Bradley and watched the television until she turned it off. He handed her a CD. "That's a list of Stewart's former students since the year 2000. We're digitizing the names of the students from before 2000. Should have them later today." He put a single sheet of paper in front of her. "On the CD we found 37 names now working in law enforcement or military. Twelve live within 200 miles. The others live farther away but could probably travel here to take part in the TLR operation." He pointed to one name—Carl Johnson. "Kind of a shock, huh?"

She said quietly, "He wanted off the case because he had a background with JFI. He never mentioned Stewart."

"No. But Stewart hadn't been mentioned then."

She knew Koberg would jump on this. "O'Brian and I will take care of Johnson. Meanwhile, remove his name and send the list to everyone on the task force. And let's start talking to the 11 immediately, like tonight. Wake them up if you have to. We want them interviewed by morning."

"No problem. There aren't that many." Ward left her with the list.

She called O'Brian. He didn't seem to care until she mentioned Johnson. "I told Ward to investigate everyone tonight. But I said you and I would talk to Johnson."

He hesitated before agreeing. "Yeah, call him in. I'll be there by 9 p.m."

He sounded down and maybe a little angry. She called Johnson at home; he wasn't happy either.

6:35 p.m.
Jacob watched Anna go into the office. She closed the door mumbling something about needing to think. Chris said good bye to Jacob and then as he stood with the door open, asked, "The Bureau interviewed your attorney and banker. What if they send someone to interview your daughters? How will they handle it?"

Chris's question added to an already deep depression—not that he hadn't been thinking of it. It was too easy to imagine the FBI agents interviewing Mary and Carol. *Has your father contacted you recently? We think he's alive and a member of the TLR terrorists—his death at sea was a hoax.* The mental image of their dismay and anguish was too much. He would have to call them. And that scared the hell out of him.

An hour passed with Anna still in the office, shutting him out. His depression was slowly replaced by anger. He was hot when she stepped in front of him. He glared up at her from the couch and said, "Let's get this over with." He stood up and walked into the kitchen, unable to look at her. "We have a job to do. I'm sorry I let my appetites get in the way. Let's try to get the job done and keep our sex lives out of it."

As he spoke, she followed him into the kitchen, her face going from shock to fury. "God damn you! You . . ." Her mouth was open, her face livid, then contorted as she sobbed and ran into the office, slamming the door behind her.

Why was she crying? She was the one avoiding him. What had he done? The door had no lock. He opened it and she was sobbing but still angry "Get out. Leave me alone, you son of a bitch." She appeared to be looking for something to throw at him. "Get out!"

Some of his anger was gone. Not all, but her tears were killing him. "Why the hell are you mad? You've been avoiding me; now you've got what you want." He closed the door behind him, sat on the couch facing the televisions but not seeing anything. His anger was gone but depression shared space with befuddlement. He didn't hear her until she stood before him again, tears running down her face, no longer angry. "You thought I was avoiding you?"

Her question saved him. She must have seen his relief as he saw her own. She straddled him as they covered each other with desperate kisses and apologies. "I'm sorry," she said. "It was stupid of me to . . ."

He stopped her with a kiss. Then said, "No, I should have known."

She held his head in her hands. "We were both stupid but if we don't stop this now we won't be ready for tonight." She smiled, kissed him quickly. "We have work to do, and not much time."

She grabbed his hand and pulled him into the office. "The last hour after Chris left I was thinking of the trap they set. We can avoid it easily but can we use their trap and turn it against them—really embarrass them? The helicopters hovering over the area, waiting to grab us. It's an opportunity, Jacob."

"Perhaps we can draw them to attack the wrong target. Another brutal, stupid raid, but this time one that is caught by the press?"

"The press will be watching, if I alert them. If it's in the news it could help push Congress to pass the amendment."

He asked, "But where, and how?" They both thought for a moment. He added, "It needs to be a crowded place. At midnight."

Her eyes opened wide as she thought of it. "Samantha's"

"I've heard of it."

"It's a bar in Georgetown. Lots of wealthy young people, many in government, or sons or daughters of people in government. Lobbyists use the bar to impress clients. Several small expensive restaurants in the area too, catering to the same crowd."

Jacob asked, "And how do we draw them in, without getting caught?"

"Send from an open programmed cell phone. But get out fast—before it begins sending."

8:56 p.m.

O'Brian did not look up as he came out of the elevator. Bradley followed him into his office. "Johnson's not here yet," she said. She sat in a chair opposite him. "The helicopters go up at 11:15. They have a grid set up. Any location within fifty miles of the Capitol building can have a SWAT team on the ground anywhere in that area two minutes after they identify the cell phone . . . if that's what they use this time. Faedester and some of his top gurus were in a little earlier to confirm some sort of electronic coordination with Linda Morrow's team and the OITC and NSA electronic surveillance. Morrow says the new technology should identify and lock on to the sending location immediately. For years the federal agencies have been hiring all the best brains in internet and computer technology." She waited a few beats before she shrugged her shoulders. "I still don't give it much of a chance."

Johnson stood at the open door looking in—nervous and defiant. O'Brian said, "Have a chair."

He sat beside Bradley. "Your name came up as a student of T. J. Stewart's."

He looked dumbfounded. "Professor Stewart?"

O'Brian said, "Some people think there's a mole in the Bureau or some other federal police organization, perhaps a former student of his."

"It's not me." He was definitely defiant now. "I liked him. So what? And I got an A in the class. It was economics and history 101. A required course for anyone in pre-law or economics or history. But I'm guessing you know that."

She smiled to reassure him. "O'Brian and I think you're a good agent and not a mole, but maybe you could help us with Stewart. How close were you?"

"I don't think he would have known me if he had seen me on the campus. But I liked him. He was sharp. And I liked the class."

Bradley asked. "Could he be TLR?"

"That's laughable. He was no revolutionary." He hesitated before adding, "Except . . . he loved liberty and hated authoritarian government."

"If he thought liberty was being lost, could he get pissed enough to fight?"

Johnson fiddled with his car keys. "I didn't know him that well."

"Did you meet him or see him at Jeffersonian Freedoms Institute?" O'Brian asked.

"No, I only started going a year or so ago."

O'Brian and Bradley exchanged glances. "Sorry you had to come in." O'Brian stood. "If you think of something we ought to know, you'll give us a call?"

Johnson mumbled, "Right" as he stood up. He turned back at the door, his face red. "I just thought of something you might not know." He was angry. "Koberg's a turd." He left the door open.

She quickly said, "I believe him." O'Brian guessed she wanted Johnson to hear her.

They discussed other options for finding the mole until, a minute later, Koberg came in and took the seat vacated by Johnson. "I noticed Agent Johnson leaving." The raised eyebrows implied the question.

O'Brian felt the depression increase. "He took a course from T. J. Stewart at Higgs U. A pre-law required course. We asked about Stewart and his students."

"Really?"

"He said Stewart was a good professor," Bradley said. "But he didn't know him. That was the only course he took from Stewart."

Koberg looked at O'Brian. "Did you believe Johnson?"

O'Brian said, "Yes. I did."

"I think you are making a mistake."

Bradley interrupted. "Johnson has been a good agent for a long time. He's not a mole."

Koberg kept his gaze on O'Brian. "Our team must be fully invested in our programs. We can't afford to be worried about him."

"He's back on the Al Qaeda Task Force."

"I'll speak to Director Proctor about him." He grinned as if they were the best of friends. "Are you joining us on the helicopters?"

"O'Brian said, "I wouldn't be any help there. But good luck."

Bradley didn't bother to answer. After Koberg left neither spoke until she shut the door. "He's going to get Johnson fired."

9:12 p.m.

Anna knew how she wanted to do it. "I'll program the cell phone and download the message as soon as you get it done. You drop me in front of Samantha's a few minutes before midnight. I'll go in, drop it in a wastebasket in the restroom and walk out to the car. If NSA has figured out how, the message will be identified a minute or two after midnight and a helicopter will drop the SWAT team a few minutes later."

Jacob said, "Good plan. Only I go in."

"Don't be silly. I can barely get in. It's . . . it's not your kind of place." She looked at her watch. "Samantha's has a waiting line. I have to get dressed, fast."

He didn't like it, but there was no time to argue and she was probably right. "I'll finish the message."

Anna was excited. She began pulling clothes out and throwing them on the bed. It was nearly eleven when Jacob finished the message and found her in the bedroom.

"What do you think?" She wore a long black wig, dark brown almost black contacts, purple lipstick and eye shadow and a blue sequined dress.

"You look . . . I can hardly wait to take that dress off you."

She laughed. "Is the message ready?"

"Yes. Please read it. I don't want to screw up again." She followed him into the office. It took her three minutes to transfer the message and addresses to the cell phone and another minute to program it to send at midnight. She wiped it off, dropped it in a thin clear plastic bag, put on black gloves and wiped the bag off. "Let's go. We need to hurry."

Jacob grabbed his keys and they stepped outside to a muggy evening. He turned left on Wilson, and four minutes later crossed the Hwy 29 Bridge over the Potomac. Samantha's was only six blocks from the bridge, just off M Street NW, on a dead end street. She had forgotten that. Easy to get trapped.

She checked her watch. "We're almost out of time, Jacob. I need to get in, drop the cell phone and get out before it sends. And you need to be here when I come out." She had seven minutes before it began sending.

"I'll drive to the end of this block and turn around. I'll try to be here at 11:59, but I can't wait in front, Anna. The street is too narrow, traffic will back up. If I'm not here, you walk to M Street, turn left and walk back toward the bridge."

She was out of the car now and leaning in the window. "If we miss each other . . . meet in front of the Kandahar Restaurant on M Street. It's two or three blocks west from Key Street."

"Good idea. Go."

Her heart fell as she looked at the line to get in. It was longer than she had ever seen it and the economy was terrible. She looked back; there were three cars behind Jacob as he began to drive slowly toward the cul-de-sac at the end of the street.

Anna walked up to the beefy long-haired guy at the head of the line and asked if she could go in, "Just for a minute to give a friend her credit card."

He said, "Sorry," with all the sympathy of an IRS agent.

She handed him two fifties. "Give me back one of them if I'm back in five minutes."

"Don't make me come find you."

She was in. The place was packed. She headed for the restrooms, but she had to work her way through the crowd and then there was a line to get in the restroom. *Dammit.* She tried to get through but some wouldn't let her. It got ugly. *Dammit . . . Plan two.*

She checked her watch. *Three minutes.* She had to get rid of the cell phone and get out quickly, or turn it off. She pushed her way into the bar and noticed a guy at the end of the bar. He seemed to be alone. She was desperate. She removed her billfold from her purse and left the cell phone in it. She walked up to the man at the end of the bar and reached around him to get a plate of peanuts. Her breast barely brushed against his arm but he noticed. She smiled, beguilingly she hoped, as she asked, "May I?" But she also used the opportunity to drop the soft leather purse from her right hand onto the floor. She pushed it against the bar with a foot.

He was younger than her, but apparently willing to believe she was hitting on him. He smiled, "Of course. Hey, have my seat. I can still drink standing up."

She said, "You're sweet." He started to get up, but Anna put her hands on his arm to stop him. "I'm Marie. I'll be right back."

She walked toward the ladies room knowing he was watching her. She looked back and he was. She couldn't walk out.

11:55 p.m.

Bradley watched the impressive display at Cencom. Linda Morrow had told her the top brains in electronic communications technology worked for NSA. No one knew how much they were paid or how many they were because they were funded through the Pentagon and that budget was never divulged. They had tied NSA into the telecommunication systems of every cellular service in the area. Their computers looked for a cell phone sending to more than 100 addresses and containing the key words that could be expected in the TLR's message signature.

The cell phone signal was identified four seconds after it began sending at midnight. The geographic position of the cell phone—within ten feet—was known eight seconds later and appeared on Cencom's real time satellite view of the area. This was all displayed on a twenty foot wide video screen together with an overlaid map which identified the street address of the cell phone's position. Three seconds later the business name appeared--Samantha's. Bradley knew it.

Each helicopter carried an identifying transponder indicating the location of its position on the same map-satellite view. The cell phone coordinates shown on the satellite-map view appeared simultaneously on each of the helicopter on-board displays. The instant the cell phone position was known, the helicopter commander in CenCom began directing the first four helicopters to positions covering the area. The narrow street in front of Samantha's was the primary drop point; three other drop areas put a total of forty SWAT and JTTF team agents on the ground within three minutes of the transmission.

Bradley watched the helicopter raid from onboard cameras the moment the TLR call was recognized. Her skeptic disbelief become incredulity and then amazement. But the regret she felt that they really might be catching the TLR surprised her.

She saw the SWAT team rope down in controlled-rappel harness. Barnes and other leaders—with mikes mounted on their helmets—followed them down.

She ran to the JTTF gathering area and ordered the agents she found there to the crime scene and she stopped at O'Brian's office to get him.

11:56 p.m.
Jacob drove to the street dead-end and turned around. He was prepared to wait in front until she came out but there were cars in front of him. Three cars ahead a convertible was waiting for someone to come out. He couldn't pass if he wanted to; the street was too narrow. After a couple of minutes he heard the helicopters coming down and started to get out and run but the cars began moving forward. By then it was too late. If he ran, he would be spotted and followed. He could only follow them out.

After Anna looked back at the guy at the bar again, he grinned sheepishly and turned away. She made it through the entry as fast as she could without attracting attention. She checked the time. It was a minute after midnight. They were sending. As she walked past the line control guy, he grabbed her arm.

"Hold on." He began looking through the wad of money in his hand.

She heard the helicopters, pulled away and said over her shoulder, "That's fine. You keep it."

Jacob was not in front and would be out the street by now. She could hear the helicopters but couldn't see them. As she walked toward M Street they were getting louder. She had just reached M Street when the SWAT teams began dropping. *My god they were fast.* She turned left walking, forcing herself not to run. Before she had gone half a block, she looked back to see SWAT troops closing off Key Street while others continued to drop. Then she saw Jacob's car coming toward her. He was grinning. They were outside the capture ring, free to drive away.

He was laughing as she got in. "I saw you in the alley ahead of me. I still had a few yards to go when the car in front stopped to look at the helicopters dropping the SWAT team. I honked and kept honking until he took off. I think I was the last car out of there. The troopers were running toward me when I turned left and drove off."

Saturday, June 7
Another

12:10 a.m.

Samantha's was less than two miles from the Hoover Building and there was no street traffic. Several people had been roughed up, most trying to escape. Some had drugs. Lots of people were angry and yelling. A young female was being placed into an ambulance together with two JTTF agents and two police car escorts.

Koberg was smug, almost pleased. "I'm glad you found time to join us. I do believe we've made our first TLR arrest."

O'Brian asked, "Why the ambulance and police escort?"

"Almost certainly the TLR female. She nearly escaped, but was shot before she could get away. She'll live to testify."

Bradley saw Barnes coming. He looked unhappy and she headed him off.

"How's it going?"

"Too many bashed heads. Some of the people in the bar came out and started running, some were drunk, some pissed. We overreacted."

"How are the interviews going?"

"Great if we're here for a drug bust. But I'm not sure we have anyone from the TLR. I wonder if they sucked us in here."

"Why would they do that?"

"Maybe they thought we would come in like a bunch of skull cracking bullies raiding a party. And maybe they knew the press would pick up on it."

"Oh shit."

"The press was here before we were. Someone may have alerted them that something was up. They saw the helicopters coming down and made a beeline. They're camped at the end of the street and I'll bet they're getting some juicy interviews with the people we release. Lots of big shots, or sons and daughters of big shots. Some surly as hell. Some are scared. I haven't seen anyone that looks like TLR to me."

An agent came walking up to Barnes holding out a purse. "I think we have the cell phone."

Bradley took a plastic bag from a pocket and let the agent drop the handbag and cell phone inside. Barnes asked, "Anything to help with an ID?"

"No, sir. Except for the cell phone, it's empty."

Bradley zipped the bag closed. "Thank you. I'll take it back to the lab for analysis. We may get fingerprints or DNA. We might even get a clue or two about their computer systems."

She held it up to O'Brian as he walked up. "The cell phone."

He said, "Great," but he didn't look enthusiastic.

"Barnes is not optimistic about finding TLR here. Thinks we were set up."

Koberg joined them as someone in the crowd being interviewed screamed, "You fascist bastards!" A moment later they heard the distinctive crunch of a nightstick and turned to watch someone dragged to a patrol car. Koberg looked concerned. "Why will some people simply not do as they are told?"

The crowd was divided into a dozen groups with two agents questioning each person from their group one at a time. One man being questioned readily admitted to having been seated on the barstool where the purse had been found. A JTTF agent brought him to O'Brian.

O'Brian asked, "What's your name?"

"Bill Polk"

"Is that your purse?"

"No."

"Let's go inside, Mr. Polk. You can show us where you were sitting."

Bradley, O'Brian, Koberg, Barnes and the agent who found the purse walked back in with Bill Polk. Polk went to a barstool at the end of the bar. "I was sitting here."

"Were you with someone?"

"No, but I met someone. Gorgeous. Long black hair, beautiful body, blue sequined dress. Dark, dark eyes." Grinning, he said, "I fell in love."

"Did she stay?"

"No. She said she had to go to the restroom. She headed that way and I couldn't take my eyes off her."

"You saw her go to the restroom?"

"Yes, well actually, she looked back at me when she got over there." He pointed. "My tongue was hanging out, so I turned around."

"When was that?"

"A few minutes, three or four minutes, before the raid started."

Bradley asked, "Where was the purse found?"

The agent pointed to the floor where Polk sat.

Bradley looked back at Polk. "Could she have dropped that purse there, without you knowing it?"

"She could have hung it around my neck without me noticing."

O'Brian turned to the agent. "We got his number if we need to talk again?"

The agent said, "We got it, sir. He's an accountant with Treasury."

Polk asked, "It's her, isn't it—the lady from the TLR?"

O'Brian pulled out a photo of Sue Thomas. "Could this be her?"

Polk held it a moment, handed it back to O'Brian and smiled. "We should surrender."

Barnes told his agents to hurry the interviews. It appeared the TLR lady escaped before they got there. O'Brian and Bradley headed back to the office. She asked. "You think it was a set-up too?"

"Of course."

"But it doesn't piss you off?"

"Maybe I'm beginning to admire them."

He sounded sarcastic and Bradley laughed, but she suspected O'Brian was only partly kidding. "The newspapers are beginning to hate them less. A lot of their readers are pissed at the federal government."

"We gave them another reason tonight."

Bradley dropped the cell phone and purse at the forensics lab and then found O'Brian at his computer reading the TLR message.

Saturday, June 7

Yesterday, as promised, we took the lives of two long-term incumbents. We deeply regret the pain we caused their families. The act was more painful and repugnant to us than many will believe. Nonetheless, we will continue removing long-term incumbents until Congress grants the American voter the right to approve or reject the term limits amendment. The Department of Justice raids on the homes of Cal Jackson and Don Hayes have made us more determined than ever.

At the direction of Attorney General John Hammar, Department of Justice SWAT teams and JTTF agents murdered Cal Jackson in front of his children. The alleged purpose for the raid was an assumed connection with the TLR. But there is no such connection, as John Hammar knows. The raids were intended to punish Cal Jackson and Don Hayes for speaking out against the growth of authoritarian government. It was also intended as a lesson to others who might speak out.

The press is beginning to discover the horrific facts. We won't dwell on them here, except to point out that these acts are precisely why we are at war with our power-mad politicians. Gratuitous brutality in the protection of political power is now standard procedure for federal, state and local officials. It will only grow worse if we do not stop it now.

We target only those long term members of Congress who will not allow the public a vote on the issue of term limits. Congress has stolen our liberty, our property and our lives. We claim the right of self defense and use the only method available to us.

Some say we oppose or ignore the rule of law but it is Congress that has opposed and ignored this nation's highest law, the Constitution. It is our Congress that is outside the law.

We know there are many who strongly disagree with us. Some love a controlling all-powerful government for the use they can make of it to enrich themselves or to control others. They argue that our nation requires professional long-term incumbent politicians in Congress because the weighty matters decided by Congress are beyond the ability of citizen-legislators to comprehend. Those making that argument are usually those who receive favored treatment from our professional Congress. Others enjoy using government to force others to contribute to their causes or succumb to their religious views. And others simply do not want to take responsibility for their lives. They want government to tell them what to do, to make their decisions, and they want others to provide for them. All the above are thieves. The Constitution was written to prevent such people from using their vote and our government to rob the rest of us of our liberty, our property and our values.

It is time for Congress to act. Voters want to decide this issue.

Today, Saturday, June 7, another long-term incumbent will be term-limited. And, if Congress fails to act today, yet another member of the congressional political aristocracy will reach the end of his term tomorrow. On Monday there will be two more if Congress fails to act on Sunday. And those professional politicians, who imagine they own us—and their seats in Congress—will continue dying until they give the voters the right to decide this issue.

*The **Term Limits Revolution***

12:10 a.m.
They drove back to the house talking constantly, pleased with the way it had gone. Anna described her problems getting inside Samantha's, her inability to get into the restroom, the guy at the bar. She did not describe the way she got his attention. "I just left the bag near his seat at the bar. So what happened to you? I beat you back to M street."

"I drove to the end of the street and turned around. There were cars ahead of me. I couldn't pass. The street was too narrow. The helicopters started getting louder. I was just a little nervous."

She held his arm, her eyes wide, as he finished. "I got a little tense. I saw you turn left on M Street, but I still had a few yards to go when the idiot in front stopped to look at the helicopters dropping the SWAT team."

She laughed and hugged him in a great release of tension. He swerved a little, but held the car on the road. "Do you realize Chris and Burton have no idea what we did tonight?" She laughed again. "We did this on our own."

He parked and they walked together to the front door. She laughed again as she stood on the small entry porch, unlocking the door. He found the zipper of the blue sequined dress.

1:50 a.m.
Bradley was exhausted as she drove back down M street on her way home. She lived a mile or so beyond Samantha's. She glanced down Key Street where the interrogation was winding down. There were still press reporters interviewing people coming from Samantha's. The papers would have a full description in the morning.

She slept until 7:45 a.m., showered, and started the coffee before opening the door to retrieve the paper. The headline was SENATOR BOARDMAN'S DAUGHTER SHOT BY JTTF. The article went on to describe a botched and brutal raid where innocent people were assaulted by an out-of-control SWAT team. Senator Boardman's daughter Monica had been seriously wounded, but was expected to recover. The senator was furious. "I'll find out who was responsible and I'll have their head on a damn platter." The article went on to say that the team was led by Agent Barnes.

Bradley wondered how Koberg managed to lay it on Barnes? She wanted to call the paper, but knew she couldn't. JTTF agents had to keep themselves out of the papers.

A second story with the TLR message was also featured. TLR
Accuses Administration of Brutal Authoritarianism. John Hammar
Blamed for Vengeance Death of Cal Jackson & Brutal Arrests. She
didn't touch her coffee as she read the TLR message with some
sympathy. She called O'Brian and was surprised he was at the office.
"You've seen the papers?"

"Yeah, Barnes and I are reading it."

"And he's pissed."

"He is, but there isn't a damn thing we can do about it. At least
they didn't get his picture."

"I'll be there in a few minutes. Any more bodies yet?"

"Not yet. But Senator Boardman wants to see us."

Bradley thought about it on the way to the office. The raid
improved the TLR's position and hurt the government's position—
which surprisingly did not displease her. *So what does that mean? I'm
damn sure not on their side.*

9:50 a.m.
Burton belonged to the New York Teachers Association and to the
National Education Association, not by choice, but because a complex
set of interwoven state and federal laws made it impossible to teach
without belonging. It was hard to determine where the union ended and
government began. Maybe they were the same thing. He despised the
unions. They used his dues to buy politicians; the politicians created
laws giving unions control of the teachers. The unions also controlled
school board elections and parent-teacher associations, behind the
scenes of course, but the control was firm and obvious to those who
looked.

Parents had no choice as to where their children attended school.
And no choice in the selection of teachers or in the selection of the
subjects their children were taught. Whose children were they?

He produced his membership card at the door and smiled at the
irony. He was the last person they should allow into this convention of
union leaders and politicians. He looked around the hall to see if he
could spot the teachers who ran the local union and the school his
children attended. They were in there somewhere.

He heard several speakers and read some handouts. The
convention had nothing to do with education—it was politics and
power. If *the children* were mentioned, it was to excuse another grab
for power, more subsidies that would go for administration cost, which
always meant the local union leaders. Congressman Marlan Grandee

was co-chair of the House Education Committee and a willing agent of the union. He was scheduled to speak in a few minutes. He was also Burton's target.

Senator Elizabeth Pinkham was speaking now. The audience loved her. She didn't speak from her heart; she spoke from their heart, and she knew it well. They frequently interrupted her with applause; she was a primary source of their growing political power. She praised Representative Marlan Grandee, and not for the first time. Like other members of Congress, they often praised each other in those reciprocal arrangements, understood by both, that provided for gushing praise in exchange for gushing praise.

As Pinkham spoke, Grandee appeared alternately proud and modest. Sometimes he amazed himself at just how modest he was. The introduction—already stretched to its rational limits—was approaching its climax when Pinkham said, "It is incumbent upon all who love the great democratic institutions of this nation that we also support and praise the dedicated leaders that make them work. Representative Marlan Grandee, a great Congressman from the city of New York, our very good friend, is one of the noblest of those dedicated leaders."

The convention rose to applaud their man.

"You know what he has done to keep your great cause at the center of the stage in our nation's capitol."

Burton seethed. *A very great cause—union control of teachers, parents and children, through political power, forever.*

"But he has done more, far more, than I can ever begin to tell you. He has proposed every education bill that the National Teachers Association has asked of him."

Again they rose to applaud a beaming Representative Marlan Grandee.

"When you've asked for his help, Congressman Marlan Grandee was always your man. Whether in the State Assembly, where for six years he fought hard for increases to the salaries and pensions of New York's teachers, or in the House where he represented you magnificently, Representative Marlan Grandee has supported the expansion of federal aid to education at every opportunity and all the other bills that supported your right to strike for fair salaries and better working conditions. He has opposed every attempt by the opponents of free public education to punish the children with public choice, or parent choice, or vouchers, or privatization of public schools. No matter the form, Congressman Grandee has always seen through their vicious attempts to destroy free public education."

After another standing ovation, Pinkham pushed on. "That is why you and this great nation must not lose his leadership." And now the audience grew quiet. "But that is precisely what the TLR terrorists propose. And there are some in Congress who propose that we yield to their demands."

The crowd began to boo and hiss.

"But great men, like Congressman Grandee and many others in Congress who defend your noble ideals, must not be forced from office by these terrorists." She paused a moment to be sure she had their attention and then spoke each word slowly and distinctly. "Can you imagine the difficulty of educating a constant stream of so-called citizen-legislators to the needs of this nation's teachers . . . and children? Would they recognize the importance of your great work? Would they protect your special relationship with government? . . . Would they?"

The crowd rose to scream their angry 'No!' and the senator added over their voices, "We must never yield to the extortion of terrorists."

Representative Grandee leaped to his feet to lead the audience in their answer, "Never, never, never, never, never . . .

When they eventually quieted, Senator Pinkham continued. "Term limits was discussed by the nation's founders . . . and rejected. Many recognized that the nation would need their services, and many of the signers of the Constitution served several terms in Congress before resigning."

She paused for dramatic effect and looked over the rapt audience. "Term limits would be a great setback for the democratic reforms we have accomplished and not just in the field of education and union empowerment but in those areas where every American is entitled to a decent retirement, healthcare, nutritional food, decent housing and respect.

"Therefore I ask your help in raising the courage of those members of Congress who believe we must yield to the terrorists and approve the term limits amendment. Please make your voices heard in the nation's capitol. Please take the time to assemble at the Capitol tomorrow and let them know that they will not be re-elected to any office if they defy the nation's teachers. I know the nation can count on you and for that, from the bottom of my heart, thank you."

The convention rose again in thunderous applause as Senator Pinkham and Congressman Grandee stood side by side with clasped hands raised in the air. Burton couldn't take anymore and he knew where Grandee's limo was parked. He would wait outside.

Burton wandered around but stayed clear of the limos. The bodyguards were thick there. Grandee's limo carried his personal plates. He could hear the applause coming from within the convention center. He made small talk with an officer and waited for the congressman's exit.

A few minutes later a small crowd emerged from the convention and Burton guessed they surrounded Senator Pinkham and Representative Grandee. He got in his car and waited. He had a direct line of sight to the Congressman's limo. And after a few more minutes he saw Senator Pinkham emerge from the crowd with Congressman Grandee, both surrounded by bodyguards. Grandee paused as he neared his limousine. Adoring fans followed both and they stopped to enjoy the attention. Their bodyguards were trying to protect them by keeping the crowds back, but both the senator and congressman reached past them to shake hands and thank constituents for their praise.

Eventually staff and bodyguards persuaded the crowd to allow them to leave. As the crowd separated the senator moved toward her car but at that same moment her staff members, the secret service bodyguards and some of the crowd came between Burton and the Congressman. He could not see Grandee get into his limousine and more important, he could not see if someone else was in the car, perhaps going with him. If so Grandee wasn't going to Elaine's apartment. The limo's tinted windows prevented Burton from seeing inside

Burton pulled into traffic behind them as the Congressman's car moved forward together with a motorcycle escort and another car for the bodyguards. The limousine stayed on main arteries, first traveling east on West 33rd street. Burton stayed back far enough that he wouldn't be spotted by the limousine or the escorts. He didn't want the driver or the bodyguard escorts remembering and maybe describing Burton's car. They probably would never put the information together with the rental car company, but there was no sense in tempting fate.

As they approached the 6th Avenue-Broadway intersection, Burton was forced to move closer. The limo could turn any of five directions; it would be too easy to lose them. But they didn't turn; they crossed the intersection and continued west on 33rd Street and Burton began to relax—they were headed for Elaine's apartment and Burton had feared he might have to follow Grandee all day. The Congressman ignored the Secret Service warnings to avoid predictable moves. Perhaps he thought no one knew about his relationship with Elaine. He had fooled his wife—how could anyone else have worked it out?

There was no need to follow the Congressman now but the limo was moving faster than Burton expected. He had to get in place ahead of Grandee. He turned right on Madison Avenue, speeded up until he could make a left on West 29th, crossed Park Avenue driving as fast as he thought he could get away with and continued on up East 29th Street. He slowed slightly as he crossed 3rd Avenue to see the limo coming fast and only a block away. There would barely be time to get in place.

He drove a half block past the apartment building—it was on his left—and turned right into the parking garage across the street. He circled back inside the garage and parked with the engine running at a point directly opposite the apartment building entrance and half a floor above it. He was in place and barely in time. His hands shook, but he was only a little surprised that he had no problem with the job in front of him. It must be done. He also had a pistol under the seat—he wouldn't shoot at police, but he also wouldn't be captured alive. They wouldn't be able to make him betray the others.

The limo was stopped, the Congressman in the back seat—with one other person vaguely visible through the tinted windows. *A bodyguard?* He would soon have choices to make and only a second or two to choose. If Grandee approached the door alone, no problem, he would trigger the bomb. If a bodyguard accompanied him he would have to choose yes or no. He thought he would choose yes.

A motorcycle cop was parked in front of the Congressman's car. The escort car stopped behind the limo. The street-side back door of the limo opened, a bodyguard got out and walked around to stand at the Congressman's door. Five bodyguards poured out of the escort car and took positions on the street, looking in all directions. One looked up at the parking garage. As the chauffer opened Grandee's door, Burton opened his glove compartment and took out the two button sending unit. His heart was racing, but he didn't hesitate. He pushed the first button, activating the unit as he glanced at the intercom.

Last week, dressed in the same white coveralls used by the building's maintenance people, he placed the tube bomb behind the intercom speaker. It was not quite head high and next to the entrance.

Grandee started up the stairs, but a bodyguard stepped in front and preceded him. Burton cursed and pounded his thigh. If the bodyguard used the intercom or even stood beside it, he would have to kill the bodyguard to get Grandee. Grandee said something that made the bodyguard stop. Maybe it would still work. Grandee was tall. He might block the force of the bomb from the bodyguard.

At the top of the steps Grandee said something else Burton couldn't quiet hear. The bodyguard looked around, and then focused on the parking garage. He seemed to be looking straight at Burton and was speaking to someone. Grandee stepped up to the door with his key out, but looked back at the bodyguard. Burton's hand shook badly as he pushed the fire button.

The blast was instantaneous. It threw Grandee into the bodyguard knocking him down the steps and onto the sidewalk. The entry door was knocked off its hinges. The gaping chauffer remained standing, as did the bodyguards from the escort car, although two dropped to the ground in a delayed reaction. The motorcycle cop fell and then got up and ran together with two bodyguards toward the bodies.

Burton was horrified and instantly ill. He opened the door and threw up. Then fear and the need to escape stopped the sick reaction. He tried to start the car. The starter motor made a grinding noise—it was still running. He put the car in gear and backed from the parking space, sorry he had not looked away when he pushed the button. He found the exit on the offside from the apartment building and drove away with the terrible scene stuck in his head in constant replay.

He did not recognize his mental state until he found himself in the driveway of the home where he hadn't lived for years. He had to get his mind working again. He backed out, thankful no one had greeted him. It was a warm sunny Saturday morning in June, his former neighbors would normally be out mowing the lawn, or trimming something, or washing their cars. He began to pull away, without having to say hi to anyone, when Bobby Schmitz yelled. Burton knew it was Bobby without turning, but he pretended not to hear. He accelerated away, cursing himself for the stupid mistake. Why had he driven there? It was still home—where he lived when he was married, a real father, lover and husband. He needed to think clearly. He pulled into a park, slumped down in the seat and rubbed his face hard. He knew it was mostly shock. He waited more than an hour, until he felt ready to drive.

Jacob, Anna and Chris were four hours away. He would return the rental and pick up his car tomorrow. He headed for the Lincoln Tunnel and a few minutes later was in New Jersey headed south on US 95. He felt better, not good but better. He had made this trip a thousand times when he was a student at Higgs U.

He wanted to talk about it, to tell Anna and Jacob how it happened and how it affected him, but not on the cell phone. By now they knew most of it. It would be on television.

The car radio was tuned to a station playing screaming-awful music. As he searched for a news station, he was apprehensive and wondered why? Did he fear their opinions?

He found a newscaster who was saying, "His death is a shock to the Democratic party and to his constituents. Here at Madison Square Garden the National Association of Teachers is in turmoil. Obviously this is the work of the TLR and the teachers here are pledging to be on the Capitol Mall tomorrow and the next day, with Senator Pinkham, to stop the TLR and their supporters from extorting a term limits amendment from Congress.

Congressman Grandee was a favorite of the National Education Association and they intend to parade in very large numbers tomorrow to make sure Congress hears them. . . ." He turned the radio off as he realized he was driving past Philadelphia.

Burton did not simply love history. He loved the heroes of history. He loved their great ideas. And nowhere on earth had there existed a greater idea and greater men than here in Philadelphia. It was the nation's birthplace, the place where the Continental Congress met, where the Declaration of Independence was written, where the Constitution was constructed and it was the first seat of the new nation's government.

This time as he drove past, he felt a fierce pride. Not that he was proud of assassinating Grandee—the explosion and the gore strewn scene sitting in the back of his mind would haunt him for the rest of his life. But on this day he had found more courage in himself than he would ever have thought possible. Perhaps Americans would regain their Congress and their individual rights at least partly because he found that courage. The entire federal government would unleash itself in the attempt to find him and the others. The founders knew their experiment in a government limited to the protection of liberty might be a footnote in the long history of mankind and tyranny. *And that still might prove true,* he thought. *But if so then so be it, I stand on the side of freedom.*

Jefferson said it would never end; liberty would have to be won over and over. Tonight the hellish scene of this morning might bring nightmares. But for now he felt pride and the presence of his heroes traveling with him.

10:30 a.m.
The 9 a.m. meeting had been unproductive. Koberg was absent. Bradley hoped Hammar was firing him. But that was unlikely. They were probably deciding how to blame Barnes or O'Brian.

After the meeting Ward stopped at her desk. "Have you seen the crowds on the mall? It's on the television now. It may get ugly."

She followed him into the lounge. There were no agents at work in the general office area, but several were watching television. Most were standing. They made a space for her. A huge crowd swarmed over the Capitol Mall, many angry-faced and yelling; some pushing. Where the two groups converged, the Park Police officers attempted to break them up. The CNN reporter, a young man she had never seen before, was on the edge of the mob followed by a shoulder-carried camera

He described the two opposing groups as he and his cameraman pushed through them. The camera panned a section of the crowd where the signs in opposition to term limits were prominent. "NO TERM LIMITS AMENDMENT, NO TO ASSASSINS". But eventually the camera moved to another group where the signs supported the amendment. "Dump the Aristocracy TERM LIMITS NOW". And some of the signs appeared to support the assassinations. "THANK YOU TLR."

As the reporter pushed into the crowd, several agents groaned. One said, "He better get outta there."

The reporter and his cameraman moved toward a yelling match between the two groups. The police were attempting to come between them. One of the teachers fell to the ground. Another, an older man with a beard, swung his sign down onto the head of the TLR supporter standing over her, causing it to blossom with blood. Another TLR supporter stepped forward and punched the bearded man in the nose.

The fight was on. The reporter tried to describe it, but was being pushed and shoved in the middle of a fighting screaming crowd. The cameraman had a difficult time maintaining a steady picture. He too, was being shoved, causing the camera to jerk from side to side. Suddenly it pointed at the sky, then to legs and feet before it went black.

CNN cut to the newsroom.

A few agents were howling. Most took it seriously. Bradley thought the TLR had started something they would regret. Ward said, "Some of that anger may be our fault. People are pissed at the . . ."

"Congressman Marlan Grandee has just been assassinated," they heard the CNN reporter say. "Let me repeat that. We have just been informed that Congressman Marlan Grandee was assassinated moments ago at an apartment building in New York. Apparently he was the victim of another TLR bomb. We have no other information at this time, but please stay tuned, we will soon have a reporter on the scene."

She found O'Brian in his office. The AG was demanding action. From time to time O'Brian said, "Yes, sir." She heard Hammar clearly. "Senator Boardman hung up on me. He accused me of running a brutal

Neanderthal organization too stupid to distinguish between a 35 year old female terrorist and a panicked girl of twenty. If we don't catch these people soon the president will have to fire me just to save his own butt. We can't afford more screw-ups. Do you hear me O'Brian?"

"Yes, sir, Of course."

"Is that all you can say? Yes, sir, no, sir . . . Can't you control your agents?"

"Assistant Attorney General Koberg . . ."

"Don't you try to blame David Koberg. Your task force let them get away."

"Sir, the TLR was expecting us. They left a cell phone for us to home in on. The cell phone had a timer that caused it to send the signal after they were out of the area. Four helicopters with SWAT teams dropped down and roughed up a lot of innocent people. I think the TLR expected that reaction from us and drew us into it."

Bradley heard Hammar's explosion before the line went dead.

O'Brian was pissed too, but mostly at himself.

She asked, "Did he mention Grandee?" O'Brian looked mystified and she added, "He'll be calling back. Congressman Grandee was assassinated. Another bomb."

O'Brian shook his head slowly and looked at the ceiling.

Bradley used the TV remote. CNN was not yet at the scene. Fox News was. Yellow tape was wrapped around the front of the building including the cars in front. A reporter stood near the tape. "We are told the Congressman was visiting a friend who lived in the building. Apparently the TLR planted the bomb in anticipation of the visit. The bodyguards thought the bomb was triggered by the Congressman when he put the key in the door. Consequently, they did not immediately search the area."

O'Brian paced. "This is great. The television stations not only know before I do, they come up with their own damn theories." He called the NYC JTTF, using the direct line that connected all Joint Terrorism Task Forces. He asked for the agent assigned to the TLR investigation and was patched through to Agent Smith.

"I'm traveling to the bomb site now, sir. Should be there in two minutes. Forensics will be there in five."

"Canvass the area, see if anyone saw anything. And get back to me when you know anything." He called the forensics lab. They were sending Marla in a Bureau jet to check out the bomb.

The FOX reporter was saying, " . . . apparently a long time friend of Congressman Grandee. She has refused to say anything on or off camera. Other tenants in the building say the Congressman was a frequent visitor."

"That's how he knew where, but how did he, or she, know when?" O'Brian asked.

"It wasn't a timer," Bradley said. "Someone in the area set it off. Someone with a view of the entry . . . so they must have waited, or?"

O'Brian called Smith back and had just told him to look for the place where someone had waited, when Koberg appeared in his open door. "You've heard of the assassination of Congressman Grandee?"

"Yes, sir, agents are on the site and forensics is on their way."

"I hope they can develop a serious lead. The political situation is becoming untenable." He slid a file across O'Brian's desk. "We need his confession immediately."

O'Brian nodded.

"The Attorney General has indicated his willingness to favorably consider the release of Mrs. Hayes and the children, after we get the confession and after Mr. Hayes gives us the names of TLR members and agrees to testify."

"What about their property?"

"You know the drill—offer hope, promise nothing. We need the carrot as well as the stick." He stood to leave. "Call me when you have the signatures. Attorney General Hammar is preparing the announcement."

11:15 a.m.
Chris sat in his study, the newspaper in front of him, reflecting on Anna and Jacob's exploits. When he first read the newspaper he was simply mystified. None of it made sense. He called Anna, she laughed and described the evening. He was shocked that they would attempt something like that without consulting him. And angry, damned angry. At first. But he held his tongue and was soon laughing with her, pleased with them both and increasingly proud of Anna.

Later, when he went back to the newspaper account, it made sense. But anxiety replaced pleasure in a heartbeat with the vibration of the CIA cell phone on his belt.

"Hi Chris, it's Luke. Sorry to call you on this phone. Do you recognize my voice?"

What the hell was going on? It was Mark Adams. Chris went along. "Of course I do Luke. What's up?"

"We probably shouldn't be using your company phone." He gave Chris a number to call. They disconnected and Chris immediately redialed on a safe cell phone.

"Thanks Chris. Please don't use my name even on this call and let's try to be careful. The electronic snoops are listening for . . . certain words. I have some news you should know about."

Chris waited, unsure what to say.

"The outfit I work for is making up a list of students, friends and associates of the late professor's. You and your sister were added to that list this morning."

"Shit."

"Yeah, that was my comment. Several hundred agents now have your names. Thought you would like a heads up. Of course they have a hell of a lot of names to chase down."

"Thanks . . . Luke. Can you tell me how you got access to the list?"

"I'm still an agent with access to the computer files."

"I don't know how to thank you."

"I want to thank you and your friends . . . for giving liberty a second chance. If I can help, I will."

"Damn, . . . Luke. You sure had me figured. I wonder how many others have seen through me."

"Must not be many. You're still walking around."

"This will change our plans. May also have saved the operation. I hate asking you to stay involved, but will you call me if you have more information?"

"Of course. Glad to be on your team."

He gave Mark the cell phone number. "I won't use it for any other purpose than to receive calls from you. We still have a hundred or so that we haven't used yet."

"Good luck, Chris."

Everything was changed. He had hoped they could pull it off without affecting his family, that somehow their identities would not be discovered. But he knew better. It was a matter of hours now. A day at the most. *I have to tell Karen.*

He let his eyes travel around the room. He loved the house, mostly because of what it represented. But now as he looked about the room, he wept, because that life, that good life, was gone forever. He sat weeping in *his* chair, the daddy chair his children called it, where they had climbed onto his lap a thousand times and frequently laughed or cried. He wept until he had no more tears to give, before he trusted himself to talk to anyone. There was so much that had to be said, to be confessed and explained. But first he needed to have a last talk that was happy and forward looking. Soon enough he would call to tell them the sky had truly fallen on their lives. Now he needed to hear them loving life.

He dreaded telling Jacob and Anna that their former lives were forever lost. And Burton. When the connection was made with Chris and Anna and T. J., someone would remember Burton. They would tackle that problem after calling Oklahoma.

He used the house phone. They wouldn't have a tap on it yet. His father answered. "Carpenters."

He tried to make his voice cheerful. "Hi, Dad."

"Chris. Well by damn it's about time. These damn kids are drivin' me nuts."

It was what he wanted to hear. "Well then, they're doin' what kids are supposed to do. I take it you're busy saddling Bill and unsaddling him?"

His dad laughed. "That's a damn fact. But it won't be long before Larry can do it himself. By golly, Chris, he's growin' fast. And Maria is too."

The conversation with his father went on for a few minutes. Some good news, but he also learned that Nicolo was getting worse. He couldn't handle the brutality and violence of prison, even in the mental ward. And his mental condition was crushing Mom, but having her grandchildren there helped. Chris spoke with everyone in turn.

The phone call lasted more than an hour and except for the news about Nicolo, he couldn't get enough. His talk with Karen left him yearning for her and a few moments after the call he was more miserable than before. The house was too silent, too lonely.

He forced himself to get up, to gather the clothes and other gear he would need during the next few days. Time to begin his new and lonely life on the run. He packed two large duffels and dropped them on the floor beside the computer. It took five minutes to remove the hard disk and the backup drive. He dropped them in a duffel and after locking the house, drove away without looking back.

He called Jacob as he drove.

"They're too close. I've moved out and I have to ditch Blue."

"Are you sure? How do you know?"

"I'll tell you when we get together. Is Anna there?"

"Yes."

"Ask her to head toward Reagan Airport. I'll call her after I've ditched it and when I'm ready for a pick-up."

"I'm sorry, Chris."

"We all knew it was coming. It's going to be hard on my family."

He left Blue in the long-term lot and called Anna as he waited for the shuttle to the main terminal. She picked him up a minute after he arrived. Her face was sad with sympathy, but not tearful. "This is where things begin turning to shit," he said.

She patted his leg. "I'm sorry, Chris. This is going to be especially hard on you."

"But not you? Hell, I was scared to tell you. You can't go back to your job. We're on the run from now on."

"I've been resigned to it for a day or two. And it's not as bad as it would have been—I have Jacob now."

"God, I wish I could have Karen and the kids hidden safely away."

"Maybe you should try."

"She wouldn't be able to do it. She would panic, look guilty and the Department of Justice would arrest her and use her and the children to make me come out. It would work, too. They should stay with Mom and Dad. I think Dad can stand up to the authorities—with Senator Penny's help.

"Are you going to warn Dad?"

"We have to, so he knows what's coming; but not yet."

"Jacob should have a say in how we handle it. And Burton."

Chris didn't like that, but knew she was right. "Yeah, I guess so." That reminded him. They hadn't spoken of Burton's success yet. "Burton did it right. I'm proud of him. More resignations, for sure."

11:40 a.m.
O'Brian and Bradley waited in the interrogation room, dreading the job ahead. A guard led Hayes in. Bradley had not seen him in the orange jumpsuit, handcuffed to a belt around his waist, a ridiculously short chain on his ankle cuffs causing him to walk in a painful shuffle. She was shocked by his deterioration. The physical pain as well as the destruction of his family appeared to have aged him 30 years. He hadn't shaved—he wasn't trusted with a shaving instrument but he probably couldn't have summoned the strength anyway. Hayes slumped into a chair and the guard reached down to handcuff him to the table. O'Brian was embarrassed. Bradley's presence made it worse. "Remove his cuffs, please."

"It's against policy during interrogations."

"Remove the cuffs."

The guard removed the hand-cuffs and shot O'Brian a surly look as he started to walk away. O'Brian said, "The ankle cuffs."

This time the guard didn't waste the surly look. He bent down, removed them and stood waiting. Hayes looked awful, like he might really pass out, or have an attack. Bradley glared at O'Brian. "He needs help."

O'Brian turned to the guard. "Get the Doctor."

The guard rolled his eyes but left. Hayes asked, "Do you have the confession?"

O'Brian looked at his folded hands. "I hate this, Don, but we don't have any options. You know what Hammar will do to get your signature."

"Where do I sign? I said I would yesterday. Stop smashing me, damn you."

"We have the . . . document. But, Mr. Hayes, please think about it."

She felt O'Brian's warning look. Hayes seemed to have just noticed she was in the room. He glanced at his damaged hand, black, blue and enormously swollen. His eyes revealed the pain. He held the wrist of the damaged right hand with his left and kept rocking, only an inch or two, forward and back. Tears ran down his cheeks. "I can't sign with my right hand."

Bradley sat on Hayes' left and put an arm on his shoulder. "Don't sign. Several members of Congress are upset over your arrest, demanding to see the evidence. You still have powerful friends. And last night, the TLR sent a blistering message about the treatment you and Jackson received."

Hayes rocked forward an inch and then back. A prison doctor walked in. She introduced herself as Doctor Moore. O'Brian nodded at Hayes. "His hand."

Without touching him she asked him to "hold it out" and then "turn it over." She asked with a tinge of anger, "When did this happen? And how?"

O'Brian answered. "Thursday evening. Rifle butt."

She was incredulous. "And he's been here untreated since then?"

O'Brian nodded again and her anger increased. "That's unforgivable. Why was I not called?" Without waiting for an answer, she used her mobile radio to order a wheel chair and an anesthetic. "This needs immediate attention. The infection has spread up his arm. It appears to be gangrenous."

While they waited, Bradley said to Hayes, "This morning 23 representatives joined with Marcus Ray to sponsor the Term Limits Amendment. The House will soon be voting to consider the Marcus Ray amendment. It appears it could pass."

A voice came over a speaker near the one-way mirror—Koberg's.

"Hello, Don. This is David Koberg. I am truly sorry to hear that your hand is in worse shape than we thought. O'Brian is trying to help, isn't he? Perhaps it would be best if we took care of your hand now. Your wife and children will wait while we hospitalize you and operate on your hand. We can get back to the confession then. They can wait."

Hayes rocked back and forth, his mouth twitching, his face grotesque. The faceless voice added anger and fear to the physical torment.

"However, Don, if you would like to speed things along, O'Brian has the confession we require and I believe I can assure you that moments after you sign the confession and while you are getting the medical treatment you need, your children will be on their way to their grandparents and your wife will be headed home. But the Attorney General is extremely busy you know and his signature is required to release your children and your wife."

At that moment a male nurse entered with a wheel chair. Hayes was distracted, his face turning one way and then the other, his voice barely audible. "I'll sign."

Koberg asked, "What did you say, Don?"

Doctor Moore helped Hayes into the wheelchair. Hammar could be heard in the background demanding that Koberg "Get that signature." Koberg said, "O'Brian, place the document in front of Don and hand him a pen."

"Right." O'Brian pushed the document in front of Hayes. Bradley leaned over and whispered in Hayes ear, "Don't do it." Koberg asked, "O'Brian, what's going on? What did she say? Is he signing it?"

O'Brian said, "She's helping him. He can't hold the pen."

Tears poured from Hayes' bright red face. "I'm sorry . . . I have to." But when his hand tried to take the pen, the pain contorted his face. His body went rigid, horror and disbelief on his face before he fell forward. O'Brian stopped his fall, holding Hayes in the wheelchair. Bradley dropped to her knees shouting, "Don, Don!"

The doctor, several feet away to avoid the negotiating, rushed to his side, examined his face, felt for a pulse, tipped the wheelchair back and ran for the emergency room. Bradley and O'Brian followed. As they left the interrogation room, Koberg's voice was still shouting after them, "What's happening? Did he sign? Answer me!"

It took too long to reach the emergency room. They ran but it was a nightmare of endless corridors, security gates, two elevators and countless doors. When they reached the emergency room, they pulled Hayes out of the chair and onto a table. Doctor Moore cut his jumpsuit open, applied the paddles and sent a burst of electricity into his heart.

She checked for a heartbeat and tried again, and again. For ten minutes she tried, but it was too late.

O'Brian was furious. At himself. At the situation. At Koberg. But grief and shame were also in the mix. Bradley pushed him out into the hall. She wept and wiped at her tears as they made their way to the underground garage. They sat in the car for some time. He despised himself for his cowardice. He should have challenged Koberg and fuck the consequences. Meg was an excuse. He had known where this was going and where it would go.

2:10 p.m.
Anna and Jacob listened as Chris sat on the other side of the kitchen table describing their changed situation. Mark was now on their team—that was the good news, but the JTTF was within a day, or possibly less, of knowing all of their identities.

Anna was pleased to hear they had someone else on the inside. She had been resigned to their exposure since the photos came out.

Jacob said, "I'm sorry, Chris."

Chris shrugged. "We don't know if *two years* was the trigger. I should have guessed they'd see through the boat accident. They put it together faster than I thought they could."

"You need to warn Karen. And you both need to talk to your parents. Getting this from the press or the FBI would be dreadful."

Chris sighed. "Yeah, we discussed that. We'll call this evening after the kids are put to bed." He wiped a nervous hand over his face. "Karen won't take it well. Neither will Mom or Dad."

Jacob ran his hands through his hair and sighed. "And I must call my daughters. Maybe this evening."

Anna asked, "What about the amendment? Congress may think we're about to be caught. Will this give them enough hope that they won't pass it?"

They all worried that issue for a moment. Chris said, "Not if we turn the heat up."

Jacob said, "In tonight's message, I can try to mislead them. Make them think they've only identified four of a great many more. That should give them pause."

"Subtle." Chris said, "Or they'll guess your intent."

Jacob stood. "I'll let you and Anna judge." He went to his laptop. Anna and Chris stayed at the kitchen table, talking of how best to break the news. They had just agreed to tell Dad first. He was the strongest and he could help the others.

When the doorbell rang they all rushed to answer it. Burton had called to tell them he was coming.

He burst in, smiling enormously, greeting everyone and radiating energy from every pore. He shook Jacob's hand while Chris slapped his shoulder. Anna stood back watching and waiting her turn. He hugged her until it hurt. She squeaked and kissed his cheek. They were especially pleased he was in such great spirits.

His face glowed. He was almost bouncing off the walls with excitement. But a minute later, while describing the explosion, Anna could see him coming down. As he spoke he looked weaker by the second. He asked for a glass of wine as he sank onto the couch.

While Jacob went after the wine, Anna asked, "Are you all right, Burton?"

He paused a moment before answering, "This is weird. I felt wonderful until this minute." Burton examined the glass Jacob handed him. "It was the hardest thing I ever did. I almost threw up while racing to get into position and then again before triggering the bomb. And I did throw up immediately after." He looked at Anna. "I saw the blast hit him."

"Oh, Burton, I'm sorry you saw it," Anna said.

"The image may never leave my brain." He gave a shudder. "But I don't regret it. It's done . . . and I won't regret it."

Chris asked, "Did anyone see you?"

He shook his head. "Not really. A bodyguard was looking at me, but I don't think he could see me. I hope he wasn't hurt. The blast threw Grandee on top of him and knocked them both down the stairs."

"The news reports haven't mentioned any witnesses," Jacob said.

"I was in the mostly empty parking garage. A perfect view from my car. Too perfect." He shuddered again. "I don't think the police saw me." He stopped to think a moment. "There were two or three other cars on that level, but I didn't see anyone."

Jacob raised his glass. "Take pride Burton. Because of you, and us, our children may know liberty."

Chris and Anna raised their glasses and Burton, smiling again, said "Thank you." Anna saw his eyes grow moist through the tears in her own. Jacob had said the words Burton needed to hear.

2:15 p.m.

They sat in O'Brian's car in the Federal Detention Center parking garage, both lost in their own thoughts. At some point O'Brian's anger and guilt had become a cold determination. He had been proud to serve as an agent of the FBI, and as an agent of the JTTF, he had felt he was protecting the nation from terrorists. That pride was gone. He wasn't proud of himself or the agency or his government. The politicians might have *a passionate vision of where they want to take the nation*— he heard that phrase in every election—but he was no longer willing to provide ruthless brutality in the service of their vision. "Fuck them!"

Bradley jumped in her seat and jerked around to look at him.

"I'm on the wrong fucking side."

She stared but nodded.

"I'm not ready to take out a Congressman and I'm not sure the TLR is right, but I won't stand in their way. And I'll screw Koberg and Hammar at every opportunity." He looked hard at Bradley as he started the engine.

She had a decision to make. Her eyes were bloodshot from weeping and her mouth was tight, but she nodded again. "I think the TLR may have it right."

As O'Brian came out onto the street he turned his cell phone on and called Koberg.

"Why the hell was your cell phone off?"

"Emergency room requirement, sir. We tried to save him, sir, but he died. A heart attack."

"We know that, O'Brian. Did you get the confession?"

"We had him ready to sign. He wanted to sign. But his right hand was . . ."

Hammar screamed into the speakerphone. "Do you know what that means? We lost Jackson, now Hayes. We needed those confessions, O'Brian. The press will tear us apart."

"Sir, I prayed he would live. I'm sorry you're angry with me, sir. I'm just overwhelmed with the way his death worked to hurt *you,* sir. But maybe we can rethink our strategy."

Hammar waited.

"May I suggest you release Mrs. Jackson and Mrs. Hayes and their children as an act of compassion. We can claim that Hayes was about to sign the confession and name the TLR members, but he died in the act. I could testify to that."

3:00 p.m.

Burton was pleased they would have Mark's help, but worried their names were about to be known. "My god, it'll be awful, especially for you three—photos and life stories in the newspapers and on television." He looked at all of them with concern. "And your families. I'm sorry."

Chris paced nervously. "We'll warn them tonight, for what good it will do. The Bureau will damn sure visit them."

"How long do we have?"

"A day, maybe.

Anna said. "Jacob won't be recognized from his photos, but I've been seen in this area."

"Let's move to Tilghman Cove now," Burton said.

"Tomorrow morning, unless they announce it before then," Chris said.

Anna went into the kitchen and began putting canned goods into bags. "We should pack tonight. We may need to get out quickly."

Burton realized how tired he was when he rose to help. "God, I am tired. I'll have no trouble sleeping on the floor tonight. Chris can have the couch."

Chris, Anna and Jacob exchanged concerned looks. Anna finally spoke. "I guess we neglected to tell you." She blushed and stumbled. "You can have the couch and Chris can use the bed in the office . . . Jacob and I . . . we share his bedroom."

It hurt. God, how it hurt. It shouldn't have, she had never returned his advances. She only joked about their potential hot affair. But he was jealous and felt stupid for not guessing. He tried to hide the pain. "Beats the floor. The couch will be great." But the heat in his face told him it wasn't working.

There was nothing anyone could say to make it better. Chris tried. "Shocked the hell outta me, I'll tell ya."

Burton turned his red face toward the television. "Yeah, Jacob over me? It's hard to understand. But Jacob has so much . . . seniority."

Chris and Anna laughed, probably from relief that he could joke. She said, "I can always change my mind."

Jacob said, "Definitely not." She and Chris laughed again.

The Minuteman appeared on television. His signboard showed Grandee marked off with a red X and three more representatives with a gray X. Burton pretended to be interested.

3:30 p.m.

Carl Johnson stood in the door, his face pink, mouth drawn tight in anger. "I don't deserve this, O'Brian." He held a box of personal items from his desk.

Bradley pulled Johnson in and closed the door. O'Brian pointed at a seat. "You've been fired?"

"It was Koberg," Bradley said. "O'Brian tried to protect you."

Johnson placed his box on the desk, most of the anger suddenly gone, replaced by a sad confusion. He slumped down in the chair Bradley had been sitting in. "I shouldn't be working here anyway."

O'Brian leaned forward, both hands on the desk. "Bullshit. You're exactly the kind of agent we need here. It's a damn shame . . ."

Johnson interrupted. "I don't want to stay now. I don't believe in what the Bureau is doing. I don't believe in what I'm doing. I feel like some mobster's enforcer . . . not a defender of justice."

"They can't tolerate dissent, not even potential dissent." Bradley said. "And after today O'Brian and I may be joining you."

"What happened today?"

"O'Brian was sent to get Hayes to sign a confession. I went with him. Hayes' injured hand was badly infected. O'Brian tried to get him some medical care . . . before he signed the confession. The pain, the infection, and the emotional anguish killed him. The Doctor called it a heart attack. Hammar and Koberg caused it."

Johnson's face revealed disbelief, then the full horror of Hayes' death. "Don Hayes? What the hell is this? It's a nightmare. He is . . . he was . . ." He looked at his hands in his lap and shook his head, as his eyes filled.

Bradley said, "It's almost enough to make you believe the TLR is right."

Johnson's eyes flashed anger through the tears. "They are right. They damn sure are." He ran both hands over his face.

"I wish you could stay with us." O'Brian said. "And help with our intensive search for the TLR."

Johnson got it. His amazement was obvious. He got up and shook O'Brian's hand.

Bradley kissed Johnson on the cheek. He smiled and picked up his box. "You've got my home phone number if you need me . . . for anything."

Bradley followed him out; she had a call she wanted to make. O'Brian searched the NSA database for information on Stewart, amazed to find the extent of the files—purchases, travel, groceries, mortgage payments, utility payments, boat hardware, prescription drugs, books he had read and referred to. The list seemed endless. A file included links to online sources for Stewart's papers and speeches. He had glanced at a couple of Stewart's papers before. This time he read them.

Thirty minutes later Bradley came back. "Three more resignations from the House and another from the Senate. The House is taking up the Marcus Ray bill. It will be debated more tomorrow and may come up for a vote Monday." She picked up the remote and sat on the edge of his desk. "And the AG has an announcement. Let's hope he took your advice."

Hammar appeared and got straight to the point.

"At 12:47 p.m. today, while being treated for a badly damaged hand in the medical ward of the Federal Detention Facility, Don Hayes suffered a heart attack. The unfortunate death of Mr. Hayes is especially troubling because he had verbally confessed to his ties with the TLR. He had asked that we prepare a statement for his signature and he was in the act of signing when his heart attack occurred. After signing he intended to name other members of the TLR."

Hammar looked up from his notes. "His heart attack was partly the result of poor medical care in the prison. Mr. Hayes' hand was hurt when he fell down the stairs of his home on the evening of his arrest. He apparently made no mention of it to the guards and it went unnoticed. The doctors believe it may have contributed to his heart attack—perhaps through infection that entered his bloodstream. As an act of compassion, I have ordered the release of Mrs. Hayes so that she may be reunited with her children. And I earlier released Mrs. Jackson, whose husband Cal died in an unfortunate incident at his home. I have also ordered the return of assets that were taken in the raids except for the records and computers that may lead to the other members of the TLR. Mrs. Hayes and Mrs. Jackson have signed confessions indicating they were aware of their husbands' work with the TLR. They have agreed to help us with our investigations into the other TLR members and will remain under our protection in their homes until we have apprehended the TLR terrorists."

He looked into the cameras with determination and said, "In spite of what you hear from the TLR and their apologists, every American should know the Department of Justice is fully invested in the protection of all your rights—those given in the Constitution as well as those granted by Congress. We will remain vigilant in that effort. The TLR may threaten to bring down your government, but they will fail. And they will pay the full price for their presumption. They may threaten your right to live in real security, but with our efforts, your prayers and God's help, the TLR will be destroyed and peace restored. Thank you. And may God always bless America."

O'Brian shook his head in disgust, remembering a sign in Hayes' office, a quote—something about tyrants being most oppressive when their actions were with *full approval of their consciences.*

Bradley misinterpreted. "Hey, it was your idea . . . and the women and children are released."

"True." O'Brian refocused on the CNN commentator who was saying, "is certain to send shockwaves through the public. There have already been mounting cries for an investigation of Cal Jackson's death and Don Hayes' arrest. The death of Don Hayes will almost certainly cause many more to join in the demand for an investigation. The charge that they were connected with the TLR seems farfetched to many. It appears Attorney General Hammar retains the support of the president and the congressional leadership, but he will have his hands full in the next few days demonstrating the need for these arrests and the manner in which the arrests . . ."

Bradley turned it off and said, "Rita handed these to me as I came in earlier." She dropped a long list of names in front of him, a list of former students, friends and associates of Professor Stewart's. She pointed to the name she had just spotted—Chris Carpenter. "The asterisk next to his name indicates he was involved in the term limits movement. The second asterisk indicates federal law enforcement."

"The CIA bomb expert. He was in here yesterday."

She nodded. "That's him."

"Hundreds of agents must have this list by now. We have an address?"

"I have his card."

Carpenter lived out by Dulles. To get onto US 66, they drove along the mall west on Constitution. O'Brian shook his head at the size of the crowd. "Three days ago I wouldn't have predicted 500 TLR supporters . . . but look at that . . . its great." The TLR supporters now looked equal in numbers to the opposition. They wore TLR tee-shirts and someone was providing signs because they were everywhere. THANK YOU TLR.

"And they're getting organized."

The crowd spilled out onto the street. He could barely drive through them. Both groups looked determined. The TLR supporters were trying to get to the Capitol Building, but were stopped by what appeared to be every horse-mounted cop within a hundred mile radius.

O'Brian crossed 23rd and turned onto the westbound onramp. As they crossed the Potomac Bridge, Dr. Galvin called with the latest from his investigations. "The cell phone left at Samantha's is one of fifty from a dealer in the Midwest. Registered in the name of Jamie Bolen— same address as the senator's. The shipping address was a P.O. Box. They prepaid for the phones."

Bradley said. "Throw-away cell phones."

"We couldn't lift fingerprints from the cell phone or purse, but we recovered DNA from a tissue. We're looking for a match from our files. If that doesn't work, it can be used for ID purposes if we catch her. That's all we could develop out of the material you brought us."

O'Brian smiled as Galvin continued, "Marla says the bomb used on Grandee appears identical to the two used yesterday. She believes it was set off by someone watching, probably from the garage across the street. The only people who could have seen the bomber were a boy and girl, both 16 years old, parked in a van twenty yards away. However, it appears they were not watching. They heard the blast, and heard noises from a car next to them and heard it drive away, but did not rise up to look. The boy said the car may have been brown and the driver was male but he has no idea what kind of car, or its age, or the age of the man, or his hair color, etc. Sorry O'Brian."

Bradley grinned. O'Brian said, "They must have been distracted."

They arrived at Chris Carpenter's home 23 minutes after leaving the office. A car was parked in the drive, but no one answered the door when O'Brian knocked. "He drives a big blue Dodge Ram—it's what he drove out of the bureau garage yesterday." They walked around the house and came back to the front door. O'Brian knocked again, then tried the door. "Call his cell phone."

"What do I say if he answers?"

"We have a very serious matter we want to talk to him about."

She smiled as she punched in his number and was pleased he didn't answer. She listened to his message and then left hers.

While she called, O'Brian retrieved a lock-kit from his car and opened the door. She followed him in. "And the reason we are going in is?"

O'Brian eyes moved over the room. "He's a potential terrorist, so we don't need a warrant. But actually he may have left something behind that he shouldn't have." O'Brian found the office and the opened computer, the hard disk missing. He had definitely skipped. They went upstairs and found a weapon's safe in the master bedroom, open and empty, a pile of clothes dumped on the bed. A chest of drawers was mostly empty.

Bradley turned the clothes over and discovered a revolver and a semi-automatic pistol. "If he doesn't need these, I wonder what he took with him."

They returned to Chris's office. O'Brian pointed to the wall. "Check the backs of the family photos. I'll start on the paper files. We want anything that might help someone guess where Chris or his family might be."

4:40 p.m.

Hayes' death devastated Jacob as much as that of Jackson. He tried to work on the message, but couldn't concentrate. Chris knew he was hurting. So was Burton. Hayes had been his friend, too.

But Burton paced the room, lashing out. "Why does any of this surprise us? Maybe their deaths will help people see the brutality of this monster. It shouldn't have been Jackson or Hayes dying, it should be the political aristocrats who think they have a right to direct every aspect of our daily lives and charge us for the service. Don's death is not the end of it. Others we love will die, and maybe we will." He looked at Jacob. "We must harden ourselves. This must be done."

Jacob tried to smile and said, "Help me with the message." Burton sat at Anna's computer editing the first draft when the alarm rang. It startled Burton, who leaped up as Anna ran in, took over the laptop and brought up the remote cameras. One of the views was of Chris's home. The remote camera showed a man and woman at the front door, their car parked in front.

Anna focused the camera, zoomed in and began recording. Chris looked over her shoulder at the screen. "Bureau, definitely." And then as the camera zoomed closer he said, "Katherine Bradley . . . and Mike O'Brian. He's Special Agent in Charge of the task force. She's second in command."

They watched as Bradley and O'Brian stepped off the porch and walked along the front of the house, but the camera lost them when they stepped around the side. Anna said, "Oh, Chris, you got out just in time."

"Yeah, damn good thing Mark warned me."

Burton said, "Well that's it then. They know who you are which means they'll soon know about Anna, and then me."

As they watched, Bradley and O'Brian came around the opposite side of the house and returned to the front door. They saw Bradley make a cell phone call while O'Brian went to his car. A second later Chris's cell phone rang. Everyone looked at the couch where his jacket lay.

The ringing stopped after four rings but Bradley still had the phone to her ears. She was talking, obviously leaving a message as O'Brian returned to the house. He fiddled at the doorknob and lock for a few seconds and then the door opened and both walked in.

Chris listened to Bradley's message on the CIA cell phone while Bradley and O'Brian were inside. He said, "That was bullshit. It was almost like *give yourself up for questioning please*. Weird."

Burton asked, "Is she stupid?"

"No. Neither is O'Brian."

Jacob asked, "A warning?"

Chris thought before he answered. "Maybe." He turned the power off and set the phone down. He had already screwed up. If they had ordered a GPS fix on that phone as soon as they suspected him they would have come through that door before now. He decided not to mention it to the others, but he listened for the helicopters.

6:08 p.m.

The house was closed up and hot when they entered an hour ago, and it hadn't cooled down. The sweat poured off O'Brian's face and his shirt was soaked. His jacket was off, but he still wore his pistol. Bradley didn't seem to be perspiring. They finished with the photos and were nearly done with the personal files. O'Brian was still unsure what he would do with the material they'd found—information on friends and relatives that might be worth talking to if an agent really wanted to find Chris. They didn't want to take unnecessary risks either. Bradley found the photo of Anna in a file and they both noticed the resemblance to a couple of the retouched photos of TLR courier.

As they were looking through the last few folders, Barnes called O'Brian. "I'm not sure if you're aware that my team turned up some names of former students, friends and associates of Stewart's. I gave Rita the list."

O'Brian wasn't sure how to play it so he let Barnes keep talking.

"Anyway, Bernie Schaeffer spotted the name Chris Carpenter. He's CIA. Bernie says Chris is the bomb expert advising you and Bradley and Dr. Galvin. Turns out he's been with the CIA for just two years. We brought up a really complete file on him when Assistant Attorney General Koberg walked in. I pointed out that Carpenter is the bomb expert the CIA sent us, and could be the person who alerted the TLR to the helicopter raid."

Shit. It was too late to stop it or turn it around. *Barnes you're too damn good.* He kept listening.

"So now Koberg wants to raid Chris Carpenter's and all the other names on the list, using intensive interrogation. We're gearing up for that raid now. Thought you'd want to know."

"Thanks for the heads-up. Bradley and I not only got your list. We also saw Chris Carpenter's name. We are going through his house now; he's already skipped. Maybe someone warned him. Anyway his computer disk is gone. He removed all kinds of stuff and some weapons. He seems to have covered his tracks—we aren't finding much."

"This will make Koberg unhappy."

"I'll call him now." He disconnected, told Bradley what he had learned from Barnes and then called Koberg.

Koberg answered with undisguised glee. "You chose the wrong time to be abroad, O'Brian. In your absence, we have discovered the TLR mole. Chris Carpenter, the CIA bomb expert you and Bradley were dealing with, is almost certainly responsible for the bombs that killed two senators and a representative."

"Yes sir, That's what we thought. Bradley and I are in his home now. We've been going through it for an hour now. Carpenter cleaned the place out before he took off."

O'Brian wiped his face with his handkerchief as he waited for Koberg to explode. Koberg's voice almost whistled with the pressure of his anger. "Damn them! Damn them!" He stuttered for a moment and then said with an attempt at control, "Get back here immediately."

O'Brian heard the phone slammed down on the other end. Apparently Bradley did, too. There was humor in her eyes and finally, a faint glow of perspiration on her upper lip. O'Brian said, "Koberg seemed disappointed. Thought he was about to roll up the TLR."

"He's going to arrest everyone on the list?"

O'Brian cocked his head and nodded.

"What about this stuff?" She pointed to the few things they had gathered that might provide a clue to finding Carpenter.

"Bring it, I'll put it in my desk and think about how we can use it. I'll come up with something in a day or two."

6:32 p.m.
O'Brian and Bradley came out of Chris's home and drove away. They carried a paper sack with them. Chris thought he'd removed everything, but they found something. He said, "Karen and Dad have to be warned tonight."

Jacob suggested, "Your dad should find an attorney. Your family can't fight the Department of Justice without legal help."

Burton added, "Even if the Bureau doesn't show up at their house tomorrow, it may be in the newspapers."

Chris ran his hands through his hair to stop them from shaking. Anna and Jacob tried to make small talk as they prepared a salad to go with the lasagna in the oven. Chris didn't hear them. He made some notes and spent a lot of time staring into space.

Burton thought he should call his ex-wife, Alice. "I don't think it will affect her much . . . and my oldest boy, Charles, is five. I don't think this stuff will get to him, either. Alice will know how to handle it."

Anna asked, "And your folks are gone, aren't they?"

He nodded. "They couldn't have handled it."

The smell of garlic, olive oil, tomato sauce and Italian sausage did not improve their appetites. Red wine helped a little and dinner was civilized but conversation was almost nonexistent.

A minute after 10 p.m. Chris and Anna went out to the car. She drove as Chris set his notes on his knee and called. Potentially the phone lines into the Carpenter ranch were already being monitored, so they drove to insure that if the cell phone was monitored and their location discovered, Jacob and Burton would not be caught.

Although Anna offered to deliver the bad news, Chris wanted to speak first.

The Carpenter farm was three miles north of Kiowa, Oklahoma. Most of the rooms in the large white frame house were unused except when family came. Karen had her own room now; it had been Anna's and still had a few of Anna's things—high school photos with friends, a stuffed animal and two dolls that her grandmother Maria made her.

Chris knew Karen loved the room—it was like the room she had always wanted as a girl in Virginia. And Larry and Maria loved the place. Chris tried to focus on those happy thoughts, but it wasn't much help.

He heard the phone ring at the other end. It rang several times and he was hoping it would be his father. Then he heard it picked up. "Hello, this is Maria Carpenter speaking."

Not good. "Hi Mom, how are you."

"Chris. I hoped it might be you. It's so good to hear your voice. We were all in the living room watching a really good movie; Larry and Maria are in bed. Will you want to talk to them? Oh Chris, they are so big and growing so fast! It makes me sad that I don't get to see them grow. I wish you didn't live so far away, Chris."

"Well maybe you will get to see more of them in the future. Mom, I need to talk to Dad, but I don't want Karen to know I'm on the phone yet, okay?"

"Well . . . I suppose."

"So could you yell at Dad that Max is on the line, and then you better go to the bathroom or Karen will see right through you, won't she?"

"I guess that's maybe right, too." She was worried. "Chris, is everything all right?"

"That answer is complicated, Mom. That's why I need to talk to Dad."

"Oh Chris . . . I . . . Oh, very well then." Chris heard her lay the phone down and prepare herself for a major deception. "Larry, its Max." She was awfully loud and completely unbelievable.

She was worried, but nothing like she would be. And then he could hear his dad coming to the phone. He braced himself and heard his mother hand him the phone and say quietly, "It's Chris."

Of course his mother would be standing nearby listening to half the conversation.

"Hey Chris, what the hell's goin on? Your mother says its Max and then has a long face on and tells me it's you. We got a problem?"

"Yeah Dad, a big problem." He hesitated, unsure where to start. His notes didn't cover the start.

"Spit it out son."

"Dad . . . from time to time Anna and I have caused you and Mom more trouble and heartache than any parent ever deserved. But we're about to make all that seem insignificant. I just hope you all can handle it."

"Well, son," his Dad's voice became soft and concerned. "If you're trying to get my attention, you sure as hell got it. Let's have it."

He told his father the entire story. It took several minutes and his father never interrupted except to curse. Then, his voice breaking, he said, "Well, you're going to have to give me . . . a moment or two."

He was silent for a few seconds. Chris heard the muffled voice of his mother in the background and imagined the phone pressed to his father's chest, his head down and his eyes closed in pain. Chris had seen him take calls about Nicolo that had that effect. Then he came back, his voice strong, "You're already into it. You knew what you were getting into. I wish you'd asked my advice, but it's way too late for that now. The whole goddamn nation has been wondering who the hell the TLR was. I sure as hell never thought it was my family."

Chris could hear his mother gasp, "Oh my God!"

"I guess I'm ready for the rest of it." His voice was stronger now.

"We're sorry for the pain, Dad. But I admit that going into this thing I was pretty sure I was going to have to do this to you. You know how much trouble our country is in. We've discussed it often enough. But in fact, it's a lot worse than you or most people know.

"I read the papers too, son."

"Either we defend ourselves and our right to own and control our lives now or your grandkids will have no chance ever to recover their lives and liberty."

"Well . . ."

"We, you and I, have watched our liberty, our right to make our own choices, slip away. We can't make the big decisions about our lives. Congress does. And every year we have less control of ourselves and our government takes more control of us. I don't want to do this. I want someone else to stand up to these bastards, but they never do. We can't vote them out; they control the elections. No one else will do it, Dad."

"I know about that, but I don't like the killing. I don't . . ."

"We don't either. I don't have to remind you of how many men have given their lives for liberty. You've watched them die. You've told Anna and me a million times that liberty isn't free." Both were silent for a while and then Chris said, "No one else is willing to stand up to these bastards. And there's no other way. They control the elections, the parties, the regulators, the judges. Us. There is no other way. Is there? And there is no one else. Is there?"

"All right, I have to trust that you've thought this out. There's no goin' back now anyway. I'm with you. What can I do?"

"You need to get ready for a visit from the Department of Justice. It may get ugly. We'll talk more about that later. In a day, maybe less, they'll know who we are. It'll be in all the papers and on TV. That won't stop us and I don't believe we'll be caught before we make Congress pass the amendment, but it may be some time before I see any of you. You're going to have to help Karen handle this. I'll tell her about it, but after I talk to her she'll need some help."

"You got that right."

"I expect you want to talk to Anna now."

"Yeah, I sure do."

Chris handed the phone to Anna and she said, "Hi, Dad."

"Hi, sweetheart. Damn . . ."

She heard him sob before he said, "I'll get over it. Are you handling this stuff okay?"

"I'm fine, Dad. I really am. How's Mom going to handle this?"

"Guess we'll have to wait and see. Hell, I don't know how I'll handle it. Sounds like the brown stuff is about to hit the fan."

"It's not all bad news, Dad. So far we're winning."

"I hope you're right, Sweetheart."

"The House of Representatives will consider a vote tomorrow, or the next day, on the amendment. We have to do this, Dad. Nicolo is one example out of millions. So is Dr Thompson. So that cocaine-using, pot-smoking two-faced lying incumbents can pretend to voters they are drug warriors. But every damn one knows the drug war is what keeps the drug lords in business. Some probably get campaign contributions from drug lords. They won't leave office except to save their lives."

"Who else . . . No I mean how much help do you have? Can you really pull this thing off?"

"Yes, the crazy thing is, we can. We aren't fighting a brave army. We are at war with a bunch of scared corrupt politicians and some others that just are inspired to run our lives. They're all running for cover. We thought this would take a month or two; but we gave them too much credit. They're about to fold. And Dad," her voice broke, "if we succeed, whatever it costs, it'll be worth it."

"I'm proud of you both. I've decided we can handle it at this end. Don't worry about us."

"Thanks Dad, now before you get Karen we need to give you some advice."

"I'm listening."

"Tonight, as soon as we hang up, call Max Carter and ask him to come over. Tell him the whole story, but don't do it on the telephone. He can advise you and start organizing a statement from the family about your position and ours. He may think he's in over his head. He may want to bring in another attorney, but you two work that out. And then call Dan Penny. He . . ."

"Hold on now; why do I need to do any of that?"

"Because the Department of Justice will soon be visiting you and they may come armed and in force. They may accuse you, Mom and Karen of being accomplices so they can throw you in a cell and interrogate you, like they did the Hayes and Jackson families. They may take Larry and Maria to foster homes, just to make Chris come out of hiding. They . . ."

"Those sons-a-bitches attempt that, they'll have a real goddamn war on their hands."

"Dad they're liars, incredibly deceitful, to themselves as well as to others and more brutal than you can imagine. You need to be smarter. You need to be ready for them so that they can't get away with it. So they won't try to make you or Karen look like accomplices. And Senator Penny is the man who can help with that."

"He'll help. He only served one term you know. He said it was all he could stomach. All right, you've thought this stuff out. Guess I better shut up and listen."

"You just need to know what you're up against, Dad."

"I'll call Max as soon as I hang up."

"I'll give the phone back to Chris now; he needs to talk to Karen. I love you Dad. Don't worry too much; we've planned this carefully and we can do this."

"Oh hell yes, I'll worry. But I see the importance of the thing, too. I'll get Karen." His voice faltered. "Good . . . luck sweetheart."

She knew he was wiping tears away and she felt her own tears flow as she handed the phone to Chris. His face was contorted from trying to maintain control.

He'd feared this conversation for two years. He heard the phone picked up off the kitchen desk at the other end. He expected Karen but it was his mother on the phone.

"Oh Chris," She was crying. "Please take care of yourself; these kids need you. Oh, here comes Karen" Her voice changed with a vain attempt to sound cheerful. "Well, Karen is here now, Chris."

"Hi, Chris."

Two words in her silky, soft, southern voice and he was undone. His voice quaked as he said, "Hi, Honey."

"You've got bad news."

"Yes. It's bad, but please . . . let me get through this without asking me any questions until I get it all out. It will take a while so you should sit down."

He heard her voice catch with fear and then the sound of a chair scooting. "All right, I'm ready." Her voice seemed harder now, as if preparing herself to hear of another woman.

"I'll start with the worst part so you know it won't get any worse . . . Anna and I are part of the TLR."

"Oh my God, no!" She was angry. And loud. "How could you do this to us?"

"Because I love you and because I love our children and I want them to grow up able to make of their lives whatever they want."

"Dammit Chris, this is . . ."

"Please let me finish. I know this is hard on you. It's been hard on Anna and me for two years. When we made this decision we did it after a hell of a lot of thought. We worried and argued for more than a year. I hoped this conversation would never have to happen. I feared that it would and I've dreaded this moment more than I can tell you."

He paused to get control of his voice and emotions. This time she waited. "I love you Karen, I would lay my life down for you and never think twice. But I also love our children and I'm unwilling for them to grow up in a world where their lives are owned by their government, where every important life decision is a political decision, a group decision, directed and regulated by government, and where their children will live the same damn way. I'm not willing to let that happen. I wish someone else would do this—anyone but me—but they won't. It's up to us, Anna and me and . . . the others, or it'll never happen."

"Do you hear yourself, Chris? This is crazy! You can't change the government."

"We aren't going to change the government. We will force Congress to give the term limits amendment to the people for a vote. The people will approve it. They hate our Congress almost as much as we do. They will elect citizen legislators and maybe they will move government back to its real job—protecting liberty."

"You're killing congressmen who were elected . . ."

"No dammit! I'm defending my right to own my life and do whatever the hell I want with it. I'm not a part of some political-social animal with its head in Washington. My life is mine. I own me. Society does not. And my children will have the right to make the same statement, if it kills me trying. I have no argument with those who want to live in a socialist paradise. They just can't use government to force me to join their insanity. I'm defending my freedom and my children's freedom . . . the only way I can."

"Why didn't you talk to me about it?" She was blubbering and angry at the same time. "Because you have to make the decisions, right? Because you couldn't trust me to make a brave decision."

"I tried, Karen. And every time I brought the subject up, you got mad and . . ."

"I saw your anger Chris and it scared me. I knew you would do something crazy. I knew it. This is what I feared."

"You were right then. But if I had told you what we were up to, then you would have been an accessory. I couldn't tell you and also keep you safe. And you would have been worried sick all of this time. And worried for me whenever I left the house or someone knocked on the door. I did what I thought was best . . . for you and our children. They needed you strong and confident those two years, and now they need you with them, when I can't be . . . at least for a while"

"So now what? You go off to prison or you escape to some place where we never see you again? Or you just get killed . . . and how do I explain that to our children?"

"If I thought those things were probable . . . if I thought we'd fail, I wouldn't have started down this road. We'll succeed."

"What do I do now? What do I tell the kids now?" She still wept, but some of the anger was gone.

"Tell them the truth . . . when you have to. For now, tell them I'm doing something important and I'll be away for a while, but I'll return as soon as I can, because I love them as much as any father ever loved his children."

"And what about me?"

"Oh, sweetheart, I want to hold you so much right now it's killing me—it's damn near killing me. Look. I don't know how, or when, but it won't be a moment longer than it has to be. I'll find a safe way to come to you, or bring you to me."

She said, "Damn you, Chris," but her voice held no anger.

"I have to hang up. Dad will explain why. But I'll call back as soon as I can. I love you, Karen."

"I love . . ." He heard her wail as the phone clattered and then disconnected. He threw the cell phone on the seat, looked away from Anna and wept.

8:03 p.m.

Bradley and O'Brian arrived back at the Bureau in time to see the task force agents headed out. Koberg was still angry but obviously anxious to discover any unsuspecting TLR member on the list. He described the operation to O'Brian and Bradley, pointing to the large overhead map of the DC area. "The list contains 93 names that live within a hundred miles. Other names live far outside the area and we've confirmed that none of those have been in this area within the last week. The addresses for the ninety-three have been plotted and marked. The teams are divided into thirty-two groups of three agents each. Each team has been given two to four names in the general vicinity of each other. They will ask the target to come in for questioning and they will point out their authority to make an arrest under the executive order amending section 219 of the Patriot Act. And they will describe the potential consequences of resistance."

O'Brian nodded. *Dig yourself in deeper, asshole.*

"I believe we can expect those who are not guilty to come willingly. Those who don't will be our real targets. The interrogation will be at the Federal Detention Facility. I will work with agents during the interrogations." Koberg looked at O'Brian. "You will advise agents that are having difficulties. The computer list fully describes our targets."

After Koberg left, O'Brian said, "You may as well go home and get some sleep."

Bradley picked up her notepad. "This will make the DOJ look even worse. Call me if something comes up."

He felt a little better about himself. He got a cup of coffee and a sandwich from the cafeteria before going to the communication center. He took a seat at a computer at the control center and pulled up the list scheduled for interrogation. He ate the sandwich as he read through the list. The OITC had provided a one paragraph summary of each person with links that went on forever, every product and service they had ever purchased; vacations; air, boat and train travel; income and sources; taxes paid; parents and siblings; marriages and divorces; children; political party contributions; think tank contributions; suspect web searches and a lot more. The detail was incredible. Most of the information came from businesses. When the federal government asked, they had to give it up. Or the company and its principal stockholders and officers could expect endless investigations and audits until it did. No one bothered to tell Congress—they used the same techniques to raise political contributions.

O'Brian ran down the list and spotted Anna Carpenter. He remembered the name from a photo at Chris's home—his sister, and a computer consultant in Arlington. He knew before he looked—Koberg and his team were going after her. They weren't likely to find her at home. Chris would have warned her. That thought improved his mood more.

The first call from a worried agent was routed through to him a little before 9 p.m. "She's a thirty-two-year-old single mom with two small children. The youngest is in diapers. What do we do with them? I can't bring them into the detention center."

"Interrogate her right there. If she seems okay leave her and go to your next target. If you think she might know something, bring her and the kids to the detention center. Koberg likes kids."

Another call came in and before he could finish with that call, yet another came in. For the next two hours he was coaching agents on how to handle single parents with children, empty houses, a large party where the target and her spouse were celebrating a tenth wedding anniversary.

Several wanted to *let their attorney know* before being taken away. O'Brian told the agents to inform them, "You may be innocent and if you will come with us to be interviewed, I'm sure we'll quickly discover that. But if you do not come voluntarily, you will be arrested on suspicion of terrorism. As a suspected terrorist you lose many of the rights you think you have, including the right to bail and to an attorney—unless we decide to appoint one for you. But you will not have the right to speak to that attorney unless we make that decision." When they scream, "that can't be legal," then tell them, "Congress has granted us this authority under the Patriot Act—to help us protect America's citizens."

10:42 p.m.
They couldn't walk back into the house weeping, so Anna drove until she and Chris regained control. Jacob and Burton were standing in the kitchen, where Burton was opening a bottle of wine. They looked at Chris with apprehension. He washed his face in the bathroom while Anna described the conversation and the reactions.

"Why would Senator Penny want to help your father?" Burton asked.

"They served in Viet Nam—Navy helicopter pilots. Penny was shot down and Dad went into some very thick fire to rescue him. They became good friends."

Jacob said, "I knew him, too. He came to Congress with high ideals. It happens from time to time. But even those few who arrive with strong principles and high ideals are corrupted by the power. Penny saw it coming. He served a single term and walked away. He's a good man. I hope he can help your family."

Chris wandered back in and Burton changed the subject. "Jacob's message should stir things up."

Jacob handed a copy to Chris. "You and Anna may want to make a change or two. We have time."

Chris had a hard time concentrating, but it helped to get his mind elsewhere. Only small changes were made. Anna downloaded the message and a few minutes later, while Jacob waited in the car, she dropped the cell phone in a trash container near the Washington Monument. The message went out at midnight as they drove away.

Sunday, June 8 message to the American people and to Congress.

The Department of Justice is one small part of a single enormous dysfunctional monster, a beast grown so large it cannot move without smashing millions of innocents in its path, a brutal and stupid creature attracting the power-hungry and corrupting those principled few who arrive in the Capitol imagining they can control the beast.

But it has no brain. It lurches in one direction and then the other, the result of the contradictory orders from thousands of federal agencies. Congress created the monster with the laws, regulations and a tax code designed to get incumbent members of Congress re-elected. The beast grows with every law and regulation and lurches awkwardly and sometimes brutally over more innocents. Congress feeds the beast with the wealth you created and with your liberty. And with your children's future.

Today, 25 percent of the wealth produced by private effort is consumed by the beast directly in taxes and fees. Another 30 percent is destroyed by stupid regulations that hobble the productivity of your wealth-producing effort without protecting anyone. But the largest amount is lost before it exists, because creative people are prevented from ever beginning. Permissions and approvals designed to protect existing license holders from competition, stop all but the most persistent.

As it grows larger, more people in its path will be smashed by the fumbling, stumbling beast as it wreaks the economy and increases unemployment. And because professional politicians speak for it, the beast cannot be trusted. It lies. It covers up.

Yesterday, at 12:40 p.m. Don Hayes was smashed by the beast for no other reason than that he loved liberty and praised it eloquently.

Attorney General John Hammar ordered the raid and orchestrated the torture of Don Hayes and his family. But the real responsibility belongs to those long-term incumbents in Congress who see to the feeding of the federal beast. They authorized and encouraged the actions of the Department of Justice.

Don Hayes was not a member of the TLR; neither was Cal Jackson, but, to rescue their children, Barbara Hayes and Susan Jackson were forced to sign confessions naming their husbands and admitting to complicity.

All of this is the result of 100 senators and 435 members of the House of Representatives each focused entirely on re-election. For each of these professional politicians every waking moment from election to re-election is devoted to retaining office and increasing their power. Our liberty is consumed in the process.

Don Hayes believed in educating the public about the importance of liberty and individual rights. He would not have supported the TLR. But words will not defeat this beast. Liberty has always required more than words.

Some members of Congress deceive themselves that we are about to be captured. A few of us may be; however, we are organized and deployed in a manner that will allow the organization to continue removing incumbents until the term limits amendment is passed. Three of our number will soon be identified, their photos and biographies published. That will have no effect on our operations.

The families of those members have been warned that the DOJ may use terror tactics on them. They have obtained legal counsel and taken other precautions. They were not given any other information because it would have placed them in greater danger.

Yesterday we took the life of Representative Grandee. Today we will remove another long-term incumbent. At least two more will die tomorrow and each day thereafter until the professional politicians that control Congress approve the Term Limits Amendment to the Constitution and offer it to the people for ratification.

The Term Limits Revolution

Sunday, June 8
They Know

12:07 a.m.

O'Brian read the TLR message as soon as it was posted. He liked the description of the beast. It would enrage Hammar, the president, and Congress. They would be blaming each other with the media goading them on.

A few minutes later O'Brian took the call from the Attorney General, who was looking for Koberg.

"I'm sorry, sir." O'Brian said. "He had all calls directed here. I can patch . . ."

"Have you read this latest TLR message?"

"Yes, sir. It's infuriating."

"It damn sure is. I didn't know Hayes' hand was hurt that bad. I would never have permitted that."

"A tragic accident, sir."

"Yes, exactly. Miscommunication. This message will drive the public over the edge. The TLR is making us all look terrible. We need to be more careful of appearances."

"Yes, sir, but we need to be tough, as you wisely said."

Hammar paused a moment. "I need to talk to Koberg."

"I can patch you through to his radio-phone. That line is encrypted and completely safe."

"Do it; you stay on the line."

O'Brian called Koberg and made the patch. "I have Attorney General Hammar on the line."

Koberg answered, "Good evening, sir. I have some very good news to report."

"I need it."

Koberg sounded smug. "We have discovered two of the TLR members. At this moment I am in the apartment of Anna Carpenter. She was the courier and probably Senator Hackman's assassin. And earlier, Agent O'Brian was in the home of her brother, Chris Carpenter, a CIA agent and the TLR's bomb expert."

Koberg was obviously expecting praise, but the attorney general asked. "We don't have them though, do we?"

"Not yet, sir, but . . ."

"You haven't seen the TLR message this evening, have you, David?"

"No, sir."

"The TLR predicted we would soon discover the identities of a few TLR members. They knew what we know."

Koberg was silent.

O'Brian added, "Carpenter is not the only mole. Someone warned him—someone in the Department or the Bureau."

Hammar asked Koberg, "How did you discover that Anna Carpenter is TLR?"

"She and her brother, Chris, are on a list of 93 suspects—students of Professor Stewart. Some others on the list are probably TLR members. For that reason, I have directed that all of these people be brought in tonight for interrogation at the Federal Detention Facility. I believe other members of the TLR will quickly confess when they learn that Chris and Anna Carpenter are identified and on the run. I also think they . . ."

"That was a good plan two days ago, David. But the TLR accused us of running a brutal and stupid organization. The media and voters are buying it. They're yelling at Congress. Leadership is yelling at me. The president is furious. I'm getting calls in the middle of the damn night. Everyone wants the TLR caught, but without making the federal government look . . . out of control."

"Sir, most of the people on the list are already in the Federal Detention Center; I believe they can help us find the TLR—perhaps in another day. Worst case, sir. We keep these people in the detention center until we catch the TLR, and that won't be long now. When we have the TLR, no one will care."

O'Brian added, "I have to agree sir. Until we catch these guys Congress will continue complaining and so will the public. You've been right all along, sir. Better to get tough now and get it over with."

12:11 a.m.
Burton and Chris were watching the pundit's reactions on television. Anna went straight to her laptop to check the internet. The red light was flashing—her apartment. She yelled and turned on the camera. People were in her apartment and going through her things. Jacob, Burton, and Chris looked over her shoulder.

The video camera—in the eye of a teddy bear sitting on a bookshelf—gave them a good view of the room. Audio was picked up through a microphone in the bear's ear. Anna saw Charlotte, her apartment manager, come in from Anna's bedroom with someone. Chris recognized him. "Assistant AG Koberg. Mark says he's Hammar's brainy thug."

Charlotte looked frightened. Koberg told her to wait outside until he had time to deal with her. One of the agents was going through the desk drawers, the other through the bookshelves, getting close to the camera. Koberg called him to the computer. Anna leaned forward. She had just said, "He better not," when Koberg's cell phone rang.

He looked at it before answering. "Yes, O'Brian."

They could not hear the other side of the conversation, but it became clear that Attorney General Hammar was patched in. Koberg bragged about the progress but his expression turned sour when he learned of the message.

Anna and Burton laughed out loud when Koberg said, "No, sir. I have not read tonight's TLR message. No, sir. I realize that, but, sir, I assure you the people we are arresting will yield all the information we need to wrap this thing up and even in the unlikely worst case, we can keep them in the detention center until we do take down the TLR. No one will care by that time."

Hammar had obviously left the conversation at some point, because Koberg's conversation was directed at O'Brian, and he thanked O'Brian for his support.

Chris and Jacob exchanged glances. O'Brian was still a mystery.

Koberg smiled and looked almost content as he returned his cell phone to his belt. But then he yelled at the agent sitting quietly at the computer. "We have work to do, agent." The agent reached down to pick up the computer. Anna's screen went dark and the sound went dead.

Anna laughed. "I love technology. A small electro-magnet fried my computer when he picked it up. It's garbage now."

Jacob grinned and so did Burton, but Chris said, "We only heard one side of that conversation. The DOJ could release our bios and photos tonight. Let's move to Tilghman Cove now."

12:22 a.m.
O'Brian had second thoughts as soon as the call with Koberg ended. He didn't want innocent people harmed. But people had to see things as

they really were. One more strong example might make the brutal beast obvious—even to those who didn't want to see it.

He wanted to talk to Bradley, but she would be asleep. He took calls from a dwindling number of agents for another forty-five minutes. Most wanted to be ordered to take the actions they were taking. O'Brian worried more about the calls he was not getting. Some agents were probably enjoying this.

When the calls dried up, he pulled his jacket off the hanger and headed home. He was desperate for sleep. He'd be lucky to get five hours. As days go, it had been about as bad as it could get, but he did feel better about himself.

He was in bed ten minutes after walking in the door. But he seemed never to really fall into a deep sleep. Then he heard the door close and someone walking toward him. He raised up and saw Bradley smiling at the foot of the bed. *Holy shit.* She unbuttoned her blouse but didn't speak. Neither did he.

One part of his brain wondered how she got in. She didn't have a key, did she? But that part of his brain seemed to forget what it was doing. He didn't care how she got through the door; he would worry about that later. She was here and she looked so good getting into the bed, and now she felt so good. She laughed and he laughed, too, while he sucked her sweet breath, stroking her. Holding her and stroking her and . . . the phone rang. He didn't care, Oh God, her tongue in his mouth . . . let it ring . . . the weight and feel of her body against his, her sweet firm little bottom . . . let it ring . . . in both his hands. She felt . . . the phone rang again and she laughed and her skin was like silk. When the phone rang again, his right leg was between her legs, her pubic mound hot against his thigh. But the phone rang louder and louder. He was furious, and awake, and he grabbed the phone, almost shouting, "O'Brian." But he looked over his shoulder, knowing she wouldn't be there. *Shit.* He felt ridiculous.

"This is Director Proctor."

Oh goddamn it. He could see the clock now; it was 8:30. He had overslept. "Yes, Sir."

"You need to be in the AG 's office at 9:30."

5:45 a.m.
They didn't finish moving into the Tilghman Cove house until nearly 4 a.m. and it was after that before they were all in bed. Jacob heard Chris or Burton up moving in the night. The anxiety level was at a peak for

everyone, except Anna. She slept softly curled against him. Jacob had slept for an hour but woke in a sweat.

The dream shook him. His granddaughter Angelina had been weeping on his lap. "Why are you dead, Granddaddy?" The dream left him incredibly sad; he was dead to her. And today he had to confront that issue. Anna, Chris and he would be identified under headlines nationwide. Carol and Mary would see the coverage and put it together. They knew Anna and Chris very well and they wouldn't hesitate a second before concluding that their father was not dead—he was involved in the TLR. And they would be angry.

He would have to call this morning and the thought crushed him. The call would be a terrible shock. My God, he dreaded that call. It frightened him far more than his appointment with Congressman Gruber. Carol would be especially hurt. Mary was tougher. She might be able to handle it.

He made no sound that would wake Anna, but the tears flowed. The sun was up before he fell back to sleep.

8:32 a.m.
For a moment O'Brian lay back, embarrassed. Dreams are meaningless, he told himself, the brain is electrical and chemical and when one is asleep the electrons fire randomly making meaningless connections. But not remembering the dream was impossible. It stayed there as he dressed. And he enjoyed it again. If he could he would have that dream every night.

Sunday traffic would be light. He stopped for a triple shot Americano before jumping on the freeway. He made it to the Bureau in time to park and walk at a leisurely pace through the tunnel to the Department of Justice building.

The receptionist showed him into the conference room as soon as he stepped out of the elevator. There were a few more people than he expected and a replacement for Hackman. Koberg looked smug, Hammar pleased. That was suspicious.

"Good morning Agent O'Brian. I believe you've met everyone except Senator Cranshaw, the Chairman of the Appropriations Committee.

O'Brian shook the senator's hand and nodded at the others. Hammar gestured toward a chair beside Director Proctor at the middle of the table, "The Congressional leadership remains concerned, understandably, with our progress. We were showing them what we have developed so far."

As Hammar spoke, Proctor gathered several photos scattered across the table and passed them to O'Brian, photos of Anna and Chris Carpenter as well as family members and bios of each. Then satellite and aerial photos of farmland with a house and barn labeled Carpenter Ranch, Kiowa, Oklahoma.

"I was just describing the success of the task force in discovering the identities of Anna and Chris Carpenter," Hammar nodded at the photos, "and the excellent background information on their families developed by the NSA."

General Faedester passed a sheet to O'Brian. "NSA has more background information on these people than I could bring. OITC has telephone records of recent cell phones calls from the Arlington area to the Carpenter farm, a twenty-eight minute call last night. We have discovered from airline and credit card records that Chris Carpenter's wife Karen and their children are staying at the farm with Chris and Anna's parents. As of 3:20 this morning we are monitoring the Carpenter phone lines. But we are also monitoring every cell and landline phone within twenty miles of the farm. If another call is made between that area and this area, we will be able to locate the cell phone quickly enough to put a helicopter team on them, even if they're moving."

Senator Harlowe interrupted. "I'm glad we're finally getting some hard information. But the TLR knew you would discover these names and that it wouldn't help. I want to hear, Agent O'Brian, that you will apprehend these people today or tomorrow."

"Senator, we've identified these two plus Professor Stewart. I'm confident we will soon identify and capture them all. But I can't promise when until I know when, Senator."

"That's not nearly good enough." Congressman MacDulmie's entire head was crimson under the thin white comb-over. "Not nearly. We have members who want to approve this damn thing. The pictures of Senator Reigns scared the shit out of all of us. Members are calling for a vote to consider the amendment. We can't stop them with anything less than a strong promise that we'll have these terrorists today or tomorrow. Now we need that promise, god dammit."

O'Brian noticed Speaker Keith said nothing. His eyes darting around the table, he seemed to be weighing, counting. He let MacDulmie make the demands. O'Brian nodded at MacDulmie and turned to the AG.

Hammar asked Senator Harlow, "If the House is unable to stand against this blackmail, will you be able to hold out?"

"Not if they keep killing our members. Hell, you've got a damn mole in your organization, John. How can we be sure you can do anything?"

"We'll have the mole in another day," Koberg said. "And that will provide us with another source of information."

Hammar said, "And the mole may know what we will be doing but he or she can't stop us. Now what if we could provide much better protection for the threatened members of the Senate?"

"What protection? I keep hearing about protection and it hasn't worked yet."

"The president will provide senators with officer housing at Andrews Air Force Base. Air Force helicopters would be used to get the senators back and forth to the Capitol."

"Dammit John, hiding won't get me re-elected. My opponent will accuse me of cowardice." He seemed to be rethinking, though, even as he spoke. "But I suppose if it were just for a week, I could get away with it." He smiled. "The helicopters landing at the Capitol will make for some good photo-ops. And we could take a press photographer with us."

Congressman Gruber nodded vigorously. "Excellent damn plan. If we can't stop the House from approving the TLR amendment, we can still stop the bill from passing. That gives John time to catch the fucking terrorists. I like that."

"I'll bet you like it," Senator Cranshaw said. "The house caves, you're safe and the TLR starts hunting senators exclusively."

"But it makes sense," Gruber pleaded. "There's a lot less senators to protect; it'll be easier to protect a few senators. All the bodyguards for 83, no, 79 senators."

Senator Harlowe rolled his eyes in disgust.

Speaker Keith said, "Let's do it, John. But what about the Carpenters?"

"That is the next decision," Hammar said. "Agent O'Brian, we were debating the advantages of immediately issuing the photos of Anna and Chris Carpenter and Professor Stewart, with the hope someone knows where to find them, or holding off and raiding the Carpenter farm tonight. Director Proctor believes we should issue the photos and name them immediately, but Assistant Attorney General Koberg believes the photos and identification may alert the family. He believes an army of attorneys and friends will flock to them. He thinks we should raid the Carpenter home tonight and release the photos tomorrow. Do you have any thoughts on the matter?"

O'Brian looked at Koberg with his question. "Won't they be ready for us anyway?"

"They may know we are coming, but what can they do? And when their parents and Chris's wife are in the Federal Detention Center, Anna and Chris will almost certainly want to join them." His smile was almost gentle.

"Perfect." Senator Cranshaw could barely restrain his enthusiasm. "They'll have to come forward then."

O'Brian asked Hammar, "You think they would give up their revolution to save their parents and Chris's wife?"

Koberg answered. "His supervisor said Chris adores his wife and children. He believes Chris would surrender immediately if he thought we might . . . if he thought it was necessary."

"But what if they have an attorney and expect a raid?" Congressman MacDulmie asked. "We need to anticipate . . ."

Cranshaw said. "What kind of attorney will they get in Kiowa, Oklahoma? A divorce and bankruptcy lawyer?"

O'Brian hoped the TLR was still a step ahead. "I think we should go with the raid tonight, and hold up on the photos until the raid is underway."

"Damn right." Gruber said. "Go get 'em, by God."

There were smiles around the table. Koberg nodded at O'Brian in appreciation.

O'Brian couldn't resist. "Any information from the people we took to the Federal Detention Center last night?"

Koberg's smile vanished. "Not yet."

Representative Gruber asked Koberg, "What people?"

"Last night we brought in 91 people for questioning. There is a strong potential link between . . ."

"Ninety-one God damn people? To the Federal Detention Center?" Senator Cranshaw was outraged. "That means still more people screaming about your rough tactics."

"Senator, we need their information to help us capture the TLR in the immediate future. Any innocent detainees will be released after the capture of the TLR, when no one will care about their detention. They have already signed statements admitting their voluntary detention. Before we release them they will also promise not to speak to anyone about their detention."

O'Brian left the meeting with another recording in his pocket. Bradley would be interested, but the tapes could never be used, without getting him caught. Barnes was waiting for him in his office. "You been to the

Federal Detention Center yet?" He didn't wait for an answer. "Some of those people are being roughed up, and they sure as hell aren't TLR."

"Two on the list are TLR. Koberg thinks the others may have information."

Barnes leaned forward, gripping the desk. "You know who else is in the detention center? Johnson. Carl Johnson and his brother Jamie. Carl isn't any more TLR than you are. Jamie probably isn't either."

"That son of a bitch." O'Brian said it before he had time to think. "Shit."

Barnes sat back in his chair, surprised at O'Brian's reaction. "Yeah, Carl's name wasn't on the list, but Jamie's was and Jamie's bio indicated Carl was his brother. Koberg arrested both of them. There isn't any information that ties Carl Johnson to Stewart, or to Stewart's friends. None."

Barnes didn't know that O'Brian had pulled Johnson's name off Ward's list. O'Brian asked, "Is Proctor aware of any of this?"

Barnes shrugged. "Who knows? Jamie made it clear he likes term limits. That pissed off Koberg and several others."

"I'll talk to Carl and his brother and I'll see what I can do. It may not be much."

10:10 a.m.

Anna eased out of the bed and slipped on her bathrobe without waking Jacob. She had a pot of espresso ready when Chris got up a few minutes later. He looked terrible. He probably hadn't slept. She let him have a sip before she gave him a hug. "You okay?"

He wrapped his arms around her. "Oh hell, yes."

They both managed a half-hearted chuckle. She asked, "Are we going to call home today . . . to find out if they've talked to Max or Senator Penny?"

He sipped his coffee before answering. "I'm scared to call and scared not to. We know the line will be tapped. I'm afraid we'll try this once too often. They have some very smart technical people."

Anna put her hand over his. "I can place the call using the internet, through a server system in Belize that provides a cutout. It will only be traceable back to the Belize server."

"Then we can call anytime. They won't be leaving the house today."

She heard Jacob in the shower and a minute later Burton wandered in. He made breakfast while Anna set up the call.

The house had fiber-optic cable service so the call would not be out
in the air to be picked up by the NSA. Her computer's firewall made
the computer invisible to anyone except the Belize server. She worried
a little, knowing the CIA bribes anyone that may help them and any
server can be compromised if the owner or his employees are willing.

After breakfast, Chris pulled up a chair and she reminded him,
"The longer we talk, the greater the chance that Dad or Mom or Karen
will say something that gets them in trouble." A few clicks later they
could both hear the phone ringing at the farm.

"Carpenter residence."

"Hi, Dad. Be careful, what you say."

"Hi, son. Oh, hell yes. I know that. Been talking to some high-
powered advisors. I talked to Max and my Navy buddy and they talked
to some people they knew. I think we're in good shape here. Damn
good thing you warned us last night. But it's you two we're all worried
about."

"Don't worry, Dad. We're in good shape. I'm just glad you have
those two friends."

"We got lots of friends and a few are visiting right now. Turns out
a few are fans of yours. My navy buddy had a long talk with Karen and
me. We all understand a helluva lot better why the TLR is needed.
Penny—aw, shit! I better let you talk to Karen before I say something
really stupid. She'll be more careful than me. Bye, Sweetheart. Bye
Chris."

Chris could hear the familiar sound of a chair being shoved back on
the Carpenter kitchen floor and a lot of muttering in the background.
Anna got up, but she didn't leave the room. She heard Karen in that
soft-sweet southern voice begin gushing as if she had been holding it
back and now couldn't stop herself. "Hi, Chris. Oh honey, I know we
don't have long to talk and I have so much I want to say. I want you to
know I've been thinking hard about this, and I think you and Anna are
probably right—no, that's not right, I'm sure you are, and I really love
you, but honey, I just miss you . . . so much." Now she was sobbing.

Chris was already choked up, and pleased that she understood. He
could barely talk. "Sweetheart, thank you. I miss you, too."

"I know that somehow . . . we'll get back together."

The doubt in her voice helped him regain control. "We will,
Sweetheart, I promise we will. But it may be a while. The Department
of Justice will be looking for me and they'll be watching you and
everyone who knows us. I can't tell you when, or how, but I will get

you and the kids back and I won't let it take too long. I promise, sweetheart. Now tell me about the kids."

The change of topic helped. She cleared her throat twice before she could speak. "Larry loves it here of course. He and your dad are pretty much inseparable. Larry follows him around asking questions. This morning I heard him say, 'oh hell yes' to Maria. He sounded just like your dad. I guess he's learning a lot; and Dad seems to love the attention. And Maria spends a lot of time with your mother and me. We've been reading a lot and she's learning fast now. I'm taking her to the library next week . . ."

"Better not, sweetheart."

"Oh . . . I guess that's right. Well, we can still get all the books we need. Some neighbors are . . . visiting. Oh I just hate not saying it, but anyway, you know. We are doing just fine. Please don't worry about us. Really."

"Yeah, I think I'm getting the picture. Damn, that's great. Listen, Sweetheart we need to stop talking now, but I'll try to call again, maybe tomorrow."

Anna returned to the laptop and severed the connection. Tears were running down Chris's face, but he was fine. He even managed a smile. "I don't know what, but I'm pretty sure they've cooked something up to protect themselves."

11:45 a.m.

As he approached the Detention Center counter, O'Brian had a flashback of Don Hayes' pain wracked face. The officer asked, "You okay?"

"Yeah. Just remembered something." He handed his badge to the desk officer, who scanned it, signing him in. "Last night we brought in 91 people to be questioned on the TLR matter."

"Yes, sir." The desk officer brought up the list.

The entries appeared with several columns. O'Brian scrolled down. "I want to see Carl Johnson."

"He's on his way back to his cell. I'll have him brought back to the interrogation room."

"Back? Has someone been interrogating him?"

"Yeah. Assistant Attorney General Koberg."

"Is he still here?"

"Good afternoon, Agent O'Brian."

O'Brian turned to see Koberg standing behind him. The smirk pissed him off, but he smiled. "I understand you've been questioning Johnson. How did that go?"

"Perhaps we should find a conference room to discuss this."

Koberg led him to a room containing a small table and six chairs. Koberg sat at the end near the door. O'Brian sat with his back to the door. The smirk was gone. "May I ask why you are here?"

"I have more than 200 task force agents working this case. I need them working together and convinced they're working for an organization that appreciates them. When an agent is arrested and accused of being a mole for a terrorist organization, it tends to get the agents talking. And when he's someone as well liked as Carl Johnson, they get pissed."

"That's ridiculous. Johnson will certainly confess. In a day or so we will have a statement from him. And the facts are so strong that I doubt any of your agents would lift a finger to help him."

"That's great. What facts?"

"He admitted to being a student of Professor Stewart's, as was his brother, Jamie. Jamie is also a friend of both Anna and Chris."

"Is?"

"He claims not to have seen them for several months, but of course he's lying. I'm sure we will demonstrate that to your concerned agents with telephone and credit card records."

"Has he been arrested, too?"

"Yes, of course."

"And has he admitted being TLR?"

Koberg didn't answer but raised an eyebrow. O'Brian nodded, as if he were buying it. "I'm not saying Johnson's not the mole, but we have to be careful how we play this. We need enough proof to justify his arrest. And I'd better look like I'm giving him the benefit of the doubt or I'll have half the agents on my team dragging their feet."

Koberg looked skeptical. "And what do you propose?"

"Time. Everyone knows we have a mole. My agents are looking at each other and wondering. But they like Johnson. Let me prove it's him. That will take a week at the most. Even if I don't get more evidence, after a week they'll have grown used to the idea, and we can negotiate a confession."

"I may have misjudged you, Agent O'Brian." He stood. "Of course, we both have the same goals. Our methods may seem harsh, but in the long run, society runs more smoothly."

As they stepped into the long corridor, O'Brian thought he caught a glimpse of Bradley turning a corner at the lobby, but he was still handling Koberg. "I'll speak with Johnson now . . . to get the process going."

"I leave it in your hands."

O'Brian remembered the interrogation rooms were wired. They could not talk there. He got the cell number from the desk officer, checked his handgun and then was accompanied by a guard down a long hall past several cell blocks. Johnson's cell was one of a hundred in cellblock C on the eighth floor. Like Hayes, Johnson wore a bright orange jump suit with the Federal Detention Center label on it and looked like hell. The guard let O'Brian in and said he would be within hearing range. "Just yell."

Neither spoke for a moment. Johnson was depressed and angry, but not at O'Brian. "There's nothing you can do."

"Maybe not, Carl, but I won't give up." It was easy to say, but he remembered being powerless to stop the treatment that killed Hayes.

Johnson's anger vanished; he looked sad and helpless. "He'll arrest my wife if I don't confess by tomorrow. I have to sign the confession to stop him."

O'Brian shook his head. "Think about it, Carl. After what happened with Barbara Hayes and Sue Jackson, he's not going to arrest Peggy. He is trying to frighten you into a confession. Don't. At least, not yet. Anyway, I got him to back off. I promised to find the evidence to convict you."

Hope bloomed in Johnson's eyes.

"Barnes told me you were in here," O'Brian said. "He's pissed. Very pissed. By now half the task force is angry. I'm going to assign two agents, with Barnes supervising, to find out anything they can to convict you. Of course when they don't find anything, it will make it difficult for Koberg to go forward."

Johnson's face brightened, but the anger was back. "Did you read the TLR message last night, about the beast?"

O'Brian nodded.

"I had just finished it when they bashed in the door. They pushed Peggy around, but didn't arrest her. They put me in handcuffs. But the TLR got it right, O'Brian. Don't get in the beast's way. It will smash you. And it will smash Barnes . . . and Bradley."

O'Brian nodded. "What about Jamie?"

"Koberg seems to want my confession more than Jamie's. He says he'll let Jamie off with a slap on the hand if I'll sign. He wants credit for capturing the mole, and he wants to believe it's me."

"He's a political animal, but he won't look good when we actually catch the mole."

"Oh, he'll take credit for that, too."

O'Brian considered that. "If the mole," and for some reason he thought of Bradley again, "gives more inside information to the TLR, it will undermine Koberg's case against you big-time."

Johnson nodded and almost grinned. "Oh, Yeah."

12:10 p.m.

After his late breakfast Jacob wandered down to the dock and sat with his legs hanging, his feet just above the water surface. A handsome yacht, perhaps sixty feet long, sailed past under spinnaker, headed toward the marina in Centreville. Anna came to sit on the dock beside him. "Let's go on a really long trip . . . after."

He took her hand in his. "Sweetheart, I am desperate to be alone with you on a yacht in the trade winds. How I long for it!"

"But that is not what you were thinking?"

"No. It's time to call Mary and Carol."

"I'll speak to them first. Hearing your voice without warning would be . . . difficult."

His eyes closed and he began nodding. "My God, you are strong." He kissed her hand. "It would be better coming from you. Then I will talk. But how can they ever forgive me for the pain I've put them through?"

Anna used the Belize server and a VOIP system again. By the time the phone rang, Jacob had gone white. It rang three times before it was picked up.

"Patrick Brownell."

Anna said, "Hi, Patrick, I don't know if you'll remember me. I'm Anna Carpenter in Arlington."

"Sure I do. How are you Anna? And how is Chris?"

"We're fine, Patrick. How are you and the family?"

"Great. Mary loves San Francisco. Jacob is growing fast. But I suppose you're calling for Mary?"

"Yes, I really do need to talk to her, but you should probably stay near."

"Uh oh—bad news?"

"Yes and no. It's complicated."

"I'll get her."

Jacob and Anna could hear him run up the stairs and his muffled voice. "It's Anna Carpenter in Arlington." Then, her voice, "Really?"

"Hi, Anna. It's Mary; what's up? Looks like you've got Patrick worried."

"Well you should sit down, Mary. I warned Patrick. It's bad news, but also good news. This will take a few minutes. Is Jacob in the room?"

"No. He's at a friends for a sleepover."

"Mary, I assume you've been reading about the TLR."

"Oh, my gosh, yes. Isn't it incredible? If Dad . . . were . . ." She stopped. Anna heard her gasp. Then she wailed, "Ohhhh, God, noooo." Then she screamed again, "Noooo!"

Anna tried to concentrate on helping Mary, but a glance at Jacob's white pain-contorted face made the tears pour from her eyes too. She squeezed his hand.

"He's in this, isn't he? Goddamn him!" Mary burst into inconsolable weeping for a moment and then added, "He's put us through this hell for . . . some damn political purpose."

The pain and anger and the sense of betrayal in Mary's voice, wracked Jacob.

Mary wept and eventually the line went dead.

Jacob stumbled from the room. She didn't know what to do. Her hands shook while she tried to reconnect, but she gave up. Jacob needed her.

She found him sitting on a log down the beach. She sat beside him, reaching her arms around him, shocked at his devastation. His face sagged as if he had aged ten years.

"It was a terrible shock for her, Jacob. She needs time to assimilate it." After a moment she added, "I should call Carol."

He nodded.

Chris and Burton were obviously worried. Burton said, "Mary really hammered him, didn't she?"

"She didn't know he was listening. And it was a really bad shock for her. I hope Carol takes it a lot better."

"You're going to call her now?"

She nodded. "Any suggestions?"

"I'm glad it's you and not me."

Later she came out to Jacob and smiled at him as she sat beside him and took his hand in hers. "Carol took it better than Mary. A lot better."

Jacob's face was still fallen, his eyes red, but they held hope. Anna said, "She was shocked, like Mary at first, then angry and she wept, but she stayed on the line. And after a minute or two, it was almost all joy. I told her you would call later but that she should expect the FBI to be monitoring their internet and telephone. She said she would call Mary."

1:15 p.m.
O'Brian wanted to reassure Jamie and get him interested in defending himself. He was on D block, which meant walking past an endless series of depressing cells with dejected, angry prisoners. Some threw curses as he passed, but most, if they bothered to raise their heads, looked at O'Brian through hopeless eyes.

Jamie was bitter and certain O'Brian was role playing—the good cop to Koberg's bad cop role. "If you really want to help me, then let me use your cell phone so I can call an attorney."

O'Brian sat down on the bunk beside Jamie. "You're a member of JFI and you were a student of Stewart's. I'm sure you know that the anti-terrorism laws are designed to prevent you from the right to an attorney. It's sick, but you know it's true. I'm a friend of Carl's, so, short of getting myself arrested, I'll do what I can to help you. Koberg told Carl, if he signs a confession the department will let you off easy. I don't want him to sign."

The surly bitter look disappeared. "Koberg said he would let Carl off if I signed."

"We need time, Jamie. Don't plea bargain and don't sign. That might make Carl give up and sign."

Jamie, surprised and hopeful, just nodded.

"We have to be careful how we fight the bastards," O'Brian said. "Don't lose hope, even if I don't get back to see you for a while. Koberg thinks I'm on his team. If you talk to him be sure you tell him I'm an asshole." He heard the guard coming and asked softly, "Who is your attorney? I may have an idea."

"An uncle, Phil Johnson. He's in the Arlington book."

O'Brian winked and said in an angry voice. "And if you don't cooperate you're going to be here a very long time." As the guard turned and bent his head down to open the cell-door Jamie nodded. As O'Brian and the guard walked away Jamie shouted, "Asshole. You're worse than Koberg."

2:55 p.m.
There were many members of Congress that Jacob knew and liked. They could be very personable. Some seemed almost modest on camera

and even sometimes in private conversations. But power, pride and public attention affected the nice guys, also. Either they failed to see that they had taken control of people's lives, or they thought it was simply appropriate that they should do so—since they were elected. Taking those lives, if the time came, would be more difficult. Congressman Gruber did not fit into that group.

Gruber was a pandering demagogue who would get behind any cause, worthy or unworthy, that would increase his power. He pretended, to himself as well as others, that he was a man of principle. Like all national politicians, he was a natural actor, affecting concern for the underclass, the middle class, the uninsured, the children, the unborn, national defense, any issue that aroused passion and votes. His performance often convinced himself and was convincing to enough voters to keep him in office. Jacob despised Gruber, but dreaded killing him.

Chris went over the weapon's operation with him and three times Jacob demonstrated to Chris he had it down pat. Unless he was badly distracted he could do it easily. Chris and Burton helped him load the weapon into the van. He looked at his watch, discovered he had time and asked Anna to help him call Carol.

The conversation went better than Jacob expected. Anna had left them to talk and when she came back a few minutes later Jacob was thoroughly enjoying the reunion. So was Carol. This time the tears were happy tears. Anna sat next to Jacob letting them talk a little more, but she eventually interrupted. It was pressing luck a little too much to let the call go on and she wanted to make sure Carol was warned about the Department of Justice.

The conversation with Carol buoyed him enormously, especially because she assured him Mary wanted to talk to him. But it was time to go.

3:15 p.m.

The relief O'Brian felt as he drove away from the detention center was clouded by the memory of all those hopeless angry faces, some— maybe many—as innocent as Carl and Jamie. No one in Congress intended the arrest of innocent people, but it happened anyway, because each of the pandering bastards was concentrated on looking tough on terrorism to win re-election. He was still in a bad mood when he got back to his office.

Of course, Barnes was waiting for him. O'Brian told what he could of the conversations with Koberg, Carl and Jamie.

Barnes seemed aware that Jamie was a long time member of JFI, that he and Carl were sympathetic to the TLR. "Good thing we don't have to arrest all the TLR supporters. You see the mall?"

"Yeah. The TLR may not be able to keep a lid on those people. The president might have used force to disburse the protestors two days ago, but the crowds are too large for that now; it would be just too damn bloody."

"There's a rumor the House will pass the amendment." He smiled. "But of course, they wouldn't move without consulting you."

He nodded. "Right. And I've also decided we will hide the targeted senators at Andrews AFB."

"Good chess move. It might work. The targets won't be at home and they won't be in their normal routine. Pre-planted bombs wouldn't do the job." He hesitated and his face brightened some. "Of course the TLR may have considered such a gambit."

O'Brian asked, "I'm guessing you wouldn't mind seeing Congress term-limited?"

Barnes looked at O'Brian a moment before he answered. "Our job is catching the TLR. I'll do my job. But I don't see a downside to getting rid of the professional politicians and I don't like the bullshit charges against Carl."

"That's why you will handle the investigation. Pick two agents to do the legwork. See if there's a legitimate connection between Carl, or Jamie, and the TLR. Use the NSA, check phone records to see if they called Chris or Anna Carpenter in the last two years, and compare credit card records that would show they were at the same place and time as Chris or Anna. And let's both hope you don't find anything, on either one."

"Thanks." He opened the door before asking, "Did Bradley catch up with you?"

"When was that?"

"She called in right after you left. I told her you were headed to the Detention Center to see Johnson. She said she would join you there. Must have changed her mind"

O'Brian remembered seeing her. "She didn't find me; I was probably talking to Koberg at the time."

Linda Morrow squeezed through the door past Barnes. "Chris and Anna called their folks in Oklahoma. Nothing I found helpful, but I sent you a recording."

Barnes asked, "Did you get a trace?"

"We traced the call back to Belize. A cutout server. Anna Carpenter knows her way around the internet. She better not use it again, though. An agent is visiting that operation as we speak. We usually get their cooperation—one way or another."

Barnes sneered. "I'll talk to you later, O'Brian."

Morrow added. "Next time she may use a different cutout server, in another country. We've alerted those that are already on the payroll."

O'Brian turned to the breaking news scrolling at the bottom of his monitor. The House of Representatives, in a special Sunday session, had voted to consider the TLR amendment tomorrow, Monday, June 9th.

O'Brian smiled, wondering if Bradley knew. He reached for the phone to call her when the Attorney General Hammar appeared on the television screen. He turned the sound up. "Good afternoon. I am pleased to announce that the Department of Justice has identified three of the TLR terrorists. They are Chris Carpenter, an administrative agent with the CIA; his sister, Anna Carpenter, a computer specialist; and their former professor at Higgs University, T.J. Stewart." As Hammar continued to speak, describing their radical political backgrounds and work history, their photos appeared on the screen. O'Brian wondered about the early release of the photos and if the farmhouse raid was underway or about to begin.

Hammar begged those in the area of the nation's capitol to "look carefully at the photos and help with their apprehension. These are bloodthirsty killers who have assassinated, in the most hideous manner, three of our nation's leaders. And they mean to murder more if we do not stop them. They must not be underestimated. The Carpenters' brother is a convicted drug dealer now in federal prison. The Carpenters were students of the radical anarchist Professor T. J. Stewart. Two years ago, Professor Stewart was reported missing and presumed drowned at sea. We now know his accident was faked. The Professor is alive and is probably the TLR leader. Other former students and associates of the professor remain followers of his radical theories and support this deadly treason. Several are in custody and are being questioned." Photos of Stewart appeared in succession on the screen as Hammar went on to describe him as a would-be tyrant, opposed to democracy and the rule of law. Hammar credited the "hard work of the Joint Terrorism Task Force for the recent breakthrough. But I want to make it clear, it could not have happened without the special authority for fighting terrorism under the Patriot Act and its successive amendments. And we do not have them captured yet."

He looked into the camera with his most serious manner. "I spoke today with our Congressional leaders. We believe more legislation is required to insure that your government is more fully protected from

these terrorists. In the coming days your elected leaders will propose
legislation that will protect the security of all Americans by giving law
enforcement the tools we need to identify and incarcerate traitors and
terrorists before they strike against the American people."

His face became sad as he said, "Some of our greatest statesmen
have died at the hands of these killers. They might well have been
apprehended, before anyone was assassinated, if we had not been
stymied by those who would give terrorists the Constitutional rights of
American citizens, if we had been armed with the tools needed to
investigate, identify, arrest and question such people before they act.
Nonetheless, even with the limited tools we now have, I can assure you
that the TLR will soon be locked away. And I know, we can continue
to count on the help of our patriotic citizens to identify them. Please
look again at these photos." The photos scrolled across the screen
replacing the image of the attorney general as he continued talking.
"Remain alert as you go about your daily business. We believe they are
somewhere in the area of the Capitol. Call the FBI immediately if you
see any of these people; the fifty-million-dollar reward remains
available to those providing information leading to the arrest of any of
these fugitives. Eternal vigilance is the price of liberty and a secure
America. Thank you for your vigilance and may God continue to bless
America."

4:10 p.m.
Jacob crossed the Chesapeake still enjoying the conversation with
Carol, his energy high in spite of last night. He smiled to remember her
description of Angelina chasing seagulls, but a flash in the distance
caught his attention. He looked for the windshield wiper control, in
case it rained. This was the first time he had driven the van. The black
clouds and lightning were worrisome. He wondered if lightning or rain
might affect the weapon. There would be a very brief moment for the
weapon to work. Another opportunity at Gruber might be difficult. And
he deserved to be a target.

Gruber was House minority leader but also co-chair of the House
Armed Services Committee. Five trillion dollars passed through that
committee, every year, subject to the deal making fully controlled by
the co-chairmen. This afternoon a sizable chunk of that amount would
be committed to several military contractors. The meeting with the
contractors was unpublished. Chris had learned of it a month earlier
through a Pentagon contact.

Jacob had known him for years. Gruber arrived in the Capitol fully corrupted from a long political career in state politics. He must be looking forward to this meeting with greedy expectation; his financial wealth would grow substantially today, as would his political capital.

A gust of wind slammed against the van, and Jacob struggled to keep it on the road. He braked hard to avoid a car that had braked in front of him. His disguise, a hat, beard and wig, slipped off the passenger seat. After today they would have to disguise themselves every time they left the house, perhaps for the rest of their lives.

He pulled off US 50 onto the county road. Chris was right, traffic was very light. He drove a quarter mile and stopped on the shoulder, waiting for a break. When no traffic was in sight, he opened the rear doors, placed the magnetic sign on the driver's side, placed one on the right side and another on a back door. Three minutes later he was back on the freeway driving a van advertising *Capitol Surveying*.

At 5:00 p.m. the radio carried the attorney general's public announcement. It was everything that Jacob feared, but expected. The photos and identifications were being made public and Congress would be giving the DOJ more sweeping powers to invade the lives of individuals, designate some as terrorists and punish them with interrogation, uninterrupted for days on end, without right of attorney or trial. And every one of the members who voted for it would look straight into the camera and declare the vote was necessary to protect the nation from evil.

As Jacob approached the exit, he glanced at the cell phone with the GPS locator chip, confirming that Gruber's limo was still at the Pentagon. Weeks earlier, Chris, attached the dime-sized GPS transmitter to the inside wheel-well of Gruber's limousine.

Jacob turned south along Indian Head Road. A few minutes later he turned left past the leveled ground to the place where he would wait. The Congressman must eventually drive past him to get home. The graded area had been residential three months ago. He stopped on the left side shoulder, the spot Chris had shown him, 300 yards from Indian Head Road. He had a clear view of southbound traffic over the leveled ground. Across the street from the graded area were three small homes that would probably be torn down in the near future. A golden retriever slept on the front step of the house directly across. No one seemed to be at home.

Jacob checked again. Gruber was still not moving. The black clouds continued to gather with a few streaks of lightning occasionally, but no rain yet and the wind had died. He opened the rear van doors and set up the surveyor's tripod within arms reach of where he sat on the van floor-bed. He mounted the electromagnetic pulse emitter on the tripod. It did look something like a surveyor's instrument. Then he remembered the hat, wig and beard and his heart sank. He should have put them on when he mounted the signs. Too late. If he were being observed, adding a disguise now would be reason to call the police immediately.

He considered leaving, but decided he would not be recognized by anyone, not yet at least. He pointed the instrument up the road and connected the cable that ran to the power-transmitter and the monitor. He looked through the optic tube and adjusted it to pre-focus on cars about a half mile up the road. He sat on the back of the van and mentally practiced. Pre-focus, acquire target, track, power up the transmitter, micro-focus on the limo's back seat, pulse. He checked the cell phone again—the blinking dot was on US 295 moving east. His stomach did a flip as he stared at the moving dot.

The bright blue limousine would be hard to miss. He pulled a rolled up drawing from the van, pretending to look at it. If he were visited by anyone he would say he was waiting for another engineer. He hoped that would not happen—he was already shaking. The blinking dot drew closer, about four miles away now and coming fast. Members of Congress used police escorts even when they weren't targeted. And they never stopped for lights. He reminded himself that Gruber encouraged the raids on the Hayes and Jackson families. And then it hit him—they know. At this moment Sue Jackson and Barbara Hayes know I brought this disaster down on them. They will hate me forever. He had to shake it off; the blinking dot was only a mile away. *Think damn it. Rehearse.*

He looked up Indian Head Highway where the blue car would first appear. He ran down the list three times, certain he had the sequence right. He looked up the road. His heart beat faster. A blue car . . . no . . . wrong blue, and it wasn't a limousine. Two more cars came into view and then he saw it. A bright blue limousine with a motorcycle escort.

Gruber.

His heart hammered as he forced himself to go through the checklist. Pre-focus. He pre-focused the lens until the bulls-eye was on the car.

Acquire target. He clicked the acquire target button and watched for a moment to confirm that the instrument was tracking. The bull's eye stayed with the car as it came closer. The instrument on the tripod turned to track it.

Power up. He powered up the transmitter and heard the faintest beep as it began sending signals to fine-tune the range and power.

Microfocus. He looked at the monitor now and used the remote to zoom in on the car, then the back seat area. He adjusted the focus ring so that it only covered a limited area. Only the back seat. He refocused as it came a little closer. The focus ring was larger than it needed to be. Adrenalin pumped so hard he could hardly think straight. The motorcycle escorts were visible without the instrument now, and a car in front and behind. The limousine's windows were tinted dark but Gruber would be in the back seat. He had to be in the back seat.

The signal grew louder. The car was probably within the electromagnetic pulse range, but Jacob wanted to send the pulse when Gruber was passing as close as possible. And it was tracking automatically now. The heart attack should be almost instantaneous, but not discovered for several hundred yards perhaps. The weapon rotated on the tripod as Jacob turned all of his attention to the monitor. He concentrated on the image while holding the remote in his right hand with his thumb above the send button.

He was incredibly tense and so fully focused on the monitor's image that when the dog leaped onto the van bed beside him, he yelled and jumped up hitting his head on the van. The dog jumped down as frightened as Jacob, who turned back to the monitor, his head in pain. The bulls-eye was pointed at the sky, the transmitter was silent. The dog had bumped the tripod when he jumped down.

The car was a hundred yards up the highway and coming fast. Jacob grabbed the instrument, the tripod legs dangling, and pointed it without bothering to focus, but he was too late. It was passing the intersection before he could do anything. He tried to bring the car into focus but trees interfered. That side was not cleared. He was heartsick, shamed by his failure. Then the rain began to fall.

There was nothing to do but pack up and go home. He removed the weapon head from the tripod and set it into its case. He glanced down the highway. The limousine was barely in sight, but it was stopped. They had pulled to the side and stopped. *Why?* He stood in the rain looking at them, completely dismayed, but when he returned to packing he noticed the remote sitting beside the monitor and knew. *I pushed the button when the dog jumped up.* He looked back down the road and grinned. *I fired the pulse, accidentally.*

The dog had started for the house but stopped and turned his head. He noticed Jacob's smile, trotted back and now stood wagging his tail.

5:25 p.m.
O'Brian had just read the notice scrolling on the bottom of his monitor. Congressman Marcus Ray had been badly beaten by a small group of angry protesters as he left the Capitol. Apparently they had been waiting for him as he left the building. When Bradley called, he tried to tell her, but she didn't want to discuss Congressman Ray. "I've made a decision; I am resigning immediately. I no longer care to be a member of the FBI or the Joint Terrorism Task Force. My letter of resignation will be on Director Proctor's desk tomorrow morning."

He heard the cold anger in her voice, but wasn't sure who it was directed toward. He was stunned. "What's going on? You're not telling me something."

"It's very simple, Agent O'Brian. I no longer care to be associated with you or the Bureau."

O'Brian was bewildered. And hurt. "Are you at home?"

She hesitated before saying, "If you're implying that you wish to come here, I will not see you."

"Oh, you'll see me. And you'll damn well tell me what the hell this is about. If I've done something to merit this treatment then you can say it to my face. I'll be there in ten minutes." He slammed the phone down and grabbed his jacket as he went out the door.

It didn't help that Koberg asked O'Brian to hold the elevator. "Heading home, O'Brian?"

He held the door. "No." *asshole*

As the elevator descended, Koberg said, "I suppose you heard about Congressman Ray?"

"Yeah, sounds like he walked into the wrong crowd."

"It's possible the crowd was tipped to the exit he would use." Koberg's smirk said he knew who tipped the crowd.

O'Brian forced himself to smile, the doors opened and he escaped, but his gut hurt and that was all Bradley. He feared this when he selected her. He was an idiot. He knew he was putting a temptation in front of himself that would lead him into stupid shit just like this. And his anger with himself grew. *I should have told her to get her ass over to the office immediately. If she wants to quit, fine. It sure as hell isn't up to me to go to her apartment to talk her out of it.*

As he pulled up to her apartment he thought, *I should turn around now, go back to the office and order her into my office.*

But he was already walking up the stairs to her unit. *I'm damn sure not going to let this get out of hand. I'll ask for her reasons, deal with them and get out. And I don't give a damn if she stays or goes.* By this time he was ringing the bell.

After he called, she changed into a blouse that buttoned at the neck, a jacket that managed to make her look flat-chested, and an ankle length skirt. She cleaned up the apartment a little, moving magazines and newspapers, and rehearsing. *Worthless bastard without an ounce of moral courage, a thug like the rest of the thugs running the DOJ, I hate him as much as I hate the damn job.*

She opened the door and stepped aside. She did not offer him a seat. "This visit serves no purpose."

"Can I have a drink? Please? It's been a rough day."

She saw anger in his eyes, but pain too. *He'll need a whiskey to hear what I've got to say.*

He followed her to the kitchen. She pushed the bottle of Jack Daniel's and a glass at him.

He got some ice cubes from the freezer. "Thank you, are you going to have one?"

"No."

He followed her to the dining room. She sat, straight-backed and glaring. He pulled a chair out and turned it to face her. He twirled the drink, took a sip and twirled it again. "Now. Why you're angry?"

She forced a hardness into her voice. "I'm not angry. I'm disappointed. You aren't who I thought you were."

"I disappoint myself, too." He took a sip. "What changed your mind?"

The memory brought the anger back and her voice was as withering and bitter as she could make it. "I could forgive your weakness, but you've given in to the bastards. You're part of their team now, one of the thugs."

She saw the question in his eyes.

"I heard you. I know about your plans with Koberg."

She watched for the collapse. He would beg. But, he didn't. He seemed relieved. She ploughed ahead. "You're helping the bastards destroy Carl Johnson. You sold yourself just to rise in the goddamn Bureau. You betrayed Johnson, and me, and yourself."

He smiled. "Is that what this is about?"

She felt her face redden—maybe she'd screwed up.

His pushed the glass away. His face grew serious. "Koberg was going to force Johnson to sign a confession to save his brother and his family. I convinced Koberg that if he did it would piss off most of my team, which would slow the investigation. I said they don't buy that he's the mole and they like him. I said we should take the time to build the case against Johnson, internally with task force agents, without forcing him to sign. When his guilt is proven, the team will accept that he's the mole. I suspect you overheard that conversation. It worked. Koberg agreed. Now I have Barnes and two other agents working to prove it was Johnson. But Barnes and I know they will never find evidence against Johnson. I bought Carl and his brother some time."

She looked into his eyes until she was sure there was no duplicity. And he looked back as if he dared her to find anything she didn't like. She looked down, embarrassed, relieved and pleased to be wrong.

"Carl and I hope the mole will strike again, in an obvious way, blowing another of Koberg's theories."

She shook her head. "I'm an idiot. Will you forgive me?"

He nodded slowly, the humor still in his mouth, his dark green eyes wide and penetrating. She liked his eyes. They ran down her face to her lips, and held there a moment. The humor returned to his face and his eyes came back to hers.

"While I'm leveling with you, can I also tell you how much I love the . . . armor you're wearing?"

"You bastard."

His smile grew for a moment, but then his face turned serious. "Kat, I . . ."

She leaped to her feet. "Stop now before you screw it up again." In two steps she stood above him, her heart racing at the risk she was taking. She ran both hands through his short black curly hair and said, "I want you, Mike."

More than an hour later his cell phone rang and she watched, smiling, as he searched among his clothes on the floor and eventually found it under his shorts, tie, shirt, jacket, pants and shoulder holster. He grinned as he answered, "O'Brian." He listened for some time without talking and then said, "I agree. Call Galvin; ask him to examine the body, and call me back when you know what happened." He threw the cell phone back on the pile of clothes and climbed back into bed, still smiling.

8:15 p.m.

Jacob expected to feel guilt, but felt reasonably good as he turned down the long gravel drive. The radio report of Marcus Ray had upset him, but even that news came with word that the House would vote tomorrow on the term limits amendment. And it was expected to pass. As he turned off the engine, Anna rushed out to meet him. She looked worried until she saw his smile, but then gave him a wonderful arms-around-the-neck kiss. He held her until Chris and Burton insisted on congratulating him.

"We've been monitoring the police radio." Burton said. "They still think the Congressman had a heart attack."

Chris clapped him on the shoulder as they walked to the house. "When they hear how it happened, it will help the House make the right decision tomorrow."

"You also fried the car's electronics," Burton said. "The engine quit at the same moment as Gruber's heart attack. They still haven't figured it out. They had the limousine towed."

Chris smirked. "I think your focus ring might have been a little larger than it needed to be."

Jacob laughed. "I think I can explain that."

He had been unaware of his hunger until he stepped into the kitchen. The aroma of the pot roast reminded him he had eaten nothing since breakfast. But he wanted to tell the story. As dinner was being served, he described his afternoon, including his failure to use the wig and beard and the dog's visit. All four laughed when he said, "I believe I could have done it without him."

Jacob enjoyed the dinner and excused himself to work on the evening's message.

Monday, June 9 message to the American people and to Congress

Late yesterday afternoon, Attorney General John Hammar announced the identities of three of our members—Anna Carpenter, Chris Carpenter and Thomas Stewart. In the next few days we expect more TLR members to be identified—perhaps several more. We expected and planned for it. The Carpenter and Stewart families were warned yesterday that the Department of Justice may torment them, as they did the families of Don Hayes and Cal Jackson, to force Chris, Anna and Thomas to surrender. They will not surrender and will not be captured. Neither will the other members of our team.

Last night ninety-one innocent individuals were arrested by the Department of Justice and are being held without charge and without the benefit of attorney in the Federal Detention Center. They are only guilty of having taken classes taught by Thomas Stewart or of having been his friend or associate.

The DOJ raids in the middle of the night are entirely within the clearly unconstitutional and unpatriotic Patriot Act passed by Congress and permitted by the Supreme Court.

With its convoluted rulings, the court has rewritten the Constitution, disregarding that document's plain language and installing a twisted, tortured logic supporting the growth of government and overthrow of individual liberty. The court and Congress call it a living Constitution to excuse the continuing torture of its plain meaning.

They have eviscerated the Bill of Rights, dividing them into 'fundamental' civil rights and 'non-fundamental' economic rights. The Constitution made no such distinction.

All rights are natural and fundamental. Property and economic rights allow individuals to provide for themselves and thereby maintain individual independence from government. But that is the point, isn't it? Our government cannot grow its power if we own and control our property. If we can determine, without government interference, who we will or won't sell to, what is a fair price, who we will hire or not, what organizations we will join or not join, then we control our lives and politicians cannot.

The property rights, contract rights and the rights of association critical to our livelihood and freedom have been stripped from us so that politicians can control us. Congress determines how much of our wealth they will allow us to keep, thereby making us as dependent on them as a child is dependent on his parent. Like a child, no area of our private lives is outside Congressional control—what we may or may not put into our bodies, our relationship with our doctor, our children's education, whether we may end our lives or not, what contracts we may or may not enter into, and with whom.

The list of laws, regulations and prohibitions is endless, and nothing, absolutely nothing, can regain us our liberty, except perhaps a Constitutional amendment forbidding professional politicians from serving in our Congress. And nothing, absolutely nothing will cause the professional politicians who rule us to willingly give us the right to vote on that amendment, except the fear of death. Power and brute force is their highest value; they will not give it up for any reason, but life itself.

A little more than an hour before this message was written, the nation learned that Representative Tom Gruber, the Co-chairman of the Armed Services Committee, died of a heart attack.

More precisely, he died as the result of a failed pacemaker. An autopsy will show the electronics in his pacemaker were fused as if by an electronic short circuit. We used a special weapon approved by Congressman Gruber and developed by the Department of Defense and the CIA for just such purposes.

We hope we soon will see an end to this. The House of Representatives will vote tomorrow on the term limits amendment. If they approve it, we will no longer target House members. We will continue to remove the senators who stand in the way of this amendment. It is our only hope for a citizen legislature and citizen legislators are the only hope for a return of our liberty.

The Term Limits Revolution

Monday, June 9
Blood of Tyrants

12:41 a.m.

The cell phone was not as loud as the phone in his apartment and this time it was no dream. She really was in his arms. And this time it was Barnes.

"You asked for Galvin's report on Gruber."

"And?"

"Like the message said, they fried the pacemaker."

O'Brian looked at the clock. "I've been asleep." *Well I am in bed.* "So tell me."

"The message said it was a special weapon the CIA and Pentagon developed to fry pacemakers. It fried the limousine's electronics, too. Makes you wonder what the hell they'll use next?"

"Maybe we should ask the CIA what else they've got."

"The other reason I called. Koberg has ordered a helicopter raid on the Carpenter ranch in 30 minutes. Thought you might want to watch. He'll run the show from the command center here."

"I'll be there in ten minutes."

O'Brian hoped the Carpenters were ready. Bradley was at the computer and read the message to him as he dressed. When she finished he asked, "How can they be ready for this shit?"

"They can't. But . . . maybe. So far they've done all right." They kissed and she said, "I'll follow in a couple of minutes."

Koberg greeted him like a comrade. "I'm pleased you are here, O'Brian. We are about to begin." Koberg took his seat at the command center desk. "Chris Carpenter will completely collapse when we have his wife and children in the detention center."

"I'm sure of it."

"Anna will too, of course, with her parents arrested for giving aid and comfort. I've arranged for official photos of the capture that will help them make up their minds."

O'Brian said, "Great idea." But he feared this too, would end in a disaster. He didn't want to watch.

Koberg pointed to the blinking display of the helicopter GPS position on the chart. "They're closing on the Carpenter ranch now." The Distance-To-Target indicated 1.93 nautical miles.

The sound of whining helicopter engines came over the speaker. Then, "Sir, we have the ranch in sight."

Koberg said. "Thank you, Conrad. Tell your pilot to set down as near to the house as physically possible. I want the Carpenters to enjoy the full audio-visual experience."

O'Brian guessed that Conrad was the SWAT team commander. He wished he hadn't come. Watching these bastards do their brutal work was not going to be fun.

"Yes, sir," Conrad said. "The pilot is turning on the landing camera and lights. You'll be able to see the area below us as we descend."

The army pilot cut into their conversation, "We have a problem." For a long moment, the only sound was the whine of helicopter engine and the rotating blades.

Conrad said, "There appears to be a crowd. It's a very large crowd, sir. Perhaps two or three hundred . . . adults and children . . . all . . . they're all around the farm. Tents and campers. Lots of trucks and cars." A moment later he said, "Sir, they're turning spotlights on us." They heard the pilot cursing as Conrad said, "It's hard to see the area."

Bradley nudged O'Brian. He turned to see her wink.

Koberg was no longer smiling. "Get over them and down close so we can see."

The pilot said, "Yes, sir, but I've got to make sure we stay above power line height until we see where we can put down." The helicopter dropped lower, but it was still difficult to see.

Conrad said, "I can make out two cars from the county Sheriff. And there's a school bus."

O'Brian's anxiety was dropping fast—maybe the Carpenters were prepared. Koberg was obviously anxious and angry. "Land that helicopter. Crowd or no crowd, I want the Carpenters captured immediately."

"Sir there appears to be a helicopter landing pad less than a hundred yards away. No crowd on it."

"Perfect. Carpenter was a helicopter pilot in Viet Nam. Land there."

"Yes, sir."

The sound of the engine changed pitch as the helicopter moved to the landing pad and began its descent. Conrad came on the line. "Sir, how do we handle the crowd?"

"To hell with the crowd. You represent the Department of Justice. Use that authority. Charge through them, take the Carpenters, bring them, no drag them, back to the helicopter and return to your base. Do not let anyone slow you down."

"Sir, some appear to be armed. Permission to fire, if fired upon?"

"Yes of course. But, do not initiate fire."

O'Brian was anxious again. The helicopter was ten feet above the large X marking the landing pad. The crowd surrounded it. Conrad wore a camera on his head that captured the action within the enormous military helicopter. His men could be seen lined up at the doors and he could be heard pumping them up. He also warned them not to shoot unless they were fired upon. The doors on both sides were open. The men stood ready to leap out and the helicopter began to settle down. As the skids touched, Conrad yelled, "Go, go, go!" and three men jumped in rapid succession from either side before he screamed "Stop. God dammit! . . . God dammit, Sir . . . God dammit, this is a pond." The men who had jumped were standing in brown-green water up to their crotches.

The engines had died. The large X had disappeared below the surface. The SWAT team stopped jumping after half were in. The surface of the landing pad had been a taut black plastic sheet resting on the shallow pond. The water was almost up to the helicopter deck. "It's shit-water, sir," someone yelled at Conrad, "it's a damned waste detention pond."

Koberg could not see anything. The view on his monitor jerked wildly from the men in the pond on one side, to the officers waiting to jump, to the pilot and to the men standing in the water on the other side, jerking badly as Conrad looked in several directions. Koberg was livid, almost ill from the jerking camera and momentarily voiceless.

Conrad pleaded. "Sir?"

"Go get the damn Carpenters and drag them back." Koberg spelled it out. "Through . . . that . . . shit-water."

Shouting into a mike does not improve the clarity at the other end. But apparently Conrad got the idea. The men jumped into the water and waded toward the crowd.

Conrad was the last to enter the water and he was therefore the last to wade to the pond edge, but his head mounted camera covered the advance of his men. As they arrived and walked up the pond side the crowd reached out to help. They seemed genuinely sympathetic.

O'Brian thought, *these people have been properly coached.* The sympathy had drained the adrenalin from the SWAT team. Koberg was yelling, "Get the damn Carpenters." into Conrad's left ear. "Don't let them stop you!"

But at the same time Koberg screamed directions at Conrad, a tall, leather-faced, tough-looking, Stetson-wearing local with a gold badge and a long barreled pistol low on his hip stepped in front of Conrad for a handshake. And he had Conrad's attention. "I'm Sheriff Doss Kutch. I'm guessin you boys're here for the Carpenters."

Conrad said, "Yes, where are they?"

"Well now, they're my guests down at the County jail. You'll want to have a look around, maybe, but I do wish you'd a called first." He turned to introduce the man at his right. "This here's Senator Penny if you want to ask about jurisdiction, and it happens the Carpenters' attorney is here too, if you need to speak to him."

Conrad cupped his hands to the mike and earpiece, "Sir?" His voice pleaded.

Koberg had heard, but his voice failed to produce anything beyond a strangled breath, his mouth twisting and working in a speechless fury.

Sheriff Kutch continued. "You boys probly wanna clean up. Step over to the barn there and feel free to use the hose." O'Brian noticed someone in the crowd panning the SWAT team with a large handheld video camera. Koberg saw it, too, and screamed at Conrad to, "Confiscate that camera!" The monitor immediately went dead. O'Brian guessed the scream hurt Conrad's ears and he unplugged his camera and radio.

Bradley enjoyed Koberg's misery, but she made the mistake of grinning when Koberg's face was turned toward the dead monitor. O'Brian saw Koberg's ears and neck go a deeper shade of red as he glared at her reflection.

10:35 a.m.
The hot sun heated the land, pulling a breeze—a cooling breeze—in off the water. It was more than Jacob could pass up. After a late breakfast he and Burton found four lawn chairs and carried them onto the dock. The smell of the seawater, the sound of the small wind-built waves lapping the piling and the feel of the sun on Jacob's skin helped to relieve the tension. He was very concerned about Anna's target for this evening, and Chris's too, of course, but he knew Anna was worried and Chris wasn't.

Burton smiled to see Jacob relaxed, his eyes closed. The faint sound of Chris and Anna, talking to their family in Oklahoma, carried out to the dock. A laugh from time to time meant things must be going okay on the Carpenter ranch, but his mind kept returning to the need for some dramatic action, something that would bring the public overwhelmingly to the TLR side and soon. The Department of Justice was getting too close.

When the idea occurred he knew it would work. "The News Hour."

Jacob's eyes snapped opened and Burton continued, "Anna can make it work. You offer to be on the PBS show. Voice only. He'll cancel the planned evening show, to get you on. The issue is too important not to."

Jacob seemed skeptical. "Will the Department of Justice allow it?"

"They'll hate the idea. But they'll probably think they'll be able to set up a trace that will catch you."

"They won't just let me talk. That would just be giving us a forum."

"They'll want someone to debate you, someone that can score points for their side."

Jacob glanced at a passing power-boat. "I hate TV debates. But it would allow the public the chance to compare both sides . . . it's a good idea, if Anna can keep our location secure."

The kitchen door slammed behind them as Chris and Anna came laughing from the house. Chris described the arrival of the SWAT team at the Carpenter ranch, as he came. In what seemed to Burton to be a fully recovered Oklahoma accent, Chris told of the helicopter, the detention pond and Sheriff Kutch—another friend of his dad.

Anna added details Chris forgot to include. "And Sheriff Kutch looked them straight in the eye and told them the big X on the plastic was a target for a cow-pie throwing contest."

Everyone enjoyed the story. Chris added, "And after they were offered barbeque, that they didn't accept, Doss had a deputy drive them back to the base in a school bus."

Burton loved that so many people had come to the Carpenter farm to protect them. "Will the local paper carry an article?"

Chris said, "Oh, hell yes. It'll be on the front page of the evening paper. The Oklahoma City TV stations have been alerted and want to interview Dad, Sheriff Kutch and Senator Penny, at the County jail, of course. That'll be great."

Anna added, "The Department of Justice won't come after them again." She said it with conviction but looked eagerly to see if the others agreed.

Jacob nodded. "Karen and the children should be in that interview."

"Max Carter suggested the same thing."

"I hope we aren't missing anything," Chris said. "The longer this goes on the more dangerous it is. The DOJ can always get lucky."

Anna asked, "Is there a way to hurry this thing along?"

Jacob nodded at Burton who said, "Maybe. If Jacob could be on the Tom Paulson PBS News Hour—just his voice—every adult in the nation would be watching. PBS would jump at the chance."

Chris and Anna considered the idea before speaking. Chris said, "The Department of Justice would never allow it."

"They don't want our ideas before the public, but they also want to catch us," Burton said. "They might think, with a few hours preparation, they could track Jacob's sending location while he was on the air. And nail him while the program was running."

"Eventually the Department of Justice will catch us," Anna said. "We need to do something that will make the Senate move."

Chris paced the dock as he worried the problem out loud. "Hammar would imagine the capture occurring on TV, in real time, with the Department of Justice swooping in to make the dramatic capture."

"While the nation watched and listened," Anna said. "His big opportunity, his road to the presidency beginning tonight."

Burton asked Anna, "Can you prevent them from tracking us? They'll have several hours to get ready."

"I think so, unless they've come up with some new technology in the last few weeks. Let me work on it."

Burton was pleased they liked his idea. "We must insist that Jacob have at least ten minutes to make his points, that he's able to talk without interruption, that only one other guest appears with him and each side gets equal time."

After sending the message to PBS Anna searched the internet for recent news. Jacob made notes of issues he wanted to cover, if Paulson agreed to the interview. He wondered who his opposition would be. PBS would find someone tough. They were subsidized by the federal government and could be relied on to present the more-government solution to any issue. They would also sell broadcast rights to the nation's other TV and radio stations. Burton and Chris remained on the dock, talking, worrying, waiting for the response, although they knew it would be a matter of hours.

When Chris's cell phone rang, everyone jumped. It was Mark, of course. They listened to the short one-sided conversation, then Chris told them what he had learned. "Yesterday, Congressional leadership met with the DOJ and O'Brian. O'Brian made a tape. Bradley—Mark's former lady friend—listened to it and told Mark. The gist of it is, the

House will approve the amendment today. The senators remaining on our list will be moved to housing on Andrews Air Force Base. The Marines will provide the senators with helicopters for the commute between the Capitol and Andrews. That announcement will be made late today."

"That's it then," Burton said. "We can't get at them in there." He looked at Chris, "Can we?"

Anna said, "What if we just announce we will wait them out."

"We can't wait," Chris said. "With enough time they'll find us. I have to get to them, on the base."

"If you're caught," Anna said, "we failed. We should consider other options including doing nothing."

Jacob said, "And you'll be the person they'll be looking for. It would be easier for me to get in. My face has changed enough they won't recognize me."

Burton was on the edge of his chair. "They haven't even guessed my identity yet."

"I'm the only one here with a military background." Chris said. "Any of you'd be obvious to military security as soon as you opened your mouth. I told Mark we would talk about it and I would call him back." He leaned forward, thinking. "I have an idea that he could help with. I can get inside, unnoticed, and I know how to use the equipment." He paused before saying, "And I'll be taking out more than one senator."

Everyone considered the implications. Jacob said, "I think it might encourage the Senate to pass the amendment."

Burton added, "It will if innocent people aren't hurt."

Chris walked to the end of the dock to call Mark. He would need help, if Mark was willing.

It was also time for Jacob to call PBS for their answer. Anna set up the call and put Jacob through.

Tom Paulson took the call. PBS had agreed to the TLR terms. "We have several candidates willing to present the opposing view, Professor. We will announce the person on our website within the next hour."

"Is this the phone number we should call tonight?"

Paulson said, "Yes, however we need you to call a few minutes before the show begins, so that our technicians can set up the sound equipment to make your voice sound natural."

Jacob wasn't buying it. "At precisely what time will you begin the interview?"

Paulson hesitated before answering. "At 7:03 and 20 seconds."

"Is there anything else you need to tell me?"

"No. I look forward to the interview, Professor Stewart."

"I will try to make it interesting."

Anna disconnected. Chris asked. "They agreed, then?"

"Yes. Jacob is on. So what happened with your call?"

"Mark will meet me with the equipment. I need to move fast before they increase security at that base."

12:33 p.m.

O'Brian turned onto 9th Avenue and cruised slowly across the mall watching the crowd on either side and reading the signs. He guessed that his union dues were paying for some of the signs attacking term limits and for the hired day laborers who carried them. He was pissed off as he pulled into the garage, but then forgot it as he began to look forward to seeing Bradley.

She smiled as he walked past. He said hi to Rita as he disappeared into his office.

Bradley followed him in to his office and said, "Good morning," before shutting the door.

He took her in his arms as soon as the door closed, his right hand behind her neck pulling her mouth tight to his. Before things went too far she pushed away. "Hold that thought . . . until tonight."

He grinned and headed to his desk as she asked, "So what does Koberg want to see us about?"

"No idea. Maybe the Johnson investigation."

"Why would he care about Johnson now? We've identified . . ."

Koberg tapped on O'Brian's door and immediately came in. He seemed cheerful and inquired about their health—as if he really gave a shit—and said he had spoken with Attorney General Hammar this morning. The House would definitely approve the term limits amendment, forcing the TLR to choose from fewer, better protected targets. Senators would be moved into officer housing at Andrews Air Force Base, making it nearly impossible for the TLR to get to them.

O'Brian and Bradley knew that. Koberg discussed the growing protesters on the mall and in the nation and asked them for their opinions. He was certain that it would all fizzle out when the TLR was shown to be impotent against the Senate.

They exchanged glances. Both waited for the real purpose of this meeting. It had to be coming. He asked for updates on the Carl Johnson investigations, took issue with every statement and asked too many questions about insignificant details. At 1:15 he checked his watch, thanked them, and left—still cheerful. Nothing had been accomplished.

O'Brian shook his head; Bradley asked, "What was that all about?"

"I don't know, but I'm worried."

Her cell phone rang and she said "Oh, hi Mark, hold on." She stood and said. "I better take this at my desk."

He was almost to the door. "Take it in here. I need to check on something." She said nothing until the door was closed. That bothered him. He could just make out a muffled, "How are you?" That sounded as if she really cared.

He walked past Koberg's office, as if on his way to the TV lounge. Koberg's door was open and he was alone. O'Brian spent a couple of minutes in the lounge watching the floor debate in the House. He purchased a Coke and headed back in time to see two agents enter Koberg's office. They were not part of O'Brian's team.

He went back to his office, knocked and waited until he heard her say, "Come in."

She closed the cell phone. "Why didn't you just come in?"

"I didn't want to interrupt."

"The guy that called is an old friend. He's an agent at Quantico."

"It's none of my business." But it came out wrong, as if he were pissed at her. His anger was with himself.

"What are you hot about?"

"I'm not hot." His eyes followed her out. *I'm stupid*

O'Brian took an hour to visit Carl Johnson and his brother Jamie, partly to get his mind off Bradley, but also to keep their spirits up and to appear to be doing something with regard to that investigation. Then, on his way back to the office, he stopped for a Reuben in the J. Edgar Hoover deli. He could hardly believe what the CNN newscaster was saying. Tonight, the TLR terrorist, Professor T. J. Stewart, would be appearing on the Tom Paulson News Hour. The implications of Stewart appearing on Tom Paulson were obvious. The Department of Justice must have approved, meaning Hammar thought Stewart could be tracked. Why hadn't he been told?

As the elevator doors opened, he heard Koberg in the assembly area, his voice pitched higher and louder than normal, probably directing the agents who would be coordinating with NSA electronic search, the OITC and the FBI cyber-crime investigation staff. O'Brian hadn't been invited, though some of his agents were in there. He took his sandwich to his office. *What the hell was going on?*

1:41 p.m.
Anna leaped to her feet when she saw the announcement. The House had approved the term limits amendment. The others were on the dock listening to the radio. They began yelling at the same moment she burst from the house to tell them. She leaped on Chris who was first in line. "They did it! We did it!"

"One down, one to go," Chris said.

Tears filled Burton's eyes. Jacob's glowed through tears, too, as he pounded Burton's back. "We are half way, Burton. Half way."

Chris grinned broadly, but Anna saw his face go from elation to worry in the next few seconds. "I need to get onto that base fast, before the Secret Service sets up extra precautions. Mark will help with the equipment."

Anna said, "You'll be alone in there."

Jacob said. "Chris has the skills to pull it off, to think on his feet, and make last minute changes. He's our best."

Anna said, "Having the skill shouldn't mean that he has to take all the chances."

Chris interrupted. "This is my call, and I am the best for this job." He looked at Anna. "It's not like anyone is avoiding risk by not going. If I'm caught it won't be long before everyone is. They know how to make me talk."

He gave himself coal black hair, silver temples and blue eyes with the mustache to match the photo ID of Air-Force Captain Matt Dunning.

Anna was amazed. "I barely recognize you . . . and I know you're in there."

He checked his watch. "I'll call to let you know what's happening. I may not be back until very late."

Chris had been on Andrews AFB many times; he knew where the officer's quarters were, but not which units the senators might be using. The important thing now was to get on the base before the new security procedures made it impossible.

Mark had already agreed to get the weapon for Chris, but he had worried. "We have hundreds in the armory, but can I get it without being seen? It won't take a damn genius to figure out the relationship if the TLR uses one later that day."

"Put it in your SUV. If you think someone might have seen you, call me. I'll do it some other way."

They arranged to meet at a shopping mall, in the normally empty overflow section of the parking lot. No one would notice the exchange of a box from one car to another.

It took an hour and 20 minutes to get to Andrews. The 2003 white Ford Taurus Station-wagon had a SAM FOX decal on the bumper. SAM FOX indicated Special Air Mission–Foreign, indicating he was a member of the team providing worldwide air service for the nation's leaders. A little dirt had helped the decal appear to have been there awhile. He found a U-Haul lot not far from the base and picked up several empty boxes, some packing tape and a broad felt marker. He visited a Salvation Army resale store and bought $200 worth of miscellaneous clothes, pots and pans and dishes. He labeled the boxes and headed for the base.

He turned onto Patrick Avenue, the north entrance, unworried about the lack of a uniform—most officers entered and left the base wearing only civilian clothes. He drove up fast and braked hard at the Force Protector gate, handing his phony base pass and ID to the security guard. It was one of hundreds of phony IDs, permits and passes he had produced at the CIA over the last two years—just in case. The Corporal at the gate—his name tag said Schaeffer—seemed to be looking at him quizzically. He looked through the windows at the boxes in back. Chris worried that he might know all the pilots that came through the gate. "Corporal Schaeffer, did my wife come through here in the last thirty minutes? She's a redhead and . . . you would have noticed."

The corporal smiled. "No, sir. She has not."

Chris banged the wheel. "Goddamn it, goddamn it." Schaeffer handed the ID back and Chris said, "Thank you, Corporal." Schaeffer turned and walked back toward the car that had just arrived.

Once inside, Chris drove immediately to the Flyway Inn. They had a bar where he might pick up information. It took a very few minutes to discover that several nearby duplexes normally used by officers on short-term assignment at the base were being vacated to make room for someone important.

Except for the colors, the units were identical. There were a total of forty units accessible from Parker Street with more located around the corner on Jasper.

He parked at the intersection and waited for his opportunity. A plain young woman drove past him and pulled into the carport of one of the units. She was inside before he could park. When she opened the door he said, "Sorry to bother you. I'm Captain Matt Dunning. My wife

Karen is coming out to join me and we've been offered one of these units, when one becomes available. She's kind of picky. I'm just wondering if the units are okay. Do you have any problems?"

"Well I guess I could let you have a look at ours." Her southern accent was even thicker than Karen's.

"Oh, God no. I couldn't come in. But maybe you could just tell me about them."

"Oh they're just real nice and furnished. I mean compared to what you'd get off base, for anything reasonable. There's two bedrooms, one bathroom, dining room is sort of in the living room, but it's real nice for the price. I'm Betty Anne by the way, Betty Anne Grant. My husband Bill is a Captain, too. Anyway I bet your wife would like to live in one of these, but it's real hard getting a unit. There's quite a waiting list, you know."

"Yeah that's what I heard. But I hear there are some big shots just staying here temporarily and they'll be moving out soon."

"Guess we aren't supposed to know yet, but its some senators hiding from those terrorists. They actually moved some officers out to make room for them. Four are staying in that light brown unit down at the corner."

He grinned. "Great. Maybe we can have the same unit the senators have. I know my wife would like that. She could brag to her friends that she slept in the same bed as a famous senator. Oh that reminds me—which side are the bedrooms on? My wife insists on an east window where the sun can wake her."

"Okay, well, see how that unit faces the street? That means they'll have two bedrooms on the east side. The senators on the other side have west facing windows."

He nodded as he looked at the units. "Maybe we'll get lucky."

"We seen their stuff arrive in a truck earlier. Two senators were in there for a few minutes. I think they're supposed to come back all t'gether early every evenin'. They'll have a limousine runnin' back and forth to the landing area, but they'll use a helicopter to the Capitol. They must be real scared—not that I blame 'em."

"Isn't that terrible?"

"It's just real sad. But those terrorists will be caught; I'm sure of that."

"Me, too. Thank you for your help, Betty Anne. If you wouldn't mind, I may bring my wife by to meet you. I know she'll be nervous moving in here. We haven't been married long and she'll appreciate your advice."

"Of course. I'd be glad to help."

He drove past the senators' duplex to the end of the block and then turned right, stopped and called Mark as he surveyed the area. Mark had the RPG in his SUV and had just left Quantico.

As he drove out of the base, Chris stopped at the gate long enough to apologize to Corporal Schaeffer for his outburst and to make certain he would be remembered.

A Radio Shack in the shopping center just outside the base provided some electrical connector wires with alligator clips and a kitchen timer. He purchased a plastic can at a hardware store, half filled it with gas at a service station and scouted out a quiet place to wait for Mark.

Mark called a few minutes later and Chris talked him over to the empty corner of the lot where he waited. "Good disguise," Mark said. "Especially that sign on the back of your car. I would have driven right past you."

"The disguise got me on the base. The sign has another purpose. Thanks for bringing this thing."

"Yeah, well, help me make a small modification so I'll sleep tonight." He crawled into the back of the Pathfinder and opened the metal box. The launcher was inside with an RPG beside it. He opened a toolbox and removed a battery-operated Dremel tool.

"Jesus! I'm embarrassed I didn't think of that."

"You would have when you opened the box." It took a few seconds to remove the serial numbers from the weapon and the firing cradle and wipe away any fingerprints. He re-closed the launcher box and passed it to Chris.

Chris carried it to his station wagon and asked Mark for advice about the remote fire arrangement he had worked out.

Mark thought the technique would work. "And if it does the Senate will approve your amendment tomorrow. I hear they're talkin tough, but wetting their pants."

Chris stepped back and closed the door. "I hope to take out at least two of the bastards tonight."

Mark took off the plastic gloves and shook his hand. "Thanks, Chris. And thank the others for me."

Chris got on Suitland headed east to the base, but stopped at Hansen Park. There were several parking areas. He found one that was empty to practice sighting the weapon and repack the boxes. He laid the weapon inside a box adjusting the approximate aim through the back car door by packing clothes and utensils around and under the box. He tore a small hole in the cardboard box allowing the weapon to be aimed using its laser sight. But the rocket propelled grenade would have to be fired through a small hole in the door. An open door would attract suspicion. He used his drill and then the Saws-all to cut a 12" diameter opening in the rear door. With the binoculars he could see the laser beam all the way to the target. He aimed at the middle of a tree about 100 yards away, closed the box and drew a line on the top of the box that also pointed at the tree.

The laser sight was pointed too high. He opened the box and adjusted the cradle elevation screw until the laser pointed six feet up from the bottom of the tree—a level line, he thought. The airbase was dead flat, his target would also be about level with his car. He covered the hole in the door with the magnetic sign praising Senator Harlowe, cut a 1/2" diameter hole in the sign aligned for the laser to sight through, moved the car one space over and re-aimed the box. From the time he stopped the car until the time the box was on target had taken two minutes—too long, but it would have to do.

Then he removed the interior lights, put the plastic gas can in the box labeled Nicolo and set it behind the RPG launcher. He set the loaded weapon into the cradle and a shallow box of panties and bras in the box on top of the weapon. If the guards looked below that he was dead meat. He had an automatic pistol and extra clips under the car seat, but he couldn't imagine a situation where he would use it.

He waited on the approach road and then timed his arrival at the Force Protector gate so that he was in front of two other cars.

As the security shack came into view his heart began pounding. Extra security and they looked like Secret Service. Too late to turn around; he would try to bluff his way through, but he knew his luck had run out. He would have to use the pistol. He could not be taken alive.

As he stopped he was approached by three men in plain clothes. He grabbed the ID lying in the passenger seat, cursing himself for not having it ready. No one left it lying in an open seat. He passed it to the big suit filling his window and Corporal Schaeffer stepped around him. "Afternoon, Captain. I think that might have been your wife that came through about twenty minutes ago."

The Secret Service guys backed off as soon as they heard the exchange. Chris did not have to fake relief. "Oh damn, thank you, Corporal."

Corporal Schaeffer looked concerned. "She was with someone else."

Chris just looked at the Corporal a moment, trying to look angry. He faced forward and drove in.

3:11 p.m.

O'Brian sat next to Bradley. She glanced up from the monitor with no emotion whatsoever—a clear signal she was still pissed. There was no one near so he took the chance. "Forgive me?"

She glowered, which was actually hopeful. But Koberg walked toward them

O'Brian said, "Good afternoon, sir. How are things shaping up for this evening?"

Koberg's smile seemed menacing. "We have on-site technicians in all of the cable and wireless companies they might possibly use. Every internet broadcast made to foreign anonymous remailers will be tracked to its source. Helicopters will cover an area within a fifty mile radius of the Capitol. No point within that area will be farther than two minutes from a SWAT team." He seemed exultant with pleasure and anger. "The TLR will be in hell before Stewart can say hello."

Bradley said, "That's great news, sir."

O'Brian agreed.

"A few minutes before seven, when the TLR makes contact with PBS, the NSA will need a very few minutes to identify them. Paulson's audience will hear a more appropriate message from Senator Harlowe while Stewart waits to be heard. And long before we have to hear Professor Stewart whining about lost liberty, he will hear my helicopter."

3:12 p.m.

Anna knew many of the foreign internet anonymous remailers were compromised—probably many more in the last few hours. She also knew that NSA hired the best and brightest techies that money could buy. She had worked with them. By now they might have created programs to identify her sending location, even when sending through the remailers. But to do that, they would need direct access into the computers of the telecom and wireless companies. It was illegal, but it wasn't as if the companies could refuse.

She sipped coffee while looking through the window across the cove. She thought a slave computer might work. *If the Department of Justice helicopters came swooping down on a slave, we could see them coming and shut down.*

A directional infrared beam could broadcast Jacob's voice from her computer to a special directional receiver hooked to a laptop sitting on the other side of Tilghman Cove. The laptop could broadcast to a local wireless net. There were several expensive homes close above the beach. Someone over there must have cable access and a wireless local area net. She could break into their net and use their cable access to send to a foreign anonymous remailer. Communications would be one-way. We have the TV here. We can hear what is being said on the television and respond over the infrared-laptop-slave-anonymous remailer. If the NSA techies ping back and discover the broadcasting computer, they will send helicopters to the slave. We will see them and shut down before they can find the link back to us.

She pulled Burton outside to explain it to him, without bothering Jacob. Burton liked it, but worried about the logistics. "You can't be on both sides and I can't operate a laptop well enough to break into a local wireless net. Won't you have to be over there to get it hooked up? Is there time?"

She considered the logistics a moment. "We take two cars, drive around the inlet and down to that dock." She pointed to it. "It's within sight and radio range. If I can't get into a local area network from the beach area we'll need to leave a car. I can't be sure of anything until we get over there."

Burton thought he saw a flaw. "If the DOJ sends helicopters in, they'll find the antennae pointing at this house." He thought of a solution before he finished naming the problem. "However, we can use one of Chris's radio activated bombs to blow it up from here."

It was complicated, but worth a try and nothing else was as safe. She liked the idea of seeing the bad guys coming, Jacob signing off and watching the antennae blowup before the helicopter touched down. "Let's do it. I have the equipment if you'll help me put it together."

It was nearly four when she was ready. They drove up the bay to Centreville in two cars and then back down the bay on the other side winding downhill on Quaker Road toward the beach. They passed a number of nice homes—homes likely to have multiple computers and a wireless home net. Quaker Road ended at the dock but it was rotted through and blocked. A gravel side road above the beach provided a place to park, but they had to walk down through the trees toward the beach to find a clear view of their house. It was up the bay less than half a mile. Unfortunately, Anna's laptop was unable to detect any wireless nets in the area.

While Burton set up the directional antennae and laptop between the beach and the gravel road, Anna would search for a nearby wireless net within its range. She backed her car around, pointed it up Quaker Road, made sure she had a good wireless connection with Burton's laptop and slowly drove up the hill while the antennae on her laptop searched for a second network. Three hundred yards up the hill, after passing the first home, she found two wireless networks.

She was confident she could get in, but how long would it take? A good firewall might complicate the job; it would take too long. Her plan was looking crazier all the time and part of her brain struggled for a better solution. Time was critical.

Her first attempt was blocked by a firewall. She played with it a moment and went to the next one. It also had a firewall, but it was a standard firewall she recognized. She easily passed through, grinning as she told Burton over the cell phone, "We're in. I see it and your computer at the same time. I'm linking up."

She was keying commands as she talked. "Out here in the woods they probably think they don't need to protect their networks."

"Until now," Burton said.

That tweaked her conscience. "I don't want to get these people hurt."

"They won't be. I doubt if the NSA will discover your transmission. Is it land line or a cable system?"

"Cable. Fast, too. I'm coming down." She walked the laptop back into the woods, confirmed the signals were still good and covered it with some brush. She was elated; they could leave with both cars. She drove back down to where Burton waited. He had placed the tube-bomb underneath the directional infrared receiver. It aimed at the house and linked to the antennae there. The laptop was beside it. She approved and he covered them with a leafy branch that did not obstruct the line to the house.

"I hope no one stumbles onto it," she said.

"That may be a problem." He pointed down the road. "I caught a glimpse of some kids while you were up above. I think they are watching us now."

"Did they see us cover the laptop and directional antennae?"

"Maybe . . . Probably. I think I better stay until they get bored and forget us."

She was annoyed and frustrated, but they were out of time. "Okay. But . . ."

He smiled as he interrupted, "I'll leave as soon as I can. I won't wait for the helicopters."

"Once the program starts, you leave!"

"I will. You need to get back to the house and get things ready."

She kissed his cheek but her face was stern. "Promise you'll leave when the program starts."

"I will, don't worry."

Jacob worried. "What if the helicopters show up faster than we expect? He may not get out." When he heard of the children he wanted to call off the broadcast.

"Burton wants this broadcast so much, Jacob. He believes it's critical. This will let the public hear the human side of our arguments. It may make the difference between success and failure. Anyway, it's too late. We are . . ." She looked at the clock. "Oh, my God. You're on in twenty minutes." She began checking her connections.

6:13 p.m.
When O'Brian entered the CenCom area, the two goons who visited Koberg earlier were talking to him. One grinned as he glanced across the room at O'Brian. Koberg dismissed them as he used his cell phone. Only after that call did he turn to look, without emotion, at O'Brian.

The cold chill up his back told him he was in trouble, but he decided he was letting his imagination get away with him. Koberg had other things on his mind. A SWAT team leader approached Koberg and O'Brian decided that's who he had called. Koberg would be going with one of the SWAT teams; he not only wanted to be in on the kill, he wanted every possible credit for their elimination. He was impeccably dressed.

O'Brian didn't hear the officer's question, but he easily heard Koberg. "No. There will be no capture. We need a clean end to this."

A department photographer floated around in the background taking photos of Koberg in the communication center. O'Brian sat at a monitor within earshot. He heard the NSA coordinator tell Koberg, "Yes, sir, we have personnel at all telecom internet servers and cable companies. The cell and landline telephone companies are tied into our system. Our foreign operations desk says we have substantial control of the remailers, ninety-five percent of them anyway. Either they allowed us to link to their systems or for one reason or another they are not operating." He seemed embarrassed with that statement, but went on. "When Stewart begins talking, we will probably know the geographic location of the sending computer within three or four minutes. Ten minutes at the outside."

Koberg seemed pleased but still cautious. "I'll contact you after we're airborne." He waved for the photographer to follow him as he walked smiling to the elevator. But he stopped to look at Bradley and O'Brian. She said, "Good hunting."

Koberg's laugh shook them both.

6:40 p.m.
Senator Morgan Harlowe looked across the horseshoe shaped studio desk at Paulson. "It's a pleasure to be with you again, Tom."

"Anything we can do to help, Senator. We value our relationship." Paulson said.

"Good. Introduce Stewart, but then introduce me and ask me a question that will allow me to expand. I will speak until he hears the helicopters."

"He's improved our ratings for tonight. I'll have to let him say a few words to satisfy the audience. His capture should excite them and improve our ratings farther."

Harlowe laughed. "And mine." A makeup artist began to touch up his glossy forehead.

"Stewart will want to talk about term limits."

"He wants term limits because he sees it leading to libertarian government. He imagines citizen-legislators would limit government and restore liberty. He's wrong. Most Americans have no idea what liberty would really mean. We must help them see. We must first get Stewart to admit complete individual liberty is his real purpose. Then make him admit what that would mean to all those people who have become dependent on the compassionate programs and agencies he would eliminate. We must help your viewers see that liberty will mean a loss of their government programs."

Paulson checked the digital clock, a little more than five minutes to airtime. "I think I can help with that."

"He and I have butted heads before. He's incredibly naïve. Americans love the idea of liberty. And they might want it for themselves, but they hate the thought of their nutty neighbor being free to make stupid decisions. And they fear the responsibility that comes with liberty. If you and I get Stewart to admit he wants to take away their favorite programs, they will abandon him."

The set director made some lighting changes—Harlowe's white mane caused some glare for the cameras. Paulson was listening to his director.

Harlowe waited until he had Paulson's attention again. "Ask the question, 'Aren't we a society? Must everyone agree to everything society does?'"

Paulson smiled. "That's where he's weak. We can't let everybody just make up their own minds about whether to pay taxes or not, about whether we go to war, or help the elderly."

"Thank you, Tom. I knew we could count on you. PBS has always been a friend to good government. It's one of the reasons we support you."

6:41 p.m.
Anna composed an email from T J Stewart to Paulson. *Mr. Paulson, I will make contact after you announce that you are prepared to begin the interview. There will be an interval of no more than ten seconds before you will hear my voice and be able to converse with me. I will hear your voice via our television. After initial contact, my responses to your questions will be without delay.*
T.J. Stewart

She used a cell phone to send the message in a microburst, then immediately turned the cell phone off to prevent the NSA from discovering their location. At one minute before airtime, she completed her circuit from her laptop to the house system and from there to a Bolivian anonymous remailer. She thought it was ironic that the people who owned the computer on the other side of the bay were probably gathered in front of their TV, waiting to hear the voice of the TLR, a voice broadcast to the nation through their desktop computer.

Paulson began the program introduction, then announced that the news summary, instead of beginning the program, would occur at the end. Anna hugged Jacob. He seemed only a little nervous. They still didn't know who would be presenting the other side.

Paulson said, "Tonight we will be discussing the term limits amendment, the TLR and the assassination of congressional leaders. I will be interviewing Professor T. J. Stewart, spokesman for the Term Limits Revolution, by telephone. Here in the studio, to present an alternate view, I have Senator Morgan Harlowe, Senate Majority Leader."

6:42 p.m.
Seconds after Koberg's helicopter and five others were airborne, the GPS position signals of each began dispersing from a single point in the center of the screen map to their designated high hover positions over and around the Capitol. They were joined by thirty others. At an altitude of 10,000 feet the TLR would be less likely to notice them. Each could be on top of any site within its part of the grid, in no more

than two minutes. If the terrain required, the SWAT teams could drop from ropes.

At 6:47 p.m., O'Brian heard Koberg contact the communications director. The television was tuned to the PBS channel, the sound muted until the TLR interviews actually began. O'Brian wandered into the TV lounge where many of the JTTF agents were watching CNN. Like other stations, CNN would be carrying a patch of the Paulson interview. But now the reporter on the mall was describing the movement of people from the mall over the last few minutes, while the panning camera revealed the Capitol Mall, littered with trash, but almost empty of people. "Most have returned to their homes or hotel rooms," the reporter said, "or wherever they can find space to watch Tom Paulson's interview with Professor Stewart."

O'Brian walked back into the Communications Center where Bradley sat at a monitor and worried about Koberg. They heard the CenCom director patch the NSA coordinator through to Koberg's helicopter, "We have several connections to foreign remailers, sir. None seems quite right. At least not yet, but three calls have just been placed. One could be it."

Koberg asked over the racket of the helicopter, "When will you know?"

"When the caller begins speaking to PBS, sir. Two more minutes. Even if his voice is not in the clear, we will still be able to identify him by comparing voice patterns coming from Stewart's voice with the different data transmission patterns going into the remailers."

A few seconds later the sound came up as Paulson began introducing the program. A minute later CenCom said, "We have it, sir. The other transmissions to remailers dropped off. It has to be the third transmission."

Koberg asked, "Where is it coming from?"

"We are tracking it now."

"Work fast. I want Stewart before he has a chance to say anything meaningful."

"Yes, sir. It won't take long. We need to identify the trunk line, the cable branch and then the house it's coming from. A matter of minutes."

The News Hour was playing on a large screen. Paulson introduced Professor Stewart first and then Senator Harlowe before he said, "Good evening, Professor Stewart. I understand you know Senator Harlowe?"

There was a short delay before Jacob said, "Good evening, Tom, Senator Harlowe."

Harlowe said, "Professor Stewart," and Paulson said, "I admit to you both and to our viewers, I am nervous about this particular broadcast. It certainly represents a first of some sort. But let's get started. I have promised to allow each of you ten minutes to make your points. I will begin by asking Senator Harlowe . . ."

Jacob interrupted. "Sorry Tom. We both know and your viewers will also want to know, PBS received clearance from the Department of Justice for this interview. During the course of this broadcast, they hope to track us down while the program continues. Since my time may be cut short, while Senator Harlowe's will not, I must insist on going first."

Paulson looked confused, but said, "If it's okay with Senator Harlowe?"

Senator Harlowe also appeared distracted, but said, "As you wish."

Paulson turned to the camera. "Professor Stewart, I will begin by asking you the question that many Americans are asking. If you achieve your purpose, if the term limits amendment is passed by the Senate as it was by the House earlier, if voters then approve it and we subsequently have citizen legislators in Congress, do you expect to see major changes in the programs that Congress has given the American people over the last 100 years?"

"First let me thank you for this opportunity. In answer to your question, yes, I hope citizen-legislators will solve the problems Congress has avoided, and the many more problems created by Congress over the last hundred years."

7:04 p.m.
Anna walked outside as she called Burton, but left the door open so she could hear Jacob.

Burton answered immediately. "He'll be great."

"Are you driving back?"

"I was just about to leave."

"Great. Get back quickly." She went in to watch the program.

Paulson was saying, "But, Professor, Americans are dependent on Social Security and Medicare. Most are unable to save enough for retirement and the cost of healthcare is far beyond the reach of most Americans. Do you believe . . ."

"Of course Americans are dependent. And they are dependent on more programs every year. Congress loves their dependency. There was never a drug lord who promoted addiction and dependency with greater fervor than Congress pushes their addictive, destructive programs. From preschool to the grave, Congress . . .

"Stewart, you're antisocial." Harlowe said. "It's revealed in everything you have ever written. You hate society and democracy . . ."

"Control your guest, Mr. Paulson, or I'll disconnect."

Paulson looked at Senator Harlowe who sat back in his chair.

Jacob said, "I do not despise society, Harlowe. I love it. I'm indebted to it for everything from the shoes on my feet to the contacts in my eyes. For everything good in my life, I depend on society. I depend on the magnificent achievements of countless men and women in medicine who have extended my probable life span by thirty years through their brilliant and amazing research. I enjoy a far happier life because of the creative efforts of countless men and women. They are society, Harlowe. Civil society, where men and women earn their livings by satisfying the wants and needs of others, and by trading their efforts in a free market. But when you speak of society, you mean political society, the institution you and your friends organize through force. A centrally planned society that promotes economic dependency and discourages individual effort. A society that attracts demagogues into government who incite class warfare and race hatred to gain votes. I hate *political* society, Harlow. It's always and only, coercive force and a plan to make everyone dependent on politicians."

Harlowe roared, "This is intolerable. Stewart wants anarchy, a government that makes no decisions and uses no force, its citizens carrying guns and fending for themselves."

Paulson said, "Please, Senator," before looking into the camera. "But what about that point, Professor? Doesn't society have a right to use force to protect its citizens?

"Yes, of course. With one exception, we entrust government with the exclusive use of force. That's why it has always attracted thugs. Every government that ever existed attracted despots, dictators, absolute monarchs, tyrants or kings. They are thugs and they hire more thugs to keep themselves in power. Government, with the power to regulate and extort, has always attracted power hungry thugs, as flies are attracted to filth. Some are attracted to that power for the wealth they can steal or extort, others for the power to inflict their religious views, moral views or personal philosophy on the public."

"What is the exception, Professor?"

"The individual has a right to protect himself from the use of force. That right is not surrendered to government. It is natural, as Jefferson said, inalienable."

"His time is up! It must be!"

That statement reminded Anna time had passed. She called Burton as she walked out the door.

He answered after the first ring. "Isn't he great?"

"Please tell me you're on your way back."

"Not yet. Three kids are crawling through the brush playing commando and watching me. I can't leave them to find our equipment."

"And you're listening to the damn radio. Chase them off and get out of there. Damn it, Burton . . ."

"I'm hoping they'll leave in a minute or two. It must be their dinnertime."

"You have to get out, Burton. They may discover our transmission."

"I'll try to scare them off."

She heard his car door open before he disconnected.

As she walked back in, Paulson was saying, "Professor, I know many very good men and women in the Congress who are absolutely sincere, dedicated, passionate even, in their wish to help the public."

"In some ways, they are the politicians most to be feared. Daniel Webster, one of the nation's first congressmen, warned us. 'Good intentions will be pleaded for every assumption of authority. The Constitution was made to guard the people against the dangers of good intentions.' The sincere members of Congress with good intentions are more dangerous than the corrupt thieves. They use government force to mold us into the golden society of their imagination. But we lose control of our lives in that blatantly authoritarian process. The religious right, the corporations who feed at the government trough, and the socialist left have found common ground in this government. I want a government that protects my rights and will otherwise leave me free to own my life and pursue happiness as I think appropriate."

Harlowe interrupted again. "Is that what the assassinations are about, Stewart . . . your happiness?"

"No, Morgan. It's about term limiting you and the other incumbents who have stolen the election process."

"We have not, we . . ."

"And you have betrayed your oath to obey and protect the Constitution. With your every act . . ."

Paulson stopped the argument and asked Jacob to finish his thought. His time was nearly up.

"Senator Harlowe and his colleagues intend to direct our lives as they think we should live them, whether we want to live that way or not. Senator, we want our lives back. And we want our children and grandchildren to be free to own and live their lives as they wish. *I own me* is a statement every American should be able to make . . . but cannot because of the political society you and your friends in Congress have created. We demand that the term limits amendment be approved by the Senate and offered to the American voters. We hope and trust that citizen legislators will undo the damage done by the professional politicians now in Congress."

"You just can't believe it, can you, Stewart? Americans want us to lead. They want strong leaders and they want the programs we bring them."

"You're right, Harlowe. Many people want leaders to make their decisions. They want your programs. They want someone else to make them secure and happy. But those people do not have a right to force me to give up my control of my life because they refuse to take responsibility for theirs."

Paulson said, "But they have a right to vote, Professor. This is a democracy."

"Under our Constitution and under any moral form of government, some actions are illegitimate and immoral even if a majority approves. A democratic vote to take something we didn't earn and redistribute it among ourselves is theft, whether or not it is legal. If the majority votes to enslave blacks again, would that be a legitimate vote? Majorities have done far worse, here and in other nations, at other times. That is why we have a Constitution—to limit government, to protect the individual from the tyranny of the majority. But the Constitution is ignored by our Congress and by the Supreme Court. That is why we need the term limits amendment."

"And you will blow my head off if the Senate fails to approve it."

"Yes! I will, Morgan! You have stolen my life. Return it, or resign, or we will take yours. Approve the amendment, Morgan, or suffer the consequences."

It had been three minutes since she talked with Burton. She called again as she walked out. He must have left by now.

7:09 p.m.
Koberg yelled. "He's been talking for ten minutes! Get me the coordinates, damn it!"

"Yes, sir," The NSA coordinator said. "Only a matter of seconds, sir. We are getting their position now."

"You've been telling me that for ten minutes. I want it now."

"Sir, we can't give you exact coordinates, yet. But we know they're sending from a computer in Maryland. Somewhere north-east of the Chesapeake Bay Bridge."

Koberg pointed north toward the bridge. "Go, go, go."

7:09 p.m.

It would be a long wait. Chris nursed a now warm beer and ate peanuts at a corner table as far from the bar and other patrons as he could get. The wide screen television was tuned to PBS. Sitting still was difficult, appearing unsupportive was impossible. Luckily other patrons seemed to like Jacob's message, but not all. Mark's call made him jump. "Hi, Luke, what's up?"

"You wanted me to find out what was going on. My friend wouldn't answer her phone until just now. Your man on TV is being traced. The cable outfits have NSA agents plugged into their computer systems tonight. They seem to think they can get the location of the sending unit by watching contacts with all known remailers. It may be working."

"Goddamn it. I better let her know."

"Apparently they can identify the computer and the house where the cable connection is broadcasting. They have a bunch of choppers in the air now; and when they identify the cable address, they'll jump on it . . . literally."

"I'll call her now."

"Good luck."

She was talking with Burton when Chris called. She put Burton on hold and told Chris they were prepared, but she told him of the problem Burton was having with the kids.

Chris tried to keep his voice down—the barmaid was coming back in his direction. "Tell him to get out now. When the choppers show up it'll be too damn late."

"What, I didn't hear you?"

He held up his beer, the barmaid turned around to get him another. "I said, tell Burton to get out. When the choppers show up it'll be too damn late."

"I will." She broke that connection and spoke to Burton. "Chris says the NSA spooks are definitely tapped into and tracing our cable connection. You must leave now. The helicopters may be on their way."

"I can't. The kids won't leave. They just go back far enough I can't get to them."

"You have to leave, Burton, It will be too late if you wait for the helicopters."

"Thirty seconds after I leave these kids will find the radio transmitter and the antennae . . . and the bomb. We've come too far to walk away now. Jacob is doing a great job. It's worth the chance. Give it three more minutes then shut him off. I'll tear it down and leave then."

"We could . . ." she couldn't think of any plausible alternates. "Okay, I'm on the dock, keep this line open. I'll yell if I see helicopters coming." She carried her cell phone to the end of the dock for a longer view of the approaching helicopters. She would see them when they first appeared down the bay, long before they could be heard. She looked across the cove at the area where Burton was, but couldn't see him or his car. He was taking a terrible chance for those kids.

Burton looked through the trees at the house and dock. He thought he could see Anna. "Are you on the dock?"

"Yes."

"I can see you."

"I can't see you. The trees are in the way."

"Story of my life. Always something between us."

"Two minutes, Burton."

"Can you hear Jacob?"

"No, of course not."

"He's great! Listen, Anna, I need to say this. If I don't get out alive, I'm just so damn proud of what we've done, what I've done, I have no regrets, about anything. We've already made a difference. Congress can't go back to business as usual. But I can't be taken alive. I know too much about our accounts, our hiding places and they would get it out of me. Torture is legal now, if they don't call it torture."

"God damn you, Burton." She was weeping. "Don't give me that shit. You get out now or I unplug the damn computer."

"Don't. We've worked too hard for the opportunity to be heard."

She wiped the tears from her eyes and looked down the bay as she spoke, concentrating on the horizon. She could easily see twenty miles, she thought. That wasn't much time. If the helicopters were traveling at 200 miles an hour they could be there 5 minutes after she first saw them, but maybe they traveled faster . . . maybe she couldn't see 20 miles. "Listen damn it. You won't get more than two minutes to get out of there, after we see the helicopters on the horizon. Two minutes is not worth your life. I'm unplugging, now."

"Burton was pleading as she walked from the end of the dock toward Jacob. She could see him through the window. He was speaking but watching her.

She heard the helicopters and spun around. They were not coming from down the bay. The sound was faint, but distinct. She screamed at Burton, "Get out! Run, Burton!" A moment later they came over the hill behind him, perhaps two miles away. She gave Jacob the cutoff sign as she yelled at Burton. Jacob nodded, half stood, but continued talking.

"Goodbye Anna." Burton said.

She screamed, "Burton, run!" But his line was dead.

She ran toward into the house and heard Jacob say, "Lie face down on the floor and wait. Do not attempt to talk to the SWAT team, or explain. Goodbye, America. Thank you."

She grabbed the binoculars and raced back outside. Three helicopters were visible as she ran back down the dock. "Burton, he's off, he's signed off." She heard crashing sounds, the antennae being knocked over? "Burton?"

She saw him on the beach. He was reaching down, putting things in his pockets. And he carried the antennae as he ran out into the water. He waded out until he was chest deep. She thought she saw him throw something farther out into the bay—the bomb, maybe—something long and thin. And then he threw the cell phone. He waded into deeper water. He hesitated. He seemed to be looking in the direction of the dock, at her, for a long moment. The helicopter was over him now.

He leaned forward and disappeared.

She screamed "Noooo!" Tears prevented her from seeing but she continued to look through the binoculars until Jacob put his arms around her.

She stood on the dock, gasping, sobbing, looking into the glasses, wiping her eyes and looking again until there was no longer reason to hope. Jacob did not ask, he held her, his own eyes flooded with tears, waiting until she could tell him.

"He's gone. Jacob, he's . . . He drowned himself." She wept bitterly as she beat softly against Jacob's chest.

Jacob held her and wept with her, barely aware of the black helicopters. Many of the docks up and down the beach were occupied.

7:44 p.m.

Two helicopters came in tight over the hill. Other choppers were seconds behind them. There was no space to land within a hundred yards of the house. One chopper dropped a SWAT team from ropes in the front yard. Koberg, in the command helicopter, was higher up, with an overview of the area.

Koberg watched the first SWAT team deploy, but his attention was attracted to a man, fully dressed, running into the water. He was carrying something. Koberg pointed at him. "Get that man! The guy in the water. He's TLR. Don't let him escape!" The pilot banked steeply and slid downhill to a point ten yards directly above the fleeing terrorist, who was now in chest high water and still moving. Koberg screamed jump but his SWAT team was in heavy battle gear. They couldn't swim any more than the guy in the water and he was in deep water. And then he went under.

Another helicopter had landed on the beach. Three men had stripped off their heavy gear and were charging into the water as fast as they could. The rotor wash threw spray into the air and made little whitecaps at the edge of the wash. They reached the area where they thought the terrorist went down, but they couldn't find him. The water whipped up by the helicopter was murky and there was a tidal current.

Seconds stretched into minutes as they searched until it became obvious there would be no capture of a live TLR member. When they left, an hour ago, Koberg had wanted them all dead. Now he needed one alive, to tell him how to get the others. "Damn them. Get me back up to that house. Maybe we can learn something there."

As the helicopter headed up the hill he said, "I hope that was Chris Carpenter."

7:45 p.m.

Chris took pride in Jacob's defense of individual rights and his heart soared when he saw the effect on the room. These people got it, even those who opposed Jacob when he began to speak. But the hope he felt crumbled and collapsed as he watched Burton wade to his death on a wide screen. A CNN helicopter had followed the SWAT teams to Tilghman Cove. Chris could do nothing, say nothing as Burton died.

While Jacob was still speaking, CNN had cut away from the News Hour to follow the swarm of DOJ helicopters as they converged on Tilghman Cove. It was all coming apart.

He saw Burton wade into the water, saw him throw something into deeper water, and sacrifice himself so they would not be caught. He had never guessed Burton had that much courage. Chris wept. He had locked the door to the restroom and wept for Burton, and for Anna, and Jacob.

And Chris wept for his own family. He knew where this was leading.

Someone rattled the restroom door several times. He had to clean himself up and get out. Cold water on his face helped. He started for the car, but stopped and walked back into the bar. CNN was still showing aerial shots. He thought he saw Anna and Jacob on the dock. The barmaid followed him to his table. She asked, "You okay?"

8:21 p.m.
First one, then two more SWAT teams had swarmed screaming down their ropes surrounding and invading the house. The neighbors stood in the street watching the Carlson home and the SWAT agents attacking it. The front door was being shattered as Koberg heard the CenCom warning that the TLR had used their wireless system. The team that entered through the battered front door discovered a terrified family of four lying prone before a television.

Koberg told the family it would be best if they did not speak to anyone about the raid, especially reporters, but not even attorneys or neighbors. Their cooperation would be appreciated by the Department of Justice, who would reimburse them for damages.

Outside, Koberg found Agent Ward waiting for him with three boys. "Sir, these boys were playing in the woods down by the beach. They saw the suspect up close."

Koberg was furious. "I'm sure that will be a big help. They can identify the body."

The kids looked horrified. Ward said, "They said he was waiting in a car for a long time and talking on a cell phone." Ward looked at the boys. "Did I get that right, boys?"

The oldest, skinny and tall for his age, maybe 10 years old, red headed and freckled said, "Yeah. He talked on the cell phone several times. We watched him."

The youngest, perhaps eight, was wide eyed, near tears and trying to stand behind his older brother, a dark haired, boy who wanted to talk. "He waved at us and smiled while he was talking on the cell phone. There was some equipment near the car. He took it when he ran down to the beach."

The oldest interrupted, "We found his laptop. He threw the other stuff in the bay." He looked at Ward to see if he had it right. Ward nodded yes.

"Anything else?"

The small boy, barely audible, said, "He drowned himself." Tears flowing, he said through his sobs. "He was . . . a nice man . . . he wanted to talk to us."

His brother said, "I better take Joseph home."

Ward received a call from his team on the beach. He seemed disappointed. Koberg watched the boys walk away and shook his head. They were nowhere. They knew nothing more than they did an hour ago. Hammar would be furious.

Ward disconnected. "They've retrieved the body, sir. Definitely not Chris Carpenter. It's being taken to the forensic lab for identification."

Koberg continued walking. "Wonderful."

"The gear thrown into the water will be recovered as soon as the divers arrive. The car will be towed in this evening."

Koberg sneered. "Excellent. The barn door is fully closed." The helicopter engine started as he boarded.

9:21 p.m.

Anna was devastated. Jacob tried to consol her, but Burton's loss had destroyed him, too. Neither could imagine going on. But stopping was not an option, either. Burton would not let them.

Chris called and Anna wept more. "I promised the NSA would be unable to trace us, but they found us. I thought up the antennae on the other side, but that meant Burton had to watch it. I could have turned the system off, but I didn't. Burton would have come back if I had just turned it off. God damn it, I caused his death. I did. Oh Chris, it's my fault." Her sobs stopped her from saying more.

Chris almost strangled in his attempt to yell without being loud enough to be heard in the bar. "That's bullshit, Anna. You do him no honor when you say you should have made his choices for him. He is a fucking hero because he knew where his actions were leading. Give the man the credit he deserves. He gave his life knowing precisely what he was doing and why. He died in a battle for liberty."

Jacob had been holding Anna and heard every word. He took the phone from her. "You're right, of course. How are you bearing up?"

"Now that I've got my anger back, I'm better. I was in a guilty, hopeless, funk too, but Burton would want us to get on with it. Seeing the helicopters so close to the house scared the hell out of me. They are closing in but we can still make it work. If I can take out two or three senators tonight, they may collapse tomorrow."

10:32 p.m.

CenCom patched Ward through. He was still at the scene. "We may not have to wait on the ID," Ward said. "The divers recovered a billfold. His driver's license says he's Burton Alan."

O'Brian looked at Bradley. "The name is familiar."

She nodded. "One of Stewart's students." She pulled up the list on her monitor. "A teacher in New York, long time friend, two children, divorced."

Ward said, "Forensics will still want to look at the body and everything else we've found. Oh yeah, we found another laptop in the brush. It was still connected to the Carlson's wireless system. Apparently it was part of a system that transmitted from somewhere around here. Maybe from a car or a boat."

Bradley and O'Brian exchanged worried looks. Ward asked, "Koberg come by yet? He was really pissed when he left the scene."

"He just needs a hug," O'Brian said.

Ward laughed at the mental image. "Any news on senators? They promised two more today."

"Not yet. Maybe they'll lay low for a day or two."

Ward said, "No way." At the same time Bradley said, "Nah."

O'Brian and Bradley moved to his office. O'Brian called Koberg to report the body was that of Burton Alan, a student of Stewart's. Koberg said he knew that and hung up. The CNN channel was full of comment about the raid, but without real news. A live shot of self-confident senators embarking on helicopters for Andrews AFB was accompanied by speculation over how many TLR remained and whether they would be captured tonight or whether they would strike again. The attorney general promised their capture very soon. Clips from the Paulson interview with Professor Stewart were shown.

Bradley received a call from Mark. "This is way after your bedtime," she said.

"Lots of excitement tonight. So have you ID'd the TLR guy?"

O'Brian rose to leave, but Bradley stood in front of the door and motioned him to sit. "His name was Burton Alan."

"God damn it."

Bradley glanced at O'Brian. "Yeah, we agree. He obviously feared our new terrorist interrogation methods."

"With good reason. Any clues?"

"You're beginning to worry me, Mark."

"Sorry."

She noticed he didn't withdraw the question. "We recovered two laptops, a digital directional radio antennae and we have divers looking for other stuff the guy tossed."

"Take care of yourself, Kat."

Bradley snapped the cell closed and looked at O'Brian. "Where the hell were you going?"

"I was just trying to give you some privacy."

"He's a former lover. That was two years ago. We're still good friends, but frankly I've talked to him more in the last few days than in the last two years. He's very interested in the TLR investigations."

11:03 p.m.

"I don't mean to be nosey," the waitress asked, "but are you waiting for someone? Should I just not bother you?"

He had seen it coming. He couldn't spend several hours in a bar drinking two beers without drawing attention. The Secret Service had been in looking around, asking for people to keep their eyes open. "I'm pretty obvious, huh? I suppose you get a lot of guys in here just to look at you."

Her grin said she liked that.

"Does it bother you? I tried not to be obvious. I can leave, if it bothers you; but I was sort of hoping . . ."

"Yeah?" Now she looked coy.

"I would like to ask if . . . but . . . we don't know each other."

"My name's Brenda. I get off at midnight."

He smiled. "Really. Can I just wait here then? I'm Matt Dunning."

"Yeah? Nice to meet you, Matt. Another beer?"

"Yeah, and a cheeseburger." He smiled, "But maybe you should leave off the onions."

"Good." As she turned to walk away, she said, "And you can look if you like."

Chris acknowledged Brenda with a smile whenever she looked in his direction, but searched for flaws in his plan. He thought the senators would be bedded down in an hour.

Mark called again. "Sorry, Chris."

"Yeah, it hurts. Anna has taken it hard."

"They know his name. Found his billfold. They also found a directional radio antennae. Some are guessing Stewart's voice may have been coming from a house nearby, or a boat or a car. Thought I better let you know."

Chris thanked him and Mark promised to call when he had more information.

He waited until Brenda was in the kitchen, walked out to the parking lot and checked several cars. When he came back in his table had been cleaned off. Brenda looked pissed, but then surprised to see him.

"I thought you left." Now she was looking a bit happier.

"No, just had to step outside a minute."

"Yeah, well, you want another beer?"

"I'm full. I'll just wait."

She gave him a sexy smile and let her hip touch his shoulder before walking away with his glass. Chris felt bad; she didn't deserve to be toyed with. He hoped later she'd discover who he really was.

He looked up to see Jacob's face—an old photo—on the screen and heard the description and the plea for viewers to be watchful. Then he was looking at Anna. His picture was coming next. *Shit.* And there it was. He looked to see if others were noticing. Some were looking at the screen. One lady looked in his direction. He put some peanuts in his mouth and stared at her until she looked away. Brenda didn't look at the screen. Thank God for that. He would leave in ten minutes.

At 11:45 he put his jacket on the back of the chair and walked in the direction of the restroom, then out the entrance. The jacket would keep Brenda from being anxious for a few minutes. And it might work for the lady who may have suspected his identity.

He drove to within a block of the senators' unit. The lights inside were dim. There were several bodyguards outside. He guessed the senators were already in bed.

He found the spot he wanted, parking the Taurus with its rear end pointed at the duplex. By moving the boxes he could aim a shot directly between the bedrooms. With the laser sight he could be accurate and the car would not alert anyone as long as the station wagon appeared to be a parked flat-tire problem.

He walked to the front and leaned down as if to look at the tire. Instead he pushed a knife through it. The air began rushing out as he walked to the back of the car, raised the rear door, removed the spare tire, emptied the air and set it beside the flat tire that remained on the car. He also got the jack out of the spare tire compartment and set it down outside. Then he replaced the weapon box, setting the boxes with the gas cans on either side and behind it. He got into the back seat and aimed the box as well as he could at the bedrooms. He turned on a flashlight and laid it on the floor pointing in the general direction of the house. If the Secret Service were watching him now with night vision glasses they were in screaming pain. He took the top off the box and flipped the laser sight on as he checked it with his binoculars and quickly turned it off. He was high and to the left, but he guessed at the change, moving the box and the internal level. That would have to do. He couldn't take a chance on the laser being seen again. He looked into the box and checked the range. It was 231 meters. He set the weapon to explode at 232 meters—one meter inside the building. He closed the back car door.

He walked around the corner away from the duplex toward the Gateway Inn. He picked a rental car first, a Chevy Malibu and similar to the car he trained on. With the strap-hook it took less than a minute to get in and another minute to hotwire the ignition. He drove out of the lot and down the back street toward the corner where his car was parked, wondering what could go wrong. Someone could have parked behind his car, or the base police could have spotted the car and towed it—it was definitely out of place, or the Secret Service guys could be examining it.

He was still going through the list as he drove around the corner, but his car sat alone and the senators' unit was still dark, except for a little light coming from the living area. Three cars were parked in front. They probably contained Secret Service agents. He stopped his car with the headlights pointed at the agents. They would not be able to use night vision binoculars with his headlights aimed at them. He quickly opened the car, reached inside, hit the timer. He had three minutes. He grabbed the spare and put it in the trunk. He pulled the car jack out and let it hit the street with a maximum amount of noise, said "God damn it," loud enough to be heard. Closed the back door, got back in his stolen car and drove toward the agents, his heart in his throat. If they stopped him, and he made a run for it, the North gate tire barriers would be up long before he got there.

As his car approached, two agents got out of a dark Impala SS sedan. He rolled the passenger side window down. One agent looked in that window and said, "Car problem?"

"Fucking spare is bad, nearest service is four miles from here and I'm dying for some goddamn sleep."

The agent shined his flashlight at Chris's dirty hands. He said, "Good luck," as he backed away.

Chris drove past and headed for the North Gate as fast as he dared. He had set the damned alarm too quick, but he didn't want to leave time to find the RPG if they decided to have a look. They might park directly behind the station wagon just as the rocket fired. He remembered Burton. Things go wrong.

A pickup was stopped at the gate. He wouldn't make it. No room to go around and he wouldn't have a chance if he stayed on the base. No room to reverse and turn. The pickup moved forward and Chris was right behind him. The officer looked bored. Chris tried to look easy while the officer looked at his ID, but Chris checked his watch. Time was up. It would blow any second but the tire barrier was down; he couldn't just floor it. The sergeant handed the ID back and said, "Have a good evening, sir." Someone inside the Force Protector gatehouse lowered the barrier and Chris started forward. The explosion occurred before he had gone three feet but Chris pushed the gas pedal down and was across before it came back up. He checked his rearview mirror after he was across. The officer stood in the middle of the road calling in his license. He kept the car moving at the legal speed until he found a residential area to lose anyone looking for him.

Then he began to worry about the agents in the Malibu. What if they had decided to investigate the Taurus?

Tuesday, June 10
And Patriots

6:47 a.m.

O'Brian woke when the sun, streaming across the bed, reached his eyes. He checked the clock. They'd overslept. He kissed her neck. "We have to get out of here,"

This would be a bad day to be late. After the carnage last night, a few heads would roll. They'd visited Andrews Air Force Base where three senators were killed and one badly mangled by a rocket-propelled grenade. The Secret Service lost an agent, too.

The weapon had been fired from a station wagon. The duplex and the station wagon were still smoking when they arrived, an hour after the blast. There was no doubt about who did it. The Gate guard identified Chris Carpenter and so did a waitress.

Ward and Barnes were waiting. Ward said, "There is more damn speculation than you can imagine. Hammar will fire Koberg, Koberg will fire you, the Senate will approve the term limits amendment today. Or it won't."

According to the Post," Barnes said, "the president asked for Hammar's resignation."

"Does anyone know anything for sure," O'Brian asked?

"For sure, the crowd on the mall is bigger than ever," Ward said. "There may be a riot if the Senate doesn't approve the amendment."

Barnes added, "Or if they do."

"Any evidence that is helpful? O'Brian asked. "From Tilghman Cove or Andrews?"

"We know who did it." Barnes said, "Nothing points to where they are. They might be in the Tilghman Cove area, based on the antennae. Or they might have been sending from a car or a boat."

O'Brian's phone rang.

"This is Director Proctor. I want you and Agent Bradley in my office right away."

"Yes, sir." The phone went dead and O'Brian felt a knot in his gut. He stood looking at Bradley. "The director wants us in his office."

Barnes and Ward stood as Bradley opened the door and walked out with O'Brian behind her. Two agents he didn't know were waiting at his door. He glanced at Bradley as they waited for the elevator. She seemed as fearful as he was.

Attorney General Hammar sat behind Director Proctor's desk. Koberg and Proctor stood beside it. They all looked angry.

Proctor said, "Give your weapons to the agents behind you."

They were finished, their careers over. O'Brian was pissed. "We deserve an . . ."

"Give them your weapons," Proctor said.

O'Brian removed his pistol and turned to hand it over. He glanced at Bradley as he did. Her face was red. Her lip trembled, but she was also angry. She passed her pistol back.

"Now your badges."

They tossed their badges on the Directors desk. Bradley's went off the desk onto the floor at Proctor's feet. He did not look at it. "Sit."

The agents left the room with their handguns.

"You betrayed me, the Bureau and this nation," Hammar said. "You are traitors."

O'Brian started to protest but Hammar said, "Shut up and listen. We have telephone recordings and videos. You have intentionally undermined the investigation. And you've passed information to the TLR."

Koberg couldn't restrain himself. "You were so obvious. Your efforts to help those traitors Hayes and Jackson, and then your effort to protect Johnson weren't clues, they were announcements. He's on his way to Guantanamo by the way." He sneered at Bradley. "I put a camera and a bug in your apartment, Bradley, and recorded the action."

"You slimy pervert," O'Brian yelled, "The video was . . ."

"Sleeping together is also against the rules, as you know."

O'Brian reached over and held her hand. It was the wrong move. She went from anger to tears instantly.

Proctor stood up. A moment later his doors opened and the agents entered. "You'll be taken to the Federal Detention Center until we decide what to do with you."

"Just for what it's worth," O'Brian said to Hammar, "when we began, it was to catch the TLR as quickly as possible. But we watched you protect your power and use the investigation for revenge. You murdered Cal Jackson and Don Hayes. And you pissed on the Constitution. You're the fucking traitors."

Koberg said softly, "Oh, you'll pay for that little outburst, O'Brian. And you will also confess. Won't you?"

O'Brian turned to leave, but Koberg stepped near. "You have a daughter. Meg will also be . . ."

O'Brian's jab, hard and swift, caught Koberg in the neck, collapsing his windpipe. Both agents brought O'Brian to the floor on his knees, his arms twisted behind his back. Koberg, his face blue, was also on his knees facing O'Brian.

Hammar, in shock, stood speechless. Proctor screamed at one of the agents to get the staff doctor. Bradley wept as Koberg collapsed and grew still. O'Brian was dismayed by the accident and everything that had happened in the last few minutes. By the time the doctor arrived it was too late. A tracheotomy was attempted but Koberg could not be made to breathe.

10:00 a.m.

According to several political blogs, the Senate might vote on the amendment today. This was the goal they all sought and agreed to give their lives for. But they could not enjoy it. Burton's suicide continued to eat at them. They could not make phone calls to family now for fear that would give their location to the DOJ.

Jacob suggested they escape now while they still had the opportunity.

Chris shook his head. "We haven't finished the job. If the vote is postponed, we'll need to take out another senator."

Anna took Jacob's hand. "Don't we owe it to Burton?"

Jacob nodded. Of course she was right. They had pledged to force the amendment through, or die trying. Burton died trying. And they were so close now. "Maybe the vote will happen today and maybe we can escape."

The bloody carnage at Andrews was constantly on TV. They all avoided watching, but worried how their families were handling it. *They must be as depressed and frightened as we are.* Jacob hoped Mary and Carol's friends would stand by them. Judging by the internet and the crowds on the mall, many people were supportive.

10:13 a.m.

"Goddamn it, you're killing me," President Herbert Kinross said. "You selected these people. Your hand picked JTTF leader is screwing another agent and they're both TLR moles. Then right in front of your fucking eyes they kill your Assistant AG. If you had picked the right person we coulda had these TLR fuckers in the ground by now."

"Herb, I know this . . ."

"I'm sorry, John," the President said. "I don't like it. You know I don't. But you also know politics. You'd do the same thing. You'd have to, if you were sitting here. The Senate is going crazy. They're going to pass that amendment and then we're all fucked."

"I can stop it, Herb."

"I'm sorry, John. I need your resignation."

"Today. I can get them today—before the Senate vote. I can."

The president was skeptical. He shook his head. "Sorry, John."

"The female agent, Bradley, was calling them on her cell phone. We have her phone and the number she was calling. No one knows of her arrest. We can make contact and get their position. We're talking about a few hours, maybe just two or three. Senate leadership can give us that much time. We can wrap this up by early afternoon. No amendment."

The president looked at the clock. Hammar did also. It was 10:20. President Kinross pushed a piece of paper across the desk. "Sign it. I'll keep it in a drawer and tear it up if you're successful."

Hammar signed and pushed it back, fighting to keep the fear from showing. Kinross said, "I'll call Senate leadership . . . whoever the hell that is now. And I'll tell them that you'll take care of the TLR problem in a few hours. But if it doesn't work out, John." He let it hang.

Hammar was on his cell phone as soon as his limo pulled away from the White House. Reporters at the gate asked, "Did you submit your resignation, sir?" He pretended to be too busy to deal with them.

When he arrived at his office, Proctor, Barnes and Ward were waiting for him. "Bradley's calls were from Mark Adams," Proctor said. "He's one of our agents at Quantico. The time stamp on Bradley's phone record matches the time of the audio recordings that Koberg's team got." He nodded at Ward. "Ward says they once had a relationship but broke it off. Adams is a libertarian and a member of JFI. He may be the actual TLR mole."

Hammar asked, "What did you get from Bradley and O'Brian?"

"Nothing useful. Apparently they were just dragging their feet, sir. The chemicals usually work. But they don't seem to know anything about the TLR we don't know. Adams may have been pumping her for the information that he gave to the TLR."

"Find out where Mark Adams is now and call me. That's where I'm going." Hammar stared for a moment before he picked up the phone and punched in a number. "I need your help. I'll have a helicopter on your pad in ten minutes. Bring your equipment." He checked his wristwatch. It was 11:23. He was out of time. He turned to Proctor. "I'm going with Barnes' team. Get three more SWAT teams in helicopters ready to go when I call." He turned to the door and said to Barnes. "Let's go. We have to stop at the CIA to pick up a specialist."

10:32 a.m.
Jacob stared at the few sentences that made up the message. There was so much to say, but he did not have the emotional energy to write more. He left it on the laptop ready to send with a single click. If the DOJ found them, he might not have time to do more. They were hopeful the Senate would vote today. If the vote were taken, they believed the vote would be to pass the amendment. They were so close. But the loss of Burton and the fear the DOJ would soon find them blocked any happier thoughts.

They all knew they would not be captured. The last thing Hammar or Congress would want would be catch them and then have to deal with the uproar from the growing numbers of people who supported them. Even worse would be to give them a trial where they could speak out. The message on the laptop would be their last chance to communicate to their families and to the world. He kept it simple.

They watched FOX News to pass the time. Three senators were filibustering to prevent the vote from happening. They took turns reading the Constitution. They appeared to be defending it. Chris called it camouflage.

"Well, it's working," said Anna. "They are stopping the amendment."

But moments later FOX cut to a studio reporter. "Moments ago we received two audio tapes from Phillip Johnson, an attorney for Special Agents Michael O'Brian and Katherine Bradley. These tapes, if they are authentic, are certain to have wide-ranging political effects. They record a meeting of Attorney General Hammar, Assistant AG Koberg, Special Agent O'Brian and a leadership delegation from the Senate and House, as they plan the raids on the homes of Calvin Jackson and Don Hayes."

Anna, already standing, gasped. Jacob and Chris leaped to their feet. The tapes could have an enormous effect on the public and the debate.

"The audio tapes are notarized and a statement is made by Michael O'Brian, the Special Agent in Charge of the TLR investigation. He was appointed by Attorney General John Hammar and he certifies their authenticity. The attorney who gave us these copies is an Arlington attorney and the uncle of another Department of Justice Special Agent who is being held at the Federal Detention Center. Mr. Johnson believes that Special Agent O'Brian and Bradley are being held by the Department of Justice and may be in some danger."

The reporter went on to read the sworn affidavit describing each of the participants in the meetings. Excerpts from both tapes were played. The reporter seemed shocked. Jacob, Anna and Chris were only shocked that O'Brian or Bradley had made them available. That was an act of bravery.

Mark called while they were glued to the television. Chris put the cell on speakerphone when Mark said, "Bad news, Chris. My friend left a message. She thinks DOJ is planning a house to house search in your area. Now I can't get her to answer. When I tried to call her cell phone, someone else answered and tried to question me. I called her apartment, no answer. I tried to call O'Brian and the same thing happened."

There was a long silence before Chris said, "I'm sorry, Mark. I'm pretty sure they've been arrested. You haven't heard about the tapes, have you?"

Chris described the broadcast they were hearing. Mark said, "They must have known they might be arrested. O'Brian must have given them to the attorney to release if they were arrested."

"If they have her, they'll pump her full of chemicals to make her talk. And they'll soon be coming after you."

"I know . . . I need to think. Too much all at once."

"You need to run, Mark. And we can help. But first get out of Quantico before they trap you."

Mark was silent for a moment, but then said, "I'm sure you're right. I'll call you back." He didn't sound like he was going to run.

The Senate chamber exploded with the news of the tapes. So did the crowd on the mall. Those opposed to the amendment lost energy as the anger on the other side grew. FOX and CNN could hardly keep abreast of the changing situation, but their interviews managed to convey a Senate in a vicious battle for control of a vote to approve the amendment. It had nothing to do with Democrat or Republican.

Jacob guessed some of those who were ready to approve the amendment included those few who felt shame for their long association with the corrupt senators. But most of those ready to approve simply feared for their lives and had long ago provided for their political afterlife. As a result of help with legislation, they were assured positions as well-paid directors of powerful corporations or non-profit organizations, or they had arranged for positions as very well-paid lobbyists for government agencies or labor unions. And some senators thought the public could be convinced to vote against the amendment. If enough money was spent to persuade them, the public could be made to vote for anything.

The filibuster collapsed a few minutes before noon, when cloture was demanded by a super majority. The amendment was scheduled to be voted up or down at 2:00 p.m.

Jacob was lightheaded with the sudden hope. Anna hugged his neck and sobbed with joy and relief. Chris nodded violently trying twice to say something, but his voice broke each time.

It seemed all but certain.

11:52 a.m.
Hammar was dumfounded by the news of the tapes. He had been on the helicopter and on his way to the CIA landing pad when Proctor called. Proctor didn't need to remind him of what he and the others had said. Politically the tapes seemed insurmountable. But nothing was insurmountable; he prayed. While flying to Quantico he silently prayed. And he rallied. He knew his purposes were pure, that everything he had done was for the good of the nation and that God depended on him and would help him. His full strength returned when he realized he was being tested. He ordered the arrest and detention of the terrorist and traitor Mark Adams until he and the CIA interrogating specialist could arrive. This would be the break he needed.

Mark Adams knew precisely the time when Hammar and the CIA interrogator arrived in his office. Mark had watched the clock while he waited under guard for their arrival. It was 12:30 when they arrived and it was 12:32 when the interrogator removed the clock. After that he guessed it took eight minutes to strip him, tie him to the chair and attach the electrodes to his nuts, stick one up his butt and test it. Maybe ten minutes. He hoped it was at least ten minutes. Since then he had lost track. Maybe it had been only another ten minutes. Maybe twenty minutes. It seemed a hell of a lot longer and time was everything. He had to stretch it out. No matter how bad the pain got, he had to keep them working on him until the vote was complete, but oh, my God, that already seemed like forever. They had stopped him at the gate. Chris had been right. If he had started running immediately he might have made it out before Hammar ordered his arrest.

Hammar did the questioning. He should have left it to the professional.

The excruciating pain was always alternated with a question and then more pain. "Now will you tell us, Mark?" More pain. "Where are they, Mark?" More pain.

If they felt he was about to give up they would keep working on him . . . and stay out of the gym bag. They gagged him to keep him from breaking teeth or biting his tongue and to keep his screams from being heard in the halls.

He stalled again, dreading the gag, acting as if he were about to speak, and then it was on and Hammar nodded and the pain took control of him again.

Their instruments were simple, electronic and left no external marks. He would never be able to claim or prove he had been tortured. No attorney would represent him. As of this moment he was a terrorist, without rights, because Hammar designated him a terrorist. He was glad they didn't have time to use the chemicals. They were more effective.

He screamed, or tried to, through the gag stuffed in his mouth, and they stopped the pain momentarily and removed the gag. Hammar said, "Tell us, Mark; you know you will eventually; no need for all this unnecessary pain." Then it started again, the pain slowly built, the amps announced as they were increased so that he could know how much more there was to come. It stopped again when he thought he heard his spine break.

He was tied into a straight-back chair on a rubber pad. Hammar was in his rolling executive chair. "Perhaps you imagine, Mark, that my strong religious views and my natural compassion will stop me. It will not. I will do what must be done to make this nation secure. The TLR will not be allowed to win this fight. They will fail. You know that. And you know we will get this information from you. You can stop the pain, Mark. Tell me where, or how, we can find them."

Eventually they would find the phone. He couldn't prevent that or whatever happened after, but he could stretch it out. He felt the drool and added some to it. He told himself to look pathetic, about to break. *Yeah that isn't tough to do.* He asked Hammar, "Why do you hate liberty?" He didn't care what the bastard thought, but he wanted to get him into a lecture. It didn't work.

Hammar nodded at the specialist, who shoved the gag back over his mouth and slowly started the electricity coursing through him. "Two amps . . . three amps . . . four amps . . ." the specialist counted as he increased the current. It went on until Mark was past enduring it. He hoped it would kill him. It didn't.

They took the gag off. Hammar looked at his watch. "We have plenty of time yet, Mark, but this is so unnecessary."

Something was damaged, the pain in his thighs and gut diminished when the current was cut, but never stopped. He blubbered, trying to appear as weak and cowardly as he felt, but he whispered something in the direction of Hammar. It was unintelligible, but he used the word Carpenter.

Hammar looked hopeful. "Yes Mark, speak up."

He let his head dangle to the left, away from Hammar and whimpered as if he didn't have the strength to do more. He tried again to speak and again it was mostly mumbling. But it sounded as if he said, "They're at . . . something incomprehensible . . . cabin." Mark began weeping as if he had just given everything away.

Hammar rolled his chair closer. "Try harder, Mark. I can't understand you." He looked desperate.

Mark whimpered it again with the words "Potomac" and "cabin" understandable.

Hammar leaned closer. "Yes, Mark?" But he leaned too close. Mark took a large part of Hammar's ear between his teeth and was biting as hard as he could.

Hammar screamed. The agent controlling the electric current panicked, shoving the current control all the way. The electrical charge caused Mark's muscles to contract. And, of course, the current passed through him into Hammar. It had the same effect on the attorney general. His muscles also contracted, causing him to jerk up and away, still screaming.

Barnes and two other agents burst through the door and saw Mark, naked, a bloody ear in his mouth, his body twitching violently. The CIA electrical interrogation technical specialist dropped his jaw in astonishment, but turned the power off. Mark ceased moving. His face began turning blue. Hammar's ear fell from his mouth.

Barnes said, "Jesus Christ, he's having a heart attack." He stepped back through the open door and yelled for a medic.

Mark was out of the chair, on the floor, the wires gone when Barnes returned. The interrogation specialist was putting his equipment back in its case. Hammar sat turned away from Mark's body, with a bloody handkerchief to his ear, beating the desk with his other hand. The agents were going through everything they could find.

"Didn't anyone read his report?" Barnes yelled. "He was at this desk job because of his heart." He was red hot and would have said more, but the medic arrived. While the medic worked on Mark, Hammar, grim faced, turned to point at Barnes. "Wait in the helicopter. Don't make any calls if you value your pension."

One of the agents held Hammar's ear out to him. "Sir, you can get it sewn on, if you get to a surgeon quickly." Hammar looked at his torn ear and threw up before he could turn away.

The medic was unable to save Mark Adams, but he was able to stop the attorney general's bleeding. A tight fitting bandage, wrapped around his head, covered the ear. That had taken several minutes. It was 1:39 p.m. as Hammar walked out the door.

1:36 p.m.
They watched on CNN as the senate began to fill the chamber. Anna was convinced the amendment would be approved. She imagined Burton watching. He would be very proud. She also knew there was still a strong probability the DOJ would soon find them. She asked Chris, "Do you think Mark is trying to get away?"

"He seemed resigned."

Jacob asked, "Do you think we can get away? You said the satellites are watching, but they may also start a house to house search."

"If we stay until after it's dark we will have a strong outgoing tide. I need to give it a little more thought but I think we can get out then." He hesitated a moment. "I want to call Mark. But that makes me nervous."

Anna said, "Call him. And hang up before it can be answered. He'll call back if he's near the phone. Even if they have him they won't know where we are. And if he calls back maybe we can help him get away."

1:40 p.m.
As Hammar's team was leaving Mark's office, an agent heard a cell phone ring once. It seemed to be coming from a gym bag near the door, a bag they had looked at three times. He still couldn't find the very thin phone until he discovered the hidden pocket. The agent gave it to Hammar as he boarded the helicopter.

Hammar flipped it open and pulled up the call history. Only one number had ever been called from this phone. That had to be the TLR.

The helicopter was airborne at 1:42 p.m. but they still didn't know where they were going.

Hammar ordered Barnes, "Get Central Communications. Give the NSA coordinator the phone number Mark Adams called—it must be the TLR. I want the GPS of that phone immediately."

The helicopters headed back toward the Capitol. Hammar sat back, his eyes closed, waiting for the call back. The torn remainder of his ear hurt like hell. The damned medic had given him nothing for the pain. Ten minutes later, with the Capitol in sight, Proctor came on the line.

"Sir, there's been a small glitch. We can't get a satellite position on the target cell phone. Apparently its GPS locator software has been modified or removed . . ."

"That's a damn glitch?" Hammar screamed.

"It's okay, sir. NSA can't see it with the satellite, but they can triangulate on it. They can put mobile equipment on three of your helicopters that will give them the phone's geographical position, the instant it's answered."

Hammar's voice betrayed his desperation and anger. "When will I get that equipment—tomorrow?"

"Sir, we suspect the TLR are in Maryland, north of the Chesapeake bridge, perhaps actually on Tilghman Cove. NSA headquarters is on your way there. The equipment is ready. They'll be waiting for you on the landing pad."

"They better be, or we'll both be gone tomorrow, Raymond."

The pilot estimated they could be on the NSA helicopter pad in five minutes. Hammar called Jack Mahoney's office. Senator Mahoney had replaced Harlowe as the acting Speaker. But the vote was about to begin and Mahoney was on the floor. Hammar begged his assistant for a delay. "Get him a note, for God's sake. Tell him we have the TLR in our sights. They'll be dead in a few minutes."

"I'll try my best, sir"

"Tell Mahoney his resignation can be considered void if we catch these people. The Supremes will give us a ruling that confirms it."

"I'm sure he'll slow it as much as he can. You get those bastards, sir."

Hammar's watch indicated 2:02 as they touched down at NSA headquarters.

It took ten minutes to get the equipment on board the three helicopters and their signals coordinated. Unfortunately there was another three minute wait for another piece of equipment that arrived by van.

It was 2:13 before they were in the air again. The NSA technician explained, "Sir, triangulation requires that we be widely disbursed if the target is some distance away. If we . . ."

Hammar could barely think with the pain, and the vote was underway. Six for and seven against. Each speaker took time to distance himself, or herself, from the tapes before voting. Everything depended on that coward Mahoney. He couldn't hear the NSA techie idiot anyway. He told Barnes, "Deal with him."

Barnes and the NSA technician decided to close on the Tilghman Cove area with the helicopters spread across the line of flight, a space of two miles between them. If the target was in that area and if they called when they were five miles out, they would have a fix on the cell phone location within a hundred feet. And they could be on top of the cell phone in under two minutes. Unfortunately, the NSA technician pointed out, if they placed the call and it was answered—for example—in Arlington, the triangulation would be several hundred yards off.

Hammar could hardly believe it. "Idiots! If the TLR is in Arlington it won't matter!"

2:06 p.m.
"Shall the amendment be approved? The roll will be called. Those affirming the amendment, say Aye, those opposed to the amendment, say No." The vote could have been electronic and over in a few seconds, but Senator Mahoney insisted on the role-call. Senators wanted to make public statements as they voted. As the secretary began the role-call, first Anna, then Chris and Jacob stood before the TV, barely breathing. This was that moment they risked everything for, the moment Burton died for.

FOX news displayed the new total for each side with every vote. Half the votes had been counted, a two-thirds majority was required and the tide seemed to be running in favor of passage. Chris had fought a battle against deep depression for several hours. He could not shake the sense of inevitable tragedy. But in the last few minutes his hope had returned. He believed the amendment could pass. He began to shake and had to sit down. Anna and Jacob felt it, too—enormous success and failure and fear, all at the same moment.

2:29 p.m.
Barnes made the call when they were five miles out. The cell phone was answered, then shut down. The NSA techie smiled. "Got him.

Straight ahead." He showed them on his laptop map, the precise location of the cell phone. A waterfront house on Tilghman Cove.

The pilot said, "I see the house. It's less than three miles ahead."

Hammar pounded his leg in frustration, the vote was moving too fast, and too many were approving the damn thing. "Faster," he screamed.

2:28 p.m.

The vote stood two votes short of those needed for passage. Six senators would never vote again, one vote was not present, only two votes remained. The tension was almost unbearable. Senator Wallis, a freshman from New Mexico, stood with tears streaming, prepared to give his reasons, but could only say "Aye."

Chris's cell phone rang. Chris grinned as he saw the identifier. It was Mark. He had run. 'Hey, Luke,' was on his lips as he put the phone to his ear, but he heard the whine of the helicopter jet. And he knew immediately. He looked at the phone and snapped it shut, his face white with terror. "Helicopters! Get out fast!" He ran out the open doorway shouting, "They're coming!"

Anna first, then Jacob followed him out. It was too late. The helicopters were a mile away and coming fast. Chris ran back inside with Anna close behind. He tore into the closet where their weapons were stored and grabbed the electromagnetic pulse emitter. It might drop the helicopters out of the air, but as he turned he leaned against the wall and dropped the weapon. It was over. If he killed DOJ agents now, it only added to the lives they had already taken. He looked at Anna and Jacob. They would not get away.

Jacob stepped inside, added Mark Adams to the TLR list and pressed the laptop's send button. The message went to all of the news organizations on their list, to his daughters, to Karen and the Carpenters, to Burton's boys.

The noise from the helicopters was terrifying. Now they were overhead and on both sides of the house. Chris looked at Jacob holding Anna and thought, *Oh Karen, Oh my God, Karen. Forgive me!*

Jacob and Anna held each other tight, but looked at the TV screen. The last senator was voting. It was Farley, the senator who offered the amendment. They couldn't hear because of the helicopters but the screen said *AMENDMENT PASSED.*

Jacob stood with his arms around Anna. She wept into his chest as the door burst open, the automatic weapons already firing.

Epilogue

The last message of the TLR was printed, broadcast and discussed everywhere.

> *The vote is underway as we write this. We are hopeful the Amendment will pass and that individual liberty will once again find a home in America. We knew we might die—liberty was worth the risk and if it succeeds, it was worth our lives. Jefferson is right. "The tree of liberty must be refreshed from time to time, with the blood of patriots and tyrants."*
>
> *We ask our friends and families to forgive us the pain we caused you and to understand the depth of our love for you. We thank all who supported us and the amendment.*
>
> *We are Burton Alan, Anna Carpenter, Chris Carpenter, Mark Adams and TJ Stewart—the TLR*

Three days after their deaths, Agent Barnes resigned from the FBI and the JTTF. He then described to a Washington Times reporter the manner in which they had died. His testimony resulted in the resignation of Attorney General Hammar.

The Author

Erne Lewis lives, sails, and writes in Port Ludlow, Washington.

He has been an architect, businessman, aquaculturist, ocean cruising sailor and traveler as well as a libertarian political activist.

An Act of Self-Defense is his first novel. A second novel, Drug War, is underway.

Find more at www.ernelewis.com

Breinigsville, PA USA
03 March 2011

256892BV00002B/72/P

9 780982 820506